Sand Roses

Sand Roses

by

Hamza Koudri

www.hhousebooks.com

Paperback ISBN: 978-1-7391047-3-3

Cover design by Ken Dawson Creative Covers

Typeset by Julia B. Lloyd

Published in the UK

Holland House Books

Holland House

47 Greenham Road

Newbury, Berkshire RG14 7HY

United Kingdom

www.hhousebooks.com

"Thus the native discovers that his life, his breath, his beating heart
are the same as those of the settler. He finds out that the settler's
skin is not of any more value than a native's skin; and it must be
said that this discovery shakes the world in a very necessary manner.
All the new, revolutionary assurance of the native stems from it. For
if, in fact, my life is worth as much as the settler's, his glance no
longer shrivels me up nor freezes me, and his voice no longer turns
me into stone. I am no longer on tenterhooks in his presence; in fact,
I don't give a damn for him."

Franz Fanon. *The Wretched of The Earth*(1963), p. 45.

Hamza Koudri

Prologue

As the dancer led him up the dark, narrow stairs, her hand softly holding his, the French officer couldn't remember how he got here from Mouloud's café. After all the drinking and smoking, the walls around him swayed and twisted, as though he was at sea.

But the officer wasn't going to miss this opportunity. Colonel Dupont was going to be very proud of him. A promotion would be in order, even.

Through his foggy eyes, he could still make out her slender silhouette, her hips sending faint ripples through her beige robe as she went up the stairs. The officer followed her through the dark balcony. He felt a little hard and tried to distract himself by looking through the arches of the balcony. He was still on duty.

Four buildings surrounded the courtyard, three of which had two floors with an arched wooden balcony upstairs. Across the yard was a one-storey building with a roof deck. Probably a stable. Quite the grand house for a dancer who doesn't do any prostitution, the officer thought, grinning. There was a well in the centre of the yard covered by a concrete lid decorated with pots of cheerful flowers that he couldn't have named even if he'd been sober.

When the dancer let go of his hand to open a door, he finally leaned back against a wooden railing. There was a sharp crack. The railing swung out from one loose end and the officer almost found himself falling onto the concrete yard. His heart raced. And he felt even more lightheaded as the dancer, thankfully, pulled him through the door.

Inside the room, he was suffocated by the smell of ambergris and jasmine. The dancer disappeared into the darkness. He heard a metallic scratch, then the room was lit by a candle on a window ledge, filling the already dense air with the scent of roses.

She sat him on a large sheepskin rug and began to make tea. The officer went over the plan in his head again. He knew how these girls operated: she would offer him tea and seduce him until he could not resist, and only then would she set the price.

Colonel Dupont had instructed them to wait until the girl produced a condom before making an arrest. They needed that proof. But the officer wasn't sure he could hold himself. The robe hugged her thighs so tantalisingly.

He looked away. The room wasn't large and furniture was scarce, humble and small. A mirror sat on a low dresser, with a wooden chest tucked beneath it, a low table leaned against the wall, and a wool carpet was spread across the floor. Was it black, or was it just too dark to tell?

When the Nailya dancer picked up the tea pot from the clay stove, the charcoal hissed with a cloud of sparks, as if protesting its separation from the pot. She filled two glasses and handed him one. As her finger brushed his, he could barely restrain himself from dragging her body down to him.

But he had to follow the plan.

'Danse?' the dancer spoke with a rusty voice. The Arab accent was clear even in that one French word.

Before he had the chance to say no, she stood up and started dancing. She swirled a veil across her face, and her hips swayed right and left, then in circles. Waves erupted from her waist and coursed through her robes in rhythm with her hips. That was it. The officer couldn't resist anymore.

'Viens,' he muttered as he struggled to stand up. He reached to the window ledge for support, but instead a piercing pain shot through his palm. It was the candle. He cursed it. Then bit his hand, losing his footing and almost stumbling over a second time. The dancer gave up her moves and rushed to put her hands under his arms, allowing him to rest his heavy head on her shoulder.

His left cheekbone hurt where he had gotten a bruise earlier in the evening. He had fought another Frenchman because of this whore, and remembering that made him more determined to arrest her. But the sweet smell of jasmine filled his nostrils as his nose brushed her naked neck. Hold it, he told himself as he kissed her neck. Focus. She wasn't going to offer herself unless he followed the procedure. Tea first, dance, conversation, then sex. He slid his hand down her lower back, but she grabbed it. She tried to pull herself away, but he held her harder.

'Arrête,' she coaxed as she tried to sit him down on the floor. 'Arrête.'

The officer felt weak against the woman's strength. She pushed him down easily, which made him furious. She was treating him like a child. It took all his power to pull her down. He shoved at her shoulders, forcing her to the floor. He put his weight on her so he could kiss her on the lips this time. Her pleas turned into shouts and curses.

'Salaud,' she kept repeating as she tried to scratch his face. "Connard."

He twisted her hands above her head and pinned them to the floor with one large hand. That made the scratching stop. But the shouting and cursing continued still, now with a mix of French and Derja, and so did the constant movement of the head. He covered her mouth with his other hand, but it couldn't muffle the screams, and her entire body started to writhe under his. No, he wasn't following procedure, but this was an exaggerated reaction coming from a slut whose profession was pleasuring men. She left him no choice but to slap her across the face. That stunned her for a moment, so he began pulling up her skirts.

The dancer squealed, and before he could slap her again something seared his eyes. The whore had thrown charcoal in his face. His whole body shivered with pain, and he instinctively rubbed his eyes, rasping them bloody red.

He could feel her trying to slip away underneath him. She was going to pay for what she did. Pay dearly. The more she wrestled, the more strength he could muster. He grabbed her arm, she pulled it free. She had nearly escaped his grip entirely when he clasped her small ankle. It gained him enough time to brush the charcoal off his face. He had just managed to open his eyes through burning pain when he saw a foot rising to meet him. She kicked him in the face. He didn't let go. She kicked a second time. A third. His face was on fire, and, despite his best efforts, his grip on her ankle loosened. She pulled it away, staggered to her feet, and ran for the door, whimpering.

The bitch opened the door and almost made it out when he yanked her back by the braid and pulled her back inside the wretched room. He slammed her against the wall so roughly he heard the thud of her skull. She let out a scream. He smiled. He could almost see his grin in her eyes. This whole situation –her fear and their panting – it all felt so familiar. He could almost taste the adrenaline he always got out of killing on the battlefield, he was going to enjoy this even more.

He put his face against hers, their eyes locked as he reached one hand between her thighs. Her hands were stuck between their bodies, and he felt them wriggle against his stomach, but he paid them no mind. Her eyes squinted with pain from his squeeze, and she shrieked again.

Her eyes stared at him. He realised her hands were no longer between their bodies, but it was too late. She already held his neck in one hand,

and something stung from the other side, just under his jaw. The pain was hot and took his breath away. He touched the wound and felt warm blood oozing out. He could taste it in his throat. Had she stabbed him?

The dancer freed herself again and staggered out of the room. Holding his neck, the officer stalked her to the balcony. This time he grabbed her robe and slammed her against the wooden column. He checked her hands for the knife, but she didn't carry any. He noticed the blood on her bracelet, then he saw thorns there too.

'What are you going to do now?' he used the weight of his body to press hers against the wooden column. She couldn't move.

Holding down her braceleted wrist, the officer clasped his other hand around her neck in a tight grip. He suddenly felt dizzy, which he didn't understand since the rush of the moment had shaken him nearly back to sobriety. He couldn't finish her with one hand. So he used his second hand too, freeing her weapon, but constantly watching it in case she made a sudden movement. She tried to scratch his face but couldn't reach it. She tried to remove his hands off her neck, but all she managed was a few scratches around his wrists.

Something hard hit the back of his head and dirt went flying through the air. His head felt heavy, and he turned to see what had hit him. She was behind him, panting and watching his reaction.

The balcony spun around him, and he was no longer able to stand. His neck was warm. He stepped back to lean against the wooden railing, but he heard a creak again, louder now. The wood snapped. The balcony retreated away from him, rushing towards the moon-lit sky until his body crashed into something solid. A wall? The floor?

As he felt the hot blood flood his head, he finally solved it all. He knew how she did it. How they did it. Colonel Dupont was going to be very proud of him.

The French officer died in the dancer's courtyard.

1935
March

One

i

The body lay in a pool of blood. His swollen eyes bulged, and his mouth was open.

Salima sat on the stairs biting her nails as she stared at the corpse. We've killed him, she thought. We've killed a man.

Her heart pounded. Her breathing heavy and her head too light. A wood splint from the balcony railing was trapped under the body, so soaked in blood it had gone a gooey black.

'…. just can't seem to have a normal life,' Fahima was saying. She was pacing around the well, avoiding the blood pool and looking at anything but Salima and the corpse. She kept sweeping an imaginary strand of hair out of her eye. 'I was this close. I was supposed to run away with him. Far from all of this. My life is ruined.'

Salima didn't respond. The courtyard was still dark and warm, so it couldn't be long after midnight. She wondered how long it had taken him to die after his fall from the balcony. I hope it took long.

'How did it come to this, Salima?' Fahima had stopped pacing.

Salima continued to stare at the corpse. 'It would have been me,' she finally whispered.

'He's dead, Salima,' Fahima said.

'It would've been me,' Salima said again, a little louder and more confident this time. She finally met her sister's eyes. 'He was going to kill me.'

Fahima slid down, resting her back against the well. She sobbed into her hands. Salima wanted to comfort her sister but all she could think was, I told you the French were all the same.

'What do we do now?' Fahima asked at last.

The question echoed in the night. Salima was certain of one thing: they had to get rid of the body. If anyone found out about what happened tonight, it would be the end of them both.

'Maybe if we go to the… to the police and tell them what happened. Maybe if we do that before they find out, maybe—'

'Maybe what?' Salima cut her off. 'They'll thank us, give us a hundred francs and invite us to dance at the next party they're throwing? You know as well as I do that they'll fucking shoot us before we even get a chance to explain. They would never believe us.' She took a deep breath. 'We have to get rid of the body.'

'Yes,' Fahima nodded, sniffing. 'But how?'

Salima fell silent. They could bury the corpse in the animal shed. But it would have to be a deep hole, and the French might still find it if they suspected anything.

'We can take it out of town and bury it in the desert.'

'Too risky,' Salima said.

One couldn't simply carry a corpse through the streets of Bousaada in the middle of the night without raising a thousand suspicions. They could chop it into pieces. The thought made her shudder. Mourad might be able to help. But she didn't know if she should involve him. What would he think of her?

Salima had always thought their mother had taught them everything they needed for life in Bousaada. She'd told them so many stories, and things had been working fine all these years. But this was different. I wish she was here now.

'I wish Mother was here,' Fahima echoed out loud. 'She'd know what to do.'

'We need to send for her. We need her help.'

Silence. Salima knew her sister was afraid of how Mother would react. Salima was scared, too, but the prospect of going to jail or being executed frightened her more.

'I'm going to find Mourad,' Salima said. 'I'll have him send a rider to get Mother from the village. Stay here, and don't let anyone in no matter what. Clear?'

'I was supposed to be on my way out of town right now,' Fahima responded. 'With him. I was going to be happy.'

Salima had more pressing issues than her sister's stupid romantic fantasies. Without a word, she went to the kitchen to clean the blood off her hands, bracelet, and face. Her beige dress was splattered with blood. She went up to change.

She tied her grey silk veil around her waist. The clay stove lay overturned with charcoal scattered around its mouth. A few pieces still glowed red each time the air breezed through the window. She cloaked herself in her white mlahfa and left.

'Clean the room while you wait, will you?' she said as she passed Fahima.

She paused at the door. Looked left, and then right, then gathered her mlahfa and stepped into the night.

ii

Salima had roamed the streets at this ungodly hour enough times to know that the city never really slept. Footfalls, laughter, and screams echoed through the dark alleyways, as though coming from a great distance. They never failed to put her on edge. The mosques would soon call for the fadjer prayer, so most men were probably getting ready to head to the mosque. Salima walked faster, winding her way through the maze of streets and narrowing alleys. It was that brief part of the night when the air felt refreshing, and the cool wind soothed her left cheek where that bastard had slapped her. Come to think of it, she was in a lot of pain. The back of her head was throbbing from being slammed against the column; her throat was tight, and she felt sore between her thighs where he had grabbed her; the palm of her right hand burnt from the coal.

There was one question she could no longer avoid. She hadn't meant to kill the man, but could she have avoided the whole fight? He was intent on killing her in the end. She could see it in his eyes, all that rage. She also knew that if she hadn't resisted, he would have raped her.

She knew he was a killer.

She had just passed the gates when a man's howl startled her to a stop. It was the adhan for fadjer prayer. The sun would soon rise, and with it went any chance of getting rid of the body in complete discretion.

Clutching her mlahfa, she crossed the marketplace as it slowly came back to life. A carrot stall was installed where Salima had danced last night before making her way to Mouloud's café. She had always found it amusing that one space could turn from a large dance party in the evening, to a quaint marketplace in the morning. And every once in a while, a place of worship, too. Today, there was nothing quaint about the scene. Every stall and every person she encountered felt like damnation. She quickened her step.

A short walk from the gate led her to the stables where Mourad was rounding up his sheep for the marketplace. He was easy to spot; he was so thin and tall that he looked like a scarecrow in his large, brown *kashabia*. He walked with the help of the same stick he used to herd his sheep out of habit, like an old man. He was glad to see her, she liked to assume. But his smile was laced with worry. He must think something was wrong, she thought. Something *was* wrong.

'Are you alright?' he asked.

'Yes,' she responded, fighting back tears.

'What are you doing outside at this hour?'

'I need someone to go fetch my mother from the village.'

'And you say everything's alright?' He turned and they started up the dirt path that led to the stables. Candlelight glowed in the window, and a man's shadow moved around. Kader, Mourad's helper.

'Can you do it?' She ignored his question. 'I need her here as soon as possible. Send someone fast. I'll give him fifty francs if he can bring her.'

'Salima, what happened?' Salima was grateful the darkness hid the bruise on her jaw. When she didn't answer, he stopped and watched her. She sat down on the palm tree trunk, their regular meeting spot.

'What are you not telling me?'

'There's something I need her help with.'

'Are you...?'

'Am I what?'

'Preh- Pregnant,' he said.

'God. No.' She waved the idea away. 'Do you have a cigarette?'

He reached through his *kashabia* and produced a cigarette case and a lighter. He lit Salima's cigarette and the familiar smoke filled her up. She closed her eyes, and, for a moment, she forgot about it all. She enjoyed the cool air against her face, and the heavy smoke in her chest. She would have preferred hashish, but she knew better than to ask Mourad for it.

'You're not going to tell me what's happening, are you?'

She let the smoke go and looked at him. 'Can you send someone or not?'

'I'll do it myself.'

'What?'

'I can take my horse. She's strong and fast. We can both ride her on the way back. We'll be here before sundown.'

'You don't have to do that,' Salima said. 'Your sheep. The market.'

'Kader will take care of that. Don't worry about it.'

'Only if I can pay you. Please.'

'No worries. I've been meaning to go see my old man soon anyway. He's very sick.'

She squinted at him as she inhaled from the cigarette. She didn't believe him; he hadn't mentioned his father being ill before. But she had no choice. She stood up to face him.

'Well, you'd better get going if you want to make it by sundown.'

She took a final drag at the cigarette and flicked it into the air as she started walking backwards. 'Oh,' she added, 'and if you don't want Mother to faint, the first thing you'd want to tell her is that my sister and I are fine.'

Without waiting for a response, she turned and headed back to town.

iii

The marketplace was crowded with people and produce now. It smelled like cow dung, and the caged chickens, ducks and geese made a deafening commotion.

Past the gate, the smells and sounds faded away. A few shop owners were opening up, and they moved lazily, slowly, to decorate the walls with baskets and lanterns.

Just as Salima turned left onto a narrow street, a chill went up her spine. She stopped. Four French soldiers came towards her. *This is it*, she thought. *This is how I'm going to die. They must've found out about the body somehow*. What could have happened to her sister? Would she ever see her again? Could they have already shot her and left her? Was she by the well in a pool of blood, just like the Frenchman? The soldiers were on her.

One of them slowed, a grin on his face. His comrade put his hand on the man's shoulder and pulled him away with a firm 'We need to go.' The soldier let himself be pulled and went with his friends, but his eyes kept flicking back to her. It was only when they'd turned the corner that Salima could finally breathe again.

When she was sure no one was looking, she ran. By the time she reached her street, she was panting. She tapped on the door using the code she and her sister always used: One tap, three taps then two. The wait felt like an eternity. The sky was turning a lighter blue, but the sun wasn't out yet. Salima glanced right and left. Something was moving behind her.

When Fahima opened the door, she was saying something but Salima wasn't listening. She squeezed in through the door and her eyes searched every shadow across the street. A light went out in one of the rooms. It was the Jew's house. Weird.

It wasn't like he was going to the mosque or anything, Salima thought. No dancer would require his services either. *What the hell are you doing up this early?* Could he have heard them last night?

iv

'...and I couldn't even sleep knowing that there was a dead man downstairs.'

Salima locked the door and turned to face her.

'What have we done, Salima? We killed a man!'

Salima put her hands on her sister's shoulders and said, 'Listen. Fahima. Listen to me. Mother is coming. Before sundown. We will find a way out.'

Fahima calmed down. But only for a moment before she found another reason to panic. 'Is this man going to lie here in our courtyard all day long?'

'No. No. We'll hide him. We'll clean the place.' She thought that would help keep Fahima distracted. *It'll keep me distracted, too.*

Salima threw off her *mlahfa* and walked to the animal shed. The shed was long but narrow, and not very high. A faint light came through a small window, and the other door leading to the little grove behind their house was locked to prevent the rooster from going to the Jew's home. She looked up to make sure he was still perched on his stick in the corner. The two goats were sleeping too, tied to their feeder.

Salima wasn't really sure what she was looking for. Then she spotted it. A large wooden cart propped up against the wall by the back door. She dragged it out to the courtyard. She rested the handles on the low wall of the well to keep it standing.

She'd tried to avoid looking at the body, but she couldn't help glancing at his face. It was chalk white. A small black rose tattoo at the base of his neck, scarred by two thin lines. It brought back distant memories. Running, blood, and killing.

'What are you going to do with that cart?' asked Fahima, snapping Salima out of her thoughts.

'Just help me.' Salima reached for the man's hands. 'Take the legs.'

The body was much heavier than Salima expected. They could barely move, much less carry him. They tried again and again, but the best they could do was get him closer to the cart, leaving a damning trail of blood behind them. It reminded Salima of slaughtering sheep.

'Let's do this,' Salima said when she realised they couldn't carry the body on their own. Not like that anyway. 'Let's both try to lift him from the shoulders. We'll pull his upper body first, then…'

Fahima had already let go of the legs and joined her at the man's shoulders. This worked better. They sat him up first, then lifted him up to the cart. But they only managed to get his upper back on before the cart moved away. The cart had no front legs, so the handles fell off the well's wall and the whole cart tilted forward, throwing the body to the ground. By this time the sisters were both covered in blood, and Salima could see Fahima was on the verge of crying. She lifted the cart up and put the handles on the well again. This time she stayed in the space between the handles to prevent the cart from moving.

'Come on!' she pressed. 'Let's try again.'

This time it worked. They first put the upper body on the cart. The cart threatened to move, but Salima held it in place with her hips. Then they lifted the man's legs, which were much lighter. They each took a handle and rolled the cart back to the animal shed where they laid the handles on a pile of straw bales. Salima covered the body with heaps of hay, then they went back to the yard and started cleaning.

The cleaning wasn't as hard, but it took a lot of time, and water too. All their water. At first, Fahima started brushing the blood, but it wouldn't come off. Having spent the whole night in the courtyard, thin layers of solid blood had formed here and there, soft and dark. Like milk skin, but red and disgusting.

The two sisters scrubbed in silence. Salima was worried her sister might throw up any minute. Ever since Fahima was young, she always had to look away when their father or mother killed a chicken or a rooster for dinner.

When they couldn't tell water from blood, Fahima went to get another bucket from the kitchen. Salima was having second thoughts. Where would they throw all this red water? Usually, they would sweep it off to the street, but that would guarantee them a trip to the grave. They could throw it into the animal shed? But it wouldn't go anywhere.

It would smell like blood for some time, and it would be all the proof the French needed to incriminate the sisters – if proof was needed.

'Stop,' she ordered her sister before she threw a bucketful of water on the floor. 'We shouldn't use more water.'

'What?' Fahima was confused. 'Why not?'

Apart from the fact that we'd have to walk all the way to the river to get more buckets of water? Salima thought but refrained from saying.

'We can't just sweep all this red water out to the street.'

'What do we do with it then?'

'The well. We can throw it in the well and close the lid again. No one will be able to see what's down there.'

They both used pieces of cloth to dry the bloody water and wring it into an empty bucket. When it was full, they removed the flowerpots from the concrete well lid. With much difficulty, they pushed it until it was a third of the way open.

Salima peered down into the deep dark abyss for the first time since they moved in, and she felt dizzy. An iron ladder went down the inner wall and disappeared into the dark, like a stairway to hell. She took a pebble from a pot and threw it into the well. It took a long moment before it landed with a splash in the bottom, the sound echoing all the way up the walls.

'It's deep,' announced Fahima.

'*It's deep, deep, eep, eep,*' repeated a thousand voices.

'Let's hope no one decides to go all the way down,' Salima said as she emptied the bloody water inside the well carefully so as not to stain the walls.

And so they went on, soaking the cloths in blood, rubbing, brushing, and wringing. The morning fresh air gave way to warmth, then heat.

Salima's head split in pain, but it didn't stop her. She couldn't stop. This labour at least distracted her from having to dwell on what they had just done, what they were doing. So, she focused on rubbing, wringing and brushing.

Around midday, someone knocked at the door. The sisters looked at each other, motionless. Another knock.

'You don't think Mourad—' Salima shook her head before Fahima could finish.

The knock turned into beating on the door. The beating got stronger, and for a moment Salima was afraid the caller would break the whole door down.

Then Nouara started shouting from outside, 'Hey Ammariya! Are you there?'

When no one answered her, she beat the door one last desperate time, then Salima heard her walk away muttering, 'You won't be getting any clients with the door locked like that.'

Both sisters relaxed again.

The sun was sliding down the western horizon and turning a bright yellow when Salima was finally satisfied with their cleaning. Not a spot of blood could be seen in the courtyard. They had even cleaned the upstairs balcony where the French soldier first started bleeding, splashing all the walls and pillars. They'd collected the debris of the broken pot and swept off the dirt. They were exhausted, but Salima felt they were in less danger now. Her mother would soon be here. She would help them get rid of the body, and it would all be over. A part of her wished there was more to clean, she scoured the floor for any sign of red. Nothing. She scrubbed some more at the well, just in case.

They threw the cloths and the brush in the well. They changed their red-spattered beige dresses and threw them in the well, too. They cleaned the buckets, and they were ready to close the well when Fahima had an idea.

'The body,' she said looking at her sister expectantly.

'What about the body?' asked Salima. Then it hit her. 'You want to throw the body in the well, too?'

'Yes! No one will think of looking there. If they do, it's too dark to see anything.'

She couldn't think of anything better to do, and it was better than doing nothing. They wheeled the cart back to the courtyard and put the handles on the well's wall again. First, they threw in the blood-soaked hay they had used to cover the body, then they pushed the body across the cart onto the well's wall, careful not to let it fall between the handles.

Fahima looked at her sister one last time for confirmation. Salima sighed and nodded. Then they did it. They rolled the body into the opening and it disappeared into the black hollow. It landed with a thud and a faint splash. The walls didn't echo the thud. It was as if the well knew what the sisters had done, and it didn't approve.

Salima looked at her sister. This time there was something in her eyes. It wasn't fear, nor sadness. Was it guilt? They were no longer just

Nailiya girls. Fahima must be thinking they were killers now. They had killed a man and hid his body; they were murderers.

In silence, the two sisters emptied a few pots of dirt into the well to cover the body and pushed the lid back to close over their fatal secret. As they put the colourful flowerpots back on the concrete lid, Salima hoped they would never move them again.

With that, they each found a spot in the shade, laid a rug on the floor and lay down to rest. Salima fell asleep despite herself. Her body granting her some longed-for escape.

What felt like moments later, she woke up, startled. Someone was beating on the door again.

v

It was dark. She stumbled to her feet. There was another knock and Fahima woke up with a sigh. Salima motioned her to be quiet, but she wasn't sure her sister could even see her.

The French. They must have come for her. Salima tried to keep herself calm, but her knees shook of their own accord.

Their mother's voice came from behind the door, 'Fahima? Anyone here?'

Salima hurried to open the door and let her mother in. Saadia kissed them both with alert and concerned eyes and said, 'Start talking. What happened?'

Salima exchanged a look with her sister, thinking of how to best tell the story. But before she could say anything, Fahima volunteered, rather abruptly, with: 'We killed a French soldier.'

Saadia's nostrils flared. She turned to Salima for an explanation.

'He was going to kill me,' she said.

Salima told her mother the whole story, and insisted it was an accident. She expected her to start screaming, but instead Saadia asked a thousand questions. She wanted to know all the details. How the struggle started in the first place. Why it started, and whether it could have been avoided.

'I tried to,' Salima explained. 'I kept trying to leave the room the entire time, but he was determined.'

'To have sex?'

18

'To rape me.'

'Well, maybe if you had let him have it, he would have just buttoned up and gone back home in peace.'

'Let him have it? You mean let him rape me? And maybe kill me like—'

'No one's asking you to be a prostitute.' Saadia rolled her eyes. 'But it wouldn't have killed you if you had swallowed your pride and given him what he came here for in the first place so we could avoid having a dead body in the well.'

She hadn't expected much sympathy from her mother. She chose not to respond.

Saadia looked up at the broken railing where the Frenchman had fallen.

'Who else knows about this?' she asked Salima. 'Mourad didn't seem to know anything.'

'He doesn't. No one else knows.'

'Where did you pick him up? The café?'

'Yes. Mouloud's.'

'No one saw you leaving with him?'

'No. I followed all the rules. I always do.'

'Who was he with at the café? Alone?'

The world started to rotate around Salima, and things became blurry.

'Was he alone at the café?' her mother asked again.

'No,' she said. She was still trying to recollect her memories from the night before. Her mother pressed her thumb and index fingers against her temples.

Salima couldn't believe she had forgotten.

'Who was he with?' Fahima was asking now.

'Another Frenchman,' Salima said. 'His friend or something. They both danced with me. His friend found another girl, and this man... he came with me.'

'Did he see you leave together? Who left the café first?'

'We left at the same time.' Salima's heart was racing.

'So you think he would remember you?'

Salima remembered the friend. How he had eyed her all evening. How he had danced with her and thrown coins her way.

'I'm not sure,' she lied. 'He was drunk, too.'

Two

i

A pointy strand of hay poked at Salima's side, so she had to shift her body, which took more effort than she was willing to put into it at the moment.

She took the cigarette from Mourad's mouth instead, put it in hers and filled her chest with smoke. Mourad lay on his stomach next to her on the haystack. He had been eyeing her for a while and she knew he was dying for a kiss.

There was also something behind that smile of his, but she didn't want to ask him what it was. She preferred not to interrupt the quiet of the night. She breathed the smoke out and took another drag from the cigarette before she gave it back to him.

'That black-headed ewe gave birth to two little lambs last night,' he said.

He knew Salima didn't care about his sheep, much less recognise the black-headed ewe, but he liked to tell her things. Unlike Salima, he felt uncomfortable with silence.

'I can sell her and her lambs for a good price, but I'll have to wait until after Eid. Everyone's looking to buy big healthy males for Eid these days.'

'Good,' was all Salima could give him. She stared at the starry sky.

'Are you sleepy?'

'A little.'

She was more exhausted than sleepy. She seldom slept before dawn, but she was too exhausted to stand up and go home.

At least that was what she liked to believe. In the back of her mind, she also knew she didn't want to face her mother's interrogations. *Where have you been? Who did you run into? Does anyone know?* Salima wasn't ready for all those questions right now.

'Too much dancing?' Mourad asked playfully.

Salima admired how he pretended that all she did was dance. He never asked about her clients or what she did with them.

'No. It's not that,' Salima replied as he put the cigarette between her lips this time and let her draw a long one.

And it was true. She wasn't exhausted from dancing. If anything, she had gotten used to it after all these years. It wasn't the client, either. That too she was used to by now, and last night's client wasn't one of those picky bastards.

ii

While she tried to avoid thinking about it, Salima knew perfectly well why she was tired lately.

It had to do with killing a man. *Accidentally* killing a man, she corrected herself. *A Frenchman,* she added in her head as if that would lighten the weight of her conscience. Living with the guilt while trying to determine if anyone suspected anything; that was the exhausting part.

When her mother arrived the night after the accident, her first priority had been making sure nothing looked out of the ordinary. She made Salima cover up her bruises and go out to dance that very same night.

Saadia had still insisted that they watch out for any sign of suspicion. 'If anyone knows anything. If they're talking about his disappearance or asking questions, we need to know about it,' Saadia liked to repeat morning, noon and evening, and in between.

Salima had been on the lookout for anything suspicious. If anyone as much as stared at her, the air would clog in her chest. Every time a French soldier walked through the door of Mouloud's café, a flush of heat would creep up her neck until it blanketed her face, clouded her vision, and pounded in her ears.

One night, Nouara came up to her and, with a straight face, told her, 'I know what you did.' A cold spasm shot from Salima's feet all the way up to her heart. Would Nouara understand? Had she told anyone already? Did anyone else know?

'I know how you won the cards game last night,' Nouara added. Salima could only afford half a smirk, but she wanted to laugh.

'You got us all high on hashish, and you kept a clear head,' Nouara explained.

'That's not cheating,' Salima shot back, regaining control of her faculties. Fahima had played cards with the girls the night before. She was the one who didn't like hashish, but Salima played along. 'Next time,' she added, with a smile now, 'decide if you prefer to win or get high.'

Nouara nudged her shoulder with a giggle and went on her way. Salima leaned back against the wall and bumped her head against it firmly. She'd been so close to revealing everything.

She felt like her life had forever changed. That she would spend the rest of her days cautious, looking over her shoulder in case two soldiers would sneak up and arrest her. Even when she was alone, she wasn't. The sticky black guilt would crawl up from the pit of her stomach and course through every vein of her body. Most nights it left her retching or crying, trying desperately to exorcise that wretched feeling.

iii

'Don't you think it's time for you to retire?' Mourad's voice shook Salima back to the haystack. It took her a moment to grasp what he had said.

'Retire?' she asked, puzzled. 'Are you calling me old?' She was only half joking.

'You know that's not what I mean,' Mourad explained. 'I mean, why are you still doing this? What do you need it for? We could just get out of here. Go back home. Make a family.'

Salima and Mourad had been betrothed for some time now, but this invitation certainly took her by surprise. They had never set a date for their marriage.

'I don't have enough dowry money yet,' was the best she could do.

In her village, it was customary for a Nailiya girl to collect enough money in Bousaada before returning to her village and offering it as a dowry for her husband-to-be.

'We don't need it,' Mourad sat up. 'You've already helped me with the stables here. I have enough to get us started. You can help me raise the sheep, and I'll come here to sell them once or twice a year.' He was getting excited, and Salima winced. 'I don't care about the stupid dowry.'

When Salima had first come to Bousaada four years earlier, her dream had been to become a successful Nailiya dancer. But she had known all along that it would only be a phase. That the ultimate goal was to collect a dowry before going back home to get married and start a family. Her mother had done that, and so did every Nailiya dancer.

Some foolish girls, like her naïve sister, dreamt bigger. They wanted to travel to big cities, their dreams feeding on false stories – myths as Salima liked to call them – of dancers who made it to Algiers, Paris or Rome. They danced for royalties and lived luxurious lives.

Salima's hopes were more realistic. For the last year or so she had started to feel content. Her sister and she had rented their own house, and they planned to hire the best dancers in town to start a *haouch*. They would be the *haouch* tourists sought when they came to town. This had always been Mother's dream.

Things had also gotten serious with Mourad. He was a strong, nice and caring man. Her marrying him was simply a matter of when, not if. So if he had asked her to get out just a week ago, she would have said yes. But now with everything going on?

She couldn't bring herself to say yes. She couldn't leave her sister alone to deal with the whole chaos she had created. She could maybe convince her sister to get out as well, but their skipping town would be all the proof that was needed. If proof was needed in the first place. It would only be a matter of days before the Caid and his nasty snitches would find them and drag them all the way back to Bousaada and throw them at the feet of Colonel Dupont. They might even kill Mourad and a score of other villagers in the process just to trade their ears for money.

How could she agree to leave with Mourad knowing it might bring all this misery on the people around her? What seemed even more daunting at the moment was having to explain to Mourad why she couldn't leave. She couldn't just tell him she had killed a Frenchman. But she couldn't think of any other good reason to stay here either.

'I can't do it now,' she said before she dragged at the nearly extinguished cigarette. 'I have to help Fahima start the *haouch*,' she added, avoiding his eyes. She stared at the sky. The darkness was fading, and dawn was upon them.

If Mourad didn't believe her, he didn't show it. Salima sat up and kissed him passionately. He kissed her long and hard while his hand caressed her leg and upper thigh. His manhood pressed against her through his thick *kashabia* and her light silk dress. He suddenly pulled away with a nervous grin.

'The herd is ready,' announced Kader behind her. 'We need to get moving before someone takes our slot at the marketplace.'

That was Salima's cue to leave. *Damn you, Kader,* she cursed under her breath. She knew Kader, like most people from Bousaada, didn't approve of Mourad's marriage to a Nailiya dancer, but why did he have to interrupt them all the time?

iv

As the sun started its ascent, casting cold light on the world, Salima slipped through the outside door, crossed the small passage and the courtyard, and went up to her room. Salima was glad the house was quiet. Her mother and Fahima must be asleep. Maybe Fahima was still with a client. It didn't matter as long as Salima could sneak into her room and sleep peacefully.

But her sleep was all but peaceful. No sooner had she dozed off than she found herself staring at the dead soldier in her courtyard. He lay in a pool of dark blood. His eyes flicked back and forth, back and forth, back and forth back forthbackforthback... she tried to scream.

She woke up to the heavy afternoon air thick in her chest and the skin of her neck damp with sweat. Her head was throbbing, and her throat was dry. The smell of tea from the courtyard downstairs, mixed with the aroma of delicious bread, her mother's bread, wafted up to her room.

She sat up lazily and looked at the sun. It was that bright yellow that preceded dusk. She must have slept for a long time, and she felt sick of sleeping. She stood up, put on a dark blue dress, fixed her braided hair, and left the room.

Salima's heart skipped a beat as she stepped onto the balcony. She told herself it was because she was afraid of falling off through the broken railing, but she knew perfectly well it was her fear of facing this place again. The feeling of the French man slamming her against the wooden column, life leaving her body as he tightened his grip on her throat.

'You're up,' Saadia declared as Salima came downstairs. She was sitting on a low stool sipping tea. A tray was laid on the table with fresh bread. 'Tea?'

Without responding, Salima got sugar from the kitchen and sat down on a low bench across from her mother. She poured a cup of tea.

Behind Saadia, the well sat under the sun, her heinous secret roasting within. The green flower-patterned tiles gleamed in the sunlight, as if they were taunting her, threatening to throw up the body concealed inside. Salima wondered if she should have risked taking the body out instead of throwing it into the well. Maybe it would have been easier to forget about the murder that way.

'I didn't hear you come in,' said her mother, interrupting her thoughts.

'You must've been sleeping,' Salima replied. She put in three spoons of sugar and stirred.

'How did it go?'

'Same as usual. I danced at Mouloud's, picked up a client and went to his hotel.'

'Is anyone talking about the French officer?'

'Not that I have heard.' Salima took a piece of the bread.

'Did anyone ask any questions?' *There goes the annoying interrogation.*

'No. Nothing,' Salima responded. 'How about Fahima?'

'Nothing,' said Saadia slowly, pensively. 'And that worries me.'

'Why? Maybe they haven't noticed his absence?' Even Salima didn't believe that.

'Don't be ridiculous. They could miss it for a day or two. Not a week. They must be investigating his absence secretly so they don't alert anyone.'

'Maybe,' Salima said between sips. 'Or maybe,' she added, 'they think it's the Ouled Brahims.' Her mother looked intrigued. 'Mourad told me they're driving the French crazy. They attacked a French farmer two days ago and stole all his cattle.' Saadia nodded along.

'You've been seeing Mourad?' she finally asked. This was what interested her most in the whole story somehow.

'Yes,' Salima tried to say casually. She then downed the last of her tea in one gulp and stood up. 'I'm going to the river,' she added. She grabbed an empty water jar from the kitchen and headed to the door.

'Wait,' her mother stopped her. 'I'm going back to the village,' Saadia announced. 'Your father needs me back home.'

'You can't stay longer?' Salima asked.

'You're doing just fine. I don't know if there's anything for me to do here but wait and brood over your safety.'

'When do you leave?'

'At dawn.'

'I'll be here to walk you out to the gate.'

As Salima headed down the path leading to the river, the street was just now coming to life with afternoon nappers going about their business. She should have asked her mother where Fahima was lest they were seen together outside, but Saadia would have told her if Fahima was down by the river.

The river was empty but for a few girls. Salima was grateful. The tea had helped with the headache, but she was still feeling grumpy.

Salima took off her dress and her jewelry, stacked them next to a rock where she could watch them, and went in in her underdress. She rubbed her body, careful not to wet her hair. She rubbed between her thighs and under her armpits. When she was satisfied, she filled the jar and sat on a warm rock to dry in the sun, fiddling with her bracelet.

She looked around at the girls as they splashed and chased each other gleefully. They reminded Salima of herself when she first came to Bousaada four years earlier, innocent and naïve. Salima always liked to think of Fahima as the innocent, naïve one, but in hindsight she realised she hadn't actually been so clever herself.

Salima felt she had spent many lives in this town, and all her experiences, good and bad, had made her the woman she was today. She was smarter and stronger than she would have ever been had she not left her village. Yet she felt trapped. Trapped by a crime she knew she would pay for one day.

Perhaps she was only partly guilty. He had tried to kill her first. But still, she was growing more convinced that there would be mercy in getting arrested. At least she wouldn't live in fear. She almost longed for punishment. Maybe if Salima paid for the crime, she would live, or even die, with a clear head. A clear conscience. A little light in her still.

But she knew she couldn't just march into the military circle and confess her crime. Not when her sister was involved, and now her mother, too.

The sun was setting when Salima felt dry enough, and more tormented than she was willing to allow herself to be. She put on her dress and jewellery and prepared to leave her thoughts on the rock.

The young girls who were now sitting to dry admired Salima's thousand-coin necklace. Just a week ago, this would have meant something to her. It would have made her feel proud. She might have even cast them a side glance with a hint of a smile, a little wink. But now she had bigger things on her mind. She picked up the water jar and made her way back home.

v

Saadia wasn't home when Salima returned, but she found her sister in her bedroom preparing for the evening.

Fahima wore a dark blue dress matching Salima's. It complimented their tall and curvy bodies. *Mother must have told her what I was wearing*, Salima thought.

'Did you go to the river?' asked Fahima without looking up from the mirror. She was putting on makeup.

'Yeah. You?'

'I was playing cards with Nouara and the girls. I can't believe those idiots,' Fahima looked at Salima, excited. 'I haven't lost a game in a long time.'

'Nouara says it's because you don't smoke hashish with them.' Salima picked up a brush and started to dab her high cheekbones with light powder.

'Maybe,' Fahima went back to carefully lining her almond-shaped eyes with kohl. 'Or maybe I'm just smarter than all of them.'

'Where's mother?' Salima changed the topic.

Salima's mind couldn't help stumbling back to the dead soldier. She knew this was her crime. Her murder. Fahima had hit the man with the pot, but it was only to save Salima's life. Yet she couldn't help but wonder if her sister had already forgotten about it. Knowing Fahima, though, Salima guessed she was only living in denial, and that only made her more sad. It wouldn't last forever.

She put down the brush and picked up red lipstick.

'She's out. She had last-minute errands to run.' Fahima was drawing the missing line in her tattoo with kohl.

When Salima and Fahima had been kids in their village, Saadia had hired the services of an *adaysiya*, a gypsy who travelled on a donkey to draw tattoos in return for food. Eggs and wheat and meat. Saadia had wanted the *adaysiya* to draw a tattoo of the Amazigh sign on both of their foreheads, right between their eyebrows.

The shape was simple. One vertical line, crossed by two slightly curved, horizontal strokes, one at the top with its sides curved upwards and another at the bottom curved downwards. This mark was the symbol of Amazigh, the freemen, and most women liked to be branded by it on their faces. On the forehead, on the cheeks or down on the chin. Sometimes in all those pl ⵝ

Salima still remembered how painful it had been. The *adaysiya* had heated a needle and used it to insert ink into Salima's skin while her mother and other women held her tight so she wouldn't move and ruin the tattoo. They had her bite down on a piece of cloth. It took all the strength Salima could muster to stop from kicking everyone around her. The skin between her eyebrows continued to burn long after that.

Then came Fahima's turn. Before the *adaysiya* even laid her hand on her, Fahima started to jerk and kick her feet. It took five women to hold her in place, but Fahima continued to scream and shout.

The *adaysiya* had just finished drawing the vertical line and the upper horizontal stroke and was about to draw the last stroke when Fahima fainted. Saadia and the other women were so worried that they gave up on the tattoo. They started splashing her face with water and slapping her cheeks to wake her up. When she finally did, she drank some water, and before anyone could do anything, she threw the copper cup on the floor and bolted.

Fahima hid in the abandoned shack outside the village all day and only came back when she saw the *adaysiya* leave on her donkey. Mother beat her until she was blue. Now she had to draw that missing stroke at the bottom of the symbol with kohl every single day. Salima respected her for it, even sometimes envied the unfinished tattoo. Fahima had this unwavering resolve. When she made up her mind no one could convince her otherwise. For all her naiveté and stupid choices she had made over the years, Fahima had grit. Salima had never told her sister this; it would go straight to her head no doubt.

vi

The sisters continued their daily routine in silence. They each fixed their thick braids in two loops around their ears. They hooked their *mlahfas* over their shoulders using *khamsa* shaped clasps, and they attached thin, red scarfs to their braided hair and draped them over their backs. Finally, they sprayed their necks and shoulders with jasmine-scented perfume from the silver atomiser. They slipped on their white shoes and left.

Downstairs, Salima saw her mother's pile by the kitchen. Salima took off a golden ring and put it on top of the bundle. She wanted Mother to take it back home with her and she wasn't sure if she would be back before her mother's departure.

'She's leaving at dawn,' Fahima announced.

'I know,' said Salima.

'I begged her to stay a while longer in case something happens.'

Salima nodded, still not sure whether to feel relieved or worried about her mother's departure. On the one hand, she looked forward to spending a day without being questioned about every little thing everyone said and did. But like Fahima, she didn't know what they would do if the French started asking questions about the missing officer.

'She says Father needs her back home,' Salima said. 'Let's go. We're going to be late.'

Taking different roads, they both headed to Mouloud's café, which had been their regular workplace for two years now. It was Fahima's turn to start the night off, so she went in through the front door while Salima went in through the back. She was to wait in the small closed off staircase.

Salima pulled the curtain covering the space under the stairs and climbed onto the pile of mattresses. She drew the curtain back, crossed her legs, and rested her back against the wall, safely hidden from the crowds.

The tunes playing in the café were barely muffled by the thin wall. From the chatter, frequent applauses and occasional roar, Salima assumed the café was bursting to full capacity, so she didn't mind hiding back there until it started to empty out. She also wasn't likely to get a client tonight – most clients took dancers back home in the first part of the evening – and she didn't mind that either. She didn't mind at all.

Taking in the small dark space around her, she wondered if this was what being in prison would feel like. It didn't seem like such a horrible place to be. Maybe she would feel different if she had to stay longer.

Salima knew for a fact her sister wouldn't be able to take it. She would rather die than spend a few hours in confinement. Lucky for Fahima, if the French found out about the murdered officer, they would certainly kill them both.

'Salima,' Fahima whispered. Salima pulled the curtain and jumped to the floor.

'Your turn,' Fahima said as she opened the back door.

'A Frenchman?' Salima asked.

'A Turk,' replied Fahima. 'I'm taking him back to the *haouch*.'

'Watch out for those French soldiers.'

'Don't worry,' Fahima said. 'I have entertained this one a few times in private before, but tonight I might—' She left through the back door without finishing her sentence.

A moment later, Salima went into the café.

vii

A little past midnight, when the music and dancing had stopped and the café was empty save for a few drunk men, Salima and the remaining girls stood out on the street for one last smoke while waiting for Mouloud to pay them for the evening. Mouloud's lads were rearranging the tables and stacking the chairs on top. He stood behind the counter, counting the night's revenues. A cigarette dangled from the side of his mouth.

The girls outside complained about the slow night. They always did when they weren't so lucky as to land a client for the night and hence depended on Mouloud's payment. Salima didn't care, she just wanted to get back home and lie down on the rooftop on her own.

Mouloud finally made his way towards the girls, a tray of coins in his right hand and a cloud of smoke tracing behind him.

Nearing fifty, Mouloud still kept an elegant appearance. He always wore well-ironed khakis with a matching vest over a white shirt. He also kept his face cleanshaven except for a carefully groomed circle beard heavily flecked with grey. There was an air of authority about the slow and graceful way he walked.

As he approached the dancers outside, they fell silent. Mouloud handed a few coins to Nouara first. 'Merci,' he said. As he moved to the next girl, Nouara counted the coins, rolled her eyes and sighed. But she didn't say anything.

'Two francs?' the next girl said. 'Are you fucking kidding me?' she shouted.

Mouloud ignored her while he carried on distributing the coins to the dancers. Salima was the last one. He handed her four francs, then turned to face the complaining girl.

'You know the deal,' he said in a controlled tone. 'You dance half the evening; you get half the price.' The girl let out a snort of frustration and turned around to go, whipping her *mlahfa* dramatically. 'Wait.' Mouloud roared. She stopped and turned to frown at Mouloud. 'There is something I need to talk to you all about.'

This intrigued the whiny dancer, and she slowly made her way back to the circle while Mouloud addressed the group.

'I know you girls probably have nothing to do with this,' he started. He inhaled some more smoke before continuing, 'but I have to ask. You don't happen to know about any Frenchman disappearing a few days ago, do you?'

Thorns, tiny daggers, dug through Salima's stomach, threatening to burst her open. She tried to keep a neutral face. No. A look of concern. She was concerned about the Frenchman. Concerned and confused. What could have happened to that poor man? She had no idea.

Mouloud waited for the girls to respond. But apart from heads shaking and pursed lips, he got nothing. To Salima's surprise, he didn't seem to notice her panic. He continued, 'A French officer came to see me today asking about his friend. He last saw him here a few nights ago before he left with a Nailiya. There's been no sign of him since then.'

The ground around Salima turned to water and she felt like drowning. She needed to lean against a wall or something, but that would be too risky. If anyone saw her react it would be obvious that she had something to do with the disappearance.

Mouloud went on, looking at no one in particular. 'Now, anything could have happened to that man. The Ouled Brahims might have gotten him. Maybe he's still in bed with his Nailiya or they're both lost in the desert. No one knows, and frankly, I don't really care, either. What I do care about is my café.

'Now, the French made it clear that they do not want you girls serving clients everywhere. I know you all have found ways around their system, and that is at your own risk, as you know. What I won't have is you picking up clients from my café. I'm trying to get my papers in order so I can get authorisation for a boarding house, but until then I don't want to give the French any reason to shut down my café. So I need you girls to pay close...'

Mouloud's voice drifted off into the distance, as if Salima was dragged away from the circle in a horse-drawn carriage. She divorced herself from the world.

She came back sagging with relief when he finally concluded his long speech, and the girls scattered, each on her own way. Salima tried to force her mutinous legs to move, but they wouldn't budge. They just stood there, shaking.

She took a deep breath and tried again. More forcefully this time. They moved. Slowly, and weakly, she walked away without saying a word.

They know, Salima thought as she trod on the cobblestoned road. *His friend has been looking for him.* Of course, he was. How could she be so naïve? How could she have assumed they wouldn't notice the sudden disappearance of a French officer? Would his friend recognise her if he saw her? What would happen if he did? What was she going to do?

Questions lashed through Salima's mind like a raging sandstorm. Her eyes stung. It was at the marketplace, having crossed the gate, that she realised she was on her way to Mourad's stable. What she needed to do was go home and tell her mother about it. That their fate was sealed. But somehow, she was now walking, almost running, to Mourad. She didn't know why she was going there or what she would say to him. Salima couldn't tell him that she had killed an officer; even her clouded mind knew that. But for the life of her, she still couldn't bring her legs to stop. They trod along the pathway like scared mares.

The stable appeared at the end of the pathway. It was pitch dark. Salima ran past the palm tree trunk and the haystack where they usually lay. She slammed against the front door of the stable with a thud. The door protested with a squeak but didn't open.

She beat on it, 'Mourad. Mourad!' Her voice was weak, shaking. Her eyes welled up. 'Mourad?' she called again, still beating against the door. The horses whinnied, and the sheep shuffled about, but no one answered. She called for Kader in spite of herself. Still nothing.

She turned around and leaned her back against the wooden door. She kicked it a few times before giving up. Her chest heaving up and down and her heart beating fast.

And then it happened. It started with one tear. A warm bead spilt out of the corner of her left eye and down the side of her nose before Salima wiped it off. Then another tear and a third, and before Salima could stop it, she was sobbing.

She folded her arms against her stomach and doubled over. She slid down the wooden door. Drawing her knees up to her chin, Salima tied her arms tight around her legs and buried her face between her knees. A little girl on the dusty ground.

She cried her eyes out.

Three

i

Colonel Joseph Dupont didn't like to bring work home.

Nevertheless, the doorman risked interrupting Joseph's breakfast to announce that Major Pierre Turrene was waiting out in the foyer.

'He says it's urgent, sir.'

'Tell him Colonel Dupont is busy at the moment,' Joseph's wife responded.

Delphine sat across the table from Joseph in a white dress with puff sleeves, her short blond hair curled in the fashion of Parisian ladies.

'Offer him a seat,' she continued, 'and ask him to wait until your master is ready to receive him.'

With an obedient nod, the doorman went back out to the foyer. Joseph wore a straight face. He split his croissant with a stab and nearly flattened it while spreading the butter.

'I got a letter from Bernard yesterday,' Delphine offered.

'How's he doing?'

'He's alright. He just finished his exams, and he's coming to visit us in April.'

Joseph couldn't help feeling concerned. His twenty-two-year-old son, Bernard, was studying law at the University of Toulouse. He hadn't visited his parents in Bousaada since his latest incident over a year ago nearly cost Joseph his entire military career.

Joseph and his wife visited Bernard in Toulouse last summer, and he often wrote to his mother. He hoped his son would have matured since then, but he doubted it.

'Good,' Joseph said.

He picked up *L'Echo de Paris*. The big news everyone was following with trepidation was the Reich's decision to rearm. Today, *L'Echo* ran a fascinating article about Italy and France's formal notes delivered to Germany to protest this act of aggression.

'He's bringing someone to meet us,' Delphine interrupted Joseph's reading. It took him a moment to realise she was referring to their son. 'He says she's his friend from university, but I think they're courting. He's already mentioned her a few times in his correspondence.'

'Good for him,' he replied without lifting his head from the paper.

Perhaps this girlfriend would keep Bernard from chasing the local girls like a mad dog.

'She's from Paris,' his wife continued.

Joseph just wanted to finish the article. The doorman showed up again. Joseph slapped the paper on the table.

'What is it now?' he demanded.

'It's Major Turrene, sir,' the Arab said apologetically. 'I told him you didn't wish to be disturbed, but he insists it's an urgent matter.'

'God damn you, Pierre!' Joseph emptied his cup in one gulp, tossed the paper to Delphine and said, 'Mr. Louis Martin wrote a whole letter arguing that the French woman should vote. I'm sure you'd like to read that.'

He wiped his mouth and left the room.

Major Pierre Turrene stood admiring a painting Joseph had recently purchased from Alexandre Ivy. The French artist was trying to make a name for himself drawing naked Arab men and women in Bousaada.

Joseph had particularly liked this painting because it didn't feature any nudity. It was a plain portrait of the beautiful Moulin Ferrero, a large building which, if not for the gable roof and the round terrace overlooking the river, you might easily mistake for a natural part of the hill on which it was erected.

Hearing approaching footsteps, Major Pierre turned to salute Joseph. Joseph returned the salute with less stiffness.

'Sir, forgive my audacity to call on you at home, sir,' Pierre started uninvited, 'but this is a matter of utmost urgency.'

'What's the matter? Out with it then.'

'Sir, it's about the disappearance of the French soldier that I reported over a week ago. Officer Cambron?'

Two weeks ago, a French soldier had dropped off the face of the earth. This was worrying, but he didn't want to jump to conclusions. He'd tasked Pierre with investigating the matter. Had he found answers? If so, Joseph had a feeling he wasn't going to like these answers of "utmost urgency."

'It's been brought to my attention,' Pierre continued, 'that another soldier has also gone missing. A medical sergeant.'

Joseph's body grew tense. 'When?' he asked.

'His comrades say they haven't seen him for almost two weeks.' Joseph was still trying to work out the math when Pierre confirmed his suspicion. 'He disappeared the same day as Officer Cambron.'

'That can't be a coincidence,' Joseph said. 'Do we have any idea what happened to them?' He tried to sound calm.

'Sir, no, sir.' Pierre said. 'We're talking to their comrades and people in town to determine where they were last seen, and we're not—'

'I want to talk to them,' Joseph interrupted. 'The comrades. Bring them to my office later today. I need to know everything that happened that day.'

Pierre looked stunned, but he didn't say anything. He fumbled with the tip of his blue and red kepi. It wasn't like Joseph to do this type of work, but this wasn't a regular situation either.

'Do we think it's the Ouled Brahims?' Joseph asked.

The Ouled Brahims tribe had lived in Bousaada for centuries. When the French came to town, they were able to gradually impose order on all the other tribes. Except for the Ouled Brahims. They were known for their inflated sense of pride and refused to submit to their new governors. They had maintained resistance, killing the French and striking terror in the hearts of residents until even the indigenous people turned on them. At that point the French took advantage of the brewing anger and threw all the Ouled Brahims out of town. The other tribes, wanting peace and favours from the French, were all too happy to help. *Divide and Conquer* at its best.

This all happened long before Joseph's time. The Ouled Brahims had now settled out in the desert where they continued to terrorise the French and natives. They attacked travellers and stole everything they could get their hands on.

Since he came to town, Joseph had heard many stories about the Ouled Brahims, but he had mostly dealt with them as urban myths. Except for the time when the former *Caid*, Si Tounsi, was murdered, the threat of this exiled tribe had never seemed real. Not even when a French farmer was attacked a few days ago.

He had a feeling he was finally going to face them. He felt that very same tingly sensation he had before facing his enemy back when he was a young soldier.

'We're not sure it's them,' Pierre responded. Joseph couldn't help but feel a pinch of disappointment.

'Well, we need to know who's responsible,' Joseph said, 'and we need to know before other soldiers disappear. Whoever is behind this will pay for it dearly.'

'Of course, sir,' Pierre said.

When Pierre left, Joseph didn't go back to the dining room. His mind was already racing.

ii

Joseph's home was in *Le Quartier Europeén*. Most French families lived in similar gated houses, safe from the litter and noise of Arabs. Arabs lived in the old part of town in ancient dirty mud houses and stiflingly narrow labyrinths they called streets.

A short walk led Joseph to Place du Colonel Pein. Joseph found two soldiers outside a café and sent them to look for Caid Kacimi in La Commune Mixte.

'Tell him Colonel Dupont requests his presence at home for lunch at noon,' he said. 'And explain that it's a matter of extreme urgency.'

Better to invite him to his home. Joseph needed to be in a position of power.

He pulled his gold-plated watch out of his breast pocket. It was almost half past eight. A group of children ran past him, shouting excitedly on their way to school. *Those natives will never be civilised*, Joseph thought, *no matter how much education you give them.*

At the centre of the square, two Arab men in Kashabias sat in the shade. Three children in shabby traditional attire played around the fountain, splashing water at each other. He shook his head in despair as he passed them.

Up ahead was l'Hotel de l'Oasis, one of his favourite places to eat lunch, a two-storey building with a huge café downstairs and tables scattered on the sidewalk under the meagre shade of naked trees.

Joseph's destination was in the alley behind the hotel. The door barely hung in place. The house, standing between the Arabs' *ksar* and the French part of town, was built with baked mud, then whitewashed. The walls inside had the wooden rooftops and flower-patterned green and blue tiles characteristic of most Arab houses. But it was also decorated with an elegantly designed walnut wood drawing room suite and a carved bookcase shipped in from Paris.

Alexandre swung the door open.

'Morning, Colonel,' Alexandre opened the door wide for Joseph.

The artist wore an open shirt revealing a dirty undershirt.

Alexandre's thick, wavy hair was kept short and flat, probably due to his habit of running his fingers through his hair while he talked.

'Alexandre,' Joseph adopted an animated tone as he removed his kepi. 'How are you doing, young man?'

'I'm alright,' the artist said. 'I was just having breakfast. Coffee?'

'I never decline a good coffee,' Joseph called after Alexandre as he disappeared into the kitchen. 'No milk. No sugar, please.'

Joseph looked around the drawing room. Despite the rich decorations, the place desperately needed a woman's touch. Books and clothes and canvases, blank, half complete and finished, lay all over the armchairs, tables and floor. The air was heavy with smoke and sleep. Was there a window they could open?

Alexandre returned quickly with two cups of coffee and handed one to Joseph.

'No milk. No sugar.'

'Thank you.' The smell of good coffee almost made up for the mess.

Alexandre cleared an armchair for Joseph and found a spot on a side table for himself. Joseph couldn't help but admire Alexandre's refreshing lack of pride.

'So, what have you been up to?' Joseph asked.

'Just the usual,' Alexandre shrugged. 'Painting, drinking, sleeping, repeat.'

Alexandre was in his late twenties. He had moved to Bousaada over a year ago and was already socialising with Arabs and learning the language. Even his oval face had picked up a permanent tan.

'What are you working on?' Joseph asked. He'd bet anything it was another portrait of some naked Arab woman.

'How about I show you?'

A short corridor led to his studio, a small parlour with large windows that flooded the space with sunlight. More canvases, at different stages of completion, hung on walls, lay on the floor and stood in corners.

Joseph spied a painting of an old man sitting at his doorstep, looking up at Joseph miserably. In another corner, a group of young girls danced merrily in a cloud of dust. A woman stood in nothing but silver anklets staring defiantly at something in the distance. Her small breasts stood perkily, and a patch of thick hair covered her private part. But the painting didn't look complete. The background was still a sandy brown, and the colours weren't very bright.

After that, Joseph saw nothing but nakedness. A group of women bathing in the river, a man and a woman lying in bed together, another woman sitting on puffy cushions. Joseph wondered if painters were just sick people who disguised their unconventional lusts in the form of artistic inspiration. He couldn't believe all those Arabs had sat, stood or lain still for hours at a time while Alexandre traced the intricate details of their bodies. But then Arabs had done much worse for him in exchange for ten francs.

'I'm almost done with this one,' Alexandre interrupted Joseph's thoughts. He pointed to a canvas that stood on an old wooden easel.

A young Arab man in a white linen suit holding a hat. The figure was complete with smooth dark skin and dimples on his cheeks, but the background still needed some work.

'Who's your model?'

'Someone from Biskra,' Alexandre shrugged. 'He's here for a few days, and I offered him bed and board in return.'

On that note, Joseph sipped his coffee and they returned to the drawing room.

'Have you read the paper, today?' Joseph racked his brains for a way to introduce the real reason he was here. Alexandre sympathised with the Arabs, and Joseph knew his type. He had to tread carefully so the artist didn't feel like he was spying for the French army. 'Everyone's worried about the situation in Germany.'

'I know,' Alexandre said. 'Everyone's afraid of another big war.'

'I highly doubt the Reich is capable of fighting another war yet. It would take another, more foolish generation. The last war is still too fresh in everyone's mind.' It was still fresh in *Joseph's* mind.

'This Chancellor, though,' Alexandre shook his head gravely. 'The things he's been doing. I wouldn't be surprised if things escalate quickly.'

Joseph didn't agree, but he wasn't going to keep arguing. Instead, he said, 'Well, let's hope the League of Nations do something about it. We've sent a message calling for an extraordinary session to discuss the German rearmament.'

'I wish other European nations would take this matter as seriously. It appears we are the only ones concerned.'

'True,' Joseph said.

His mind was too occupied trying to find ways to talk about the disappearance of his soldiers. Alexandre wasn't always willing to share the information he had as readily as Joseph would expect from a patriotic French citizen. When Joseph had bought his painting, the artist's tongue loosened up a little, but he didn't share everything. He just had to be patient.

'How are things with you, Colonel?' Alexandre asked.

'Good, good,' he said. 'We're dealing with a difficult situation right now though. Two soldiers have gone missing. It's like the earth has swallowed them whole.'

Alexandre looked quizzical. 'Any idea what might've happened?' he asked.

'We have theories,' Joseph shrugged. 'Nothing concrete yet.'

'And you came here in hopes that I've picked up some chatter that might be of help to you,' Alexandre guessed.

There was no point of keeping up the pretence. Joseph said, 'Anything you know might be of great help.' He sensed desperation in his own voice.

Alexandre pressed his hair down then shook his head. 'I'm not really sure.'

'Have you heard anything about the Ouled Brahims?' Joseph didn't bother skirting around the subject anymore. He usually wouldn't ask a specific question like this so as not to influence his interviewees, but Alexandre was smart. 'They're among our prime suspects.'

'I thought they were a myth.'

'That's how they always operate,' Joseph said. 'They strike when and where you expect them least. Then they disappear and wait till we forget they exist. Suddenly they're back at our throats.'

'No one's brought them up in front of me, if that's what you're asking.' Now Alexandre was being blunt. Joseph could work with that.

'What's your take on this?' Joseph probed. 'Any idea who might be behind these disappearances?'

Alexandre shrugged, his hand caressing his hair. 'I can ask around?' he said.

'That would be very good,' Joseph conceded as he stood up to leave. 'Please keep an eye out for any discussion that might be of help to our investigation.'

Alexandre nodded reassuringly.

At the door, Joseph turned to face the artist. 'If whoever killed our men goes unpunished,' he said gravely, 'more Arabs will be eager to do the same. No Frenchman will be safe.' He paused to let that sink in, then added in dramatic conclusion, 'I pray to the Lord we can stop this before it becomes a war.'

iii

When Joseph left the artist's home he didn't feel reassured in the least.

The visit had been a complete waste of his time and pride. Joseph had a feeling Alexandre was hiding something. His assimilation with the indigenous population was a priceless opportunity to collect valuable information, but his loyalty was starting to become questionable.

Joseph headed to the military circle, a massive walled fort that housed French soldiers, an office building, and a whole military hospital with a section for civilian use.

Upon entering his office on the third floor, Joseph removed his coat and opened the window to let in some fresh air. The sky was clear, but the air felt cold and wet on the tip of Joseph's nose. Joseph's office window commanded a view of Place de Pein, which was pleasantly quiet today. On market days, he would suffer a million noises and smells rising from the crowded square to contaminate his office.

Joseph was just flipping through the correspondences on his desk when Turrene came in with a younger officer who reeked of rubbing alcohol. After the salute, Turrene took a chair. The younger officer remained standing.

Major Turrene spoke first, 'Colonel, per your request, this is Sergeant Jean Larrey. He works with Sergeant Brossolette who disappeared two weeks ago. The other comrade is currently on guard duty at the fort.'

Joseph nodded then asked Jean Larrey, 'So, what happened to your comrade?'

The young man was taken aback. 'Sir, I er— I'm not sure,' he said.

'Surely you have some theory,' Joseph pressed on. 'Killed? Kidnapped? Lost? I want you to be honest with me, Sergeant.'

'Yes, sir,' he tried again. 'I'm honestly not sure.' Joseph whipped his head to the side with a tsk-tsk, and Turrene's eyes bulged. Jean Larrey didn't seem to notice. He was gazing at something in the distance, far behind Joseph.

'When did you last see him?'

'March ninth, Sir. We worked together at the hospital until about four or five, then I saw him at that Ferrero party in the evening.'

'And you only reported the disappearance when? Yesterday?'

'Sir, after that weekend, I took a week off, and I resumed work Monday. On Tuesday, when Brossolette didn't show up for work, I assumed he was sick or something, but then he didn't turn up yesterday either, and that wasn't like him. When I asked around, no one had seen him for almost two weeks. That was when I realised I needed to report that to Major Turrene.'

Joseph took out his small notebook and pencil from the drawer and started scribbling.

He asked if anyone had seen Brossolette since March ninth.

'I've already gone around the hospital asking other officers and staff. No one could remember running into Brossolette since that weekend, but they hadn't noticed his absence either. He always kept to himself. Didn't have many friends at the hospital.'

'His supervisor?' Joseph asked, unable to fathom how no one had noticed a doctor's absence for two whole weeks.

'Work was slow,' Turrene replied, 'and everything went on so seamlessly they hadn't noticed someone was absent.'

This wasn't enough, though. Joseph needed more concrete information. Something to act on.

'Do you two have any reason to believe Brossolette and Cambron's disappearances are somehow related? Were they friends?'

Without shifting his gaze, Jean Larrey shook his head, dissipating Joseph's last glimpse of hope. He was about to write no connection on his notebook when Jean Larrey spoke, and for the first time today, Joseph heard something he could work with.

'No, they weren't friends,' Jean Larrey said. 'In fact, they had a big fight that same evening. On March ninth.'

'A fight?' Joseph was incredulous. *And you didn't think this was worth mentioning?* 'What was it about?'

'I don't know the details. I ran into Brossolette at the Ferrero party that evening, and I noticed a cut on his lip. He seemed preoccupied, but he didn't say anything. He didn't stay long. But people were talking about a fight in town between Brossolette and Cambron. I'm afraid I don't know what it was about.'

Joseph was no longer sure the Ouled Brahims were behind the disappearances. Nothing was conclusive yet, but Joseph probably had a whole different case on his hands now. An internal matter. Disappointing.

'Do me a favour, Major Turrene,' Joseph said. 'Bring me Cambron's comrade as soon as he's off his guard duty. In the meantime, I need you to see if the officers' belongings are still in place. Check for their clothes, their weapons, pictures, anything. Check the hospital too for Brossolette's belongings.'

'Oui, Colonel,' Turrene said, and he left with Jean Larrey.

Looking out the window, Joseph lit up a cigarette. Place de Pein didn't seem to have changed since the morning. The two men in *Kashabias* were still sitting in the exact same spot, and the three Arab boys were still splashing water at the fountain. It was like time had frozen.

Joseph often felt time was experienced differently by the indigenous. It was like their time was circular. Never ending cycles. To him, time was linear, constantly marching forward. That was why Arabs struggled to progress, they kept running in circles.

Joseph sat back in his chair and looked at his notes.

He twirled his pencil between his fingers. Maybe things escalated between Brossolette and Cambron, and one of them ended up murdering the other? In a fit of panic, the murderer might have hidden the body and run for the hills.

But there was no proof. He had to know what they'd fought about.

Joseph drew a hard line under the word *fought*. Then he added three question marks next to it.

He hoped his next conversation with Cambron's friend would clarify more.

iv

It was noon when Colonel Joseph Dupont left the military circle.

He was going to be late for his lunch appointment, but that would only put the *Caid* on edge, and the Lord knew Joseph needed to have the upper hand today.

As intended, *Caid* Malek Kacimi was waiting outside Joseph's home. The *Caid* was well into his forties, but he acted like a seventy-year-old man. He moved at an infuriatingly slow pace and used a wooden cane he didn't really need.

Today, *Caid* Kacimi wore a beige turban and his usual clean white *burnous*. A long, silver dagger hung from the left side of his leather belt and a long barrel pistol hung from the right. Perhaps these weapons were mostly for decoration. Kacimi didn't strike Joseph as the fighting type. But then you never really knew with these barbaric Arabs.

'*Caid*,' Joseph called with feigned cheerfulness. 'How long have you been out here in the sun?'

'Ah, this is nothing,' Kacimi replied, ready to start the all too familiar speech on true desert heat. Joseph clasped Kacimi's hand in a strong handshake. 'I actually think the weather is a little cool today.' Kacimi chuckled at his own joke.

Compared to most of his compatriots, Kacimi's French was good; correct, at least, though his pronunciation of *U*s and *R*s was a little off, like the Brits. It had a weird ring to it that made Joseph's ears itch.

'Well, let's get you inside,' Joseph had no intention of apologising for his tardiness. He led the way to the back garden where a round wooden table was set up in the shade of fruit trees.

'How have you been, *Caid*?' Joseph asked as the two men took a seat.

'Busy. We've been pollinating palm trees for two months now.'

Caid Kacimi's family wealth came from their enormous palm tree plantations. However, they both knew that Kacimi's 'busy' work with the pollination didn't extend any further than overseeing the labour done by dozens of poor farmers.

'Well, that's good,' Joseph said. 'I'm sure it'll all pay off during harvest season.'

'Inshallah,' Kacimi said.

'How's your family?' Joseph asked. 'How's your daughter doing? What's her name? Karima, is that it?'

Men here weren't supposed to ask about other men's female relatives. However, he had recently done Kacimi a big favour by ensuring his daughter's enrolment into the European elementary school in town. Of course, Joseph only did that to ensure the *Caid*'s obedience back when Kacimi was showing some reluctance to accept his position.

If Kacimi was offended by Joseph asking about Karima, he didn't show it. 'She's good,' he said with a broad grin. 'She's already in her final year.'

'Serious? It feels like it was just yesterday that we got her into that school. I can still remember how shy she was on her first day.'

'True,' Kacimi nodded, grinning. 'And now she has friends. She can speak and read French like a little *roumia*. All thanks to you, Colonel. Thank you.'

It takes more than speaking French to become a European, Joseph thought. Aloud, he said, 'Well, I guess she needs to go to Algiers to finish her education. High school and maybe even university.'

He chose his words carefully to give his guest the impression he was promising to help with that without committing to anything. Kacimi's grin waned, and his eyes narrowed. According to this Arab, completing primary education was more than enough for his daughter, and it was now time to groom her for marriage.

'But you don't have to worry about that now,' Joseph reassured him. 'She still has a few months to go before you have to make that decision.'

'Thank you for your kindness, Colonel,' the *Caid* said sheepishly.

Joseph's housekeeper came out of the kitchen, and with a constantly nodding head, he whispered a *bonjour* and a quite unnecessary *merci* as he served them both lemonades. Then asked in barely comprehensible French, 'You like lunch now? Ready.'

'Yes,' Joseph said. 'You can serve us lunch now.'

'Oui, merci,' the housekeeper bowed and nodded again before heading back to the kitchen.

'Tell me *Caid*,' Joseph lifted his glass and encouraged his guest to do the same. 'What's the word on the street? Any recent developments I should be aware of?'

The guest shifted uneasily in his seat and put the glass down without tasting the lemonade. 'Nothing that comes to mind,' he replied with a slow shake of the head. 'Everything's going well. Things are safe.'

'How about the Ouled Brahims? Have you heard anything about them lately?'

'Nothing out of the ordinary,' the *Caid* shrugged. 'I mean sometimes I would hear of some hero or another killing a score of them, but I'm sure you're always the first one to learn about that.'

One of the old practices that Joseph found in place when he took office was the ten-franc payments in return for killing Ouled Brahims. Until this day, Joseph still paid Arabs who took up manslaughter as a profitable venture. Every week, they would go out to the infinite desert hunting for Ouled Brahims and come back with their victims' right ears strung on a large ring of bloody copper string.

He wasn't sure about the efficiency of this practice, though. He must have paid for thousands of ears in the last year or so, which should have been more than enough to cleanse the whole tribe. Yet, somehow there was always another ring of Ouled Brahims. Joseph felt like these savages had devoted their whole lives to breeding little monsters who would grow up to kill more French.

It was like the story out of Indochina about a French governor-general who had set a bounty to encourage locals to kill rats in the sewer system. To avoid having to deal with thousands of rat corpses, the general-governor introduced a one-cent bounty for a rodent's tail. The French soon learnt that instead of exterminating the rat population, the bounty mysteriously caused the rodents to multiply. The locals not only resorted to cutting off tails without killing the rats, but they even started to breed them for profit.

Joseph didn't think it below the Arabs to set up human farms outside of town to breed people and use their ears for money. Had they been cutting ears off without killing them? He felt nauseous at the thought of being raided by an army of earless Ouled Brahims.

'Has anything happened?' the *Caid* inquired. 'Forgive my honesty, Colonel, but you seem to be looking for specific information.'

'True,' Joseph nodded. 'Let me be candid with you. Two of my men recently disappeared, and I have reason to believe the Ouled Brahims are behind this.'

'I'm terribly sorry to hear that, Colonel.' Kacimi's face looked genuinely sorry.

'I'm now leading the investigation myself, and I was hoping you had information.'

'Nothing I can think of. But now that I know what you're looking for, I'll keep my eyes and ears alert.' Joseph was inclined to believe him.

'And *Caid*, this needs to remain discreet. If people hear of the disappearance of two soldiers, I won't be able to contain the fear around here.'

Joseph's housekeeper reappeared with another tray. The sweet smell of steamed meat and vegetables flooded Joseph's nose.

While he ate, occasionally chatting with his guest, Joseph felt more positive about this meeting. Kacimi hadn't provided any useful information, but Joseph believed that for the first time the *Caid* was in his corner. Joseph usually sensed reluctance in the way Kacimi provided any service. It was as though he regretted accepting the *Caid* position.

But today Kacimi either felt bad for the missing young men, or ashamed of his own race. Whatever it was, Joseph saw genuine empathy and a determination to help in the man's eyes.

v

Officer Mercier came to see Joseph late that afternoon with more information than everyone Joseph had interviewed that morning put together, including Turrene.

The young soldier was too dark, undoubtedly from the long hours he stood guard, and was marked by two matching brown moles, one under each of his tired green eyes. They gave you the eerie impression that he had four eyes watching you. He looked familiar.

At first, Mercier's account mostly aligned with what Joseph knew. Additionally, Cambron had not taken his belongings with him.

This was already helpful. Cambron's intact belongings meant he probably hadn't disappeared by choice. If Brossolette's things had disappeared, it would almost confirm Joseph's theory that Brossolette had hurt Cambron and skipped town.

He asked Mercier, 'Do you know why Cambron and Brossolette fought that night?'

'Yes, sir,' Mercier replied. He hesitated a little, but Joseph gave him an encouraging nod. 'It was about a girl.'

'A girl?'

'Yes, sir. It was a Nailiya girl.'

'A prostitute?' Joseph couldn't believe his own ears.

Two of his men had gone missing, and he was already spending more time than he should on this stupid case, and this was all for what? A stupid dancer? He hoped to find the two young men alive just so he could kill them himself.

'Respectfully, it's not like that, sir. Cambron didn't fight the doctor for the girl's eh... love or anything. Cambron and I were part of the tax evasion task force.'

After the new ban on undocumented brothels, some prostitutes had found ways to service clients secretly, refusing to pay taxes or undergo periodic medical checks. They claimed that Nailiya dancers weren't prostitutes. They only danced for clients.

In retaliation, Joseph and Turrene had put together a taskforce of young officers to approach these self-proclaimed virgin dancers and try to catch them in the act. It turned out Cambron and Mercier had both been part of this taskforce.

'Then why did your friend fight with the doctor that evening?' Joseph asked.

'I'm not sure,' Mercier started. Joseph was growing sick and tired of that answer. 'Cambron and I... We were sort of competing over the number of girls we brought in.' He lowered his face, clearly not too proud of the childish unprofessionalism. 'We were aspiring for a promotion.'

Joseph could relate to that. He grinned as Mercier continued, 'So we didn't share a lot of information about our targets. All I know is that Cambron was following a girl he thought was practicing prostitution illegally, and he was determined to expose her.'

'Do you know who this girl was?' he asked.

'No, sir,' Mercier said. 'The last time I saw Cambron was that evening when he left Mouloud's Café with a girl.'

'Do you think Cambron and Brossolette both wanted to go with the same girl? Is that why they fought?'

'No, sir, I don't think so. The fight had taken place earlier. The doctor wasn't at the café when Cambron and I were approaching our targets.'

'Then why did they fight?' Joseph strained not to show his frustration.

'I'm afraid I don't know. All I know is that they fought over a prostitute. Cambron himself told me but didn't mention any details.'

'Do you think it was the same girl Cambron left with that night?'

'Maybe,' Mercier said. 'I couldn't be sure.'

There was a two-tap knock at the door and Turrene let himself in.

After a salute, Turrene said, 'Brossolette's belongings have disappeared, Colonel. Most of them, anyway. Clothes, books and other personal things...'

This solidified Joseph's theory. Brossolette killed Cambron and disappeared. His instinct was right. At least this didn't mean the whole French army was under immediate danger. Now he just had to find Brossolette.

'...green bag was always hanging in the back of the—' Turrene was still speaking for some reason.

'Thank you, Turrene,' Joseph interrupted him. 'That's very helpful. What I need you to do now is find out how Brossolette skipped town and where he was headed. Check with bus drivers, people with automobiles, Arabs with camels. Anyone who could have helped him get anywhere. He couldn't have walked out into the desert on his own.'

Turrene nodded, and Joseph turned to the young officer. 'Officer Mercier,' he said. 'I need you to look into the fight. Ask other comrades. Do whatever you need to get to the bottom of it. I need to know why the two men fought over some random prostitute.'

'Yes, Colonel,' Mercier nodded.

'Also,' Joseph added, 'try to find this girl they fought over. Whoever she is, I need to have a conversation with her.'

Mercier nodded again.

'And Mercier,' Joseph squinted as he thought about it. 'Why don't you start with the whore Cambron left Mouloud's café with that night?'

Four

i

'Come on, Ammariya,' Nouara begged. 'Last round. I promise.'

Salima had spent most of the afternoon on the roof of Soltana's *haouch*. She sipped tea with the girls, traded gossip and played knucklebones; and Nouara had won most rounds.

'You said that last time,' Salima said as she lit a cigarette.

'I mean it this time,' Nouara was giddy. 'Come on.'

She had also said that last time, but Salima let it go. The spring sun was dropping behind the hills, but they had enough time for another round. The other girls shifted on their rugs. They didn't seem to be enjoying the game but didn't say anything. They were young and less accomplished, so they went out of their way to please Nouara. They'd started acting like this around Salima too.

That was one of the reasons Salima liked having Nouara around her. Unlike her, Nouara embraced people's attention like a lover. She rolled in it and rubbed her body and soul with it like a chicken bathes in warm dirt.

Nouara dropped the five stones, spreading them by her feet. She picked up one of the five pebbles, threw it in the air, no higher than her head, picked a second pebble and caught the first one before it dropped to the floor. All in one fast swish. She did the same with the remaining three stones. She squealed with triumph and went on to the next phase. And so the game went on, with Nouara flying seamlessly through the stages, now scraping two pebbles at a time off the ground, now throwing all four stones in the air to pick up a fifth.

With the cigarette in hand, Salima watched the pebbles rise and fall into Nouara's cupped hand. She felt relaxed. Like she didn't belong to this world of pressure that Nouara was living in. Maybe it was fatigue.

Salima felt drained from worry. She wouldn't be able to run now even if the ground started to shake with an earthquake. But she also felt safer. It had been about two weeks since Mouloud mentioned the French officer. Salima had been terrified to death. She would be killed, and so would her sister, and maybe even her mother.

But no one came looking, and all those fears gradually dissipated. Salima and Fahima had gone back to their regular life, dancing and working and making as much money as ever. The guilt was still lodged like a thorn in her throat though. She kept reminding herself that he would have killed her. She would've been dead.

Salima forced herself to focus on the game. Forming a small bowl by cupping her hands together, Nouara was now trying to pick up the pebbles with her two forefingers, one at a time, and throw them inside the small bowl of her hands.

The game was finally broken off when a young lad in dirty white clothes came up the stairs. It was Mouloud's errand boy, a skinny lad of about ten or eleven who was light on his feet, quick-witted and acted with an air of manly authority that rivalled that of the Caid. Akshish, everyone called him, meaning boy in Berber.

'There you are girls,' Akshish announced as though he was addressing a group of five-year-olds. 'I figured I'd find you up here going about your womanly things.'

'Would you like to join?' Nouara pretended to seduce him. 'You figured that out all on your own?' someone else asked between giggles. Salima contributed with a dull 'I guarantee you it's not as exciting as you'd imagine.'

The boy raised his chin and looked away from the women like men often did in public. He said, '*Ammi* Mouloud wants you at the café a little early tonight.'

'Did he say why?' Salima asked casually. She wouldn't allow fear to take over again.

Akshish eyed Salima with his eyebrow raised and an impish grin Salima couldn't help admiring despite the condescendence it carried.

'Since when does *Ammi* Mouloud have to tell me or you why he wants something?' he took one step down the stairs before pausing to say the one phrase Salima hated the most in this town, 'Regular girls only.'

That meant Nouara and Salima only, and everyone on the roof knew it.

ii

As the warm afternoon gave way to a chilly evening, Salima hugged herself and walked up the Street of Joy.

Once home, Salima crossed the yard to the animal shed to check on her rooster. The small window didn't bring in any light, but Salima didn't usually have trouble spotting the cock perched up on his wooden stick. He wasn't here now, though.

'Damn you, rooster,' Salima hissed. The goats chewed as they eyed her with mild curiosity.

This meant one thing. The stupid rooster had gone to Fadhila's coop again. Salima hated that woman, and the only thing she hated more was having to talk to her about her dumb rooster.

The rooster kept going back to the Jewess's chickens because the dogs had eaten his hen, so he went out and found himself a group of chickens to fuck instead. *Why am I surprised?* Salima wondered as she left the shed. She would have to get that stupid rooster a new chicken.

Salima went out and crossed the street to Fadhila's front door. It took all her determination to not turn around and leave that useless animal to his own mess.

When Salima knocked on the door, no one answered. She knocked again, a little harder. Something moved above her.

'Ayash isn't working now,' Fadhila's voice, high and squeaky came from a slit above the door. 'It's late.'

Salima rolled her eyes. 'My rooster ran away again,' she said. 'I think he's in your coop.'

I should slaughter the damned cock as soon as I lay my hands on him, Salima thought.

'I don't know,' Fadhila said. 'It's too dark to see. If I see it in the morning, I'll throw him out.'

'I don't want him to sleep here tonight,' Salima was exasperated. 'It'll be even harder to break his habit.'

A ruckus came from the coop to the side of Fadhila's house. Chickens and roosters flapping their wings and crying. Then it died as suddenly as it had started.

'Well, if you're so concerned about your rooster's habits,' Fadhila said, 'why don't you lock him up?'

This is ridiculous.

'Come on, Fadhila,' Salima knocked on the door. 'We don't need to do this. Just give me the fucking rooster, and let's not talk to each other ever again. Deal?'

'That foul mouth!' Fadhila screamed. 'I have no idea what we've done to deserve such vulgar neighbours. I told Ayash, I said if these shameless girls move to this street, we need to move out, I said. I told him. They'll just bring sin and filth to our doorstep. And we have our daughter's reputation to keep.'

You think your girl is the Virgin in flesh and blood, don't you? Salima kept this though to herself.

'Come down here and I'll show you what real sin and filth feels like, you piece of shit!'

She was still hollering profanities at the Jewish woman when the door creaked open, revealing the weak figure of Fadhila's daughter, looking as pale and scared as ever.

Without a word, Yamina produced Salima's rooster. Despite the dark, Salima recognised his red-feathered neck, his white back and black dotted wings.

Salima stood still thinking this may be a trap until Fadhila's annoying voice descended again, 'Yamina! What are you doing? Yamina? How dare you open the door at this time? Do you not realise how dangerous it is out there? You get back in right now and lock the door behind you. Yaminaaaaaaaa!' She dragged that last *Yamina* like the call of someone falling off a cliff.

Salima took the rooster, mouthed a thank you and winked at Yamina before holding the bird towards the window slit in defiance. She wanted to call the woman some more foul names but chose not to in front of her daughter.

iii

Exhausted by the stupid rooster, Salima locked the bird in the shed and went upstairs to her room. She smoked a cigarette while she threw on a blue and black striped dress with large sleeves, fixed her hair and applied makeup before heading back out.

Salima heard something. She stopped at the first step of the stairs and listened. She recognised the sound of Fahima's sobbing from the courtyard.

'Oh crap,' Salima whispered. 'What is it now?'

Looking over the wooden railing, she couldn't find her sister in the dark. The uncontrollable sobs echoed from below like the cries of a tormented ghost. With a shudder, Salima moved to stand over the large flowerpots that had replaced the broken wooden railing. She saw her.

Fahima was slumped against the wall of the well, knees drawn to her chin. Her body shook compulsively with the sobs.

'Oh shit,' she hissed again. 'I don't have time for this.' Then out loud she called, 'What the fuck is wrong with you?'

Startled out of her dramatic fit, Fahima stopped shuddering and looked up. 'Go away. Leave me alone.' She turned away, but didn't resume her sobs.

'What happened?' Salima insisted. 'Why are you crying?' She tried to hide her irritation, but her voice betrayed her. 'Are you crying over the Frenchman?' Nothing. 'I can't believe it. That excuse of a man doesn't deserve your tears.' This time, Salima managed to hide her irritation better.

'That excuse of a man was the love of my life,' Fahima started sobbing again. 'And I've lost him.'

'*Love* of your *life*?' she said. 'You stupid naïve girl. You really think he loved you? What did you expect to do? Go to Paris, get married and live like a princess? He'd never do that. Never. He was playing with you, and you believed him.'

That didn't seem to help. Salima knew she had to go, or else things would get ugly. She didn't want to fight with her sister. Not today. Not when she was finally feeling relaxed. She dashed down the stairs and crossed the courtyard toward the entrance.

'Had he really loved you,' she said, turning to Fahima, 'he wouldn't have done what he did.'

To Salima's surprise, Fahima emerged from behind the well like a monster rising above a hill. Fury and death in her bloodshot eyes. Salima was scared. She had never seen her sister like this.

Fahima picked up a flowerpot and hurled it at Salima. It rolled in the air, end over end. Salima ducked just in time to avoid it smashing into her face. The pot crashed into the wall instead, and exploded into mud shards and dirt, showering Salima.

'It was you,' Fahima the monster was roaring. 'It was all *because* of you, you *cunt*! I would still be with my man now if it weren't for *youuuu*.'

She picked up another pot and threw it at Salima, but Salima was more prepared now. The door was ajar. She slipped through it and closed it before the pot hit the door.

'You're fucking crazy,' Salima shouted.

'*You're* crazy!' Fahima called back, her typical childish reply.

'Clean up the mess,' Salima called as she walked away.

She sensed a movement through an open window in the Jew's home. Salima wasn't sure, but she knew someone had been watching her. Had probably been watching her and her sister fight.

She shook her head and walked away, but she couldn't shake off the unease that was growing in her stomach. *If they've seen this*, she wondered, *what else could they have witnessed?* The thought made the hairs on her arms stand up. *If they'd really seen anything*, she tried to convince herself, *they probably wouldn't have stayed silent all this time.*

She forced the idea out of her mind and picked up her pace as she headed to Mouloud's.

Why is the world so determined to ruin my day?

iv

When Salima went into Mouloud's café, staying in a good mood became the least of her worries.

The café was empty save for a small congregation of Ouled Nail girls standing in uncharacteristically solemn quietude. Their stern faces and crossed arms gave Salima the impression that someone had just passed away in front of them. Salima stood at the door, taking in the motionless scene. If it weren't for Mouloud's waiter shuffling around, it could have easily been mistaken for a French tableau.

Approaching the group, Salima noticed three men and a woman in the back by the counter. The woman sat in one of the low stools usually used by the musicians, her back to Salima. She was facing three tall men, all standing like the minarets of a mosque. One of them Mouloud. The other two men, to Salima's horror, were French officers.

Her sore heart began to thud in her throat and the blood drained from her face. She continued walking towards the other dancers, her eyes fixed on the back of the room. One French officer wrote on his notepad. The woman seemed to do most of the talking. The other officer occasionally said a word or two, which Salima couldn't make out. Mouloud looked deeply concerned as he squinted at the cigarette between his fingers.

Salima stood between Nouara and Djamila, crossed her arms, barely able to breathe. The girls glanced at her briefly then looked towards the back of the room too. She wanted to ask what was going on but was too scared of the response.

'It's about the missing soldiers,' someone said, as if hearing Salima's thoughts.

'Soldiers?' she asked, puzzled. Was there more than one soldier? 'Mouloud talked about one missing.'

'There's a second one,' Nouara whispered. 'It's definitely the Ouled Brahims. Who else would kidnap two soldiers? And I say they're dead. Why would they kidnap them? They killed them and threw them out to the wolves.'

'So why are these officers here?' Salima asked.

'They're investigating,' it was Djamila who answered now. 'One of them was last seen here apparently.'

This place suddenly stifled her and she wanted to run away. Not back home. Not to Mourad's stable, either. She had to escape all of this. To go out to the desert and lie there until she died. But she couldn't. She could only stand and watch. At least the other girls also seemed scared.

It felt like ages before the woman stood up and joined the girls. Mouloud called for Djamila next, who sat through another interview, then another dancer replaced her. Salima was dying to know what questions the Frenchmen were asking, but she couldn't bring herself to inquire.

Then it was her turn. When Mouloud called her name, Salima walked slowly towards the back. The urge to run away was strong. The three men stared at her with impatience until Mouloud motioned for her to hurry up already. One French officer, a lean man in his forties dressed in a khaki uniform, asked her to sit down. She obeyed, collecting the seams of her dress in front of her.

'This is Major Turrene,' Mouloud started. 'He's investigating the disappearance of two French officers.' He spoke mostly in French, but since moving to Bousaada Salima had learnt to understand the language. She still spoke it with difficulty, though.

'He wants to ask you a few questions,' Mouloud continued. 'Please answer to the best of your knowledge. Don't be scared. They're just doing their work.'

Salima tried to nod.

'Mademoiselle Ammariya,' Major Turrene started slowly, pronouncing the nickname she and Fahima had come to be known as with great difficulty. Then he looked down at his notepad and asked, 'Where were you the evening of March ninth?'

Salima knew what evening he was referring to. She faked a puzzled expression. Then smirked at Mouloud. 'They expect us to know the dates?'

'It was the evening Ferrero hosted a party,' Mouloud explained patiently. 'About three weeks ago.'

Salima nodded, then she said in broken French, 'Here. I remember I worked here that night.'

The three men nodded in unison and Turrene scribbled something.

'Do you know a French officer by the name of Cambron?'

Salima didn't have to fake any puzzlement this time. She gave him an expectant look, and when he didn't explain further, she couldn't help saying, 'We don't check our clients' papers here.'

Turrene continued to stare at her, clearly not happy with that answer.

'Ammariya,' Mouloud warned.

'I don't know anyone by the name of Cabrone,' she said in French, throwing her hands up.

'Cambron,' Turrene corrected. 'He disappeared the evening of March ninth, and he was last seen here at this café.'

Salima shrugged.

'Tell me, Mademoiselle, did you go back home alone that evening? March ninth?'

'Yes,' she nodded, trying to hide a fresh rush of fear.

Salima didn't have any official authorisation to take men home, so she would have lied about going back home alone even without the incident. She had often lied about taking men home, and she liked to think she was a good liar, but this was different.

'I only dance,' she added.

'Can someone testify that you went back home alone? Someone you met on the way back?'

'I don't remember. I'd have to ask.'

'Tell me, Mademoiselle Ammariya,' Turrene flipped the pages of his notepad and produced a small photograph. He handed it to her and asked, 'Have you seen this young man before?'

As she took the picture, her throat tightened. Her hand shook frantically. Turrene saw that. She knew he saw that. The photograph showed a young man in a dark beret grinning at her. He was leaning his elbow on the hood of a car, a glass bottle in his hand. A chill crept up her back and put its weight on her chest. It was like staring a ghost in the face. The young man's skin was pale in the photograph, his dimpled cheeks looked puffier, swollen. The black rose tattoo at the base of his neck was invisible – hidden under the shirt, Salima assumed. But it was him. The same lazy eyes, dark and glittery under bushy eyebrows. The man who had tried to kill her.

She still remembered the anger in his red eyes and the grip of his hand on her neck. She recognised the grin in the picture in front of her, cunning and mischievous. Like he was in control. Like he was going to get his way.

Salima forced herself to focus on the men in the room. She tried to shake her head, but it only moved slightly. Mouloud jumped in, saving her from having to talk.

'We have a lot of clients in this café, sir,' he said cautiously.

'I only have one last question,' Turrene said, snatching his photograph back. 'Have you heard of a fight between two French officers?' Salima frowned. 'We know the two men had fought here in town that evening. It was over a— over a dancer. Did you see or hear anything about that?'

Salima remembered a bruise on Cambron's face. She shook her head again.

Turrene sighed and with forced courtesy concluded, 'Thank you for your time, Mademoiselle.'

Salima needed no further encouragement. She sprung up and joined the circle of dancers. The men had barely enough time to interview one last girl before the first clients trickled into the café.

Salima tried to calm her heart while she watched the last of their discussion. Turrene's face was solemn. A statue. To his left, Mouloud was easier to read. He was all concern. He sucked at his cigarette with such intensity you would think he was trying to burn his mouth.

Mouloud's only concern was that his own business was at risk. If the French succeeded in tracing the soldier's death back here, Mouloud and his café were both going to be in an unenviable situation. Salima couldn't help feeling guilty. Though she knew that if it came to that, her fate would be a whole lot worse than his.

She looked at Turrene again. Still nothing. And then, another French officer came through the back door and a surge of panic nearly overwhelmed her. Those green eyes and the matching moles right underneath them   .

She had seen him several times before, including the night of the incident three weeks ago. He had come in with his friend, *what was his name again? Cabrone? Cambron.* When Salima had left the café with Cambron, this man with the moles left with another girl. They had laughed drunkenly as they walked down the street, and Salima had wished they'd be more discreet.

But as she stood here staring at him, she had no doubt. The Frenchman whispered something in Turrene's ear then stood behind him. His eyes wandered the place until they fell on Salima, and he glared at her. Salima looked away, her face burning red.

Did he remember her?

v

When they were done, Mouloud offered the French officers a table and served them drinks.

The dancers went out the back door to smoke, which Salima was in desperate need for. As the girls whispered their theories about what happened, often circling back to the Ouled Brahims, Salima's mind was preoccupied by the man with two moles.

She couldn't figure out why he hadn't said anything. Was he not sure? Or maybe he just didn't want to mention it in front of his superior. After all, soldiers weren't supposed to go home with unauthorised Nailiya girls, either.

Something else bothered her about this man. She had seen him before. Just like Cambron, he was a murderer, and Salima had witnessed that first-hand.

Salima was in no mood to dance, but the French officers stayed for the rest of the evening and she couldn't afford to raise suspicions, assuming she hadn't done so already.

She forced herself to move to the beat of the music and sway her body to the hungry eyes of men. Her own eyes often flicked back to the French officers. Turrene was completely immersed in the party, sipping at his beer, swaying with the music. But his companion worried Salima. He was constantly staring at her. More than once, they locked eyes for a moment before he looked away. Sometimes he would stare at her in defiance until she broke off the gaze. Salima would have given up all her possessions to find out what that man was thinking.

As soon as it was appropriately late for her to leave, she slipped out the back as if for a cigarette and didn't return. She rounded the café and emerged on the main street, walking back home in long hurried strides. The night had gotten cooler. She didn't know what to do about the man with two moles, and all she wanted was to get home, lock the door and think about it when she was calmer.

She had just turned left onto the street leading up to her home when she heard something behind her. A faint thud of a boot. Or the click of a heel? She looked back and saw nothing. The corner was just behind her though, and someone could be lurking behind it.

Memories from the cursed night a few years back rushed into her mind like sharp sand grains on a sudden gust of wind. She remembered the horror, the screaming, the chase. The cold fear and hot blood. It had happened on this very street. The thieves had chased them, and no one was there to save them.

Fear grasped onto Salima's chest, and the sound of footsteps behind her sent her running. She didn't risk a glance over her shoulder. She ran all the way to her doorstep. She had already produced the key from her bosoms. She quickly opened the door, dashed in and locked it.

She leaned against the door, breathing heavily. Her foot jolted up. She'd stepped right onto a sharp mud shard. *Fucking Fahima*, Salima cursed under her breath. *I told you to clean up the fucking mess.*

The footsteps came closer now. She stood still, wishing for them to pass and disappear down the street. The cut in her foot throbbed in rhythm with her heart.

The footsteps stopped right outside her door.

She willed them to resume their walk, longed to hear heavy boot thuds on cobblestone.

There was a bang on the door.

Five

i

The outer door shut with a loud bang. Someone was violently beating at it. Something was wrong. Fahima sat up in the darkness of her room and listened.

She had cried herself to sleep, and she didn't know how late it was. Her eyes still swollen from all the weeping.

This was the first time she had cried in weeks. She had finally succumbed to her hollowness and admitted to herself that she missed him. She loved him, René. She loved his tenderness and his care. His smile and soft skin. The way he touched her. Kissed her. She missed all of that, and it was too late now. He was gone; he left her alone, drowning in her pathetic sorrow, trying to find traces of him, of his scent, in the sand rose and the Eiffel Tower postcard he had given her.

She didn't know why it had taken her this long to let it out. To cry rivers. She probably didn't want her sister to judge her. To make fun of her, and to scold her the way she had earlier that evening.

Had he really loved you he wouldn't have done what he did. That had done it for Fahima. The way Salima talked, as if she didn't know she was the reason behind all of this. Fahima had exploded, hurling pots at her sister in a frenzy of rage. She couldn't say she regretted it.

The door downstairs rang with more banging. There was talking, too. A male voice speaking in French. A drunk client? As she got up, she had to close her eyes to stop the walls from swirling. She tip-toed out onto the balcony, careful not to reveal herself. Standing away from the wooden railing, she peered at the courtyard below.

To Fahima's surprise, Salima had let the man in. He emerged from the passage and strolled into the courtyard with the casual air of someone who owned the place. The same casual air most French soldiers had when dealing with locals. He inspected the place in silence, taking stock of the animal shed, the kitchen, and then peering up at the balcony. Exactly where Fahima was standing.

Fahima didn't move. It was dark, and she knew the shadows of the walls would cloak her like a magical burnous. She could see him clearly, though. His skin was tanned, his eyes green, and a pair of matching moles under his eyes looked like they were peering at you too. Fahima realised where she had seen this four-eyed man before.

It had been at Mouloud's café a few weeks ago. Fahima had spent the entire evening avoiding him and his friend for she had suspected they were those secret officers who arrested Nailiya dancers for tax evasion.

Not seeming to notice Fahima upstairs, the man's eyes continued to sweep the place until they fell on the broken section of the wooden railing. The part from which his countryman had fallen to his death a few weeks ago. Fahima and Salima had never gotten around to fixing it, so they had placed large flowerpots there instead. To Fahima's relief, his gaze didn't linger there for long. He turned to the well while Salima fidgeted with her bracelets.

Was she planning to hurt this man? Had he found out about the body in their well? This man looked stronger and soberer than the one they had murdered the other night. The bracelet would not be enough.

'Nice place,' the Frenchman remarked politely as if he was a dinner guest. Salima made no response. 'Is this where you did it?'

She tilted her head and frowned– feigned puzzlement, Fahima knew.

'My friend,' the man explained. 'Cambron.' Despite the darkness, Fahima thought she saw the colour leave her sister's face. She seemed to recognise the name. It had to be the man they had killed. An unnaturally cold shiver swept up Fahima's back, and she fought back bile. This was it. They knew.

'I know he left Mouloud's café with you that night,' the man continued.

He had resumed his casual stroll, this time towards the door.

He looked down with mild curiosity as pottery debris cracked under his boots. He said, 'The last night … seen. I remember... saw you...'

Fahima strained her ears but could only make out a few words. She snuck down the balcony and stood outside Salima's bedroom, near the large flowerpots.

'Don't play games with me, Ammariya,' the man was saying. He knew their name. 'I know you're involved in my friend's disappearance.'

'If you're that certain,' Salima said in broken French, 'why didn't you say anything earlier?'

How her sister had the courage to defy this officer right when he was about to arrest them, or maybe kill them, she would never know.

A patronising smile graced his face. 'Good question,' he said. 'I'm giving you one last chance to tell me what happened to him before I bring the full force of the French army down on you.'

He squashed a pot shard under his boot until it became tiny red grains of sand.

'You're mistaken,' Salima said. 'Maybe he did come home with me that night. I don't remember. But I had nothing to do with his disappearance.'

Salima was careful not to say death or murder. Smart. But the man didn't seem convinced. He gave Salima another condescending snicker and stepped closer.

'You know I can just shoot you dead right here and now, and no one will know about it until worms are eating your flesh, right?'

'I know,' Salima said. They were now standing under the balcony where Fahima was hiding. Fahima noticed something else on Salima's face. Not fear. She looked angry.

'It wouldn't be the first time you did that, would it?' she asked.

He ignored her, 'But you know what? I think I'd enjoy watching you rot in prison. To see you humiliated and dragged across town. Then shot or hung in public. Wouldn't that be satisfying?'

Fahima and Salima swallowed a lump in their throats.

'So, one more time. This is your last chance,' he said.

Fahima moved closer to the edge of the balcony. Her toes accidentally knocked into one of the flowerpots, nearly sending it over the edge.

'Tell me what happened to my friend, or next time I'm back here, I won't be alone.'

Fahima's blood rushed to her head as she kneeled down and placed her small hands on the heavy pot.

'Wait,' Salima said. Fahima paused. 'Your friend back in the café. Monsieur Turrene? Why didn't he say anything? Why did you let him waste his time with all those girls? Or were you afraid he would know that you and your friends have been playing with Nailiya girls outside of authorised places?'

'I wasn't sure until I saw you at the café,' he said, almost defensively. 'Now that I know for sure, I'll have to report it to my supervisors.'

Fahima's hands were back on the pot. She started pressing just enough for it to tilt ever so slightly. But the man had walked towards Salima, too far for the pot to fall on him. Salima, moved closer to him, locking eyes with his.

'Oh, but that's not all,' Salima said, forcing the man to retreat backwards until he was back beneath Fahima. 'I know what you do in your free time. When you need an extra franc.' Fahima couldn't see his face, but she assumed he was just as confused as she was. 'You kill dancers,' Salima was saying. 'You kill Nailiya girls and steal their jewellery.'

Fahima pushed hard. A voice spoke in her head, was it her mother's? It tried to warn her, to stop her from killing the man, but she wouldn't allow it, she couldn't make out the words. Didn't want to. She had to do this. This was the only way. If she let him go, it would be the end. The pot was weightless under her touch.

It didn't turn in the air or roll like the small pots did. It fell sideways, the top side diving first, the leaves of the plant flapping like wings. Fahima saw the Frenchman look up as dirt drizzled on his face, his eyes wide open, his moles staring upwards. It fell right on his head and they, man and pot, dropped to the floor with a crash.

When she stood up to get a better look, he was lying on his back exactly where his friend had lain not very long ago. He was covered in dirt and mud shards. There wasn't any blood this time. Had she pushed the pot hard enough? She stared at his feet, his fingers.

Salima stood so close to him she could have easily been hit by the pot herself.

She looked up at Fahima. 'He killed Naima.'

1931
March-September

Six

i

Fahima felt joy radiating from the city before they even laid eyes on it. The *zurna* flutes whistled, the drums beat, and the *kerkabos* rattled. Their music was carried out by the evening breeze along with women's ululations and echoes of men clapping. She forgot all about their long journey and her sore feet. She imagined herself swaying with a group of beautiful Nailiya dancers, charming the French soldiers, wealthy tourists and local merchants. Fahima couldn't wait to have her first coin necklace and collect so much money it would cover her entire chest.

She would quickly rise to be the most popular dancer, and girls would hear her stories just like she had long marvelled at the tales of the famous Hizia, who danced around the world.

Their small caravan had set off from their village before dawn, led by *Ammi* Messaoud, who was making the journey to Bousaada with his seventeen-year-old son, Mourad, and a herd of sheep to sell. There was also Said, a merchant who told everyone he was bringing food back that people in the village had never even heard of; he spoke of mangos from Mali and watermelons the size of a cow that you couldn't even carry. You had to roll them all the way back to the village, he said. Fahima wondered how he kept it from breaking when he rolled it down those rocky hills that separated them from Bousaada.

A woman in her early thirties was accompanying her younger sister, Aida, to become a dancer. Aida was shy and mostly kept to herself. Fahima thought of talking to her, but her mother, Saadia, had strictly forbidden such contact. Mother wasn't concerned about people from their village finding out that Fahima and her sister were going to dance. Everyone including her father and siblings knew about it. But discretion, Saadia kept repeating, was key to the success of their deception scheme.

Everyone in Bousaada would try and take a part of your earnings, Saadia warned. The café owners would keep a share of your hard-earned income, and the house matrons would charge you for rent and more if you brought a client over. Even the French military would take taxes. Fahima didn't understand the difference between money and taxes.

And with two sisters working, those thirsty leeches would be making a fortune on their backs. But Fahima and Salima looked so identical they could easily fool the whole town into believing there was only one of them. That way, they would only pay for one sister while they earned double.

Fahima had to admit it was a genius plan. Although it would be hard to keep up the lie with so many people, she was excited by the prospect of keeping a secret with her sister.

Right now, though, some conversation would've kept Fahima's mind off her sore calves and the burning kernels of sand that kept creeping into her sandals all day long.

'And *that* is Bousaada,' her mother declared when the small caravan came upon the edge of the hill, and Fahima finally caught her first glimpse of what she had spent her entire childhood dreaming about. 'The City of Joy.' Mother enunciated every word emphatically.

The City of Joy sat low between naked sand and rocky hills. Fahima had never imagined there could be so many houses in one place, hundreds and hundreds of them built close to one another, on top of one another even, house on house after house. The sandy colour of the walls made it look like they had erupted from the ground in an earthquake, exactly like Fahima had heard in stories. Thousands of palm trees shot up in ones and twos from inside the buildings, like hands sliding through bracelets. Others clustered in dark green patches here and there inside the city and around it, providing much longed for shade during the day.

Now, at dusk, darkness hung low like a cloud above the city, but small dots of warm light were nonetheless everywhere, on the walls and under palm trees, like a starry sky in a clear summer night. Full of life.

When her sister, Salima, asked Mother about the tall, thin building at the centre of the city, she said it was the minaret of the mosque. As if hearing its name called, the white minaret replied with the adhan. The whole city, its music, its clapping and its youyous, all fell silent as the minaret sent loud yet peaceful echoes of the call for prayer. The warm evening air carried the words above the buildings and lights, and Fahima imagined them floating around the high hills, reaching up to her, gently brushing her face, inviting her in.

'It's getting late,' Saadia said after the *adhan*. 'We need to move.'

ii

Outside the city gate, Ammi Messaoud agreed to keep the cart with everyone's luggage until the other travellers secured their lodging. All Fahima and her sister had was a small bundle of clothes, but Saadia still preferred to come back for it later once they'd secured a room at Hadda's. Something about having the upper hand while negotiating the price. Fahima and her sister didn't argue.

Crowds were gathered outside the city walls in raucous circles, clapping, cheering and laughing. The open area would usually have been shrouded in darkness if not for the light of the moon and numerous bonfires. Smoke hung thick in the air, blended with a strong dung odour and the smell of rotten grapes.

As Mother led them through the crowds, Fahima's stomach tingled, and she walked sideways trying to take in everything around her. Her mother kept jerking her hand to get her to walk faster. They shoved their way past a circle of faces painted red by the light of the flames, cheering as a topless man with a sweaty torso breathed fire. Another group swayed awkwardly to a confusion of musical instruments, and a few men clapped overexcitedly to the slow beat. Three men played music for two Nailiya girls who danced absent-mindedly around the circle, their feet moving with very short steps as if floating on a cloud of dust. A smaller ring huddled tightly around an old man in shabby clothes. He was bent over a wooden board where he shuffled three white cards as men around him shouted. Most of the people out here were men wearing thick brown hooded *kashabias* with beige turbans. Some sported western-style suits and red tarbushes, and many European couples walked gracefully through the crowd, flaunting their fancy hats and colourful gowns.

'You have to hurry if you don't want to sleep with the donkeys,' Saadia threatened as she tugged Fahima's hand for the hundredth time. 'We'll come back here once we've secured a room for the night.'

Fahima tried to hurry, but she was soon distracted by the largest and loudest group of them all. Half of them were Europeans, and their clapping and shouting threatened to overwhelm the fast-paced music. Dust rose in a thick cloud around them as they tapped their feet in excitement. At the centre of the circle was a dancing figure. With her hands above her head, she swayed her arms in mesmerising loops while her belly rose and fell rhythmically with each drumbeat. Her legs moved freely as if each had an independent life. Yet, the anklet on her foot swerved in circles, always complementing the beat of her hips.

Fahima stood still. She was enchanted by the music and dancing. And how the performer dazzled everyone around her. She wore a bright red dress embroidered in gold with fluffy sleeves and a large girdle right below her breasts. The big golden rose adorning the belt must have cost her months of work. A grey silk veil around the dancer's head covered most of her black hair except for two thick plaits that looped around her ears and lolled to her shoulders. Two black ostrich feathers decorated the veil and brushed the air as her head swayed right and left. Another veil, striped in beige and white, was tied around her waist and cascaded almost to her ankles, leaving an opening through which she revealed the length of her leg. Layers of coins covered her chest and forehead clinking and dancing to their own music. Even her olive skin danced in harmony with her body, the fire casting shadows across her perfect face, her full lips in a slight smile, her thin nose and her large gazelle eyes ringed by thick eyeliner. She was like the legendary dancers from the stories.

In her plain, brown dress, covered in layers of dust, Fahima felt like a beggar. Now that she saw a dancer for the first time, she wondered if she would ever enjoy a moment like this. If people would ever gather to admire her as she performed a breathtaking dance. If she would ever stop young girls in their tracks.

'Come on!' Her mother's voice snapped Fahima back to reality.

It was then that she realised that even her mother had allowed herself a moment to enjoy the show at the risk of spending a night with the donkeys. The same fascination danced on Salima's face, too. Even though Salima's annoying sense of righteousness would never allow her to admit it, Fahima knew very well that her sister harboured the same dreams to be a successful Nailiya dancer. The difference was that Salima just wanted to collect a fortune and start her family, while Fahima dreamt bigger. She wanted to travel the world with a reputation that preceded her.

'We're late,' their mother said as she resumed walking. Her daughters followed, and they all walked faster this time. 'For a dancer her age,' Fahima's mother said more to herself than anyone else, 'she must be very popular to have collected that many coins this early in her life.'

A *guezzana*, an old woman with a toothless mouth, recognised Saadia and insisted on reading Fahima and Salima's future. Saadia declined politely, saying they were in a hurry.

They rushed past the city gates where crowds of people walked up and down the wide, cobblestone street. Fahima had never seen so many people in one place before. The two-storey buildings she'd seen from above now rose on each side of the street, with long, narrow windows and low walls around them. It was too dark to be sure, but she guessed the houses were yellow. Every once in a while, they would walk past a building larger than others with more traffic than most.

'This is a hotel,' Saadia declared. She also pointed out some closed shops, explaining where to get wool, cloth and wheat.

'Don't ever come to this jeweller,' she warned her daughters as they walked past a small shop, as if they had just asked to go in with all the money they didn't have. 'I know a Jew that makes the finest jewellery.'

She turned left into a narrower alley. It was dark and empty, the houses smaller and pressed closer together. The dirt path weaved and twisted until the women turned left again to another wide street. Most houses here were only one-storey squares with half palm tree trunks sticking out of the walls near the roof.

'This is the Street of Joy,' Saadia announced as they passed under some oil lamps hanging from the walls of the houses.

Many women stood idly by the doors, their eyes following passers-by. One man in a tuxedo and black hat stood with a Nailiya dancer as she moved slowly against the door frame, cigarette between her fingers. Two young soldiers shuffled past the doors, nodding with wide grins at a girl that was barely wearing any clothes. Not paying attention where they were going, one of them slammed into Salima.

'Hey,' the soldier growled at her.

Fahima could barely take her eyes of the handgun attached to his belt. But even though it was dark, Fahima noticed a tan on the soldier's face as well as matching brown moles, one under each of his green eyes. Strange. She couldn't understand what he said next but from the way he spat out the French words, she knew it was not an apology.

Salima stared him down. The frown above her dark bulging eyes reminded Fahima of the way her sister looked at her before slapping her in the face. Salima and the soldier stood like that for a long moment. Fahima thought she saw the soldier's hand flex towards his gun.

It was her mother who finally stepped between them, apologised to the soldiers, and hurried the girls away. The soldiers stood their ground watching them go.

'Don't ever do that again with French soldiers,' Saadia warned when they were out of sight. 'They might shoot you just for staring at them.'

Fahima looked at the two-storey house they had stopped in front of, it must have been painted white many years before but was now turning red from the fine sand that had covered the rough clay walls.

Mother pushed the shabby door open and they all stepped down into a yard filled with the smell of freshly baked bread. In the far corner, a stout woman sat flipping a round loaf in her hands before putting it into a clay oven.

'*Khalti* Hadda,' Saadia said cheerfully. 'So, the rumours are true!'

'What rumours?' the woman responded without turning around, her voice raspy. She used a metal rod to manoeuvre two loaves of bread inside the oven, then stood up to face them.

'That *Khalti* Hadda is no longer the young, slim dancer she used to be,' Saadia said as Hadda squinted at her. Fahima assumed the woman was at least forty, like her mother, though the creases around her small mouth made her look much older.

'Look who's talking,' Hadda shot back. 'You couldn't even keep an old man entertained for two minutes.'

Suddenly Saadia laughed and embraced Hadda. When she pulled away, Hadda playfully swung the metal rod at Saadia and sat back on the stool to resume her baking.

'Are these your daughters?'

'Salima and Fahima,' Saadia said. 'You can call them both Ammariya.'

'Just like their mother. They want to be dancers?'

'Only Fahima,' she lied. Saadia discreetly gestured for both her daughters to stand against the wall in the dark. 'She just turned fourteen.'

A woman's moaning came from a dimly lit window downstairs, and Fahima wondered if the woman was in pain and why Hadda and Mother were ignoring the sound.

'And the other one?' Hadda asked. 'With those generous bosoms, she'll attract a lot of clients.'

'Maybe next year.'

'Virgin?'

'Yes. Both of them.'

Hadda was now working on another loaf of bread. She spread a ball of dough flat against the outside of the clay oven.

'How is business?' Saadia asked.

'You think I'd be making my own bread if business was good?' said Hadda, beating at the dough between sentences. 'It's not like it used to be in our day. Those French bastards are constantly watching us, looking for ways to get pleasure for free. Tourists are stingy. Watching from a distance and flashing those machines at you. I swear it was those machines that turned me blind. I know it.'

'Yeah, I know,' Saadia smiled. 'Those tourists with cameras must be knocking on your door every day.'

Fahima was intrigued by this new side of her mother, teasing Hadda and playing with her. She was funny.

'And as if that's not enough,' Hadda continued, ignoring Saadia's comment, 'you can't even trust a young dancer, you know. Take her in and groom her to be successful. Once she has used you, she switches to another woman with a bigger *haouch* to make more money. People'— She threw the disc of flat dough inside the clay oven and turned around— 'People these days just have no morals, you know.'

'I don't remember people having any morals back in our day either.'

'You must be tired.' Hadda stood up, clapping the flour off her hands. 'Let me take you to your room.' She waddled her way across the yard.

Their room was downstairs across from the outside wall. It was the last room on the left, just by the stairs. Fahima didn't know what to expect; she'd never been in a house before. The room was about the same size as their tent back home. Small, but enough to fit all three of them comfortably. Across from the door sat a wooden trunk under the window and three rugs were spread out on the floor, one by each of the remaining walls. An oil lamp glowed in the middle.

'Twenty francs upfront,' Hadda announced. Fahima didn't know how much that was. 'When she starts earning, I'll take two thirds of what she makes, including her virginity bid.'

'I'll give you ten,' Saadia replied as she searched through the top of her dress between her breasts. 'And she'll give you half of what she earns.' She produced a coin and gave it to her. 'Twenty francs from her virginity bid,' she finished.

'I wouldn't expect anything more from you,' the stout woman said as she took the coin and handed Saadia the key. 'I'll have someone bring you dates, bread and milk. After that you're on your own.'

'I wouldn't expect anything more from you,' Saadia shouted before she closed the door.

The grin she had been wearing faded.

iii

When a girl brought them food, Saadia took the platter at the door, and Fahima locked it immediately behind them. They placed the platter on the floor and huddled around it. The milk was cold and smelled of goatshit, but the bread was warm and soft.

'Listen, girls,' Saadia took a sip from the milk jug and passed it to Salima. 'You have to remember. You can't be seen together in public. No one can know that you're sisters. Not even the girls working here can know that there's two of you in this room. *Khalti* Hadda's almost blind, so it's easy to fool her, but you have to be careful with the other girls. You can never trust anyone. Not even the ones you think are your best friends.'

Salima threw a sardonic laugh. 'You really expect this to work? Have you seen how this idiot dances? Like a duck.'

'And you dance like a fat cow,' Fahima responded.

'You have to take it seriously,' Saadia said, a little agitated now. 'You heard what Hadda said. No one's your friend. They're all here to make money. To be successful dancers. And they'll do whatever it takes to get there. So if you want this to work, you have to protect your secret. Do you hear me? Any girl would be more than happy to rat you out to Hadda or the café owners.'

The daughters nodded.

'Now that rule starts tonight.'

Saadia decided that only one of them would be accompanying her to the stables to get their luggage from *Ammi* Messaoud. Against Salima's protests, she picked Fahima. She was better at finding her way.

'She'll also slow you down,' Salima whispered as she locked the door behind them.

iv

Fahima jumped back. A roaring car sped past them on the wide cobblestone street. *It will take time to get used to this*, she thought.

The crowd outside the gates was thicker and louder than before, but Fahima didn't stop to stare this time. Someone clutched her wrist and pulled her downwards.

'You're back!' shouted *Khalti* Baya, the seer.

Fahima called for her mother, scared that she would leave her behind. Saadia turned and looked down at the *guezzana*.

'Sit down,' *Khalti* Baya pointed to the empty stool across from her. 'I'll tell you what tomorrow has in store for you.' She forced Fahima to sit.

'We're in a hurry,' Saadia protested, but too weak and too late. The seer already had hold of Fahima's right hand, placing it on her knee and tracing a slow, sinuous path through her palm. Saadia rubbed her hands together, clearly uncomfortable, but Fahima knew her mother couldn't protest more without raising the seer's suspicions.

Fahima, on the other hand, didn't really care to resist. She had only spoken to seers when they travelled through their village, and it was always fun to run after them with the other children, throwing stones at them and calling them names. She'd never had her future told before.

'Mmm,' started *Khalti* Baya, sounding curious. She was staring through Fahima now, not quite at her. 'I see success, and I see fame. Those will come in twos. Your dance puts others to shame, and to admire you men will stand on toes.' She smiled tightly.

Success and fame. Out of the corner of her eye, Fahima saw her mother's face loosen up, and she turned and smiled up at her.

The seer continued still, 'Money you shall have. That and even love.'

Money. And even love. And then as if the poetic jinn left her for a moment, she looked up at Saadia and said, 'Most dancers never experience love no matter how beautiful and skilled they are.' Saadia barely nodded.

Baya frowned suddenly and her eyes shot venom at the empty stool next to Fahima. 'You stay right here, you lazy scum,' she hissed at the stool. 'Come back here, I said, and do your job.' Turning to Saadia again, she added, 'I honestly don't know why I keep this dirty snake around if he always leaves in the middle of my sessions.'

Fahima didn't know who Baya was talking about. Her skin tingled with fear, but she couldn't free her hand from the old woman's grasp. And besides, she wanted to hear more.

Baya looked back at Fahima and continued, 'Men will only have eyes for you, and for that women will envy you.' Then she tilted her head sideways, her rough finger marking a stop in the very middle of Fahima's soft palm and said slowly as if she couldn't quite comprehend what she was seeing, 'You and someone else. Your sister?'

Fahima felt her guts twist. How did this woman know about her sister? Saadia fumbled in her bosom and produced a coin. She shoved it at the seer and motioned Fahima to get up. Baya thanked them and gently brushed Fahima's left elbow as she stood.

The seer suddenly threw her head back and groaned in pain. Fahima stopped and stared, her smile passed away. The old woman's eyes had gone white and her head was shaking frantically. Saadia shook the seer's shoulders. But that didn't help.

'Death!' shouted the seer. Fahima and Saadia stood motionless. 'I see death,' the old woman continued, 'I see a lot of death. And fire. I see darkness, and the living sleeping with the dead in the dark.'

A streak of foam seeped between the woman's lips. Saadia looked around them. Fahima wanted to disappear into herself. Luckily, Baya's voice was mostly drowned out by the music and clapping of the crowds.

'You'll be our downfall, young lady.' She was screaming now. 'You and your sister will bring death and misery to this town.' Saadia dragged a feeble Fahima away as the old woman continued to shriek behind them.

'Your daughters will be our undoing, Ammariya!'

'They will bring God's wrath upon us!'

'They will bring ruin!'

'And death!'

'Death!'

Seven

i

'I won't repeat myself,' shouted the fat café owner, his thin moustache bouncing about with every word. 'If you don't take your slut of a daughter and leave now, I'll beat you with this fucking cane.'

This was the fourth café Fahima and her mother had courted this morning. Like all the others, this owner refused their services before Saadia even started talking.

'Your loss,' Saadia called back as she pushed Fahima out to the street. 'Bastard.'

Fahima was puzzled. *Why are people treating us like this?*

It was almost the middle of the day, but the sun still felt frigid. Shop owners were shouting, and passersby bustled past them as if they didn't exist. Fahima ignored them too; she was far too worried about how she was going to become a successful Nailiya dancer if no one allowed her to dance.

'Mother?' Fahima asked, treading carefully. 'Do you think they're treating us like this because of what that *guezzana* said?'

Fahima didn't truly believe what the old woman had predicted last night, but rumours might still have spread, and perhaps people wouldn't let them work because of it. That was how things worked back in the village.

'Don't be silly,' Saadia said. 'No one takes that woman seriously.'

Saadia occasionally stopped to check out a carpet, and Fahima didn't understand how her mother was taking it all so lightly. Just a moment ago, she'd been shouting back at the café owner.

'Let's try Aissa,' Mother said when they reached another café. 'Hadda says he'll take you.'

Saadia smiled as if this was this was the first café they were courting, and they both went in. This one was empty except for two men who were cleaning.

'We're not open yet,' said a stout middle-aged man. He squinted at them.

'Excuse me, sir,' Saadia said, her voice soft, while she approached the older man. 'I'm here to offer you my daughter's services.' She pushed Fahima forward before he could protest and added, 'She's an exquisite beauty, and very skilled at dancing. She would make an excellent companion for your clients, French or locals.'

'I'm sorry, sister,' the man replied. 'I'm sure—'

'She'll even do two days for free,' Saadia cut him off. 'Just try her out and see what she can do.'

'We're not looking for new dancers.' He smiled apologetically, there was nothing he could do.

'Have I mentioned she's a virgin?' Saadia asked in a last desperate attempt. The man's arms closed around his large belly, and he looked Fahima up and down. 'You may get a cut of her virginity bid,' Mother added.

He remained silent for a moment, then he said, 'I'll have to see. I'll look for her if I need her services. Where's she staying?'

'Hadda's *haouch*. Look for Ammariya.'

'Ammariya. I'll remember that.'

'Thank you, sir. You won't regret it.'

Back out on the street, Saadia whispered to her daughter, 'He'll never look for you.'

Fahima grunted. She hadn't expected it would be this hard to find a place to dance. She had imagined she would enter any café and start dancing for clients. Or maybe for a group of people outside on the street like the beautiful dancer from the night before. Now she doubted she would ever get to dance.

'What do we do now?' Fahima asked her mother.

Before Saadia could answer, someone came out of a store. Fahima did her best to avoid him, but her face still slapped against his chest.

Fahima looked up to apologise, but Saadia beat her to it. She started to say something in French.

Saadia looked up to meet the tall man's eyes and stopped mid-sentence. Her face turned red. Fahima's gaze shifted between her mother, the tall man, and the blonde woman accompanying him. All three were around the same age. Fahima had no idea why her mother was acting so strangely.

The man's face also flushed bright red. The blonde woman looked as clueless as Fahima.

Saadia shook off her surprise and tried to edge past the couple when the French woman said something to her husband. The man's face grew tense. His Adam's apple jolted up and down in his long neck. Then he said something else in French and Fahima caught her mother's name somewhere in the middle of all the gibberish.

The conversation was all fake smiles and forced laughter. She could tell they were all feeling very uncomfortable, though she didn't know why. She did pick up that the man's name must be Monsieur Dupont.

Fahima felt something else: admiration for her mother.

Joking with Hadda last night, cursing café owners and now conversing with French people? Saadia suddenly stopped being the mother from their little village. The more time they spent in Bousaada the more Saadia acted like a woman who belonged to the city. Someone Fahima barely recognised.

At one point, the blonde woman interjected the man with an 'oh' and a loaded look. He was in big trouble. A final goodbye and Saadia finally hurried past them. Fahima smiled at the couple and hurried after her mother.

'Who was that?' Fahima asked when she finally caught up to Saadia.

'No one,' answered Saadia. 'Someone I used to know when I worked here.'

'Was he a client?' Fahima was intrigued.

'He's back in town for a new position with the military.' Saadia said. 'A colonel or something.' She then added, 'Let's go back home. I'll take Salima out later to see some other cafés in the evening.'

ii

By the time they were back at the *haouch*, the midday sun was warm above their heads and three girls stood in the courtyard, each holding a water jar.

'There you are,' said one of them, a thin girl in a dark purple dress. '*Khalti* Hadda told us to take you to the river with us. We've been knocking for a while.'

'We thought you'd already started working,' said another girl with a smirk.

'I'll just take a nap,' Saadia addressed Fahima. 'You should go and get us water.'

Fahima didn't want to go alone with girls she had just met. Before she could even think of an excuse, the girl in the purple dress pushed her jar into Fahima's arms and picked up another one. The three girls left the *haouch*, but Fahima didn't move until her mother gave her a push.

Fahima tried to keep up with the three girls, but the jar kept slipping. She wondered why they couldn't just use goatskin bags like everyone in her village. This mud jar was heavy, even though it was empty, and Fahima didn't want to think about returning with the jar full of water.

The girl in the purple dress said her name was Naima, and she did most of the talking. She told them about her adventures from the night before. A group of rich gorgeous young Frenchmen took her and two other dancers out to the desert for a party in the wide open air. Drinking, dancing and pleasure until the sun came up. She was still tired, but she loved every moment. Good money, too.

They passed through a part of town Fahima had never seen before. There were fewer stores and people, and the houses soon gave way to palm trees. Mountain Kerkada always loomed above them wherever they went. The palm trees grew thicker and taller until Fahima heard water in the distance, splashing against rocks. And girls giggling. Fahima wanted to break into a run. But her arms were aching and besides, she didn't want to arrive alone.

As they emerged into a clearing, Fahima stood stounded by the magic of it all. The clear water ran through and over big, rounded rocks. She couldn't tell where the sparkling river came from, and she couldn't see where it really ended; it just merged with the horizon.

Across the river, a hill provided generous shade in which a dozen young girls perched on large rocks or lounged on colourful carpets. Three girls were washing their clothes, spreading, kneading and slamming their white dresses against the stones. At the water's edge, two girls stood naked, washing their armpits and splashing each other. The water only came up to their waistlines, leaving their breasts out on display. Fahima decided she was not doing that.

Meanwhile, the three girls from Hadda's *haouch* put down their water jars and jumped into the river with their clothes on, screaming and laughing. Fahima sat on a warm rock and watched.

No one paid her any mind, and she didn't mind it. That, however, didn't last long. Naima soon came back for her. 'Come on in.' She grabbed her hand and drew her towards the water. 'You'll dry in no time under the sun.'

Fahima was half excited and half afraid of getting into the river. She nearly lost her footing on a slippery rock, and if Naima hadn't held her steady, she would have slammed her face on it. When she finally managed to stand properly, she looked at the water running around her legs. She felt a little dizzy.

She tried to stand still, stiff legs and arms spread out to keep her balance. As if that wasn't enough, half the girls were laughing at her. Her face turned red hot. Somehow, she managed to throw herself against the nearest rock, climb, and perch herself on top, letting her feet dangle in the cool water. The girls were still giggling, so she didn't lift her gaze from her feet.

'You're new here,' said a voice behind her.

Fahima turned slowly, careful not to fall, and she immediately recognised the stunning woman lying behind her. She could recognise those gazelle eyes anywhere. This was the dancer from outside the gate the night before. The one everyone worshiped while she danced. As she lay in the sun, propped up on her elbows, her long hair tickled the rock.

'Do you speak?' asked the woman.

'Yes,' Fahima finally said. 'I – I just came to town last night.'

The woman nodded and looked away, allowing Fahima to take a deep breath. A while later, she asked Fahima how old she was. Fourteen. The woman, Nouara was her name, said she was thirteen when she started working in Bousaada. Silence. Fahima said the spot was beautiful.

'You should see the waterfalls,' said Nouara. 'Some rich Italian man bought the whole thing. Built a mansion around it. Moulin Ferrero, it's called. Makes loads of money.'

Fahima didn't know how to respond to that.

When the other girls were done washing their bodies and clothes, they all sat talking in the shade and ate dates and bread. Fahima joined in the circle. One girl said she had been to a party the *Caid* had thrown the night before. She met a lot of young men and made a lot of money. Another one said she had taken a client back to the *haouch*, but his wife followed them and dragged him back home by his ear. They all cracked up with laughter.

'Men,' said Naima with a sigh. 'They're never satisfied with what they have.'

'Can you blame them?' said someone on Fahima's right. 'What if she doesn't know how to do it right?' They all started laughing again.

'It's how they want them,' said another girl. 'Right, Nouara?' she looked expectantly, clearly seeking her approval. 'Men play around all their lives, and when they want to get married, they want a clueless virgin. No?'

'True,' said Nouara. 'Do you know the Hmaida story?' she added and giggled. Two other girls giggled too. Nouara needed no encouragement.

'This guy was looking for a virgin wife,' she began. 'When he married the first one, he pulled out his dick on their wedding night, and asked her if she knew what it was. "Of course," said the wife. "It's a dick." He sent her back home immediately. The same happened with a second wife and a third. The fourth one was something different. On their wedding night, he pulled out his dick and asked if she knew what it was. "Is it a date?" she asked naively. The man was pleased with his virgin wife. "No," he corrected. "This is a dick." The wife was puzzled. "Really?" she asked. "Because my cousin Hmaida has a dick, and it's as big as a cucumber."'

All the girls burst out laughing. One of them fell to her side and beat the carpet with her palm. Not sure what was funny, Fahima smiled, but when Nouara looked at her, she forced a laugh. The girls passed around more bread and dirty jokes.

When the sun turned a bright yellow, they filled their jars with water and returned to town in groups. Fahima balanced the full jar on her hip, relieved that it wasn't as heavy as she had expected it to be.

'Do you want to go dancing with us tonight, Ammariya?' Naima asked Fahima when they arrived back at the *haouch*. 'We'll start outside the gate then see if we can get into some cafés.'

'Yeah, thank you!' said Fahima. Her ears thudded with excitement.

'Great. Get ready. We leave at sunset.'

Fahima waited for the girls to go up to their rooms before she knocked on her bedroom door. One tap, then three, then two. Just like her mother had instructed.

iii

'That's not fair,' Salima complained to her mother as Fahima pranced around, getting ready to go back out. 'She's the only one who's been out since we got here.'

'Shush,' Saadia whispered. 'You can too, as long as you go to separate places.' Salima fell quiet, but Fahima could still see she was annoyed. 'What's more important,' Saadia continued, 'is that you report to each other what happened. You can't miss any details.'

Saadia had already covered the morning tour of the cafés, so she made Fahima report on everything that had happened out by the river. Her mother kept interrupting with questions. Who did she go with? What were they wearing? What road did they take? What did they talk about on the way to the river? Mother was not kidding when she said not to leave out any detail.

Saadia even made her retell the story of Cousin Hmaida. Fahima felt very uncomfortable, but her mother just listened while braiding Salima's hair. She neither flinched nor laughed at the joke. Was this what Mother intended for them to do for the rest of their lives? Just sit here and narrate all the details of their days? Now Fahima understood why Salima had been sceptical about the whole plan.

'That's good,' Saadia finally commented. 'Make sure you tell each other everything every single day. Understand?'

Fahima nodded while putting on her large silver hoops. By the time she had tied the red veil around her waist, there was a knock at the door. Knowing it had to be Naima, Fahima skipped to get the door. Her mother stopped her before she could answer it.

'Do you know where you'll be dancing?' Saadia whispered.

'Outside the gate I guess.'

'So Salima and I will stay away from that area. You be careful, alright?'

Outside, Fahima stood for a moment under the arched walkway, admiring the festive creature Naima had transformed into. She had wrapped her thin body in silk clothes that made her bosoms look even bigger and donned heavy jewellery and a large feather on top of her head. Fahima noticed her necklace had dozens of coins, which spoke to her experience and wide success. Her big lips looked more sensual in bright red.

Naima was also looking Fahima up and down with a smirk. In her simple clothes and light decorations, Fahima felt almost naked, but she liked to think her beauty made up for the lack of accessories. She had large eyes, a small mouth and high cheekbones, and has often been told that her beauty was otherworldly. She was finally going to put that to the test.

Fahima and Naima ran into another group of dancers on the way, and they all headed towards the gate. Fahima recognised two of the three girls from the morning trip to the river, but apart from a glance up and down, the girls didn't pay her much attention. It wasn't like they were ignoring her, Fahima thought; they treated her as if she had been going out with them every night for years, and she liked that.

A few men called after them here and there, some saying some very nasty stuff, but the girls pretended not to hear any of it. Outside the gate, the nightly festivities had already started at the crowded marketplace.

The group of girls strolled between circles of people, curious to see who was performing. One circle featured a drum beater, a flute blower and one girl dancing to a small audience of three. Everyone looked at Fahima's group expectantly, almost begging them to join, but the girls continued their tour.

Fahima was starting to feel impatient to dance when Naima tugged at her and motioned her to follow.

'Let's go find us a better spot to dance,' she said.

The two girls toured the place until they found a small circle with an audience of about a dozen people. The music was lively, though, with five middle-aged men playing drums, flutes and an oud. Without any invitation, Naima jumped inside the circle and started dancing. A roar went up among the audience, and the clapping became more passionate.

The ring soon grew bigger and denser. Naima danced with her hands up by her head, waving in circles right and left. Her hips and belly moved to the beat and her dress rippled in dancing waves.

Fahima wanted to join her, but each time she tried to make that first jump, she felt sick to her stomach and the blood rushed to her head. It wasn't until Naima swayed her way towards Fahima and dragged her inside the circle that Fahima was finally able to start dancing. Another encouraging roar went up around her.

Fahima danced slowly and shyly at first, barely moving her hips. Her hands just hung in the air, unable to move any which way. But the clapping continued, and the beat got stronger, and Fahima started to lose control. She imagined she was dancing at a wedding back in her village, and the people around her faded away.

The spinning made everything look hazy, like seeing through a white veil. Her shoulders shook of their own accord and her head whipped her hair round and round. Her feet carried her like the wind carries a feather. Sometimes she danced by Naima's side. Other times they were back-to-back. At one point, Fahima thought she glimpsed a smile on Naima's face.

As she moved about, Fahima knew in the back of her mind that the audience was getting bigger. This was good. It meant people liked their dancing. Fahima glimpsed several men staring with hungry eyes. One bit his lower lip. They roared again when two more dancers broke into the circle. A Frenchman held his crotch and thrust his hips back and forth, his tongue sticking out to the side. She quickly averted her eyes and tried to dance as far away from him as she could without being obvious, careful not to lock eyes with that man again.

The music played on, and so did the dancing. Every now and then, something hit Fahima on the head or shoulder. A pebble? A coin? She never had time to look. The dizziness was taking over, she was losing breath, but she didn't want to stop. She couldn't. Her back broke into cold sweat, and her feet felt sticky from the dirt.

Then the music stopped. The four dancers continued to move uncontrollably for a moment before they could finally bring themselves to a halt. Fahima was incapable of standing still. The ground span around her, so she kept walking in circles until she could stand in one place. The music had stopped because the old men needed some rest. Fahima could use a breather too. She looked for Naima, and when their eyes met, Naima gave her a smile.

Fahima felt exhilarated. *I made it*, she thought. *I'm a dancer*. One of the two other dancers, to her surprise, was Aida, the girl from her village who had travelled with them yesterday. She looked at the third one, and her heart skipped a beat. There, in all her majestic beauty and grandeur stood Nouara. She bent over, her hands on her knees and her head down.

Fahima couldn't believe she had been dancing with *the* Nouara. She almost fell when Nouara raised her head and her eyes met Fahima's. Panting heavily, Nouara winked at her, but all Fahima could offer was a meek half-smile.

A young lad quickly collected the coins off the ground and distributed them to the musicians and dancers. He gave Fahima four coins. She looked at them, unaware of their worth yet very proud of her very first payment as a dancer. She tucked them into her bosom.

The crowd started to clap again urging the performers to resume the show, and the old musicians obliged. The beat started off slow, and the four dancers moved lightly trying to find their rhythm. But before they could reach that high place of mindless movement, a fat man approached the musicians. Fahima thought she'd seen that thin moustache and that cane hanging from the hook of his elbow before, but she couldn't remember where.

The man said something in the flute blower's ear while slipping a few bills into his front shirt pocket. Without breaking air, the flute blower made eye contact with the other musicians, and they all stood up slowly in unison so as not to interrupt the beat. They started to walk to the gate.

Nouara followed them, dancing and swaying, and so did Aida. Fahima looked to Naima for guidance, and Naima said the fat man was taking them to dance at his café. 'He wants us to lure all these people to his café so they spend money there.'

It was then that Fahima remembered where she had seen the man. It was the café owner who had threatened to hit her and her mother with a cane that morning. Unsure if she should follow the procession, Fahima stood there for a moment. But when all the people darted past her, clapping and smiling she realised this was her first opportunity to dance at a café. She couldn't afford to miss it for the sake of dignity. The man probably wouldn't even remember her anyway.

Fahima ran to catch up with the other dancers.

iv

The street was crowded and Fahima's procession walked slowly behind the musicians. Right before they arrived at the café, a horse-drawn carriage sped towards them so fast she thought it would run them right over. The wheels didn't seem to roll, but rather bounce off the pebble stones.

In no time, the crowd parted for the carriage. Fahima caught a glimpse of the two men riding it. In the front sat a young man in a grey shirt lashing the two black horses with a long whip.

Behind the coachman, lounging comfortably in the open carriage, was a stout man in a beige turban and a white *burnous*. He looked straight ahead as if the whole world around him was unpopulated. Fahima could sense his wealth.

'That's *Caid* Tounsi,' Naima announced. 'Our local leader, they tell you. But everyone knows he works for the French. The locals are the least of his worries. It's the colonel and the generals that he likes to please, and they let him do as he pleases.'

Behind the *Caid*'s carriage, riding an elegant mare was a slender young man in a matching white *burnous*. Everyone stopped and watched the cortege ride by.

A man trying to get out of the way stumbled on the uneven road and fell forward. The carriage driver didn't seem bothered. The man tried his best to crawl away. But the front wheel rolled across his foot. He screamed in agony. The man finally managed to stand up and shouted something at the *Caid* as he limped his way to the side of the road.

The carriage stopped. And so did the music and all the noise on the street. The whole world came to a halt. The crowds stood motionless. For a moment, the injured man was the only one moving, still limping away from the scene.

'His funeral,' whispered Naima in Fahima's ear.

Without waiting for instructions from his master, the rider led his white mare toward the limping man. The man didn't need to look back to know someone was coming for him. He tried to disappear among the crowds, moving surprisingly fast. Undoubtedly painful.

The rider followed him, and Fahima's back went cold when she caught the rider's eye, dark and unfeeling.

He led his mare right into the crowd. But the limping man hurried into a narrow alley and disappeared into darkness. The rider paused until *Caid* Tounsi, produced a sound between grunt and a 'hey' and motioned the rider to follow.

The rider followed obediently. The coachman lashed his whip again and the whole world was whipped back into motion. As the carriage took off, the crowd went back to their business. First, they moved about, then a drum was beaten, a flute was played, and the whole street was vibrant with noise and dancing again.

v

Once inside the café, the audience settled down in the narrow space, and musicians stood against the counter playing their instruments.

Nouara and Naima danced between tables, smiling at this man and that. Fahima and Aida followed suit. When an old man pinched her buttocks, she swirled around and pressed her back against a pillar. The man and his friends roared with laughter. Fahima smiled nervously as she moved away from that table. They danced for the best part of the night while the customers clapped and shouted and drank. They spent money, and the café owner was happy. Fahima was happy too. Dancing at a café was the first step to becoming the successful Nailiya she had always dreamt to be.

As the customers started to leave, a man put a coin in Aida's hand. With a grateful smile, she slid it down her dress. The café owner's face turned red. Without a word, he dashed towards her with his cane and struck her so hard she collapsed to the floor.

Fahima didn't understand what had just happened. She had no idea why he had done that. He then said, 'You. Whoring. Thief.' Each word came with a strike on the poor girl's back. 'Stealing. My. Customers. Money. In. My. Own. Café.'

Naima and Nouara jumped to her rescue. Nouara tried to drag Aida out while Naima came between the man and his victim.

'She doesn't know,' Naima said. 'She's new.'

Fahima didn't know what to do until Nouara called her to help with the injured girl. They shouldered her between them and helped her out to the street, wincing and groaning. Fahima didn't understand what had happened, but she certainly wasn't going to stay and ask.

'Let's take her back to our *haouch*,' Nouara said, panting. 'Her sister will take care of her.'

Naima caught up with them, cursing the old man. Before they'd gotten far, Fahima realised the whole world around them was motionless again. They were the only ones moving. They stopped, and Fahima looked around to see what was going on. *Haven't we had enough for one night?*

Then it happened, right in front of her.

The limping man from earlier that night was on his knees in the middle of the street. Two strong men flanked him, gripping his shoulders. The *Caid* had climbed off the carriage and was walking slowly towards the man. There were bruises above his left eyebrow and under his right eye. His clothes were torn, bloodied and wet. He was sweating, and crying, his lower lip quivering. The man was soaked in fear.

Once upon him, the *Caid* held a fistful of the captive's hair and raised his head until their eyes met. He unsheathed a dagger and pressed it to the man's neck.

'What did you say to me earlier?' *Caid* Tounsi said casually.

The man made no reply.

The *Caid* hit him on the temple with the handle of his dagger. 'Tell me what you said.'

'I'm ssorry,' the injured man mumbled. 'I d-d-didn't know it was—'

But before he could finish, the *Caid* slit his throat open. Blood gurgled out as the man's head drooped forward. Fahima let out a gasp and looked away.

When she finally looked back, the *Caid* was using the man's shirt to clean his dagger before putting it back into its sheath. He then climbed back onto his carriage and disappeared down the street.

The two men who held the injured man dropped his corpse in the growing pool of blood. They stepped back, and Fahima lost sight of them among the silent crowds.

This time, it took a long while before the world went back into motion. Slowly and quietly tiptoeing at first. When passers-by finally resumed their normal activity, the once-jubilant street never really regained its former joy.

What is this town? Fahima thought. *The City of Joy?*

Eight

i

'Did he hurt you?' Saadia asked Salima for the hundredth time.

Fahima wanted to stop the interrogation. She knew Salima wanted to be left alone. She refused to say much about what had happened the night before, but Mother was relentless. In that respect, Salima and Saadia were equally stubborn.

'No,' said Salima, 'I'm just tired.'

'Lift your dress.' Saadia kneeled down by Salima's side. 'Let me see what happened down there.'

Salima crossed her legs and shot her mother an incredulous look. Fahima didn't want them to fight. Especially not after what Salima had done for her.

'Let's go, Yemma,' Fahima begged, pulling her mother's elbow. 'She wants to rest now. You can do this later.'

Saadia stood up, miraculously abandoning her quest. She then asked in a softer voice, 'Do you want anything to eat?'

Salima shook her head and looked away. Fahima knew her sister was just waiting for them to leave so she could cry in peace. Had it been her, Fahima wouldn't have been able to hold back her tears. Her sister was much stronger. She had been brave enough to take the first customer.

This client had originally been intended for Fahima. The night Mother came home to announce the deal, she had lain in her bed for hours wondering what the man would do to her. Girls often said it hurt first, then the pain would give way to pleasure. 'Provided you relax,' Naima always cautioned.

Fahima had always known it would come to this. It was a necessary part of becoming a successful dancer, but somehow it had never felt real.

The next day, she got cleaned up in the river and wore the new blue dress Mother had made from the piece of cloth the client had offered them. Fahima was hoping for some expert advice from her mother. There had to be something about the first time, as with all first times, that Fahima didn't know. Saadia didn't say a word.

As she put her makeup on, her vision blurred. It wasn't until her mother shouted, 'You're going to mess up the makeup!' that Fahima finally realised she was crying. She tried to stop, but the tears kept pouring. She started to sob. She didn't care about her makeup.

'What's wrong with you?' Saadia asked.

I'm scared, Fahima wanted to scream. *I'm frightened. I don't know what's going to happen. I'm not ready to give myself to some old stranger. How can you be so oblivious to all of this?*

But she didn't say any of that. She just buried her face in her hands and cried. When she lifted her head, Salima was sitting by the mirror putting makeup on.

'I'll do it,' Salima said.

Her mother was confused, and Fahima sensed disappointment, too. Salima quickly prepared herself and left the house without another word. Mother followed her.

So now that Salima was back from the hotel, it was the least she could do to give her some peace.

ii

Fahima and her mother walked as if they were racing to the jewellery store. Not a word was spoken on the way.

Fortunately, the Jew's store and dwelling weren't far from Hadda's *haouch*. It was on a wider street though, with bigger, fancier houses painted beige. No peeled off patches; no fallen bricks. The walls were like newly washed bedsheets.

When Saadia knocked, the heavy iron door was answered by a girl around Fahima's age with lighter skin, fancier clothes and more jewellery. The girl was pretty, but she had an air of weakness about her.

Without a word, the pale girl held the door open for Saadia and Fahima to go in. Saadia led the way like it was her own home, taking them through a short hallway to a large courtyard.

A blue-tiled fountain, pale and dry, stood in the centre of the courtyard. A few small tiles had fallen off, or someone had removed them to form a grey gap in the perfect shape of a pyramid.

About half a dozen women were gathered around the fountain, and Fahima knew from their clothing that they were all Nailiya dancers. She spotted Naima. Naima met her eyes and immediately abandoned her group to join Fahima and her mother.

'Made a fortune last night and came to cash it in for jewellery?' Naima teased.

'Not as big a fortune as yours, I'm sure,' Saadia shot back with her most ingenuine of smiles.

'Well, you came to the right place,' Naima said.

A short, stout woman approached them wearing a black velvet jacket embroidered in gold. A light blue scarf was tied right underneath her right ear and draped down her shoulder in hair-thin threads. She was elegant. She was rich.

She took annoyingly short strides, her chin held high with one hand resting on her hip.

'What can I do you for?' the lady asked with a smile that was somehow even less genuine than her mother's. Her voice was high and squeaky like a child's.

'We're here to make a necklace,' said Saadia. She made some effort to be pleasant.

Saadia had decided to use Salima's virginity bid to buy them both necklaces for their coins. It would take years before they were heavy with success, but it was a start. Fahima had been impatient to get her own necklace, but she had never imagined it would come at the cost of her sister.

'My husband's out running errands. He should be back shortly. Please wait out here with the other... dancers.'

The Jew's wife cast another ingenuine smile and walked away in the same, unnecessarily slow, proud manner she had come.

'Fucking slut,' Naima hissed. 'She thinks she's so much better than the rest of us.'

'Why does she act like that?' Fahima asked.

Uninterested in this discussion, Saadia left to talk to a woman she evidently knew.

'She thinks she's better than us because we're prostitutes,' Naima said.

'But we're not prostitutes,' Fahima said.

Naima rolled her eyes. 'Please. We're luxurious prostitutes. We dance and sing and entertain. But at the end of the day, we still let men fuck us for money. Those whores have it easier than we do if you ask me.'

Fahima had never seen it that way. She was a dancer. A Nailiya dancer. For her, that was very different from being a prostitute. It was better. Prostitutes were poor. Fahima wasn't a whore.

Naima read her mind, 'Listen. I know you think we're better than prostitutes, but when you look at it, we're all doing it for the money. We're selling our bodies.'

That did make some sense, but that still didn't mean Fahima was a prostitute.

'Actually,' Naima continued, 'I think most people are prostitutes one way or another.' Fahima shook her head, but Naima went on, 'Everyone sells their principles for money. Those sneaky little spies calling themselves men. They're always running back to the *Caid* with secrets on this tribe or that tribe for a five-franc coin. They sell their own kin for money. The *Caid*. Oh, don't get me started on the fucking *Caid*. He's no better than those boy prostitutes. Seriously. All he does is serve the French for money and power. He's selling his home and his countrymen for money. Prostitute.'

Naima lowered her voice in a conspiratorial tone, 'Have you heard of those *brave men* hunting for Ouled Brahims out in the desert?' She rolled her eyes when she said 'brave men'. She went on, 'They go out every day, killing men and women and children, then they cut off their right ears – it has to be the right ear to make sure they're not double counting – and bring them to the Colonel who pays them ten francs per ear. They call themselves Muslims. They say they're defending the town from the outlaws, but they're not just killing Ouled Brahims. They'd kill anyone in their way for that ten francs. If that's not prostitution, sister, I don't know what is.

'Ouled Brahims are the real men if you ask me. At least they wouldn't put up with the French. We call them outlaws, but they're the only ones who stood up to the French.'

Naima paused for breath. This was too much for Fahima to take in.

'This woman? The Jew's wife who thinks she's better than all of us? She's a prostitute, too. If her religion or principles tell her to judge us for what we do for money; if she doesn't approve of it, then why does she let her husband take our money? The money we made on prostitution. Why does she force herself to host us here at her home? Isn't she selling her beliefs for money? How's she better than us?'

Fahima didn't know how to answer these questions, and she fortunately didn't need to.

'What I'm trying to say is,' Naima kept going, 'in this town no one is better than the rest. The French, the *Caid*, the Jews, the Ouled Nails, the prostitutes. We are all the same, yet we spend our lives judging each other.'

The door behind them opened and in walked a tall man with sharp cheekbones and a greying goatee. The chatter in the courtyard died out. He must be the Jew.

Without a word, the Jew went into his workshop and his wife called in the first client. When it was Naima's turn, she went in and out quickly.

'We're trying to get into Mouloud's café tonight,' Naima said to Fahima on her way out. 'His usual girls are out camping with some French youth, so we're thinking tonight or never.'

It hadn't taken long for Fahima to figure out that all cafés in Bousaada had their own rank. Nailiya dancers had to start at the bottom and work for years before entering such prestigious cafés like Mouloud's with their wide open space and wealthy customers.

Being allowed into those places was like finding a treasure in the desert. The customers tipped a week's worth of pay, and most of them went there scoping for girls to take back to their rooms, which meant more work and more money.

Fahima was still trying to make her way into lower-level cafés. Naima had made it to the medium ones. But could they just show up at Mouloud's?

'Do you want to join?' asked Naima.

'Yeah, sure,' said Fahima. 'Knock on my door when you're leaving.'

Naima smiled at her and left for home.

When Fahima and her mother went into the Jew's workshop, he was sitting at a wide table counting franc coins.

'What do you need?' the Jew said in a deep rusty voice without looking up.

'I need two coin necklaces.' Saadia reached into her bosoms and produced a pouch she'd made of an old checked handkerchief. 'There's fifty francs here. Twenty for each necklace. Ten for your fees.'

'I charge ten francs per piece.'

'That's expensive.' Saadia frowned. 'I always paid you five for necklaces.'

'When was that?' The man looked Saadia up and down. 'Thirty years ago?'

She could see that Saadia wanted to argue, but he was infuriatingly spot on so she held her tongue. To Fahima's surprise and relief the Jew slid Saadia's money into another pouch and said, 'Your necklaces will have fifteen coins each. Come pick them up in two weeks.'

iii

They walked briskly out of the workshop. Fahima knew better than to say anything lest her mother explode with rage. When she realised they weren't on the way to Hadda's *haouch*, Fahima asked cautiously, 'Where are we going, Mother?'

Saadia was silent for a while, 'We're going to see Dahmane.'

Dahmane was the café owner who had connected Mother to one of the first bidders on Fahima's virginity. Saadia had cancelled the deal because Dahmane had wanted a cut of thirty francs.

'I hope the deal still stands,' Mother said. 'We have to sell your virginity tonight. If word spreads about Salima's bid, we won't be able to sell yours for good money.'

Fahima could never get used to her mother talking about her virginity like it was some trinket they were trying to get rid of.

'Yemma,' Fahima probed carefully. 'Are we prostitutes?'

Saadia slowed down. 'Where's this coming from?'

'Naima,' Fahima started after taking a deep breath. 'She said one way or another we're all like prostitutes because at the end of the night, we all let men fuck us for money.'

Saadia's face was turning red. She was about to suffer the full force of her mother's fury that had been simmering since the night before.

Saadia slapped Fahima across the face. Then she followed it up with another smack to the back of her head. She pinched her ear and yanked it upwards.

Fahima stood on her toes to try and ease the weight off her throbbing ear. She squinted and howled. Mother twisted her ear and hissed, 'If you think this is going to be another excuse to get out of this virginity bid, it's not going to work this time.'

Fahima tugged at her mother's hand, but Saadia didn't budge.

'You're going through with it this time,' she went on, 'even if I have to take the man's cock in my hand and shove it between your legs. Do you hear me?'

Fahima strained to offer a slight nod.

'Good,' Saadia said. 'Now we're going to Dahmane. We're going to take his bidder even if he offers half the price he did last week, and you're going to dance for him, and you're going to open your legs for him. And if I hear this talk about prostitution again, I'm going to pluck your eyes out.'

Saadia released her ear but followed with another strike to the back of her head and spat in her face. Then she just walked off.

Breathing hard, Fahima wiped off her mother's spittle and followed her away from the small ring of people that had gathered to watch.

iv

Located on a side alley, Dahmane's café was small and empty save for a group of three youths in brown *kashabiyas* playing dominos.

By the time Fahima and her mother made it there, Fahima had cried and dried. But her ear still throbbed, and her eyes were bloodshot.

Dahmane immediately understood Saadia was back here because she had no better offer, so he wanted a bigger cut for himself. Saadia tried haggling, but he wouldn't budge. She finally conceded to giving him thirty-five francs, and he agreed to let Fahima and the client use a room above his café instead of hosting him at Hadda's haouche.

By cutting Hadda entirely out of the deal, Saadia ended up with an even bigger cut, yet showed no sign of pleasure.

The appointment was set for tomorrow night.

Fahima's stomach felt like a pitless well.

v

Later in the afternoon, when Saadia finally calmed herself to sleep, Fahima told her sister everything that had happened as they lay side by side.

Salima's mood hadn't improved much since the morning, but she was at least no longer staring absentmindedly at the roof. Now it was Fahima's turn. She preferred not to think about it.

'Naima wants us to try and get into Mouloud's café later tonight,' Fahima said.

'That's impossible,' Salima sniffed.

Fahima repeated what Naima had said about Mouloud's dancers being away.

'I doubt it will be that easy,' Salima said. 'Naima maybe. She's been at this for some time now. But you? You're just getting started. Mouloud will chase you away with a broomstick.'

Fahima didn't understand why her sister was being so pessimistic.

They both fell silent for a while. Fahima whispered, 'Naima said something interesting about prostitution.' When Salima didn't react, Fahima explained. 'She said one way or another we're all prostitutes.'

That got Salima's attention. She turned to her sister, confused. Fahima explained the whole point about how everyone sold their values for money, and that no one was better than the prostitutes. Not even Caid Tounsi and the Jew's devout wife.

'That's crazy,' Salima said with a snort. 'Why would Naima say something like that? To be honest, I don't trust that girl. I think she feels threatened by you. By us. And she wants to get us in trouble or make us quit. Don't let her nonsense get into your head, alright?'

Fahima nodded, but she wasn't really convinced. She didn't think Naima had any bad intentions. She was fun and spontaneous. Whatever was in her heart was on her tongue, as the saying went.

'If I were you,' Salima added, 'I wouldn't go with her to Mouloud's café tonight. I don't think it will end well.'

vi

Attempting to get into Mouloud's café didn't end well.

Fahima left the houach with Naima and went to the main street where they met another girl named Djamila. Djamila was apparently the one behind the whole idea. She and Nouara were from the same *houach*, and that was how she knew they were away at a camp.

Djamila was short and had slightly lighter skin and a puffy face. Her green cat-like eyes gave you the impression that she was constantly shocked. While her type of complexion wasn't uncommon in Bousaada, you didn't see them on Nailiya dancers very often. Rumour had it they all came from *roumi* fathers.

'What took you so long?' Djamila asked when Naima and Fahima approached her. 'Some other dancers might've beaten us to the café.' She glared at Fahima. 'Who the hell is this?'

'This is Ammariya.' Naima said. 'She's new here. I'm bringing her with me tonight.'

'She's pretty, but one more dancer is one more excuse for Mouloud to refuse us.'

'Why don't you let him decide on that one,' Naima said as they walked. 'Let's just agree on something. Whatever happens, we all go in or we all leave. He can't take one of us and leave the others outside.'

'Great,' Djamila snorted.

Fahima couldn't believe she was about to dance at Mouloud's café in her first month in Bousaada. What made her even happier was that she already had friends that wanted to help her.

The café's lights flooded the street outside, and Fahima's heartbeat faster as they came closer. Naima seemed nervous too.

The café wasn't too crowded, but many people had already been seated. Fahima noticed there were no dancers inside. A good sign.

A young waiter rushing between tables eyed them in the doorway. A wide smile flashed across his face and he howled like a wolf. A loud roar went through the café; clapping, howling and whistling. Fahima could swear she heard a faint jingle too.

She couldn't believe this was happening. Salima would certainly think she was lying when she told her about this warm welcome. *This is what being successful feels like.*

The uproar went down as quickly as it had gone up. The faint jingle Fahima heard earlier got closer and louder. It was behind her, she realised. Someone shoved their way past her. It was a girl. Two girls. Three. Five.

Five dancers, swaying their hips with arrogance and seduction, went right through the door into the café.

'What do they think they're doing?' Djamila asked.

These five dancers had clearly been booked, and they were showing the world that they had graduated to the luxurious café of Mouloud. The five dancers wasted no time; they immediately started to perform in the small round space at the centre of the café.

Fahima watched as her dreams dissipated into thin air and wafted away. She wasn't going to dance here tonight. Or anytime soon. She would still have to work her way up like all the other girls.

Djamila wasn't ready to give up, though. Standing on her toes, she peered through the crowds. The young waiter saw Djamila, and he put down his tray to come over.

'What?' he said.

'We want to dance,' said Djamila as if it was normal to just show up and demand to work. Her voice was soft, as if she was trying to seduce him.

'We already have our dancers,' the waiter said. 'You can't see them?'

Djamila's face turned red. Fahima willed Djamila to hold her tongue for once. Causing a scene would get them banned for life.

Someone came through a backdoor with his cigarette dangling from the side of his mouth. 'Mouloud,' Naima whispered.

'What is this all about?' he asked. 'You're blocking the entrance.'

'These girls want to dance tonight,' the waiter replied. 'I told them to go away, but—'

'We just want a chance,' Naima cut him off. 'We know your girls aren't here tonight.'

'I already have dancers.'

'They're not your usual dancers. You're giving them a chance. Why don't you do the same for us?'

Mouloud squinted while he pulled smoke from his cigarette. Maybe he was considering the request. A good sign.

Djamila pressed on, 'We promise you won't be disappointed.'

'Fine,' Mouloud finally broke. Fahima could barely believe it. 'But I only have room for two more dancers.'

Fahima's heart sank. She waited for her companions to persuade Mouloud to keep them all. *We all go in, or we leave.*

'Fine,' said Naima as she darted past Mouloud into the café, and Djamila followed.

Of course, Naima and Djamila would want to dance at Mouloud's. Still, Fahima would have appreciated if they had at least checked with her first. They had gone in without even looking at her, as if she didn't exist.

Mouloud flicked his cigarette in the air and went back into his café. The young waiter shrugged helplessly and went back in.

vii

Fahima was alone on the street, unaware of the crowds walking around her. What should she do? Where should she go? It was as if she had been kicked out of her own home with no place to spend the night.

But she did have a place to go. She could go to Dahmane's café. It now occurred to her that since Dahmane had gotten her the virginity deal it might give her the right to dance there.

As she made her way to Dahmane's, Fahima was seething. Naima was her friend. How could she have just left her?

Dahmane's café was poorly lit. Only one lazy drummer played for about a dozen clients slumped over their teas or coffees like soulless *kashabias*. This café might be her only option. She had to make it work for now.

Dahmane was sitting with a client and his lips drew back in a smile as he rose to meet her.

'You're the one I was looking for,' he said with exaggerated enthusiasm. Fahima took that as a good sign, though. 'Is your mother coming, too?'

'No,' Fahima replied. Dahmane frowned. 'I'm only here to dance,' Fahima said trying to sound confident.

The client Dahmane had been sitting with turned to watch. He was big with receding white hair, and his neck was so thick Fahima thought he might break it when he turned. His smile revealed a row of brown teeth.

'Dance?' Dahmane frowned. 'That's not why I sent for you and your mother.'

'You sent for Mother?' Now Fahima was puzzled too. 'What for?'

'Your client,' Dahmane wrapped an arm around Fahima's shoulder and walked her outside the café. He whispered, 'He was excited to learn that you had agreed to– you know. To offer him your maidenhood.'

Fahima nodded, blushing.

Dahmane continued, 'In fact, he's so excited he doesn't want to wait until tomorrow.'

A numbness crept into her bones. Her feet weren't hers anymore.

Dahmane whispered, 'He's here right now, and he'd like to have you tonight.' He made the announcement sound like good news. Like the return of a lover.

'I sh—' Fahima cleared her throat. 'I need to consult my mother first.'

'Of course,' Dahmane nodded. 'I've already sent for her. She should be here anytime now.'

'I don't know,' Fahima was running out of ideas. Things would only get worse once Mother arrived.

'Oh, you're playing shy,' Dahmane said. 'Your client loves that in a girl.'

The panic was making Fahima nauseous, but Dahmane took her hesitation to mean she was being coy. *I could run,* she told herself. Of course, she would have Mother to deal with, but she would worry about that later.

'There you are!' Fahima was relieved to see her mother rushing towards her. 'I was looking for you everywhere. I see Dahmane's already found you. Are you ready for your big night?'

Just like Dahmane, Mother was trying to make it sound like it was her wedding night. *The big night.* Saadia turned to Dahmane, 'Is the client here?'

'He's inside,' he replied.

Fahima couldn't help noticing that their animosity had entirely subsided and they were now talking to each other like lifelong partners.

'Can you give us a moment?' Mother asked Dahmane.

He went into the café with a smile and a nod.

'Are you alright?' Saadia asked, cupping Fahima's face in her hands.

'Yes,' Fahima lied, but her tears betrayed her again.

'Don't cry,' Mother tried to soothe Fahima, keeping a stern face. She wiped her tears and said, 'You'll see. It'll go fast and easy, and you'll realise there's nothing to be afraid of. If you're lucky, he'll come before he even enters you.'

Fahima snorted.

'I haven't even bathed or—' Fahima started, but Mother shook her head.

'Those filthy pigs never know the difference,' she said. Mother reached her hand through the neck of her dress and produced a crumbled condom. 'Be sure to use this,' she said. 'No. Matter. What. Do you hear me?' Fahima nodded. 'Let's go.'

viii

Having paid Saadia, Dahmane led Fahima and the client around the café and up a flight of stairs.

Fahima walked behind Dahmane, the big client breathing heavy behind her. She'd never felt smaller. At the top of the stairs, Dahmane opened the door and let them both in before closing it from the outside.

The room was almost as large as the café downstairs. It was poorly furnished; a candle burnt on a low table in the middle. And a thin, worn-out mattress was pushed against the wall, the wool poking out of a dozen small holes. The walls were cold. Fahima hugged herself.

The man sat down and patted on the mattress, inviting her to join him. The candlelight cast long shadows beneath the creases on his forehead and around his mouth. His fair skin was now the colour of sunbaked mud. He could have easily been a Frenchman, but the brown *kashabia* told Fahima he wasn't. The man smiled at Fahima, exposing his browning teeth.

She remembered that she was supposed to entertain him first. She asked him if he wanted her to dance, but he just patted the mattress again, a little harder this time.

Her feet moved slowly. She sat down as far from him as she could manage without offending him. He didn't seem to care. He slid himself closer until he was almost touching her. He smelled of dung. Her hands started to shake uncontrollably.

He put his hand on hers, 'Don't be scared.'

Fahima couldn't help flinching away. To her surprise, that didn't offend him either. His patience and ease made Fahima wonder how many times he had done this before. Did he only do it with virgins?

'I'll be gentle,' he added with a knowing smirk that all but reassured Fahima.

He kissed her lips. His breath was rank. Some mixture of tobacco, rotten eggs and dung. Pursing her lips tightly, she fought the urge to throw up. The man was still not discouraged, though. His kiss lingered. Then he parted his lips and sucked at hers, engulfing her mouth entirely in his and licking her up and down. Fahima felt like she was being licked by a dirty cow. She kept her eyes shut and hoped for him to be done.

Fahima's ordeal didn't go fast enough. The man's mouth was now covering all her face, his lips and tongue working tirelessly against her skin. He cupped her breast in his hand, gently at first then firmer. He stroked and squeezed one breast through her dress then moved to the other, grunting with pleasure.

Fahima tried to send her mind somewhere more pleasant, but the man's hand squeezed her nipple so hard she recoiled in pain. He drew back, a lousy smile on his face, then removed his *kashabia*. If this was already painful and disgusting, what would she feel when he penetrated her?

The client didn't seem to notice any of her discomfort. He threw his *kashabia* on the floor. His large beige pants showed a lump between his legs.

Catching her staring, he grabbed her hand and pressed it to his erection. It felt thick and hard. The man pushed Fahima onto her back and kneeled between her legs. He slipped his grimy hands under her dress and felt her skin all the way up to her thighs, hiking her dress up.

His hands moved closer and closer to the spot she had been dreading, but he stopped before touching her. He just looked at her down there. He lifted his head to look Fahima in the eyes before biting his lips in an expression of pathetic lust, he stroked her with rough fingers. Fahima wanted to squeeze her legs together, but his head was in the way. His stroking was getting rougher, and rougher, and rougher but there wasn't anything Fahima could do.

When the man finally stopped stroking, he climbed on top of her. One elbow on the mattress, the other around his cock, he shoved it against her aimlessly. Fahima grunted in pain, but he didn't care to notice.

She thought of giving him the condom, but he had thankfully already pulled one from his pocket and was placing it over his manhood. He brought his hand to his mouth, spat in his palm, then brought the hand back to his cock and stroked the used condom. His fingers searched between her patch of hair and thrust his penis inside of her. Hard. She screamed, and he pulled away.

This was enough. She was getting out of here. That was what Salima would do if she was here. She would smack him on the face and run off.

She tried to sit up, but the man forced her back down. She tried to wriggle herself out from under him, but he pinned her in place. His smile had disappeared. It felt like a threat. It was a threat. She laid still.

The man went back to his cock. He thrust himself inside her again. This time it went even deeper and the pain was much much worse. Fahima couldn't hold back a grunt of pain. He was killing her from the inside.

He pulled back again, but not all the way out this time, and then he pushed it back. Fahima grunted again. The third thrust hurt a little less, the fourth less still. Then Fahima was able to handle the pain. She stared at the ceiling while the man slid in and out of her. Several palm tree trunks ran across the room above her, carrying the weight of the whole structure. The beams were stacked so tightly together Fahima could not tell if they were used whole or cut in half along their lengths. A few trunks were riddled with holes and cracks, and Fahima imagined them giving in to the weight and crumbling down to bury her and this monster in rubble.

His thrusts got faster and closer together until he shuddered and grunted with pleasure. He pulled out once and for all. He let himself fall onto her. His heavy head buried in her neck. She felt sticky between her legs. She wasn't sure if it was her blood or his ejaculate. Probably both.

As the client's repulsive breath coated her skin, Fahima wondered if this was what Salima had been through last night.

Nine

i

'You'd better watch out for your jewellery,' Nouara warned on their way to the Street of Joy.

The night was warm, and Fahima was boiling after dancing at Dahmane's cramped café. The three other girls skipped down the deserted alleys, their heels clapping on the cobblestones. Their laughter echoed off the close walls like trapped spirits.

'The thieves are back,' Nouara whispered. Fahima and her companions stopped giggling and listened to Nouara's murmurs. 'I heard three dancers from Dodja's *haouch* were robbed off their jewellery last night. One of them tried to resist. So they cut her throat!'

Fahima touched her neck as if to make sure it was still there. She counted the coins on her necklace. Saadia had used most of the money from Salima's virginity bid to get the sisters coin necklaces, and since then they had amassed a modest sum of coins.

Yet Fahima's necklace was an impoverished trinket compared to Nouara's, which boasted a dozen layers of closely-knit coins covering the dancer's entire chest and part of her stomach. Fahima's necklace had three small ringlets on which coins were placed with embarrassing distance between them.

All the same, she had forced herself to dance with filthy men and take their violence for it. The modest fortune around her neck was all she owned in this world.

'Who are these thieves?' one of the girls asked.

'They're no one,' Nouara replied with a hint of a smile. 'They could be anyone,' she added, her big eyes flicking from one girl to another. 'They're men, I'll tell you that. Some say they're Ouled Brahims, but it's easy to blame it on those that aren't here to defend themselves, I say.'

'Some say they are *roumis*,' another girl suggested. 'European youth from Algiers on vacation wanting to fill their pockets.'

'Maybe,' Nouara said. 'Maybe it's just locals. Those bastards enjoy our services at night and curse us at the mosques during the day.'

'True.'

'Maybe it's a different group each time,' Nouara continued. 'Everyone knows we carry our wealth on us. They don't need to break into any house. All they need to do is corner a weak little girl with a chest full of jewellery.'

Fahima could almost feel her gold necklace snap against the back of her neck. If she didn't have her coins, she would have nothing.

'Aren't you scared, Nouara?' Fahima had to ask.

'Of course, I am. But fear won't save me. Each year dozens of girls get robbed. Some get injured. Or murdered. They were probably all scared to death, but that didn't keep them safe. I say you need to be prepared. If they attack you, be ready to fight back. Know that they're there for the money, and they wouldn't hesitate to kill. To them, we're just trash. If you scream for help, no one will bother to save you. You have to take matters into your own hands.'

Nouara's tone had changed. She was no longer trying to scare them. They needed protection.

'How?' Fahima asked, unable to fathom how a woman could face a group of ruthless bandits.

'These men are secretly cowards. If they'd been any braver, they wouldn't resort to lurking in dark corners waiting for a girl with coins. All you need to do is show them you're not afraid to die. You need to always carry a weapon with you and be ready to use it. Here's mine.'

Nouara lifted her hands. Bracelets covered her forearms all the way to her elbows, thick rings dotted her fingers, and a golden snake coiled around her upper arm.

She rotated a thick bracelet on her right wrist. The silver bracelet had intricate triangles and lines and circles, and some zigzags too. Fahima was surprised to see four short studs sticking out. The tiny spikes had dull heads, but the side edges were perfectly sharp.

'This looks like a harmless decoration, yeah?' Nouara said. 'But it's lethal.'
Nouara slid the bracelet down to the heel of her hand and swished her arm in front of her.

'You can dig those spikes into a man's neck,' she added as she rotated her hand in circles.

Below those pretty features and the skilled dancing, Nouara was hardened. Like now, in a rare moment when she wasn't smiling, you could see some weariness in her eyes. Some practiced numbness.

'You only need to attack once,' Nouara was still explaining as they emerged onto the Street of Joy. 'You don't even need to kill them. Just one serious blow with confidence is enough to show your attackers that you're not afraid. *Et voila!* They'll escape as quickly as they appeared.'

Entangled in Nouara's mystery, they'd followed her like children following the adventures of a hero, but the band of dancers had to separate. Nouara threw one last warning in Fahima's direction: 'Again, I'd watch out for my jewellery if I were you.'

She winked playfully and disappeared through the door, leaving Fahima alone with the ghosts of dispossessed dancers and angry bleeding men.

ii

Hands shaking, Fahima pushed the *haouch* door closed and crossed the yard. All was quiet except for a man moaning coming from a window upstairs.

As Fahima tried to unlock her bedroom door, something moved. She whipped her head to the right. There was no one.

Fahima went back to fidgeting with the key, and when it finally popped into place, she heard the noise again. Louder this time. It sounded like the muffled mooing of a cow. Fahima frantically shook the handle hoping it would unlock before the thief jumped her.

A silhouette moved in the dark. It was long with bulges that shifted slowly like sand dunes. Now higher and now lower.

Fahima couldn't hold back her tears. The door unlocked, and she pushed it open, clashing it into the wall with a bang. She was just about to dash inside when the monster rose to meet Fahima. She shrieked. The shape stopped. She was about to cry again when someone addressed her.

'Ammariya?' a familiar voice called. 'What's wrong?'

Fahima's eyes adjusted to the darkness. It was Hamid, Hadda's help. He had been sleeping there under a sheet.

'You startled me,' Fahima said with a hand on her chest.

'Who did you think I was?' Hamid chuckled with a hoarse mocking voice. 'A ghoul?'

'Thieves go after dancers, you know.'

'Those cowards wouldn't dare go into any *haouch*,' Hamid said reassuringly. 'Much less one that's guarded by me.' Another chuckle.

'Of course not,' Fahima conceded.

Hamid helped Hadda in every aspect of managing the *haouch*, from running errands to standing up to the violent drunkards, but he was kind to the girls. He reminded her of her father.

'Sorry I woke you up,' she added. 'Go back to sleep.'

Hamid lay back down, and Fahima went into her room, calmer now. She locked the door behind her, walked blindly to the middle of the room, and squatted down next to where she believed the oil lamp was.

Unable to see anything in the dark, she placed her hands on the brass lamp and removed its small glass chimney, then turned the small knob to raise the wick. Her hands found the lighter immediately. She lit the wick, and the room went aglow. Placing the glass chimney back to cover the torch, she turned the knob a little to weaken the flame.

Every time she used the oil lamp, Fahima felt excited. She had never used one before coming to Bousaada. It was small things like this that made her grateful for being here. She wondered what joys lay hidden in bigger cities.

Fahima removed her jewellery and placed it gently inside a wooden chest. She took a moment to admire the small collection she had earned after months of hard work. She had danced every night until her feet hurt and occasionally given stinky men pleasure. She wasn't complaining, of course.

Things had started to change once she sold her virginity. She still cringed whenever she thought about that awful night, but time had dulled the pain. Time and experience with clients that Dahmane and Hadda had brought for her and her sister over the weeks. The job hadn't gotten any easier, but she had gotten used to it.

Nevertheless, Fahima was glad to be dancing at cafés. Of course, she wasn't dancing at any prominent ones yet, but since she had started dancing at Dahmane's, other café owners were easier to approach. The competition between these old men worked in her favour.

For now, she and her sister made enough money to pay for rent, dresses and jewellery, and they even spared some money for their mother to take home to their family back in the village. She dreamt of rising higher. Perform in Algiers or Paris? A circus in Rome? Who knew?

Saadia had also taken a bundle of cloth, dates and fruits. She had left Bousaada almost two months ago, leaving Fahima in tears.

'You'll be fine,' Saadia had told her daughters. 'Take care of each other and remember what I said.' Saadia also took that opportunity to remind them of all her rules. For the hundredth time. 'Protect your secret. Don't be seen together. And don't trust anyone. You're here to make money, and so is everyone else. Some people will do whatever it takes to get that one franc instead of you.'

Fahima had learnt this last truth the hard way.

She was still thinking when she heard Naima's voice outside in the front yard. *Naima will live a long time*, Fahima thought. Tradition had it that if someone walked in when you were talking or thinking about them, it was a sign that they would live to be old.

'I highly doubt that,' she heard Naima say. 'I think I would've known.'

'I don't know,' Salima said. Fahima sensed a feigned nicety in her sister's voice. 'Anyways,' Salima brought the conversation to an end. 'Good night, Naima!'

'*Bonne nuit*,' Naima called in mock French, dragging the words longer than necessary. She then added in a serious tone, 'Oh, and remember, if you change your mind about that trip tomorrow, you let me know, yes? We leave at dawn.'

'Alright,' Salima said. 'Though I'm pretty sure I won't change my mind.'

'Your loss,' Naima called out as she went upstairs.

Fahima heard her sister gasp loudly. She must have walked into Hamid sleeping outside. Fahima chuckled. Salima rushed in and locked the door, leaving Hamid to snore his dreams away. Fahima was still smiling when Salima turned to face her.

'What the hell is he doing here?' Salima asked.

'I guess he sleeps here now. The nights are getting warmer.'

Salima shook her head as she took off her shoes. She removed her necklace and tossed it into the box like it was burning hot. Salima rubbed her neck as if she had been freed from an iron collar.

'Where did you dance tonight?' Fahima asked her sister as she stripped down to her own underdress.

Salima shrugged. 'Outside,' she said. 'Then we went to this small café. Can't remember the name. You?'

'Dahmane's,' Fahima replied then sat down on her mattress and added, 'What was Naima telling you about the camp tomorrow?'

'It's nothing. She wanted me to go to this overnight camp with some tourists and dancers. I said no.'

'What? Why?' This was a great opportunity to get more work. The tips were good, and you would also be invited to more wealthy camps and house parties. 'Are you crazy?'

Salima shrugged again. 'I just don't trust Naima. That's all.'

'What does Naima have to do with this?' Fahima struggled to keep her voice low so Hamid wouldn't hear them arguing.

'Have you lost your memory or are you just plain naïve?' Salima hissed back. 'Have you forgotten what she's done to you? She abandoned you like some stray dog outside Mouloud's! You said it yourself.'

In hindsight, Fahima might have been a little bitter that night, but that was two months ago. She hadn't held a grudge against Naima. Obviously, Salima hadn't forgotten, though.

'So what? This isn't her camp. What can she possibly do to you?'

'You never know with that snake. And I'm not willing to find out while stranded in the middle of the desert.'

Fahima snorted. 'You just don't trust anyone. That's your problem. If you don't want to go, I will.'

'And that's your problem. You never learn. You're so naïve you trust everyone no matter what they do to you. You *are* like a stray dog. A bitch they kick around who comes back for more kicking.'

'You're the dog!' was all Fahima could say, and she hated herself for sounding like a child. 'I'll go with Naima in the morning and there's nothing you can do about it.'

'Fine,' Salima said as she lay on her back. 'I hope she slaughters you and leaves you there for the wolves to feast on.'

Fahima turned out the torch in the oil lamp and crawled back to her bed.

iii

The next morning when Naima came down the stairs at first light, Fahima was already waiting under the archway.

'Look who decided to join us,' Naima said with amusement. Her dress was too tight for her big bosoms.

Fahima tried to hide her excitement. 'I could stay if you don't want me to come along,' she said.

'Nonsense,' Naima shook her head. 'Let's go. We're already late.'

And just like that, Fahima was on her way to a camp. The two girls hurried to the gate where seven or eight people had already gathered.

Two Nailiya dancers sat cross-legged on a small rug in the middle of the marketplace. Not very far from them was a small group of *roumis*, three men and two women, standing idly under a palm tree. Their brown sunglasses made their eyes look like cat eyes. With them was a local man with a large grin on his face. He was apparently the one organising the trip.

Fahima and Naima squatted beside the two other dancers. One of the *roumi* men kept checking his watch. Fahima had learnt that people did that when they were in a hurry. The two other dancers said they were waiting for the rest of the group and the camels.

Much to the tourists' annoyance, the sun had already risen and started radiating heat when the rest of the group arrived: three other men and one woman, and a younger local man with a herd of camels.

Each of the *roumis* was helped to mount their own camel. Fahima and the other three dancers rode in pairs and the younger man led the small caravan on a graceful white palfrey that looked and moved like she was too pretty to be ridden. Bringing the rear was the older man leading three donkeys heavy with luggage.

The party set out into the desert. Fahima asked how things worked and what was expected of them.

'Didn't I explain last night?' Naima said, uncertain. Fahima held her breath. *It must have been Salima.* 'These camps are usually organised in the winter or spring,' Naima went on, 'when the weather isn't too hot. You'd go out until there's nothing but you, the sand and the stars. You'd have a nice dinner and a musical night. Then you'd sleep or do other things under the starry sky and head back the next day.

'To be honest, I'm not sure how much of that we'll be able to do today in this heat. It might still be magical, though.'

Fahima smiled.

The *roumi* tourists didn't seem to mind the heat. They chatted and laughed. They pointed excitedly at every rock or tree like they had never seen one before.

The trip wasn't exhausting, not like the first day Fahima had travelled from her village to Bousaada. Riding on the camel sure made it a lot easier, and she also enjoyed passing the time chatting with Naima while watching the tourists.

Naima talked about the village where she had grown up, and how it had been difficult to get started in Bousaada. She was the only girl in her family, and her brothers had tried to stop her from going, but her mother wouldn't allow them. It was just as important to her mother as it was for Naima that she should pursue her dream of becoming a dancer.

'Do you think people like you and me can make it? I mean like Nouara?'

Naima snorted. 'Nouara? Darling, that girl has nothing on us. Have you ever seen your reflection? You're pretty as the Virgin, and your dance is enchanting.'

'But I'm not the one walking around with a heavy coin necklace.'

'Just be patient. Nouara wasn't born with that necklace, you know. Though it sure helped her that she was born here in town.'

'What?' She turned to look at Naima. 'Serious?'

'Yeah, some say she was Hadda's daughter, given all the stories between them and all.'

Fahima had heard a lot about the complex relationship between Nouara and Hadda, but she assumed it was the regular stuff that often happened at those *haouches*, especially when a girl tried to shift allegiances. She didn't know Nouara was Hadda's daughter.

'You think so?'

'I don't know. But it would explain how she had a head start.'

Fahima agreed, though she still had a lot of admiration for Nouara's beauty and dancing.

It was late in the afternoon, the sun blazing right ahead of them, when the caravan arrived at the camp.

Tents had been set up by three men who had arrived ahead of the group. Fahima was amazed that the tourists still had enough energy to go splashing and squeaking in the river as soon as they dismounted. Later, while the two guides made dinner, grilled meat and bread baked in the sand, the tourists climbed up the small rocky mountain and sat facing the west.

Naima said they didn't want to miss the sunset, but Fahima couldn't fathom how watching the sun go down was worth all this exhaustion. One thing she had learnt since her arrival to Bousaada, though, was that the Europeans were different.

iv

After sunset, the campers ate around the fire while three guides played quiet music. Fahima and the other girls ate in the back and sipped tea, watching the *roumis* giggle as they drank their wine.

Then the beat of the music grew faster and louder, and that was the dancers' cue. The three girls rose to their feet in union, and Fahima followed suit. They danced their way to the middle of the circle and swayed their bodies to the surprised and excited roar of the small audience.

As Fahima moved around the fire, she was ecstatic. Dancing out here in the desert felt different from the crowded marketplace or Dahmane's stifling café. Here, the whole desert was hers.

Back in Bousaada, she was always competing with other girls for clients' attention. Here, there were only four girls and more than enough clients to go around. She didn't worry that her companions would steal them away from her. She was so glad she had decided to come on this trip. She couldn't believe Salima had missed out on it.

At first, the tourists cheered and waved their bottles in the air, then a man stood up and started moving aimlessly next to Naima. The others burst into laughter. Then another woman joined. Then two men. Soon the whole place was one loud party with people dancing and laughing like they were in a whole different universe. As if they were no longer flesh and bones, but rather the large free shadows cast by the flames of the fire.

Fahima didn't know how long this lasted, but the *roumis*, drunk and unaccustomed to long hours of dancing, were first to tire. They dropped down one by one, their faces red.

At some point, a man snuck away with a woman in a yellow dress. Their attempt to be discreet was ruined when someone whistled at them. The couple giggled without breaking stride.

Then another man, a quiet one who had not participated in much of the evening festivities, retired to lie down on a rug nearby and stare at the sky, reminding Fahima of her sister.

Two men danced around a Nailiya girl some more, then they too, snuck away with her to their tent. And so before long it came down to Fahima, Naima, the musicians and three young Frenchmen whose faces continued to gleam with hunger.

One of the young men danced with Naima. She got a little closer to him, rubbing her body against his then moved away to entice him some more. That encouraged the man to wrap his arms around her waist. He moved one hand up, and slowly, pulled her dress down the side of her shoulder.

Naima didn't seem to mind that, and neither did the two other men sitting around the fire. One of them whistled and the other one howled like a wolf. The dancing man giggled then pulled the other side of Naima's dress over her shoulder. She didn't let that interrupt her dancing. He stepped around to face her, the grin still looming large, and in one swift movement he pulled her dress all the way down to her waist revealing her two bosoms, large and shining with sweat.

His two friends sprang to their feet and jumped up and down, shouting and howling. Naima covered her nipples with her hands and kept on dancing. The musicians turned away from the nudity, but their instruments continued to send their tunes.

Fahima stopped dancing and stared at Naima's naked upper body. She had seen many dancers, including Nouara, lose their garments in cafés late in the evening when everyone got drunk and excited, but it hadn't happened to Fahima yet. She had danced naked for a client or two, but that was in private. Though she had always known this was part of the work, Fahima felt uneasy.

The two young men stopped jumping and approached Naima. The three *roumis* were circling her like prey. One of them touched Naima's breast and moaned with pleasure. Naima smiled faintly, but Fahima sensed Naima was no longer comfortable. Was she afraid?

Another man pulled at her dress to slide it all the way down, but Naima stepped away. They booed in fake disappointment, but weren't discouraged in the least. They followed her and circled her again. This man pressing her breast and that one stroking her behind.

Fahima was growing worried. These men intended to take Naima all together, and Naima didn't seem to want that. Fahima didn't know what to do. She thought of screaming for help, but she highly doubted the other people would leave the comfort of each other's arms to save a miserable dancer.

Naima was still recoiling, careful not to anger the drunk men, but her predators were relentless. Her eyes, now glittering with tears, fell on Fahima's and the two women held each other's eyes for a moment.

There was something else in Naima's gaze. Fahima wasn't sure what it was.

Naima said something in French. Fahima assumed it was a supplication for the men to leave her alone. It wasn't the common 'lâche-moi' phrase that Fahima had learnt to say. But Naima was better at French than she was. Fahima couldn't understand why Naima, with a faint smile, pointed at her.

It wasn't until the following day that Naima would confess having told her predators that Fahima was a virgin.

The three men's eyes fell on Fahima. A cold spasm ran up her body as their lips pulled back into smirks and their heads tilted sideways. They walked, crept, like a pack of wolves approaching a lone gazelle.

Fahima's first instinct was to run. But she realised she could never outrun these young men. She had seen them tirelessly run up and down the mountains that day. The desert, which not long ago had felt like her own limitless universe, was a prison. A bird's cage.

They were upon her before she could think. One of them said something in French. A question. But Fahima didn't understand. A hand groped her breast. Another pulled her dress down. Fahima shot Naima a look, but Naima averted her eyes as she pulled her dress back over her shoulders. Fahima realised Naima must have sent them to her but didn't know how.

The man continued to address Fahima in French. Asking her questions followed by a 'huh?' Another one bit his lower lip as he pulled her dress down. They exploded in laughter at the sight of her underdress. He pulled it down, too, leaving her upper body naked against the warm night.

Fahima hugged herself. She kept repeating, 'Lâche-moi. Lâche-moi. S'il te plait. Lâche-moi.'

Her supplications only resulted in another fit of laughter. Then a foot swept Fahima's legs off the ground, throwing her in the air and on her back. A stab of pain shot up her spine. She shrieked, but the men didn't stop. One of them was already on top of her, still asking her the same question in French.

Then there was commotion.

'Ey. Ey,' a male voice said as it inched closer. 'Arrêtez. Ey!'

A fourth *roumi* had joined and reached his hand for the one on top of Fahima, but the other two men pushed her saviour away. They argued in loud voices and more people joined.

The man on top of Fahima had already started groping her breasts and rubbing his body against hers, his breath sour with wine. But when the commotion grew too loud, he stopped and stood up, irritated by the interruption.

Fahima's saviour, a tall blonde with blue eyes, extended a hand to help her stand. She rose to her feet and pulled her dress up over her shoulders, shaking.

The music had long stopped playing, and the old men had disappeared into their tents. The three predators stomped off into the darkness muttering French profanities. Naima was nowhere to be seen.

The French woman in a yellow dress offered Fahima tea as she sat down by the fire, and the man, her husband, Fahima thought, covered her back with a rug. They nodded at the tall blonde man and walked away.

The tall man sat quietly next to Fahima. She was grateful for that. She felt safer that way.

He said something she didn't understand. So close to her, his blue eyes looked vast. The flames glowed on his kind face, illuminating his long, thin nose and full lips. He seemed young, in his late twenties. A long strand of slick hair tumbled freely over his eyebrow.

'Merci,' Fahima said to the blue eyes. He smiled and nodded.

'Merci,' she repeated, shivering.

v

The next day, Fahima rode behind Naima, ignoring her countless apologies.

Salima's words rang in Fahima's ears loud as drums. *You're so naïve you trust everyone no matter what they do to you. You're like a stray dog. A bitch they kick around who comes back for more kicking.*

Fahima took a deep breath, trying not to cry.

The whole caravan rode in silence. Fahima's attackers were thankfully shunned by their friends, and their camels had fallen behind the caravan.

Upon entering Bousaada, Fahima received her payment. She stomped off without looking back. Naima called after her: 'Ammariya, wait up. Please, Ammariya.'

But Fahima walked fast until she arrived at the *haouch* and locked herself in her room. Naima knocked on the door begging Fahima to open, apologising some more. Fahima finally allowed the tears she had held back all day long to pour down like the Moulin Ferrero. Eventually, Naima gave up and went to her room. Fahima cried herself into a deep sleep.

Salima turned the dreadful light on. Fahima sat up slowly, feeling stiff in her clothes and jewellery. Should she tell Salima about what happened to her? Her sister would scold her, but Fahima and Salima had to share everything. She blinked some more sleep out of her eyes.

Salima had been crying too. She was still crying, Fahima realised. Her sister ignored her presence and collapsed on her mattress like a sack of beans. Fahima's chest went numb with terror.

'What happened?' Fahima asked, dreading the answer.

Salima's eyes screamed, *do you really not know what's happened? Can't you see?*

Her coin necklace was missing.

Salima had been robbed.

Ten

i

During Salima's first autumn in Bousaada, she attended the camel race. As promised, it was a day she would never forget.

Salima had heard so much about this yearly event, but no one had told her that the race itself was short, and, most likely, the least important part of the day. People came out for the festivities more than anything else.

It was a warm afternoon and after the long months of excruciating summer heat, warmth was a relief. A faint movement in the air made the relentless sunshine bearable.

When Salima and Nouara arrived at the clearing near the river, the place was already swarming with people.

Makeshift tents had been set up in the far ends of the clearing, offering spaces to rest and drink tea in the cool shelter of palm trees. Bonfires sent columns of smoke into the blue sky, carrying the mouth-watering odour of meat and a thousand different spices. Stands to sell fruits, souvenirs and assortments of homemade food had sprung up by the river. The younger ones elbowed their way around the crowd, trays strapped around their necks, shouting their world-famous goods and unmatchable prices.

The reason most locals were so excited, though, was the return of tourists. For months now, Bousaada had been abandoned by its regular visitors who, according to Nouara, preferred the fresh salt air of a beach than the oppressive heat of the desert.

Except for prominent cafés barely surviving on a trickle of local regulars, most places had closed over the last few weeks, their owners fleeing the hot hell too.

Salima also suffered the loss of tourism, as did most Nailiya girls. Having been robbed of her necklace at the beginning of the summer, she would barely have been able to pay for rent and food had it not been for Fahima's money.

This weekend, however, the City of Joy was coming back to life. She was a woman recovering from a heavy fever, longing to breathe new air. Groups had arrived in cars and carriages yesterday, and this morning's bus spilt more tourists too. It was nothing compared to the winter and spring periods, but it meant more life for everyone.

The locals also emerged from their houses and congregated on one side of the clearing. Women in *mlahfas* and henna-covered hands and feet clapped and chatted cheerfully.

Salima and Nouara joined other Nailiyas and watched three old musicians tickle their instruments and some friends of theirs dancing along.

'I've missed this,' Nouara mouthed with a large grin. Salima smiled back.

Everyone in the crowds gossiped loudly, having to shout over the clamour and noise. Is that the Caid's brother back there with Djamila? Check out Elyakout acting like she's a good dancer. And do you think that old man came without his wife? He looks like he's here to spend money.

Salima nodded and smiled but didn't say much.

'You girls won't believe this,' Nouara shook Salima's arm.

Salima followed Nouara's gaze until her eyes fell on a surprising sight. Yamina, the Jew's daughter, was walking next to a young roumi man. She looked as timid as always, her head low and hands clasped, but there was no mistaking the intimacy between her and the young Frenchman.

'Isn't that…' Nouara started.

'Bernard,' called the girl sitting on Salima's left. 'He's Major Dupont's son.'

Salima had seen Major Dupont in town and his son looked just like him. The same tall figure and long neck. Bernard was handsome, slenderer, and his hair was dark and glossy in the fashion of young *roumis*, but the resemblance was uncanny.

'That little bitch,' Nouara hissed. 'I bet her parents would love to learn that their shy little girl is frequenting the high military ranks.'

'It would teach her mother to be less judgmental,' Salima couldn't help adding.

'Are you seeing what I'm seeing?' someone had just fallen on their knees right next to Salima.

Salima turned to see that the voice belonged to none other than Naima. Salima immediately turned away, her face flushing with heat. Fahima and Salima had both been ignoring her. Naima had apologised again and again, but Salima still couldn't bear to look at her for what she'd done to her sister.

'Yamina?' Nouara responded eagerly. 'I can't believe my eyes.'

'I can't wait to tell her mother,' Naima said. 'I would die to see the look on her face.'

'Let's take a walk,' Salima said to Nouara. 'I suddenly feel choked here.'

'Come on, Ammariya,' Naima begged. 'Could you please stop it with...?'

But Salima had already stood up and was walking away. Nouara gave in and caught up with her to take a tour of the place. Kids chased each other with gleeful shrieks. A group of tourists applauded a band of male dancers when they shot their rifles into the sandy ground with great flourish, sending a cloud of dust and smoke over the audience. The smell of salty meat grew stronger on the locals' side. Some boys were already participating in slow camel races.

ii

Salima and Nouara found their seats; the official race was starting.

The crowds grew silent, and a wide path formed along the shallow river. Young men with turban covered faces led sturdy camels to the start line. The camels' heads were decorated with colourful silk braids and large earrings.

A rifle shot declared the start of the race and the camels took off in a flash of thunder. Their legs reached impossibly forwards, and their hooves beat the earth like large stones falling from a mountain. The group that had started in a line soon merged into one murky cloud of dust and fur.

The crowd booed and heckled as the camels thudded past them, ruthlessly striving for the lead. They flashed past Salima, allowing her a glimpse of the riders. They were young slim boys, rocking up and down with their heads bent down against the wind, one hand firmly clasped the reins and the other frantically beat the sides of their mounts with sticks.

Up close, the mounts seemed like giant beasts, not camels. Their muscles flexed dangerously beneath their skin and their legs reached so far and so fast it was like they were floating above the sand cloud.

One camel stood dumbly at the starting line, jerking his head right and left while his rider screamed at him and beat his poor side with a stick.

The crowds roared as the racers approached the finish line. Salima couldn't tell who was winning. She didn't really care, anyway. The winner paraded his camel back up the path, accepting cheers and applause. Once the obligatory race was officially done and congratulations were bestowed, people quickly reconquered the racetrack and went back to eating, dancing and laughing.

Salima danced, more than glad to make a few francs. Autumn was just starting, and the season promised more nights and customers. When she tired, she sat down to catch her breath, sweating like a pig.

'Wasn't that great?' Nouara asked, lighting a cigarette.

Salima was going to comment on how short the race had been, but Nouara waved her cigarette in front of Salima's face, and said, 'I've never seen you smoke. You should try it.'

'No, thanks.' Salima shook her head, still panting.

'Come on,' Nouara wined. 'You'll like it. Just try one.'

Salima took the cigarette. She had seen many people smoke and liked the way it smelled, but she had never had the courage to do it. Even now she heard her mother in her head. *Put it down, you stupid girl. If I hear you coughing, I'll add to your suffering.*

Salima put the cigarette between her lips and inhaled. The smoke filled her chest before she exploded into a coughing fit. Nouara burst out laughing and took the cigarette away and smoked some more.

Salima took the cigarette back, and this time she didn't cough.

iii

The night had gotten cooler when Salima headed back to town with Nouara and Naima, letting them do most of the talking.

When they came upon the eastern gate of town, Nouara excused herself to go to Mouloud's café, leaving Salima and Naima to walk the rest of the way on their own. Salima warned Nouara to be careful and took off, not waiting for Naima. Naima tried to keep up, attempting to make small talk, but Salima was determined to ignore her.

Naima ran past Salima and blocked her way. The narrow alley was dark and empty.

'Please listen to me, Ammariya,' Naima said. 'I know you're angry with me. And you have—' Salima rolled her eyes and tried to go around her. Naima grabbed her shoulders and pleaded, 'Hey, hey. Please. Just listen. I know what I did at that camp was unforgiveable, and I'm ashamed of myself. But I was so scared. I was scared for my life.'

'And that's what you do when you're scared?' Salima addressed her directly for the first time in months. 'You push others to their own death?'

'I know it doesn't justify it, and I've hated myself since that night. I don't know how to live with this guilt—'

'Good,' Salima interrupted, freeing herself from Naima and shoving her to the side. 'You should hate yourself.' Salima shot past her, but Naima wouldn't leave her alone.

'Ammariya, please,' she called behind her. 'What do you need me to do or say to prove how sorry I am? Just say the word, and I'll do it. I'll do anything.'

Salima stopped and turned to face Naima. 'Anything?' she asked with the ghost of a smirk.

'Yes, anything.'

'Then how about you never talk to me again?'

She stepped into Naima's space, their noses almost touching. Naima's eyes widened.

'*Ever*,' Salima added. 'Pretend you don't even see me on the street. If we're dancing together, don't even smile at me. Forget I even exist. How about that? Because you're a worthless piece of shit, and I *despise* you. I despise you like I've never despised anyone in my life.'

Naima was silent for once. Salima turned around and went her way, glad Naima wasn't following her this time. Her relief didn't last long, though, for she soon heard Naima running behind her again.

'Ammariya,' Naima shouted. 'Ammariya, Run. Ammariya.'

Naima didn't stop beside Salima. She grabbed her elbow and continued to run, dragging her along. Without looking back, Salima bolted. She heard footfalls behind her. Someone running. Gaining on her.

'Thieves,' Naima was saying between breaths, 'Run. Run.'

Forgetting all about her anger, Salima ran as fast as her legs could carry her. They screamed and shouted for help, but no one was around.

The thieves weren't discouraged by the shouting. They chased them down the street, around a corner and up that narrow alley. They were almost on them when they turned onto the wide street where the Jew lived. Her knees felt like water. Her throat burnt dry.

A man was walking up the street. Naima and Salima jumped on him, begging him to save them from the horrible thieves. They turned to point out their aggressors. The street behind them was empty. Not a soul could be seen. The man was already wiggling himself free of their grips, cursing and growling at these silly girls and their games, and he walked away.

The two dancers kept running, but their legs wouldn't carry them much farther. As soon as they got to the Jew's house, they slammed against his front door with a thud. The iron door groaned but wouldn't budge open. They beat it. Called for help. No one answered. They took one last look behind them. The thieves still weren't there. They must have been spooked.

They started towards the Street of Joy. They just needed to get home, somewhere safe.

A man appeared from a corner further down the street in front of them. He wore a long shabby coat and a hood over his head. His grin was not happy, and hunger emanated from his green eyes. He had a mole under each eye.

The thief approached slowly at first. Something flashed in his hand. He carried a knife. He had a knife. Behind him was another man in a matching coat and hood.

Salima and Naima retreated, horror struck. They started beating at the Jew's door again, hard. Knuckles on iron, as hard as they could, tears streaming.

'Go away,' Fadhila called through the slit above the door. 'We're closed.'

'Open up!' Naima and Salima called. 'Someone's trying to kill us. Help. Please.'

There was a brief moment of silence. It lasted for ages. The two men were still approaching, hyenas circling their prey. Keeping them in sight, Salima kept beating the door.

'You reap what you sow, girls,' the woman declared. 'No proper lady should be out this late, exposing herself to such perils.'

'You fucking cunt,' Naima called back, a resignation in her voice that frightened Salima.

Salima, Naima and the thieves broke into a run at the same time, like race camels to a rifle shot. Salima lifted her dress over her knees to run faster. Naima did the same. Their jewellery clinked and tinkled with their footfalls as if they were dancing.

Salima's chest was aching, and the sound of her mother's words rang in her ears. *Never fight them off. Give them what they want and spare your life. Your life is worth more than a thousand necklaces.* But Salima didn't think her predators would spare her life if she stopped and handed them her meagre collection of jewellery.

The footfalls gained on them. Of all people, why was she the one to get attacked twice? What had she ever done to deserve this?

She heard heavy breathing first, and growling too. Then she felt his touch on her shoulder, his fingers brushing the back of her dress. She ran faster. His shoulder rammed into her back and his arms wrapped around her waist in a horrid embrace. She fell. Her hands just barely catching her before her nose cracked against the ground.

His whole weight was on her. She managed to turn and hit him in the face, but the slap didn't faze him. He was busy adjusting himself on top of her until he was sitting on her chest and had her wrists pinned under his bony knees.

Salima's legs were still free, she kicked the air like a cockroach turned upside down. She pressed her feet down and tried to raise her upper body. The man was too heavy. So heavy. She hit his back with her knees, but he was too far up her chest.

Salima heard Naima running away, fast at first, then slower. She stopped and screamed, 'Ammariya, no. Leave her alone!'

Then the whole world around Salima started to fade as her lungs struggled under his weight. The thief pulled at the necklace, trying to tear it off her neck. The copper strings resisted and stung her. She was sure they would pierce right through her neck, slicing her head clean off.

The man released and a few coins clink-clanked against the cobblestones. He used his knife to cut off the strings instead. His first strike came up empty, and the second one sliced Salima above her shoulder blade. Hot blood trickled down the side of her neck. He paused for a moment.

He had lost his hood in the run, and his dark lazy eyes peered under bushy eyebrows. A black rose tattoo was drawn at the base of his neck. Salima had seen this face before, but she didn't have clarity of mind to remember where. Her vision was blurry, and her limbs were weak.

The man tried to cut the necklace again with his knife. His eyes widened with shock, or pain? Naima appeared behind him, trying to stab his neck with her spiked bracelet. He moved away from her, and she scraped his neck instead, leaving two thin bloody fissures across his rose tattoo.

Naima had come back to save her, and they were going to survive.

Naima was on the ground next to Salima, another person on top of her. The thief with the two moles.

The injured thief sitting on Salima dropped his knife and pressed his neck, glaring at Naima. He lost interest in her and joined his friend who was sitting on Naima's chest.

'Run, Ammariya. Run!' Naima shouted. The thief tried to subdue her hands besides her head. 'Now! Go!' Naima screamed.

Salima forced herself to sit up. Her head spun circles, and blood flowed down her chest, warm and ticklish. It took all the strength she could muster to get herself on all fours. She was trying to stand up when she saw the tattooed thief kneel beside Naima.

He groped for the knife. Naima continued to yell at her, oblivious. She told Salima to stand up and go. She told her to leave her. Salima reached for the knife, but she was too slow. Too feeble to move.

The thief grabbed it and drove it between Naima's ribs.

Naima's shouting stopped mid-sentence. It turned into a wet guttural howl; her eyes bulged unnaturally. Salima couldn't look away. The thief kept twisting and twisting the knife inside her small body until she stopped moving and screaming. Naima didn't look like herself. Her face was contorted in an uncanny expression she'd never seen before. Air gurgled in her throat like boiling water before grace had left her body. It was a mockery of its former self; it was so limp. Her eyes silent, matte, dead.

Salima awoke to the world again and got back on her feet, gasping. She took in Naima's motionless face one last time. Her dark blood spouting into a pool around her. She didn't know what to do. She wanted to drag Naima away. To thank her. She wanted to hit her.

You stupid girl, she thought. She opened her mouth wide to scream, but a low wail came out.

Why did you come back? You stupid girl?

The thief– the murderer, the one with the rose tattoo– now got on his feet, his hand on his bloody neck. He shot Salima one look, and she turned to run.

You stupid girl, she wiped her eyes, but it did little good to clear her vision. She didn't even run fast. She didn't care if the murderers caught up with her.

But for whatever reason the men didn't give her chase.

You stupid girl.

iv

They buried Naima at dusk the next day. They wouldn't wait for her family lest the body swell up in the heat, but her cousin was there to accept condolences.

For Salima, the whole ritual felt barely more dignifying than burying a cow. Two Imams had refused to lead a prayer for a woman who had led such a dishonourable life, to borrow their words. At the mosque, one of the pious women had taken that opportunity to ask Salima and Nouara what they had learnt from what had happened to their recently deceased friend. Repent to Allah, they advised.

The sisters at the church had also refused to wash Naima's body, and they, too, seized the chance to tell Salima and Nouara about Jesus and Mary, and how they could avoid Naima's fate by embracing the Lord's mercy.

So Hadda and a few old women washed the body as best they could and wrapped it carefully in a white sheet. Hamid oversaw a group of paid lads as they dug a grave in the Southern outskirts of town, just down the river from where Etienne Dinet had been interred. They stayed to help lower Naima's small body and close the grave, and the girls helped with handfuls of dirt, too.

The funeral was fast and simple, attended only by Ouled Nail dancers, sad and quiet as Salima had never seen them before. The women didn't say a word. Why did the world keep moving? Why didn't anyone do anything? Find the murderer? Bring Naima justice? Bring these Nailiyas justice?

Why did you come back for me? Salima asked the fresh grave. She stayed long after everyone had disappeared. She didn't expect answers from the dead, but she had to ask the questions. She had to scold Naima.

Did you want to redeem yourself? To make up for what you did to Fahima out in the desert? Is that it?

If that was the case, it was hardly worth sacrificing herself like that. They hadn't even been that close. They were here to work and make money.

Or did Naima see things differently? Had Salima been wrong about her? Maybe Fahima was right. Fahima always saw the good in people. Maybe Naima wasn't a bad person. She might have done bad things, but that didn't necessarily make her a bad person.

Salima had judged Naima. Harshly. Salima was like the Jewess.

Forget I even exist, was the last thing Salima had told Naima. *Because you're a worthless piece of shit, and I despise you. I despise you like I've never despised anyone in my life.*

She suddenly felt an urge to get out of here. To go back to her village where no one got murdered for money and jewellery. She would lead a simple life with her family without having to be afraid at night. She didn't see why she had to stay here and work anyways if each time she collected a small sum of money, someone would rip it off her neck, and maybe kill her while they were at it.

With a heart still as heavy, she stood up and brushed the dirt off her dress.

'Thank you,' she said to the pile of sand, and she turned to leave.

She had only walked a few steps when she glimpsed a robust woman walking briskly towards her.

Salima didn't believe it at first, but it was her mother. Salima hadn't seen her in months.

'Here,' Saadia said as soon as she was within earshot. 'You'll need this for protection.'

Skipping the kissing and greeting, Saadia took Salima's hand and placed a bracelet in it. It was a silver piece with intricate carvings of large flowers and small rhombi and other shapes Salima couldn't make out. What stood out to her, though, were the spikes. Five short but sharp studs on the outside of the bracelet like the menacing teeth of a lion's snarl.

'I got one for your sister, too,' Saadia added while Salima turned the decorative weapon in her hand. 'I need you to wear it at all times. If someone tries to as much as touch you, you plant those spikes in his neck until he bleeds to death. You hear me?'

'Don't let anyone hurt you,' Saadia ordered.

Salima nodded as she slipped the bracelet on her right hand, then turned it around her wrist, feeling the cold silver against her skin.

As mother and daughter returned to the City of Horrors, Salima didn't wonder if she was ever going to have to use this weapon. She wondered how soon.

What she should have wondered, was how many times she would drive that bracelet into a man's throat, how many times she'd watch a man die.

February 1933-
January 1934

Eleven

i

Fahima had never realised how much furniture and clothes they owned.

She and her mother were on their third trip to the new house. They drove a donkey-drawn cart loaded with a chest full of dresses and layers of mattresses, sheets and blankets topped by a table and three stools. In the past two years, the sisters had acquired more possessions than they had owned in their entire life.

As they went up the Street of Joy, Fahima was glad for the midday sun which had finally melted the morning chill. This was a good day. Fahima and her sister were moving out of Hadda's *haouch* and into a big house all for themselves. It wasn't on the Street of Joy, but the sisters had established such a reputation that they were sure to have a steady flow of clients even if they lived out by Moulin Ferrero.

Fahima couldn't say when exactly in the last two years their luck had turned. She could still remember the time when everyday seemed to pour new suffering on them: theft, attacks, humiliation, abuse.

Then came a period of prosperity. Bad things happened less and less, and money poured a lot more freely. Of course, it helped that they had started dancing at hotels and prestigious coffee houses like Mouloud's, but Fahima wasn't sure if that really was the cause.

Whatever it was, Fahima was glad. Perhaps she would soon be able to leave and dance in other cities. Her mother was also happy, Fahima reflected as she glanced over the donkey at Saadia, walking with her head held high, chin prodded forward.

Saadia had come to town a few weeks ago. She'd decided the jewellery and coins that Salima and Fahima had together was enough to rent a big house for a few years.

For days, Saadia inspected every single house in the Quartier des Ouled Nails and beyond. She even barged into dwellings that weren't for rent and offered the owners a good price. In the end, she found exactly what she was looking for.

The house was located on the cobblestoned street where many well-off locals lived. The neatly painted beige houses were almost as big and beautiful as those in *Le Quartier Européen* or *La Commune Mixte*.

Fahima didn't like that their new dwelling was right across from the

Jew's home though. Dealing with his snobbish wife each time they needed his services was more than enough, especially since Fadhila had refused to shelter Salima and Naima against those murderous thieves. Yet the new house was so spacious and reasonably priced that both sisters were ready to deal with Fadhila, or ignore her for that matter.

ii

Fahima produced her key, overly excited about opening her own front door.

Salima was still upstairs placing the first two loads in the two bedrooms. Fahima had wanted the one near the stairs, but Salima called it first. Below their bedrooms was a kitchen, larger than Fahima had ever seen, and a living room.

Fahima moved the pile of blankets and sheets up to her bedroom and went back out to the balcony. She stopped right outside Salima's bedroom, taking in the whole place.

To her left was a third building, across from the front door. The landlord stored his belongings in those rooms. One part of the house was more than they needed anyways. Until they decided to start their own *haouch*.

The toilet, a tiny space with a hole in the ground, was between that third building and the animal shed. The rooftop above the shed overlooked a little date palm grove.

The midday sun shone on the vast cemented courtyard and reflected off the flower-patterned tiles of the well. Fahima wondered why it was covered with a concrete lid. Perhaps it had gone dry. She was so used to bringing water from the river every day anyway that she couldn't see living without her daily trips and the friends she met there.

Fahima leaned against the wooden railing, how could this whole place be theirs? The planks creaked, threatening to break and drop her to an early death. She stepped back.

They took a break to eat bread with cheese and dates. Then Fahima continued to set up the space while Salima and Saadia went to buy more things from the market.

Hamid, Nouara and other girls had offered to help move, but Saadia had cordially refused. Instead, she invited everyone for dinner that night. For *baraka*, Saadia said. Good omen. But Fahima knew Mother was only doing it to show off her daughters' success.

Not long after Saadia and Salima left, Hadda came snooping around and asking Fahima if they planned to start their own *haouch*, clearly not happy about a potential rival. Fahima neither confirmed nor denied her suspicions.

To Fahima's surprise, Saadia and Salima came back with another pile on top of the cart: a sack of semolina, another one of flour, a heap of wool, two rolls of silk cloth, several empty mud pots, three roosters and a chicken tied together at the legs. Trailing absentmindedly behind the cart were two young goats.

Saadia killed two roosters for dinner and spared the smallest one to live with his hen.

'Just feed them leftovers,' she instructed, 'and there's already enough dry straw in the shed to feed the goats for years. You'll need the eggs and milk.'

The sisters prepared tiny light pieces of bread for *Zvitti* while Saadia cooked spicy gravy with tomatoes, green and red peppers. She ground fresh coriander, olive oil and garlic using the new brass mortar and pestle she had bought. They boiled the two roosters so they could pluck out the feathers, then seasoned them with garlic before cooking them golden over a warm crackling wood fire.

iii

Before their guests arrived, Fahima inhaled the delicious meal with a cup of *leben* and hurried out to dance at Mouloud's café. Only Salima got to stay back and receive guests so they wouldn't see them together.

On her way, Fahima ran into their new neighbour, Fadhila, who was sweeping the small corridor behind her door. Meeting the Jewess's eyes, Fahima hesitated for a moment, uncertain if she should be nice to her.

It had been over a year since Naima died, and now they were neighbours. Should they continue to be hostile? Fahima knew where Salima stood on this. She would take her grudge to the grave.

Salima and Fahima had still continued to use the Jew's services. He did the best work in town, the price was reasonable, and he was an honest man. But every time they came to his house, they completely ignored his wife.

She was still mulling over whether to wave at Fadhila when she stood up and eyed Fahima. Shaking her head with a loud sigh, she smacked the door shut.

Hostility it is, Fahima thought. It was almost dark. She hugged her *mlahfa* and walked on her new path to the main street. Even though Fahima had seen all the parts of the city these last two years, there was still a sense of novelty about this new route from home to work. Like the night she and her sister had first come to town.

Mouloud's café was already half full of clients, and three girls stood smoking outside. Tonight, less than two weeks after Eid and after a short hiatus during Ramadan, business was almost back to normal. As Fahima joined the knot of Nailiya dancers outside the café, Djamila immediately held out a cigarette for her.

'No, thanks,' she said. 'I just smoked,' She lied.

Djamila's eyes widened in disbelief. Salima would never have done that. She'd take a cigarette while one was still between her lips. *It's why her voice is so rusty.*

Fahima was saved by the old musicians. They started playing a low beat to warm them up and attract the customers' attention. The girls crushed their cigarettes and went inside, smiling seductively at the welcoming applause.

Fahima danced with moderate effort tonight. She saved her best performances for big nights, usually weekends, when she was targeting a specific client who could offer a steady income. Tonight's attendants, however, were mostly locals and young French soldiers who wouldn't offer much.

Fahima had barely danced five pieces when a familiar tall figure appeared across the street. Her heart skipped a beat.

iv

He was wearing a long brown coat and a matching hat covering most of his blonde slick hair. Still as a rock, he watched Fahima dancing.

Feeling the blood rush to her head, Fahima struggled to keep calm and continue dancing. *What is he doing? He can't be here now.*

When no one was watching, she snuck out of the café. She stomped across the street to René.

'What are you doing here?' she hissed. 'It's still early.'

'I know, ma chère' he said, his smile widening. His deep blue eyes stared right into hers, making her uneasy. 'I wanted to take you out earlier tonight.'

'Why?' she asked.

René was Fahima's favourite client—for what else could she call him? Lover? Not really. She met him a few times a week. Sometimes here at the café; other times they would go out for a walk, and very often, they would end up in his home or hers, making love and chatting away the night. But there was an unspoken agreement between them that all of this had to happen after she was done working. She still had to dance and entertain clients privately to earn money, and he seemed to understand that. So why was he here?

'I'll tell you on the way,' he said in a calm voice, the one he used to whisper in her ear when they lay in bed. 'Let's go.'

She hesitated a moment, not wanting to lose tonight's pay. Mouloud would be mad at her for leaving so early when the café was still bustling with customers—

'Alright,' she responded.

They walked side by side towards the gate. The street was crowded with people going back and forth between coffee places and whatever was happening outside the gates.

René reached inside his coat pocket and produced a piece of paper the size of a picture, mostly white except for some lines and scribbling. He handed it to her, a broad smile on his face.

Confused, Fahima took the card and examined it. The paper was thick and sturdy, but Fahima couldn't make anything out. She couldn't read, and he knew that. She did recognise one shape, though. She had seen René draw it so many times that she could recognise it anywhere: a heart. The shape was slightly crooked on one side, but Fahima loved it. She asked him what the rest of the writing said.

René said, 'It says happy Valentine's Day, ma chère. From Paris.'

'From Paris?'

She turned the piece of paper around, and there it was. A massive structure stood against a clear sky.

'It's the Eiffel Tower,' René announced. Fahima already knew that.

She had seen pictures and paintings hanging on walls in cafés and hotels. But somehow holding this picture in her hand meant more. As if she now owned the tower. Like she and René shared it together.

'Today's Saint Valentine's Day,' René continued, 'so I wanted to give you this postcard, you know.'

He shrugged and averted his eyes. This whole thing, his present and shyness, filled Fahima with joy till it was sprouting from her fingers and toes. But she didn't know what to do or say. She wanted to kiss him. She wanted to lie with him and feel him inside her, but alas that was not possible here.

'What's Saint What Day?' she asked, trying to distract herself.

They saw people gather in clusters, hugging their coats and watching different sorts of performers. Dancers and musicians, magicians and tricksters, animal trainers and seers.

René cleared his throat and explained: 'Saint Valentine's Day happens on the fourteenth of February every year. We celebrate Saint Valentinus who was martyred for performing secret weddings for couples to prevent men from going to war. To honour him, every year on this day people send flowers and cards to friends and loved ...'

René's voice trailed off in the distance as Fahima spotted a familiar face.

v

Sitting on a low wooden stool with her toothless mouth stretched into that sheepish yet impish smile of hers, *Khalti* Baya, the *guezzana*, squinted through the crowd, hunting for her next prey. The old woman frowned and the Amazigh tattoo disappeared between the folds of her forehead.

A wave of panic washed over Fahima. She still remembered the first night they had come to town and Baya insisting on telling Fahima's future. The seer had said Fahima and Salima would bring death and wrath. There was something about sleeping in the dark with the dead that had terrified Fahima.

Still, Fahima didn't believe in clairvoyance, so she couldn't understand why she was scared of catching Baya's eye. She took René's elbow and diverted him away from Baya's path, her heart beating fast.

'Ammariya!' the old hag's voice a piercing shriek.

René turned around before Fahima had the chance to stop him.

'Why don't you and your man come let me see your future,' the seer said. The sneaky *guezzana* knew there was nothing Fahima could do to keep a Frenchman away from this exotic experience.

'Let's go,' Fahima pulled at his sleeve.

'Let's try it,' René said cheerfully. 'Let her predict our future.'

She wasn't going to let that old woman touch her again.

'You go ahead and do it,' Fahima said. 'I'll watch.'

René sat on the low stool in front of the seer. Baya returned a triumphant smile, revealing toothless gum. She took René's hand in hers. As she traced a wrinkled finger across his palm, René looked up at Fahima with childish giddiness.

'Mmm,' the *guezzana* started, faking an intrigued voice, like she was already seeing something. 'I can feel your heart from here. It is beating for someone.'

Fahima rolled her eyes, annoyed by the woman's lame poesy. Baya could read faces alright. René was clearly falling for it.

'Can I assume your heart is beating for our beauty here?' Baya asked. '*Ammariya?*'

The man's face reddened as he glanced at Fahima. Baya didn't wait for an answer.

'Your affection for her runs through your veins,' she went on.

And then, just as Fahima had feared, trouble started.

'But be cautious,' Baya warned. 'She's going to break your heart. I can see it.' She nodded with authority. 'And you'll break hers, too.'

'René,' Fahima tapped his shoulder. 'Let's get out of here.' But he ignored her.

'She'll bring you absolute happiness and the deepest sorrow,' Baya went on. She threw her head backwards in that dramatic way she always pretended to communicate with the jinn. 'She'll be your demise,' she was screaming now. 'The fire will eat you alive.'

Everyone within earshot was staring at them, eerily silent. Baya's screaming voice was everywhere. People looked at Fahima, then down to René, and at the shrieking *guezzana*. Fahima couldn't take it anymore.

vi

Fahima didn't look back as she elbowed her way through the crowds back to the gate.

Everyone was still staring at her. Her eyes stung with tears. She didn't know why this stupid bitch was so bent on embarrassing her.

Fahima wondered if Baya was right about bringing death upon the city. Indeed, Fahima and her sister had seen more violence here than they had seen their entire lives, but she had always assumed a big city like this with hundreds of tourists drinking and fighting, was bound to have some violence.

'Fahima!' her thoughts were interrupted.

It was René. She ignored him, but he caught up with her.

'Hey, what's wrong?' he asked.

'Nothing,' she shook her head. 'I just want to go home.'

'Hey, hey.' He grabbed her elbow.

They were close to the gate. Behind her, people sauntered up and down the main street.

'Hey, don't let her get to you.' His voice was soft, and his eyes were begging to meet hers. 'She's just a seer. She makes money by saying stupid things like that. I thought you knew that. It's just for fun. None of that is going to happen.'

'I know,' Fahima said. She didn't know what else to say.

A wave of screams rampaged the main street. Fahima turned to see what was going on. Someone ran past her, ramming into her shoulder. She hardly had time to see anything at all. A local man in blood-stained clothes. There were spots on his face, too. He vanished among the crowds.

Fahima couldn't see much with the crowds running and screaming bloody murder. But then the crowds thinned out, and the wide street grew deserted. Quiet.

Then she saw three people squatting not far from the gate. For a moment, Fahima couldn't see what was so terrifying, but then she perceived a fourth person. He was lying in a pool of dark blood. One of the men was shaking him, trying to wake him up.

René dashed towards the scene, evidently not scared of whatever had terrified the crowds. Fahima moved forward too, but only a few steps. Around her, people were breathing a million panicky whispers.

'He stabbed him,' someone said.

'Were you here when he killed that man in the middle of the street?' another asked.

'He drove the dagger right into his heart.'

'Must be the Ouled Brahims.'

'He had it coming.'

'It was his men who did it, not him.'

'He works for the French!'

'He can't survive this.'

'He was after them for years.'

'Still, he ordered them.'

'He's the *Caid*.'

Fahima was shocked. *Caid* Tounsi had been stabbed. And on the very street he had slit a man's throat open some years back.

René kneeled by the *Caid*'s side and placed two fingers on his neck, then he felt his wrist too. Fahima could only see René's back, but the way the three other men stared at René, then down at the *Caid*, told her everything.

Caid Tounsi was dead. Murdered.

Twelve

i

Sitting with her entire family around a low table, Salima realised that the village had changed a lot since she and Fahima had left.

Across the table sat her youngest sister, Farida, nibbling a piece of bread. At six, Farida's front teeth had fallen out, and she looked much bigger now. She no longer smudged her face with *leben* when she drank.

Next to Farida sat their only brother, Amar. At thirteen, he'd already started to look and sound like a man, and he certainly acted like one now. He spent most of his time with their father taking care of the sheep and goats, or hunting birds with other boys.

A month ago, when Amar came back in the evening to find his elder sisters in the tent, he didn't run to hug them. Instead, he approached them casually and kissed them on the cheek like he would a distant relative.

People used to say that Salima was Amar's second mother. As a kid, she was the only one who knew how to calm him down and get him to sleep. He had been so much like her in character, just like Farida took after Fahima.

Now Salima felt he had suddenly detached himself from her without a warning and she hadn't been allowed to bid Amar the boy goodbye.

Washing her pain down with a big gulp of *leben*, Salima shifted her gaze to their father, Afir. Father had thick dark skin that resisted old age, and his hair had neither thinned nor turned grey since they'd left.

Afir was the exact opposite of Saadia. He was calm when she was irritable. He was reclusive while she was intrusive. She was shrewd and he was naïve. His only job was to take care of the animals, and he happily let her manage most household affairs, including Salima and Fahima's finances. All the same, Salima and her siblings favoured Afir over their mother, and they never hesitated to show it.

On Salima's right, Saadia ate as if she had somewhere to be. They had to get to a wedding, but that wasn't till late in the afternoon. Mother had recently gotten a new tattoo on her chin– three black dots that complemented the two crosses she already had on her cheeks.

Ever since Salima and Fahima had arrived a month ago, Saadia hadn't missed a single opportunity to show off her daughters. She would make them wear their finest dresses and put on all their jewellery, much to Saadia's delight and her daughters' embarrassment.

Saadia even rejoiced in Farida and other girls silently following Salima around everywhere, staring at her with bewildered eyes.

Salima remembered herself as a kid always dressing up as her own role model, a mythical dancer named Hizia, who toured the world with a famous circus managed by an Arab man in Italy. Back then, she had been completely oblivious to what it would take to even be allowed to dance at a café, not to mention all the violence and injustice rife in a town like Bousaada. She didn't want her little sister to suffer what she had gone through, but this was her fate. Most of the village women had been through this.

Fahima sat to Salima's left, eating with an absentminded smile. Her Amazigh tattoo was missing the lower horizontal stroke. Fahima hadn't bothered covering it up. Fahima seemed to enjoy her visit to the village a lot more than Salima. She had immediately found her childhood friends and spent many evenings playing knucklebones with them.

'I'll make you some bread for the road back,' Saadia said. 'And we can spare some dates, too. To give you strength. With this heat, you'll need it.'

The air outside was so heavy you could barely breathe. Salima wondered how they would get past all the hills and dunes without protection from the sun. Nevertheless, they would have to join the group travelling back to Bousaada tomorrow. Salima and Fahima had already been gone long enough, and if they didn't show up at Mouloud's café in time for the first wave of tourists, he might assume they weren't coming back at all and would hire someone else.

Salima couldn't stand spending another week here. Time in the village seemed to drag on. She was bored. She didn't remember things moving this slow. She marvelled at how quickly she had gotten used to a place she had hated.

'I want to go to Bousaada,' Farida declared, flashing a toothless smile. 'Fahima, can you please please take me with you? Please?'

Farida hopped as she begged, her braids bouncing up and down.

'You're too young,' Fahima said. 'I promise you'll be old enough in no time. Your teeth will grow back, and you'll be ready to become the most beautiful dancer in the city.'

Farida threw her hands in the air, never letting go of the piece of bread, and squealed with delight. 'So when my teeth grow back, I'll go with you?'

It's not your teeth that need to grow, Salima thought and smiled at her own dark joke.

'Of course,' Fahima nodded patiently, sending Farida skipping with elation.

Father shook his head and smiled, and Salima realised that Farida had become the new joy of this family, young, and above all, still innocent.

ii

After lunch, Father and Amar went to lie down while Fahima cleared the table and Salima prepared tea in the shade of the tent outside. Saadia sat down across from her.

'Do you have everything you need for your trip?' Saadia asked.

'I think so,' Salima shrugged.

'I've gotten you three large sacks of wool from Ami Messaoud,' Saadia said, her eyes fixated on Salima, as if checking for some reaction. 'You can use them to make new mattresses and cushions,' she added. 'It'll cost you close to nothing. Better than paying a fortune for wool in Bousaada.'

Salima saw the sense in that, but there was an obvious concern. 'How are we going to take three large sacks all the way to Bousaada?'

'Mourad offered to take them on his cart,' Saadia said, smiling knowingly.

Salima knew where this was leading and had no way of preventing it. She focused on the teapot in front of her.

'Speaking of Mourad,' Mother added, dragging Mourad's name. 'His mother talked to me about you two. He wants to marry you.'

Salima nodded, hoping against hope that this would be the end of the conversation.

Salima had known Mourad since childhood, though they had only been on nodding terms. When she ran into him in Bousaada, she would greet him politely, or chat briefly about news from the village, but nothing more.

Since her return to the village, though, she and Mourad had been seeing each other secretly almost every night. It started the first week when she couldn't sleep. Having grown into the habit of working until late in the night, Salima had found it hard to go back to the old village ways, sleeping shortly after sunset and waking up at dawn.

On her first night, she tiptoed out of the tent and trod stealthily to a small rise just outside the village. It was perfectly safe, of course, and

Salima enjoyed the quiet as she lay on a flat rock, searching the starry sky. Soon she was there every night.

One night, she heard footsteps pressing softly on the pebbles behind her. She turned to see the shape of a man in a large *kashabia* approaching her. Her throat went dry, and her mind was flooded by images of Naima's death. Her pale graceless face.

She stood up. Her left hand went to the spiked bracelet on her wrist. She hadn't used it since her mother had bought it so she didn't know how much protection the piece of jewelry could offer, but it was her only weapon.

'Relax, it's me,' Mourad's familiar voice came from the dark.

'What are you doing up this late?' she asked him, her voice still trembling. She felt silly now; who would attack her here? This wasn't Bousaada.

'What am *I* doing up?' Mourad asked.

'I couldn't sleep.' She sat back down.

Mourad joined her. They sat together until dawn that first night looking at the clear starry sky, and Salima liked his silent company. She also liked that he shared his cigarettes, which were a rare commodity in this place.

Mourad showed up again the following night and lay next to her on the rock, but he didn't touch her. He grew chattier as they grew familiar with each other, but as long as he didn't expect her to participate in the conversation, Salima didn't mind.

He touched her the third night. Salima smiled, so he took that as encouragement to kiss her. On the fourth night they made love until the first light. They did that almost every night since then, and Salima loved it.

Sex with Mourad was nothing like what the men did back in Bousaada. He kissed her tenderly and held her with such ferocity that she didn't want him to let go. She liked feeling his strong muscles around her and when he slipped inside her, he filled her with warm ecstasy.

After that, they would lie down and smoke quietly.

When Mourad knew she and Fahima were going back to Bousaada, he asked her to marry him, and Salima said yes. She knew it was only a matter of time before she would have to find a husband and settle down, and the prospect of spending long nights in Mourad's arms was hard to resist.

iii

'I'm assuming you've already said yes to him,' Saadia said, joy glittering in her eyes.

This was the climax of Mother's pride, Salima thought. Her daughter getting engaged at sixteen, and to a prosperous young man whose family already owned a wealth of sheep. Salima's dowry would only bring their prospects higher and would be enough for the couple to live comfortably for years at least. Her mother's over-sweetened pride made her want to decline his offer.

Salima nodded again.

'Well, you know you don't have to get married now,' mother explained. 'They don't expect you to give up dancing anytime soon.'

Salima already knew all of that. She and Mourad had talked it over. Mourad was hoping to build a stable in Bousaada just outside of town to facilitate his sheep trade, and Salima's dowry would help him build that stable.

'How about Fahima?' Saadia asked, ready to marry off her other daughter in the same go.

Salima was saved from this topic by *Amti* Tamani's arrival, father's twin sister. She had his face, except she wore it much better: high cheekbones, thick hair and glowing skin. Salima and her siblings all had those features, too, though people often said they were more like Saadia.

'What are you two up to?' *Amti* Tamani said, taking a large rock for a stool.

Amti Tamani lived three tents away from Salima's family, and both families went back and forth between the tents several times a day. She needed no greeting or invitation to join them.

'Just making tea,' Saadia replied.

Salima assumed they weren't ready to share her engagement news with her aunt yet.

Amti Tamani came to ask for Salima and Fahima's help in introducing her fourteen-year-old daughter, Souhila, to Bousaada, but Mother was quick to refuse with little subtlety.

'Have you heard what has been happening in Bousaada lately?' Mother warned. 'The thieves? The Ouled Brahims? You know *Caid* Tounsi was murdered out on the street in front of everyone. You want to send your daughter alone? I wouldn't advise that. Maybe give her one more year or two until she's able to fend for herself.'

Everyone knew that if Souhila waited until she was sixteen, she would be too old to get started as a dancer. *Amti* Tamani nodded gravely, avoiding Saadia's eyes.

'But,' Saadia resumed, 'if you're sure that's what you want, my daughters will be happy to take Souhila with them tomorrow.'

If this was Saadia's attempt to patch things up, it was weak and too late. Now *Amti* Tamani couldn't say Saadia and her girls had refused to take her daughter. Salima was as always, surprised by her mother's slyness.

Amti Tamani left without a word.

'Why did you do that?' Salima asked.

'*Why?* Can you imagine what would happen if you took Souhila under your wing? You'd have to give her lodging, too.'

'And how's that a problem? We have more than enough space.'

'How's that a problem?' Saadia was hissing, her rage simmering. 'Haven't you thought that she might reveal your secret?'

The stupid secret again, Salima thought. Mother was willing to do anything to protect her daughters' little secret, but Salima didn't see why. It wasn't like they had gained much by hiding it from everyone in Bousaada. And it wasn't like they had killed someone. They weren't going to get thrown in jail over this. She was surprised they had gone this long without being discovered. Salima had only gone along with the whole game because she didn't expect it to last more than a week, but time had flown by without anyone noticing anything. It proved just how little people in Bousaada actually knew each other.

Salima kept these thoughts to herself. Saadia was already boiling with rage.

'Or am I the only one who thinks?' Saadia stood up and knocked the teapot off the fire, spilling the tea all over the dry ground. 'And I thought Fahima was the fool,' she turned to go.

She stopped face to face with Fahima, who was standing at the edge of the tent, having heard everything. Mother looked at her. She was startled but said nothing. Then she stormed past her.

It was late in the afternoon when Salima and Fahima dressed up to go over to the bride's tent. Saadia insisted they wear all their jewellery, and the sisters complied. They couldn't stand another confrontation with their moody mother.

The three women walked the short distance to the bride's tent. The sound of drums and clapping came from the well where the men were already congregating.

Aida, the bride, lived in one of two large tents occupied by her family of fourteen. The two tents were separated only by a veil between the male and female sections.

Saadia entered the female section to help the older women with the cooking while Fahima and Salima joined the five or six girls who had occupied the male tent and were preparing the bride for her big night. The air inside was thick with the smell of salty meat and flowery perfumes.

Aida looked like a creature from another world. She sat majestically cross-legged on a sheepskin rag in a magnificent beige dress, a white veil covering her head and two thick braids falling over her shoulders. She already had kohl outlining her large eyes, and her lips were made fuller and redder than usual. Another girl was on her knees brushing Aida's cheeks until they turned pink.

'Aida!' Fahima squealed. 'You look fabulous.'

Salima thought so, too. As she and her sister went around the tent kissing everyone on the cheeks, she couldn't help wondering how Aida hadn't made a successful life as a dancer back in Bousaada. She had an attractive body, and she was a good dancer, but she never qualified for hotels or Mouloud's even though she and Salima had moved to Bousaada in the same caravan and started dancing on the exact same day.

Fahima had told Salima the story of how on her first night, Aida had innocently taken a coin from a client and the café owner had beaten her so badly she stayed at home for over a week. Perhaps Aida had never really recovered.

Nevertheless, Aida's short career was enough for her to collect a decent dowry for the man she wanted to marry, and her eyes now shone bright with joy.

She wondered if she too should put an early stop to her career and get married. Her success would allow her to continue for a few more years at least, but she wasn't sure it was worth all the violence and hardships. The last year has been more or less safer than their first, but Salima could still feel danger lurking around every corner.

Mourad probably wouldn't mind if she decided to stop now. He would find a way to build his stable in Bousaada without a larger dowry.

Salima's thoughts were interrupted by Farida, who skipped into the tent, flashing her toothless smile and holding her still uneaten piece of bread.

'Fahima,' she called out and said, 'Krimo wants to see you behind the tent.'

Farida's attempt to whisper those words had failed miserably, and the girls in the tent heard everything. This excited them, and they gave Fahima playfully vicious smiles. But Fahima seemed to be the least excited about Farida's news. Krimo was their cousin, *Amti* Tamani's eldest son, and he had spent the past few weeks trying, and failing, to woo Fahima.

'Tell him I'm busy,' Fahima told Farida with unconcealed irritation.

The other girls roared their disapproval. 'Come on,' Aida said. 'Go see him behind the tent.'

They all giggled, and Fahima pretended not to mind, but her face was reddening quickly. The girls insisted that she couldn't dismiss the bride's wish on her wedding day, so she finally went.

No sooner had Fahima gone than all the girls went to the far end of the tent, each finding a small hole to look through, straining to control their giggles. The bride stayed back at first, then jumped to her feet and found her own hole. Salima joined in, too.

Salima spied Fahima standing next to Krimo. He fidgeted while Fahima stared him down. She opened her mouth to speak first, and, to Salima's surprise everyone in the tent could hear her. Salima hoped, against hope, this wouldn't cause any trouble.

'What?' Fahima said aggressively. 'What do you want?' Fahima sounded just like their Mother.

'I just wanted to talk to you,' Krimo said with a quivering voice. The girls in the tent covered their mouths to suppress a laugh.

'I'm here. Say what you want.'

'I want to ask your hand in marriage before you go back to Bousaada.' The girls held their breath in anticipation. 'I'm going to ask my mother to talk to yours later tonight.'

Krimo clearly didn't know he was being watched, but Fahima kept glancing in the tent's direction. *Walk away*, Salima thought. *Take him on a stroll.* But Fahima didn't seem to think of that. *Or maybe this is what she wants*, Salima thought. To humiliate him in front of the girls. *Fahima? When did you get this sneaky?*

'I told you so many times,' Fahima said. 'I don't want to marry you. So don't talk to your mother. Not today. Not ever.'

Salima winced as a few girls snorted besides her.

'But why?' Krimo asked.

Salima knew why. Fahima had naively fallen for that French doctor who had saved her from being raped at that camp. Salima had tried yelling and reasoning with her sister, but she never listened. Salima had even tried humiliating her, asking her with disgusted disappointment what she expected from a relationship with a *roumi* who was clearly toying with her. Fahima argued that she was aware she couldn't marry him, but they could travel together. To Algiers, Paris, or Rome where she could prosper as an exotic dancer.

And he's not toying with me, Fahima insisted. *He's nice and honest, and he loves me too.* Salima couldn't believe that, but her sister was still crazy about him.

Salima's heart was beating fast. What if Fahima brought up the French officer in front of everyone. People would talk about Fahima for years – about how she had turned down a man from her own village to stay with a *roumi*– Mother would be furious.

Salima stepped away from the hole and spoke aloud for the girls to hear her, 'Listen. I think they're coming to get you, Aida.'

The girls ignored Salima and focused on the scene outside. Feeling down with desperation, Salima retook her spot and peeped through the hole.

'... to work in Bousaada for years,' Fahima was saying.

'I can wait for you,' Krimo said, desperate. 'Two, three, five years. Take as much time as you want.'

'You're not listening, Krimo. Why would I marry you when I can marry any man I want?'

Without waiting for a reply, Fahima pushed past him and headed back to the tent. One of the girls near Salima snorted a little, and that sent everyone into a laughing fit.

Krimo heard them. He looked at the tent. His face was shocked to notice the holes for the first time and rage took over.

The girls stepped away from the holes, but he could still hear their laughter. Fahima came in with her head down and took a seat in the far corner. The girls followed her with their silent stares, glee on their faces.

Just when Salima thought the spectacle had ended, Krimo burst into the tent, and the girls screamed in shock. Krimo stood at the entrance, looking in dismay and rage at the girls, and probably realising that by the end of the wedding tonight, everyone in the village would hear about it.

The elder women from the next tent ran to inspect the cacophony. Saadia and Aida's mother appeared first, with the other women at their heels. They stood in shock, puzzled by the man in the bride's tent. Then *Amti* Tamani stepped out of the group of women, marching across the tent to her son.

'What in the world do you think you're doing in the bride's tent?' *Amti* Tamani shrieked. 'Have you lost your mind? Do you want people to say my own son is a crazy monster who peeks into naked girls' tents?'

The young man stormed off and his mother and her wrath followed him outside.

Salima glanced at her mother who had evidently understood what had happened, her eyes were fixated on Fahima who was hugging herself in the corner. Salima realised that while her sister had purposefully caused her cousin humiliation, she clearly hadn't enjoyed it any more than he had.

Before anyone had a chance to say anything, the sound of drums grew louder and closer. Too close, Salima thought.

'They're almost here,' Saadia announced. 'Come on, is everything ready?'

The elder women ran back to their tent to finish the cooking, and the younger ones surrounded Aida to fix her hair and clothes.

Then they went out to welcome the procession with ululation. The group of men stopped outside the tent, playing their drums and flutes and clapping with great enthusiasm. A large circle formed in the middle and young men danced inside it. An old woman joined, then young girls jumped in, too. They danced alone, together and with other young men, whipping their hair in circles and heaving their bellies up and down.

When they tired, the women brought out large bowls of couscous with meat and everyone sat down to eat in small knots.

After eating, Aida came out of the tent under her father's arm and a white *burnous*. Father and daughter were met with great applause before they all wandered back to the well together where they congregated in a large flat clearing.

They sat the bride on a thick carpet. Then they brought the groom out and sat him next to his beaming bride, surrounding them with music and dancing. Horses danced, bands of men competed with rifles, shooting the earth and sending clouds of dust and smoke in the air.

Salima clapped, watching the joy radiating from the couple. She noticed Mourad not far behind them. He had been looking at her, and when their eyes met, he smiled warmly. She smiled back, understanding.

She wondered when they would have their own wedding. She wouldn't wait long. She would work for a few more months, maybe help Fahima set up a *haouch* at their new house, then come back and get married here.

She would make her own happiness.

v

While the procession prepared to accompany the couple to their new tent, the two sisters slipped away. They had to wake up early for their trip to Bousaada.

Salima didn't want to bring up what had happened with Krimo, knowing Fahima would bring it up when she was ready. But Mother wasn't willing to wait.

They found Saadia already in the tent, stroking Farida's hair on her lap. Farida opened her eyes, gave her sisters a toothless smile then drifted back into her dream, her hand still clasped around the now stale piece of bread.

Saadia didn't greet them. 'What happened with Krimo?'

Salima decided to stay out of it.

'He keeps asking for my hand in marriage,' Fahima said, a tremble in her voice. 'I keep saying no, but he won't listen. I had to do it in front of the girls to make him stop.'

'And why don't you want to marry him?' Mother asked.

Strangely, Saadia didn't sound angry. In fact, she sounded curious. Maybe she had someone else in mind for Fahima.

Amti Tamani stormed into the tent. 'Saadia!' she shouted. Farida twitched in her sleep. 'Who do you think you are? You and your girls, huh?'

Mother stood up, hands on hips and chin in the air.

'First, you refuse to take Souhila to Bousaada,' *Amti* Tamani continued, 'And now you humiliate my son in front of the girls? Everyone in the village will laugh at him.'

Salima's aunt addressed all three of them as if they had all conspired to humiliate Krimo.

'Maybe it's because he *is* a joke,' Mother started, angry, but still in control. 'He caused himself this scandal, and he should take responsibility for it instead of running to his mother like a little girl.'

Amti Tamani stepped closer to Saadia, too close, but Saadia wasn't intimidated. They locked eyes like cocks about to fight.

'How dare you humiliate my son! And I've always considered you family. My beloved brother's family. I loved your kids like my own, but I should've known that a snake like you can't be trusted. You know what? I blame my brother. He's too nice. Had he beaten you, you and your cocky daughters, you wouldn't have gotten out of control like this.'

This was way out of line, Salima thought. She stepped between the two women. 'Hey, hey, hey....do you want to offend Amar and Farida, too, while you're at it? Maybe blame them for your son's humiliation, too?'

Amti Tamani was shocked. She clearly hadn't expected Salima to speak up. Salima was surprised, too. She couldn't help feeling good about it, though.

'I won't stand here and let you offend everyone,' she pressed on. 'Do you hear me?'

Amti Tamani squinted at Salima then at Saadia. Adopting a quieter voice filled with hurt, she said, 'You're ganging up against me now, is that it? You're taking your mother's side?'

That was a stupid thing to say. Did *Amti* Tamani expect Salima to take her side over her mother's?

'You'll regret it, trust me.' She nodded gravely, then looked at

Fahima, who was hiding behind her sister and mother. 'You'll all regret it. You hear me?' She stormed out. 'All of you!'

Her mother smiled at Salima, but Fahima held her breath, no doubt expecting a scolding.

'Looks like you still need your sister to stand up for you,' Saadia joked.

Salima realised her mother was right. Life in Bousaada might have taught Fahima to be conniving, but she still couldn't get herself out of trouble. Salima had to protect her.

She couldn't leave Fahima alone in Bousaada.

Her wedding would have to wait.

Thirteen

i

Colonel Joseph Dupont loved the traditional flatbread his housekeeper served this morning, warm and mushy. Delphine took a bite of the bread and sighed with pleasure.

'Where is Bernard?' Joseph asked. 'He should come eat while the bread is still warm.'

'He's still asleep,' she said avoiding Joseph's eyes. 'He came in late last night.'

'He's been doing that a lot lately,' Joseph said. 'Where does he go?'

'With friends, I guess.' Delphine shrugged.

She took a sip of her coffee, then picked up the newspaper, trying to put an end to the conversation.

'I hear he's been spending a lot of time with an indigenous girl,' Joseph said. Major Turrene had mentioned it a few days ago.

'Me too,' she replied absentmindedly, still looking at her paper. 'Elizabeth told me at church the other day.'

'Do you know the girl?'

She shook her head. 'Elizabeth says it's a Jewess. Her father's a jeweller near the Street of Joy.'

Rage brewed in Joseph's chest. That couldn't be good. What did he want with her? It wasn't like he could just marry a Jewess. Why was Delphine fine with this?

'Have you talked to him about it?' Joseph asked. 'Told him he should stop seeing her?'

Joseph didn't want to speak to his son about this juvenile love affair.

'I will,' Delphine said, then something on the newspaper caught her attention and her face lit up with excitement. 'Hey, look at this. They're releasing *Le Simoun* in Paris this coming Friday.'

The whole town was excited about *Le Simoun* because they had shot some scenes in Bousaada back in May. The crew and cast had spent days out in the dunes working late nights under blinding light projectors. Every night, hundreds of Bousaadans watched with bewilderment as the crew blew up a sandstorm for the film using two airplanes.

'Do you want to go see it while we're in Paris?' Joseph said. They were planning to go there for Christmas.

Before Delphine could answer, the doorman appeared.

'Désolé, Monsieur Dupont,' he said, his eyes fixated on the floor. 'Si Madani's here to see you. I told him to wait until you're done with breakfast, but he says you'd want to see him immediately.'

Joseph's mood deteriorated. The world seemed determined to not give him a moment's peace.

ii

Fatah Madani was a big Arab with even bigger aspirations.

He had been grovelling since the former *Caid*'s murder back in February, with the clear objective of securing the position now that it was vacant. Fatah's family was one of the three most prominent families in Bousaada, and the traditional providers of *Caids* in this town: The Madanis, the Kacimis and the Tounsis.

Since the deceased *Caid* belonged to the Tounsi family, Joseph would now need to appoint a new *Caid* from the Madanis or Kacimis to make sure power didn't permanently reside in one family. Also, taking turns in power ensured a lifelong rivalry between the three families, meaning they wouldn't combine efforts against the French administration. Instead, they dedicated their lives to pleasing the colonels and bringing each other down. Divide and conquer.

Joseph needed a *Caid* he could rely on to keep the indigenous people in check and be his eyes and ears in the town. The late *Caid* Tounsi had failed miserably at his task, and now the office had been vacant for almost a year. Joseph couldn't afford to make the wrong decision.

Looking at Madani in his intricately embroidered caftan and his sly grin, Joseph was sure he wasn't the right person for the job. No amount of flattery or bootlicking would change his mind.

'Si Madani,' Joseph said, not trying to hide his annoyance. 'What could possibly be so urgent you couldn't wait until I'm at work?'

As they shook hands, Madani raised a small jar in his left hand, his sly grin permanent on his face.

'I brought you the best honey from Constantine. When I tasted it, I said, Colonel Dupont has got to taste this delicious, sweet, natural honey.'

He chuckled, and Joseph had to match it with a forced smile. Madani handed him the jar.

'That's very nice of you,' Joseph said, incapable of meeting this feigned kindness with attitude. 'Delphine will love it, I'm sure.'

Madani smiled meekly.

'How's everything at work?' Madani asked, and Joseph knew where this was leading.

'All's good. It's busy, but we're doing our best.'

'Have you been able to find the old *Caid*'s murderer?'

'Still working on it. But we're pretty sure it was the Ouled Brahims.'

'That's what I thought. They must have taken revenge for the killing of one of their men.'

'What do you mean?'

Caid Tounsi had made a lot of enemies and had definitely been behind the killing of many Ouled Brahims, but as far as Joseph knew, none of these killings stood out. Madani's face lit up as he realised he might know something Joseph didn't.

'It happened more than two years ago. There was some sort of confrontation between the *Caid* and one of Ouled Brahim's fighters. Later that night, the *Caid* executed the man in front of everyone. I told them then. I said they'll never forget that. They will come back and kill the *Caid* for it. And look what happened. They killed him the same way. The exact same location.'

Madani seemed very proud of himself. Joseph could barely contain his fury. This incident apparently happened before Joseph's time. How had no one at his office made that link before? And now this slimy Arab was telling him about it?

'It's a very sad situation,' Madani resumed, shaking his head gravely.

'True,' Joseph agreed.

'But you need a new *Caid*. You need one of the locals to be on your side. To be your right hand.'

There we go, Joseph thought. 'We're working on it,' he said.

'If it pleases you, Colonel. I'd love to be at your service. I know everyone here, and I'll be able to control everything. The whole town will be at your service. You know— my grandfather was a *Caid* a long time ago, and he was loyal to Colonel Pein. They were best friends. Ask anyone.'

Madani was proving more resourceful than Joseph had thought, but he still didn't qualify to be the *Caid*. Joseph had another man in mind, Malek Kacimi, who was much wiser and less annoying.

Malek Kacimi seemed a little reluctant though, but whatever virtues or principles made Kacimi hesitant, Joseph was sure they had a price. He had come to learn that all Arabs had a price.

On the other hand, Joseph didn't want to say no to Fatah Madani until he had a new *Caid* in place. A little grovelling can be useful.

'I appreciate your loyalty,' Joseph said. 'I'm sure you would make a great *Caid*. But you know how the bureaucracy works. It takes a long time before we can officially appoint someone new.'

'I understand.'

'But I promise I'll keep you in mind, alright?'

Joseph went to the front door, and Madani followed.

'Thank you, Colonel. I really appreciate it.'

'We do our best to reward loyal people,' Joseph said as he opened the front door. 'Thanks again for the honey.'

iii

Joseph always told himself that the desert cold, bone-chilling though it was, was still the desert cold. It was nothing like those harsh winters in Paris. But it didn't feel that way now as he walked up Rue Gaboriau, his nose growing frosty. When he emerged onto Place de Pein, the sun was bright but conceded very little warmth.

At the military circle, Major Turrene was already waiting for Joseph in his perfectly ironed khaki uniform.

'There's a couple of things that need your attention, sir,' Major Turrene started after the salute.

'Tell me.'

'First, a few Arabs have been hunting for Ouled Brahims, and they've collected quite a few rings of ears. They're demanding their payment.'

When Joseph took office, the bounty system was already in place. Joseph found the practice needlessly expensive and was planning to put an end to it. But then the old *Caid* was murdered. If he stopped the bounty now, they'd think he was caving for the Ouled Brahims.

'You can go ahead and pay those Arabs for their bloody ear rings,' Joseph conceded. 'Once this *Caid* story has blown over, we'll make sure we're not giving money away to people plucking ears from cemeteries.'

Turrene winced, but he knew better than to voice misgivings about Joseph's plans.

'There's also the Ouled Nail dancers,' Turrene moved on. 'We received communications from Algiers inquiring as to what we've done to organise er... the working girls.'

One of the main objectives he was tasked with when he took office was to organise the prostitution trade. There were concerns that the working girls weren't clean and safe enough because they'd caused a few health issues among their clients, especially French soldiers.

Joseph's superiors in Algiers were also concerned that there was a huge trade in Bousaada they weren't taking advantage of. His task was to make sure all working girls had regular medical checks and were only allowed to practice if they had authorisation, hence paid taxes.

'Let's write back to Algiers,' Joseph improvised. 'Tell them we're running all the Ouled Nails through our military hospital, and we're working to have all girls and pleasure houses registered so they can start paying taxes.'

Turrene frowned at this obvious lie.

'And needless to say,' Joseph said, 'let's send a communication out to the town. Make sure every pleasure house knows they have to register before the end of the month if they want to keep their business.'

'And every girl working without a permit is to be imprisoned,' Turrene offered.

'And every girl working without a permit is to be imprisoned,' Joseph nodded.

Turrene performed another salute and left the office, eager to get started on the new task.

Joseph felt a lot less enthused. He had every intention to reinforce those laws, but the colonel couldn't even begin to imagine how complicated it would be to navigate the local system without a *Caid*. Even prostitution wasn't the same as in France. Back in Europe you could just walk into a whore house, receive the service of your choice, pay and leave. Simple.

In Bousaada, you had the brothels, but you also had cafés and you had girls who worked independently at home. It would take ages to track them all down. There were your common variety prostitutes, but there were also girls who didn't provide quick pleasure. They expected you to commit to a few sessions of private entertainment, dancing and music and conversation, before they let you touch them. Joseph felt sorry for the men who had to go through that long process. There was also the 'purer' type. These were dancers who didn't provide any pleasure services. They only danced at cafés and parties, and that was it. They might get naked if forced, but never let a man touch them.

As far as Joseph was concerned, they were all the same.

iv

Malek Kacimi lived in *La Commune Mixte*. Well into his forties, he had already taken ownership of his family's palm tree plantations, their large wealth and the indigenous people's respect. And that was exactly what Joseph needed to stay in control of the locals.

The problem was that Kacimi seemed a little reluctant. Since *Caid* Tounsi's death back in February, Kacimi had to know he had very good chances against his only rival, Fatah Madani, and Joseph had expected Kacimi to express his interest eventually.

Back in the summer, Joseph had even slipped into discussions that he was considering Kacimi for the new position as a Caid, knowing very well that word would get to Kacimi before Joseph even stood up to go. But to no avail. Kacimi had never come to Joseph about the position.

So now Joseph had to be bolder. He was willing to give up a little leverage if it meant he wouldn't be stuck with Madani as Caid.

A servant ushered Joseph into Kacimi's sunlit courtyard where he found him reading the Quran. Kacimi closed his book and placed it gently on the table in front of him. He stood up with the pace of a seventy-year-old. *A seventy-year-old who's in no hurry to please his French superior,* Joseph thought.

'Si Kacimi,' Joseph said cheerfully.

'Colonel,' Kacimi said as they shook hands. '*Zaretna baraka* as we say here. A blessing has honoured us with a visit. Please come. Sit down and have some tea.' His rolled Rs rang loud in Joseph's ears.

He sat on a cushion across from Kacimi. There was a tray on the table with a tea kettle and three used glasses. There was also traditional bread, a plate of dates and fresh butter. It smelled fresh and warm.

Karima,' Kacimi hollered towards what looked like a kitchen in the lower floor and shouted some orders in Derja.

'No need to bother anyone,' Joseph protested. 'I'm not going to stay long.'

Kacimi smiled at him, but Joseph knew his host wouldn't call off the tea. Local hospitality didn't permit that.

'Try these dates,' Kacimi pushed the plate to Joseph. 'It's our finest.'

'Thank you,' Joseph said. The date was soft and fleshy, and tasted of pure ripe sweetness. Joseph helped himself to another. 'How's business?'

'All is good. It keeps us busy. How are you doing, Colonel?'

'We're busy, too. And we're looking for someone to help us with everything going on. You know, the Ouled Brahims and the Ouled Nail. Since Caid Tounsi's death, we still haven't been able to find a new man for the job.'

Joseph paused, giving Kacimi the chance to take the bait, but Kacimi only gave a sympathetic nod. Joseph would probably have to place the offer right there on the table next to the tea set and the dates. At the same time, he didn't want Kacimi to feel too essential. He needed to know that Joseph's good graces was a privileged but precarious place to find oneself.

A young girl with two thick braids, probably about nine or ten years old, tip-toed out of the kitchen carrying a new tea kettle. Smiling wide, she served them both. Kacimi followed her movements with a proud smile as she left to tend to the kitchen again.

'This is my only daughter,' Kacimi announced. 'Karima. She's my pride and joy. Nothing like her brothers.'

'She's very sweet,' Joseph agreed, trying hard to hide his irritation at being interrupted.

'Thank you. Sorry, Colonel. You were saying?'

'I was telling you we're still looking for a new Caid, and I was hoping you'd take the position.'

Joseph couldn't afford being implicit anymore.

'Me?' Kacimi looked genuinely surprised. 'I never thought about it.'

'Why not? Your father was a *Caid*, right? And others in your family, too.'

'I'm not sure I can do it.'

'Of course, you can,' Joseph said. 'I mean you're well connected to the community. People respect you. And you have the wisdom it takes to be a *Caid*.'

'That's very kind of you, Colonel,' Kacimi said, but that didn't sound like an acceptance.

'Do you have any concerns?' Joseph sipped at his tea. It had a bitter aftertaste.

Kacimi cleared his throat. 'I'm not sure what would be expected of me if I were to take the position.'

'Not much. You would be the liaison between the administration and the locals.'

'Between the French and the Algerians?'

'Mostly, yes. I mean the European community here is very small. It's not like in big cities.'

'What else?'

'I'd like you to also keep an eye out for potential issues. If a problem arises, I'd like to know about it before it becomes a real problem.'

'Like the Ouled Brahims.'

'And any other threat to the community.'

'A threat to the *European* community?'

'The Ouled Brahims are a threat to everyone in Bousaada.'

Kacimi nodded, keeping his eyes down. The man seemed to be losing enthusiasm. Joseph didn't want to sound desperate, but he'd already lost a lot of ground in this negotiation. What was another few meters?

'And I'm sure you're familiar with the rewards that come with this position,' Joseph said. 'On top of your monthly salary, you'd have exclusive rights to certain business opportunities. Lands for sale. Crops. Cattle. You'll also have the full support of the French administration. You'll enjoy full immunity. All your crimes, past and future, will be forgiven. Even murder.'

'That's the last thing I intend to do,' Kacimi said. 'I like to live by the guidance of Allah. There's nothing more precious than human life.'

'Of course. Sure. I know you enjoy great popularity here, but you're undoubtedly going to have a few enemies. The Ouled Brahims for one. So you'd need to protect yourself. And needless to say, we're going to provide you with the best protection possible.'

'That's very nice of you,' Kacimi said, still not meeting his guest's eyes.

'You don't have to give me an answer now,' Joseph spat out the words before he even thought about it. He did need an answer now.

He didn't like the prospect of having to wait a few more days, especially not now that Turrene was probably going around town to cafés and brothels with new commands, but it was still better than a firm no.

'Take your time. Think about it.'

Joseph stood up to leave, and Kacimi stood up, too.

'I don't need to think about it. I have an answer for you now, Colonel.'

Joseph's heart skipped a beat. He hoped it didn't show on his face.

'As much as I appreciate you coming all the way here to offer the position, I'm afraid politics is not my thing. I'm a businessman. I don't feel comfortable informing on my own brethren.'

Joseph nodded. He turned around and left without a word.

v

By the time Joseph turned to Rue Gaboriau, he had forgotten about the cold.

He had practically begged this half-wit Arab to fill a position others would kill for, but he thought he was too noble to work for the French. He was too loyal to his people. They would sell him out for a piece of bread.

What was Joseph going to do now? Should he appoint Fatah Madani instead? Everyone knew Madani was sly, and Joseph couldn't rely on him to earn the indigenous people's trust.

No. This wouldn't do. Joseph couldn't take no for an answer. Not from an Arab.

Joseph kept mulling over the situation while he ate his lunch alone. Delphine was out, and Bernard was still sleeping. Joseph had half a mind to go throw a bucket of water on his son.

After lunch, Joseph was surprised to see the honey jar that Madani had brought still in the foyer, exactly where he left it on the table. Had no one bothered to put it away? Joseph didn't know why this was bugging him so much. As he picked up the jar to inspect it, the doorman burst in.

'You're here, sir,' the doorman said with a bow. 'Would you like me to bring you coffee?'

'Yes. And take this jar to the kitchen.'

'Isn't this the jar Si Madani brought for you?' the doorman asked.

'Yes, and no one bothered to pick it up all day.'

The doorman looked like he had something to say.

'What is it?' Joseph asked.

'I... It's not my place, sir.'

'No, say it. Let me decide if it's your place or not.'

'It's Si Madani, sir.' Joseph nodded encouragingly. 'Well, the only reason he brought you the honey is because he's after the *Caid* position.'

'I already know that. Do you not think he should take the position?'

'Again, it's not my place, sir. But he only wants it for his own interests.'

'What interests?'

'His business deals. He wants to be important. And to threaten people. He's already violent with everyone. And if he becomes *Caid*, he'll kill people right and left. He also wants his son to go to the French school, and to have a big...'

'Wait, wait, wait.... Say that again? About the French school?'

'Yes, sir. All important men want their kids to go to school. A French school is the best of course. Their kids will be able to study in Algiers or Paris to become doctors or pharmacists or lawyers...'

An idea lit up Joseph's mind like a kerosene soaked torch. He left the house, shutting the door behind him while the doorman tried to say something about the coffee.

At Place de Pein, he spotted Turrene crossing the square towards the row of cafés with four soldiers in tow. He was probably distributing the communications they had discussed this morning.

Joseph hurried towards *La Commune Mixte* as if in a race against Turrene. He had to have a new *Caid* in place before his new orders led to public riots. Luckily, he ran into Kacimi near the Gendarmerie.

'Si Kacimi,' Joseph said, feigning a casual tone. 'Look at us running into each other twice in one day. I could get used to this.'

Kacimi flashed an overly polite smile. 'I'm on my way to the mosque.'

'Alright. Don't let me hold you up. Please.'

Kacimi nodded and started to waddle away when Joseph said, 'Oh, by the way, Si Kacimi.'

Kacimi stopped and turned. His useless cane barely touched the ground.

'I just thought of something. Your daughter. What was her name again? Karima, right? Beautiful girl.'

'What about her?' Kacimi asked, his voice cracking just a little.

'I've seen how smart and energetic she is,' Joseph started, 'and then I thought what a shame she doesn't go to school.'

'She goes to the Quranic school,'

'That's good. Good for her. But I'm sure she can do much more. She needs proper schooling. A French school.'

'The French school isn't for our kids, Colonel.'

'It can be,' Joseph smiled. 'I'm sure we can arrange something with the director.'

Kacimi fell silent.

'That is, of course, if you want your daughter to receive a proper education.'

'Certainly, Colonel.'

'Well, this is your opportunity. Karima can be anything she wants. A doctor maybe? In any case, education will prevent her from becoming one of those Ouled Nail dancers.'

Kacimi's hands curled tightly around the cane. He knew exactly what Joseph was doing. This was a threat.

'Of course, I have no doubt you'll make the right decision for your daughter, Si Kacimi.'

'I'll think about it,' Kacimi finally said.

'I'll need an answer right now I'm afraid,' Joseph pressed. 'We've already waited too long, and besides, I have other people dying to be appointed *Caid*.'

Kacimi took a deep breath. Behind him, across the square, Turrene emerged from the lobby of L'Hotel de l'Oasis and marched towards the café next to it.

'So, what's it going to be, Kacimi?' Joseph pressed again.

'Fine,' he said, in a barely audible voice.

'Well, congratulations,' Joseph exclaimed. He shook the new *Caid*'s hand.

Across the square, a group of people were already stirring up some commotion outside L'Hotel de l'Oasis.

Joseph pointed in the direction of the hotel. 'Looks like your work has already started,' he said, laying a heavy hand on his shoulder, '*Caid*.'

Caid Kacimi turned to follow Joseph's gaze, then mumbled something in Derja. Joseph didn't understand what he said, but he had the feeling it meant something along the lines of 'God help us.'

'Amen,' Joseph nodded. 'Amen.'

Fourteen

i

The poor chicken lay shapeless. Lifeless. A large hole was where her chest should have been, revealing dry flesh.

Salima looked in horror at the dead bird, her feathers soaked in blood, and her head nowhere to be seen. A puff of feathers, small and light, was scattered not far from the body. The dogs had barely eaten anything as if they had only killed her for the sake of it.

The rooster wasn't there, and Salima assumed the stray dogs had taken him. The goats ate from their feeders, seemingly oblivious to the massacre that had taken place in front of them.

The shed door was ajar, letting in the morning light. Of course, the dogs had found their way through the door and attacked the birds while they slept, blind in the dark. Salima took a deep breath.

'Fahima, you stupid bitch!' she shouted. 'What did you do?'

Fahima came out of the kitchen and hurried across the courtyard.

'When did you come back from the camp?' Fahima asked.

Salima had spent two days with some tourists and had made it back late last night, going straight to bed.

'Look what you've done.' Salima pointed to the dead chicken.

Fahima covered her mouth. 'The dogs ate her?'

'No, the goats did,' Salima said. 'Of course, the dogs. You left the door open, you stupid fool.'

'I forgot,' Fahima said.

If Salima stayed a moment longer, she would start throwing punches, so she picked up an empty water jar and left without a word.

She went to the river where a group of girls were already bathing in the sun. Some washed their laundry on the banks, but none ventured all the way in. The morning air was cold, and the water was painfully icy.

Salima leaned her jar against a rock and crossed the river on a path of stones. The girls basking in the sun stopped laughing and stared as Salima joined them.

Salima didn't like how they looked at her, even if it was out of admiration.

'So, Ammariya, how was the camp?' Nouara was the first to break the silence.

'It was alright.' Salima shrugged as she lit a cigarette.

'No one gave you trouble about authorisations or taxes?' Djamila asked.

'No, but we only danced. Nothing more. The men organising the camp didn't want to take risks.'

Since Colonel Dupont had introduced the new regulations over a month ago, requiring Ouled Nail to have authorisation and proof of medical checks, business in Bousaada had almost died out. Cafés no longer allowed dancers to work. In fear of having to pay heavy penalties, many *haouch* owners closed down while they waited for their documentation, and most camps were put on hold. French soldiers were everywhere, asking people for papers right and left, and many girls had been arrested.

But then, just two weeks ago, someone had found a loophole. The rules only concerned prostitutes. If the girls only danced, then they didn't have to comply with regulations.

Everyone soon started dancing. Cafés were working again, and camps were organised. *Haouch* owners like Soltana and Hadda didn't make much money off dancing, and the paperwork was taking forever, but the girls still had to pay rent.

'Has anyone applied to get authorisation?' one girl asked. 'I think it's the only way out. I started working on it a few weeks ago, got my medical check. I'll have my papers soon.'

'Good for you,' Nouara said mockingly. 'Then you'll have to pay half of your earnings in taxes.'

Everyone laughed, and the girl's face went bright red.

'My mother said they've always had this law,' Djamila said. 'But they haven't always been strict about it. Every once in a while, some colonel came and tried to show them he's the man. I guess it's Dupont's turn now.'

'Maybe if we just wait it out,' Salima suggested, 'they'll forget about it again, and things will go back to normal.'

'But how long do we have to wait?' a girl asked. 'What are we going to eat in the meantime?'

Fahima and Salima had figured out a way around the regulations, but Salima couldn't risk sharing that information. She shrugged as she put a cigarette in her mouth.

'I know a girl who moved in with one of her clients,' Djamila said.

'With his own wife and kids. Can you believe that? This way he has his way with her and she doesn't lack for anything.'

'I'm thinking of going back to my village and getting married,' someone said. 'I don't know if I can do this much longer. It's not worth it, honestly.'

Salima stayed a bit longer, listening to stories and complaints until she felt hungry. She stood up to leave.

'Wait up.' Nouara put her hand on Djamila's shoulder for support as she got on her feet. 'I need to pick up a ring from Ayash. I'll walk with you.'

ii

Salima filled her jar with water from the river and turned to walk back home with Nouara when she noticed a man sitting between some palm trees.

'Who the fuck is that?' Nouara asked, then she immediately changed her tone. 'Oh, it's him, Alexandre!'

Most of his body was hidden behind a large frame which Salima soon realised was a canvas. French people often came here to paint whatever drew their attention: men, women, river, trees, houses, anything.

'Alexandre,' Nouara called out. 'What are you doing here?

Alexandre smiled at Nouara. 'Bonjour, Nouara,' he said. 'I'm just watching.'

'What are you painting?' Nouara asked and walked around the canvas to look. Salima did the same.

'It's nothing yet,' Alexandre said.

The canvas was mostly blank save for a blue line snaking its way across the painting, some small shapes in different colours right above the line, and a few bigger forms in brown. Salima recognised the painting to be the scene directly in front of them: the river, the girls gathered on the other bank and the tiny hills rising beyond them.

Alexandre had been secretly watching them, and Salima felt naked.

'That's beautiful,' Nouara said with exaggeration.

'Thanks. Is this your friend?' He smiled at Salima.

'Yes, this is Ammariya,' Nouara announced.

'She's beautiful,' he said. 'I love the shape of your face. Your cheekbones.'

'Hey,' Nouara scolded him, 'You're not going to paint her in my stead, are you?'

'No, don't worry. I have to finish your portrait first.'

Nouara turned to Salima and explained, 'Alexandre is going to make a painting of me. Naked. And he wants to take it back to Paris, and maybe I'll go with him, too. Can you imagine?'

Salima couldn't imagine, but she forced a smile. 'Exciting.'

'I could also paint you if you wish,' Alexandre addressed Salima.

'Yes, sure,' she said.

'Nouara, bring her with you when you come to my house tomorrow, will you?'

'Yeah, I will,' Nouara said. Salima sensed some irritation in Nouara's voice.

The weight of the jar grew heavier on Salima's shoulder, so she motioned Nouara to resume walking.

'Well, I guess I'll see you tomorrow,' Nouara called over her shoulder.

'Sure, and bring Ammariya with you, alright?'

Nouara didn't say anything. On the way back home, she told Salima how Alexandre paid her good money and what she was going to do in Paris when the painting was done.

None of this appealed to Salima: posing naked for days and going to some strange place full of French people. She preferred to stay here and save her money for her dowry. *Fahima would love all of this*, Salima thought. But then she remembered that Fahima had left the door open for the dogs that morning.

iii

Salima put down the water jar in her courtyard and joined Nouara outside the Jew's house.

Yamina, the Jew's daughter, ushered them into the courtyard, which was empty but for two other Nailiya girls. If dancers didn't make any money, they didn't buy any jewellery either.

Fadhila emerged out of a side room, and she walked slowly, one hand on her hip like a bride.

'How can I help you, girls?' Fadhila asked in her squeaky little voice.

'I'm here to see if my necklace is ready,' Salima said coldly.

'And I'm checking in on my ring, too,' Nouara said, more nicely, 'I paid Ayash over two weeks ago, so...'

'Let me ask him.' Fadhila headed to her husband's workshop.

Yamina had already covered herself in a *haik* and was heading to the door.

'Where do you think you're going, young lady?' Fadhila's high-pitched voice rang in Salima's ears.

'I told you. I'm going to Afaf's. They had a new baby so they're hosting a dinner.'

'You need to be back here by sunset, you hear me?'

'I know, mother,' Yamina said as she hurried outside.

As Salima and Nouara stood idly, looking around the house, Salima eyed the blue-tiled fountain at the centre of the courtyard, dry and dusty, and wondered if there had ever been any water in there. A few tiles had fallen off leaving a pyramid-shaped gap as if it had been done on purpose. *Some kind of Jewish ritual or something,* Salima thought.

A few hens waddled around lazily, pecking at things only they saw on the ground. Her own old chicken and rooster had become some stray dogs' meal thanks to stupid Fahima.

Suddenly, a chicken bolted past the two girls, cackling and squawking. She was being chased by a rooster who seemed to be enjoying himself immensely. He had a red-feathered neck, dotted wings and a perfectly arched tail of black and brown.

'That's *my* rooster!' Salima called. 'I thought the dogs ate him.'

Indifferent to Salima's happiness, the rooster continued to chase the chicken until she stopped, all on her own, and lowered herself, ready for him. He got on top of her, took her comb in his beak and thrust himself, only three or four times, and just like that it was all over. He unmounted her and stood looking at her sideways. The hen ruffled her plumage and shook her body, then went about her business.

Salima approached the rooster. He didn't seem afraid of her. When she was close enough, she grabbed for his wings. She only caught one, and the cock flapped his other wing and squeaked aloud until Salima put the two wings together. The rooster writhed some more, then calmed down, surrendering to her grip.

Just then, Fadhila came out of the workshop, 'Sorry girls, but it seems that...' she stopped when she saw Salima holding the rooster.

'This is my rooster,' Salima said before Fadhila had the chance to scold her. 'He must have come here when the dogs ate his hen.'

'How do I know this is really yours?'

Salima rolled her eyes.

Nouara changed the topic. 'So they're not ready yet?' she asked the Jewess.

'No, sorry,' she replied, her face reflecting all but an apology.

Salima left with her rooster. Nouara followed.

iv

For the first time in weeks, Mouloud's café was at full capacity. When Salima entered, Djamila was already there dancing and people were cheering her on.

'No special clients,' Mouloud told Salima before she started dancing. 'Not at his hotel, not at your home. Nowhere. Do you hear me? I still don't have my papers in order, and neither do you, I guess, so let's not risk anyone going to jail tonight, alright?'

'I'm only here to dance.' Salima raised her hands in surrender.

She was lying, of course, and Mouloud didn't seem to believe her. But nor did he do anything about it.

Salima and Fahima had a plan to take in clients without raising suspicions, and it was working just fine so far.

She went to the middle of the café to dance, and Nouara joined soon after. There was one other girl, but none of them danced with the full-hearted engagement they usually did. They danced with the spirit of a kid who was forced to eat something they didn't like.

A middle-aged man, small with thick grey hair, caught Salima's attention. He was neither local, she judged, nor French, which was the safest choice. Most importantly, his eyes were on her, and his clothes whispered of wealth. A perfect catch. She gave him occasional winks and faint smiles, and she let him watch her bottom as she danced.

When the musicians took a break, Salima and the other girls went out to the main street for a cigarette.

'Have you seen Fadhila this evening?' Nouara asked with the hushed voice she often used when she had some gossip to share. 'She's running around town like a crazy woman. She can't find her daughter anywhere.'

'Didn't we see her leave earlier today?' Salima asked, giggling at the image of that vile Jewess running around like a headless chicken. 'She said something about a friend and a new baby or something.'

'She did. But it turns out she was lying. Her mother didn't find her there. And now she's freaking out because she doesn't want her husband finding out that Yamina's gone missing.'

'I guess we all know where she is,' Djamila said. 'Curling up in bed with the colonel's son.'

The four girls exploded into laughter.

'I can't wait for her mother to find out,' Nouara said.

The old men inside the café resumed their music, so the girls crushed their cigarettes on the ground and went back in.

Salima danced closer to the middle-aged man, her target, until she she could see lust scintillating in his eyes. When the men were drunk enough to start dancing, she let her target touch her. She rubbed her body against his just enough to arouse him. Then, when the time was right, she whispered, 'Wait awhile then leave. Wait for me out by the gate.'

Fortunately, this man knew the rules of the game. He sat down, drank some more, then paid and left. Salima gave it another moment before she went through the back door. As planned, Fahima was hiding under the staircase behind a curtain.

'You're up,' Salima said.

'You got a client?' Fahima asked, but Salima didn't answer. She was still angry with her sister.

Fahima went into the café to dance for the rest of the evening while Salima left through the back door.

Salima didn't let her client take her that night. She wasn't a prostitute, she told herself. Instead, she danced for him naked and let him touch her breasts. He paid her eight francs.

v

Salima couldn't help feeling a little satisfied on the way back. Her mother had been right to insist on them hiding their secret. Thanks to Saadia's shrewdness, the sisters were now able to go about their business, taking clients without having to pay taxes or wait months for their paperwork.

While most other girls had to content themselves with dancing and selling their jewellery for food, Salima and Fahima continued to increase their wealth. Salima might even be able to collect her dowry and get out of here soon. Marry Mourad and raise a family of her own.

She was snaking her way through the narrow alleys when the hairs on her arms prickled. The place was empty. It was nothing. Footsteps? No Nailiya dancer had been robbed or murdered for over a year now.

She pressed on. She was almost home. But there were footsteps ahead. Someone was running in heels, panting, and Salima's heart was racing. She wanted to run back, but before she even turned, a girl slammed into her.

'Help me,' the girl begged. It was Yamina, the Jew's daughter.

'Please, help me. He's trying to rape me.'

'Who?' Salima asked. She knew the answer to her question.

Bernard, Colonel Dupont's son, was upon them. His glossy hair was dishevelled, his face red and his clothes a mess. He was obviously drunk and his bloodshot eyes bulged at them.

'Come back here, you slut,' he addressed Yamina. 'You think this girl's going to save you?'

She didn't understand what was going on. Everyone in town knew these two people had been together for a long time.

'You leave her alone,' Salima somehow found the courage to shout at the drunk man.

'Get out of here, bitch,' Bernard retorted. 'This is none of your business.'

'Bernard, please,' Yamina begged, hiding behind Salima.

They both retreated, but Bernard followed, fists clenched.

'I told you you're mine,' he said.

Yamina squealed. 'I can't. My father will kill me.'

Salima understood now. Tonight was the big night Bernard had decided he was no longer satisfied with kissing and touching.

Salima told Yamina to run and they bolted towards the main street. To Salima's horror, Yamina was limping.

'I can't,' Yamina screamed. She stopped and leaned against a wall. 'I twisted my ankle.'

Bernard was approaching fast.

Salima turned to face him. Her hands shook, but she forced herself to stand her ground. She might die.

'Go away, you fucking asshole or I'll—'

Bernard punched Salima in the face, his fist connecting with her jaw with such force that the whole world went dark for a moment. She was on all fours, her head drowning in pain. She didn't know how long she stayed down, unable to open her eyes.

Yamina screamed.

Salima ignored her burning jaw and forced her eyes open. Bernard pressed Yamina's body against the wall and clutched her arms above her head.

Despite her dizziness, Salima took a deep breath, and stood up. Her head went swimming. She wouldn't let herself fall again.

Bernard hiked Yamina's dress up to her waist while she wiggled and cried and tried, in vain, to free herself.

Salima opened her mouth to tell Bernard to stop, but the pain in her jaw was unbearable. Nothing came out. She closed her eyes until the pain receded, her left hand toyed with the bracelet on her right wrist.

Bernard unzipped his pants and took out his cock. This was Salima's last chance.

She fixed the bracelet on her wrist, pressing the heel of her hand against the side with two studs. Since her mother had given her the bracelet, Salima had often found herself daydreaming about another attack in a dark alley. And how she would drive the spikes deep into the thief's neck until he bled to death.

She hesitated. A part of Salima told her to run. This wasn't her friend; she owed this girl nothing. Naima hadn't been Salima's friend either when she sacrificed herself to save Salima. What if this was Naima? Would Salima leave her to be raped and killed? Would she have died for Naima?

Bernard was starting to thrust himself into Yamina when Salima grabbed a hold of his left shoulder and drove the spikes of her bracelet into his pulsing neck. The metal broke through skin and flesh. It felt like cutting a chicken thigh.

Salima plucked the tiny spikes as quickly as she had planted them. Bernard screamed and he slapped the place where Salima had left two small holes.

He turned to face Salima. his eyes wide with shock and anger. Blood seeped through his fingers in thin rivulets.

He took his hand off the injury and was even more surprised to see blood. He looked at Salima's hands and frowned.

Salima braced herself, expecting him to attack. Instead, Bernard placed his hand back on his neck to stop the bleeding. But the blood kept coming, soaking his shirt and drip dropping to the cobblestones. Bernard leaned his back against the wall, his face paling.

Yamina stepped away from him to stand behind Salima. She was crying. She pulled her dress down.

'Thank you,' Yamina whispered.

Salima didn't reply lest her jaw hurt again. Bernard was squatting now, his cock still out, dangling limply like a crazy man's penis. Salima wondered if he was going to die. She didn't know what to do. Beside her, Yamina seemed even more disoriented.

Salima heard footsteps approaching. *If it's Bernard's friends*, she thought, *or French soldiers. It will be the end of us.*

1935
January-March

Fifteen

i

The dancer across the table was lying through her teeth.

Colonel Joseph had left her in the cold cell overnight. He had tried intimidating her, reasoning with her and bribing her, yet she wouldn't confess. They were now interrogating her at the military circle in a dimly lit room, and Joseph was exhausted.

'We know you've been practicing prostitution illegally,' Turrene said, standing behind Joseph.

The girl stared at Turrene with wide green eyes. Cat eyes. She'd said her name was Djamila, but he didn't believe anything that came out of her mouth.

'Well, if you know that, why have you spent a whole day questioning me?' she said, tartly.

She's got us there, Joseph thought. It had been over a year since Joseph had allowed Turrene to introduce the new regulations, but those girls soon found their way around the system. *I only dance* was the most common excuse. There was no law to regulate dancing. Not even dancing naked for customers in private. Turrene had suggested taxing that too, but Joseph didn't want a riot.

Joseph cleared his throat and said, 'We're offering you a great deal here. Tell us who else is working illegally, and we'll let you go.'

Djamila leaned across the table until Joseph could smell the smoke on her breath. She acted as if she was about to confide her deepest secret, but Joseph wasn't fooled.

'I. Only. Dance,' she whispered.

Joseph's eyes held hers, his blood boiling. Then, without breaking his gaze, he punched the metal table with both hands. She didn't flinch. She drew back with a hint of a smile that made him want to shoot her. The dancer and he had been playing a game. She was winning, and he hated it.

There was a knock at the door, and Turrene went out while Joseph paced around the room. Turrene quickly came back with a knowing look on his face.

'The doctor's here,' he announced as much to scare the dancer as to inform Joseph. 'He knows what he has to do.'

Djamila's face turned from mocking to curious. If she was afraid, she was doing a great job of concealing it.

'The doctor,' Joseph said, placing his open palms on the cold metal table, 'is going to check if you're telling the truth.' He was pleased to see her frown. 'He'll check you down there to see if you recently had sexual intercourse, and don't you dare say it was with your husband.'

The girl's large eyes opened even wider, straining to hide the terror growing in her, and Joseph's blood cooled down. It was as if he had sucked the calmness right out of her.

'You can't do that,' she said, her voice faltering.

Joseph smiled, then he headed for the door.

'You can't do that to a girl,' she called out again.

In the corridor stood two young men. They saluted Joseph.

'This is Dr. Brossolette,' Turrene said, referring to the man in white scrubs.

'I need you to do a thorough check,' Joseph addressed the doctor. 'Both.. er... you know...'

Brossolette nodded and lowered his head.

Joseph turned to the soldier who had summoned the doctor. 'You go in with him in case she needs restraining.'

'Yes, Colonel.'

Waiting outside with Turrene, Joseph lit a cigarette and paced up and down the hallway. The door did little to muffle the bellows of the girl inside the room, but Joseph ignored her.

He couldn't believe a bunch of sluts were fooling him every single day, evading taxes and lying to his face. If it weren't for the tourism they brought to town, he would simply have thrown them all in jail and been done with it.

He needed a distraction while he waited for the doctor to complete the examination.

'Major Turrene,' Joseph said, stopping next to his underling, 'How was your trip?'

Turrene had gotten back from a month-long trip two days ago.

'It was nice,' he said, quickly warming up. 'We went skiing every day. Christmas in Marseilles, and we saw Tartarin de Tarascon. It was hilarious.'

Tartarin de Tarascon was yet another movie that had been shot here in Bousaada last year, and Delphine had been dying to see it. It was impossible for Joseph to take time off at the end of last year though. Delphine wasn't happy about it, and not just because she missed the movie.

She had wanted to visit their son, Bernard, in Toulouse. Joseph didn't think they needed to visit him twice a year, especially not after the scandal that almost caused Joseph his entire career. Someone had found Bernard bleeding on the street with his pants down. It turned out he had tried to rape a local girl and she, or someone else, had attacked Bernard leaving two deep holes on the side of his neck, like the bite of a desert viper.

Joseph was forced to pay the man who had found him in exchange for his silence, and as soon as Bernard had recovered from the injury, Joseph sent him to Toulouse where he was now studying law. Joseph and Delphine had visited him in the summer, but father and son had barely spoken.

'That's good. Well, now that you're back,' Joseph said, 'we should focus our effort on the taskforce.'

'Yes, Colonel,' Turrene said enthusiastically, 'I've identified a small team of our finest men. Young, smart and very competent. We can meet them whenever you want.'

Before leaving in December, Turrene had come up with this idea to put together a secret taskforce, a group of talented officers who would go undercover and solicit Ouled Nail dancers. When the officers caught the dancers in the act, they could arrest them.

'Let's gather them this afternoon,' Joseph said. 'We'll brief them on their mission, and they can start immediately.'

'Yes, Colonel,' Turrene nodded.

Dr. Brossolette came out of the room with the other soldier and shook his head gravely.

'No sign of recent sexual intercourse,' the doctor said.

This couldn't be. The girl was working, Joseph knew, and nothing in this world could convince him otherwise.

'Are you sure?' Turrene said.

The doctor nodded. 'I did a thorough check. As far as I'm concerned, the girl's telling the truth.'

With that, he gave them a salute and left. Joseph and Turrene exchanged a confused look.

'What do we do?' Turrene said.

Joseph's hands were tied. He knew something was wrong. The doctor might have missed something, or maybe she offered him free sex in exchange for lying. But Joseph couldn't prove any of that. He could go back in and check himself, but he wouldn't know what to look for. He would only make a fool of himself.

'Take her back to the cell,' he told Turrene while he squashed a cigarette butt under his boot. 'Release her in the middle of the night.'

He strode to the stairs to go up to his office.

'And let's move faster on that taskforce, alright?'

ii

The taskforce was a small group of young men. Joseph counted about nine when he stepped into the room and the first thing that struck him was that all the soldiers Turrene had selected were, much to Joseph's irritation, very good-looking young men.

The officers rose to salute their colonel, and when he allowed them, sat sternly and watched as he paced up and down like a teacher in the front of a classroom. Major Turrene sat behind a desk facing his group.

Joseph stopped, studied their faces for a moment, then started to speak. 'Do you know what you're here for?' he asked.

'Sir,' one young man started, 'Major Turrene called us for a special taskforce.'

Joseph couldn't help thinking the whole business sounded like they were after the most dangerous mafia in the world. If word got out that Colonel Dupont had created a special taskforce to hunt prostitutes, he would be the joke of the French military. All the same, this was necessary.

'Do you know what the task at hand is?' Joseph asked, and when no one replied, he added, 'Every taskforce needs a specific task, no?'

Blank stares. A few eyes risked a glance at Turrene.

'We'll tell you what your task is,' Joseph started. 'It doesn't give me joy to talk about this. But we can't go on ignoring it, especially not when our regulations are being violated every day and the health of our soldiers is in great jeopardy. I'm sure you're all familiar with the Ouled Nail dancers.'

The silence in the room grew thick, and some soldiers swallowed hard.

'Maybe most of you have even enjoyed their services, and, before you deny it, we're not going to look into that. That's not why you're here. You're here to help us catch those dancers who practice prostitution outside the law.'

The young men relaxed a little as Joseph explained: 'Many Nailiya dancers claim all they do is dance, but they take clients home for private services. Not only do they not pay their taxes, but they never go to the hospital for mandatory checks. Instead, they spread their dirty diseases among the ranks of soldiers, civilians and tourists.'

Joseph then gave the floor to his underling, Major Turrene, who explained the role of the taskforce.

'What we need you to do,' said Turrene, 'is to help us catch those prostitutes in the act. Of course, we can't just hide in their rooms and watch, and we can't possibly time our raids to catch them naked and entangled with their client, but what we can do is have their clients arrest them. And you will be those clients.'

The officers' faces showed everything from excitement to fear. There was uncertainty, and, much to Joseph's disgust, some lust.

Turrene continued, 'We want you to go as potential clients. Show them you're interested. Offer money. Do whatever you need to do to get them to take you home. Go along with the whole process until you prove they're committing prostitution. That's what we need to arrest them.'

A young man raised his hand, a handsome youth with a scar across the side of his tattooed neck. It looked like someone had gone for this fellow's life and failed.

'Sir,' the young man spoke. 'How do we proceed with the arrest? Do we go back and report it?'

'What's your name?' Joseph asked, though he knew he wouldn't remember the name.

'Officer Cambron, sir.' said the young man.

'That is a great question, Officer Cambron,' said Joseph. 'If you leave her behind, the girl might escape. You'll need to arrest her on the spot. Assuming you're able to physically restrain a scrawny young girl, that is.'

Everyone stifled a laugh.

'Sir,' said the young man sitting next to Cambron. This one had two matching moles on his face, like an extra set of eyes. 'What if word gets out that we're secretly arresting illegal prostitutes? Wouldn't they be more cautious?'

'Officer Mercier, right?' said Turrene. 'That's exactly what we want. We want them to be so paranoid they won't take risks. We want them to realise that their only way out is to follow our regulations.'

Mercier nodded.

Joseph and Turrene took turns answering questions about the operation. Someone asked if they should go in their military uniforms, Joseph told them to do that sometimes and go as civilians other times. Turrene instructed them to generally disperse, hit every café and hotel in town, taking turns, and changing targets.

One shy officer asked a practical question that caused another round of snorts: what was considered as catching them in the act? Should they arrest them after the intercourse? Joseph set condoms as cause for arrest.

He had already thought about this question before. He knew that all Ouled Nail used condoms, albeit old, dirty and holed, because they didn't want to get pregnant. If the client was wearing a condom, there was no other explanation except that they were about to have sex. He assumed most of these young men would probably enjoy themselves first before making the arrest, but Joseph didn't want to think about that.

It was almost five when Joseph left the room with Turrene, having officially declared the taskforce active. Joseph was mostly pleased with the group. They looked competent, and they asked important questions.

'Thanks for putting this together,' Joseph complimented Turrene as they went into his office.

'Thank you, Sir,' Turrene's face lit up.

'However,' something still bothered Joseph. 'I'd like you to add a few more members. Four or five.'

'Yes, Colonel. I can do that.'

'And Major Turrene, please bring in some older men, fatter, the types that look like the usual clients, the ones who would have trouble finding girls to sleep with.'

Joseph could almost see Turrene's brain processing this instruction.

'I understand, sir.'

'We're putting together a taskforce of soldiers to catch prostitutes, for God's sake. We don't need them to be the prostitutes.'

iii

The Moulin Ferrero was probably the most beautiful building in Bousaada. As Joseph climbed down off the horse-drawn carriage that evening, he admired the edifice, taking in the gable roof and the round terrace overlooking the Bousaada River. The building looked like it had been dug out of the mountain, and the thin waterfalls nearby completed the beautiful tableau.

Joseph helped Delphine out of the carriage, and the couple walked the short distance to the entrance. Him in black pants and a white blazer, and her in a blue evening dress, long and slender underneath her fur coat.

They were invited to a dinner party hosted by Gabriel Ferrero, the current resident of the moulin. There were too many Ferreros in the world for Joseph to keep up with, all rich and prosperous, and he was never sure which of them resided here in Bousaada. All the same, he always made sure to attend their parties. Their influence in Algiers and France was too big to ignore.

'Colonel Dupont,' a cheerful voice called out. It was Gabriel, a short fellow with a heavy build and a conniving smile. 'Welcome, welcome. We're glad you could make it.'

'Thank you for having us,' Joseph said.

The host shook Joseph's hand and kissed Delphine on the cheek. He led them into a wide hall lit up by a thousand candles and oil lamps. Soft music flowed from a corner where two young men played violins. About a dozen people were gathered in groups near a fireplace. As soon as Joseph and Delphine walked in, a young Arab waiter served them drinks.

Gabriel was talking very fast while he guided them across the hall, 'It's so cold outside. I know they say you shouldn't underestimate the desert cold, but still, I always forget how harsh the winters are.'

Before Joseph had the chance to make up some generic response, they had joined a group of three women.

Gabriel introduced them: 'This is Colonel Dupont and his wife Delphine. Colonel, you already know my wife, Elizabeth.'

Joseph nodded. Elizabeth ran the local school in Bousaada, and she was a good friend of Delphine's.

'These are my cousins, Emilie and Mathilde. Their father, Uncle Antoine, is the man responsible for this great moulin.'

Around fifty, the two women were in great shape. They wore matching green dresses, with grey veils draped over their naked shoulders. Their faces were also identical. It was as though he was seeing double.

Clearly used to this reaction, the twins looked bemused as they gave Joseph their gloved hands to kiss. Elizabeth was much warmer, hugging Delphine with a gleaming smile.

'You have a beautiful city, Colonel,' said one of the sisters. 'We don't remember it being like this when we were growing up.'

'Thank you, Madame,' said Joseph, 'Your family's had great impact on Bousaada, as you can see.'

Emilie or Mathilde accepted the compliment with a graceful smile.

'We're taking them into the desert for a week-long camp,' Gabriel announced. 'Music and dancing and great food.'

'They're going to love it, I'm sure,' said Delphine. 'How long are you here for?'

'Two weeks only. But we'll come back again in March.'

'Half the Ferreros are coming down to visit in March,' said Gabriel, still speaking as if he was in a rush to get somewhere. 'We're throwing a small party. I want to get some Nailiya dancers. Musicians. We'll invite some young people. We want it to be a fun event, you see.'

Joseph cringed inside. Young people, drinking and Ouled Nail? That couldn't be good. On the other hand, it would be a great opportunity to hunt some illegal prostitutes. He made a mental note to sneak a few members of his new taskforce into the party.

'Have you seen the little art exhibit?' Elizabeth asked. 'It's this young

French painter who moved to Bousaada just a year ago and he's been doing great work. Let me show you.'

Joseph and Delphine followed Elizabeth to a wall covered by a dozen paintings.

'Please, meet our young talent, Mr. Alexandre Ivy,' said Elizabeth.

Alexandre, who had been engaged in conversation with another lady, turned to face them. He had a tan and wore a black *jabador* with golden embroidery in the style of rich Arabs and Jews in Bousaada.

Joseph had heard about this young artist. He had apparently assimilated quickly to the local culture, and Joseph had thought he would make the perfect asset. The next Etienne Dinet, if rumours about Etienne's work as an informant were to be believed. Joseph was glad he had come to this dinner.

As Joseph and Delphine shook hands with the artist, Elizabeth said something about how she and Gabriel wanted him to do some more paintings.

'Let's take a look at your work,' Joseph said.

Delphine stepped closer to the wall too. Joseph's eyes first fell on a group of naked girls, Ouled Nail, washing in the river, and he strained not to groan at the crude scene. There was an image of a bearded man embracing a girl from behind, and another of a young girl holding a large water jar on her head. *This one's tolerable*, Joseph thought.

Joseph was disgusted by the nudity in most of these paintings, and even more disgusted by how these respectable people pretended to admire the artistry, ignoring the inappropriateness of it all. But he kept his opinions to himself. He didn't want to be shunned from Ferrero events, and most importantly, he wanted to get closer to this young artist.

'This is gorgeous,' Delphine said, pointing to the painting of the little girl holding a jar. 'Have you seen it, Joseph?'

'Yeah, it's nice. How about this one?' He pointed to a painting of the Moulin Ferrero. 'Wouldn't it look great in our foyer?' he asked Delphine.

'Oh, it would be perfect.'

Joseph didn't really care for the painting, but he had to keep up the pretence.

'Is this for sale?' he asked, and Alexandre nodded, his eyes gleaming.

I got you, young man, Joseph thought. *You're in my hands.*

iv

It was almost ten in the evening when Joseph and Delphine climbed out of the carriage in front of their house on Rue Gaboriau, and, much to Joseph's irritation, Major Pierre Turrene was waiting for them.

Joseph handed Delphine the painting he had purchased and told her to go inside.

'What is it?' Joseph asked. What had the Ouled Brahims done now?

'It worked,' Turrene said. 'The taskforce is already working.'

Joseph sagged with relief, then he found himself even more irritated. *Couldn't this wait until tomorrow?* he thought.

'They've caught four dancers,' Turrene added. 'All red-handed. They're at the military circle now, and none of them denied their crimes.'

'Of course, they didn't,' Joseph said. 'How could they?'

'Our taskforce is working,' Turrene repeated. 'We'll catch them.'

'We'll catch them all.'

Sixteen

i

The lazy-eyed Frenchman was too insistent.

Fahima had come to Mouloud's café with no intention of taking private clients – she was planning to see René tonight – but this young man had spent the entire evening following her every move. Now that the men got up to dance, he wouldn't leave Fahima's side. He kept touching her and whispering in her ear despite her clear disinterest.

Of course, this kind of behaviour wasn't new to Fahima. Many men, especially drunk clients, didn't know when to back off. She had to be careful, though. This man could be part of Colonel Dupont's special group who, rumour had it, were out hunting for women working without permits.

Fahima and Salima's switch plan had been working just fine these past months – *thank you, Mother* – but Salima was out with Mourad tonight and Fahima couldn't risk it. Mourad had recently moved to Bousaada and used Salima's dowry money to build a stable outside of town.

Fahima avoided the young man's fixed stares, slipping away from his touches and ignoring his clumsy seduction attempts. Something about him was very unnerving. His lazy eyes looked conniving; she couldn't read him. He had two thin-lined scars across a rose tattoo on his neck that spoke of violence.

The predator was with a friend, a green-eyed youth with tanned skin and two matching moles under his eyes. She didn't trust him either. He had eyes for Nouara and he danced close behind her, hands on her hips.

She was grateful when René showed up outside the café, and even though she left early, Mouloud still paid her. Nouara also received her payment and left alone.

Fahima and René strolled up the main street towards the gate where the last of the people watching the outdoor performances were scattering, discouraged by the cold. Fahima kept checking over her shoulder to see if the weird man was following her. René noticed, and she told him what had happened.

'I warned you, ma chère,' he said. 'You have to be careful.'

'I *am* careful,' she assured him. 'I knew something was off about those men.'

'You have no idea how many girls Dupont has made me inspect to check if they've been recently penetrated. This whole business is disgraceful.'

'And hypocritical,' Fahima said. 'Dupont should be the last person to go after us like this. Especially after what his son did last year.'

'What do you mean?'

'Didn't I tell you?' she wondered out loud. 'You remember Dupont's son? Bernard? Well, he was going steady with this young Jewess. My neighbour. Then one night, when she refused to sleep with him, he tried to force himself on her. Right on the street. She was lucky someone saved her.'

Fahima was careful not to mention that Salima had been there.

'Are you serious?' René was flabbergasted. 'That explains a lot. That's why he sent his son away so quickly. He said Bernard wasn't safe here in Bousaada, and people assumed the Ouled Brahims were targeting Bernard to get to his father.'

Fahima wasn't supposed to go around sharing details from that night in case it attracted the wrong attention. Salima had been adamant about that. But she hadn't really revealed much. René would never know she'd been there.

'Oh crap,' Fahima said as they passed a souvenirs shop. 'I forgot to buy an oil lamp.'

Fahima had stopped partly to change the topic, but also because she was indeed supposed to buy an oil lamp to replace the one she had broken.

The shop displayed countless sand roses, little figures, paintings and wicker baskets, but no oil lamps. *Damn it*, Fahima cursed, *Salima's going to kill me.*

'I have candles if you need some light to get you through the night,' the vendor said with a knowing smile, no doubt assuming René was her client.

'I'll take them,' Fahima said. *Salima would have to make do with candles for now.*

When Fahima paid the vendor and turned to leave, she was surprised to see René behind her holding a sand rose. He paid for it without haggling.

When they left the store, Fahima was about to mock René for acting like a tourist when he offered her the sand rose.

'It's for you, ma chère,' he said.

'Why?' she didn't know what else to say.

'Do I need a reason to give you a present?'

She wanted to say yes.

'Besides, I was meaning to give you something for Valentine's Day two days ago.'

Fahima's mind wandered back to that night, two years ago, when René had told her all about Valentine's Day. She still had the Eiffel Tower postcard in her bedroom.

'You remember Valentine's Day, right?' he said, holding the sand rose out to Fahima.

She took it and examined it, caressing its grainy petals.

'Of course, I do,' she said. She wanted to say it was the day the old *Caid* had been murdered in front of them, but she didn't want to ruin the mood. 'This is beautiful,' she said, flashing him a coy smile.

'Just like you,' he said. 'Beautiful and strong.'

Fahima's heart melted. This man was so kind to her— kinder than anyone had ever been— and she didn't know what she'd done to deserve it.

'Did you know,' he went on while they walked out the gate, 'that sand roses are just like diamonds?'

Fahima snorted. 'Now you're just being poetic,' she said.

'No, I'm serious. They're both types of crystal. It's just because diamonds are rarer to find that they're worth so much more than sand roses. But as far as I'm concerned, my sand rose is the most precious thing in the world.'

She didn't know what to do with herself. She had never imagined being so consumed by love; she was at a loss for words. How could she have been so lucky?

Thankfully, she didn't have to say anything. Seeing them from a distance, Djamila approached, all glee.

'Hello, Ammariya,' she called out. 'Hello, handsome,' she gave René a wink which Fahima didn't like one bit. 'What are you love birds up to?'

'Just strolling around,' Fahima replied. 'You?'

'I was with Nouara. And I just heard the best news ever!'

'Do tell.'

'The Ferreros are throwing the biggest party you can imagine. Everyone's excited. Dozens of Ferreros are coming to town, including some handsome young men with deep pockets.' She winked at Fahima. 'And they say they'll invite dancers to perform. We need to get invited!'

This was Fahima's chance to perform in front of rich people. They might take her to other cities if they liked her.

'But how?' Fahima asked. 'How do we get invited?'

'We have to talk to Mouloud tomorrow,' Djamila said. 'I'm sure they will ask him to bring his dancers.'

'Yeah, let's do that,' Fahima said.

'I won't hold you much longer,' Djamila said, wearing that seductive smile again. Shifting to French, she added, 'Oh, by the way, Monsieur

Brossolette, I haven't had the chance to thank you for saving me the other night.' She tapped Fahima's shoulder and added, 'I'd be in jail right now if it weren't for your handsome man here.' Then back to René, she whispered, 'And my man is also grateful. He says to let him know if there's anything he can do to thank you. Now, the man transports crops and cows back and forth to Biskra, so I'm not sure how on earth he can thank you, but I can think of a few ways to express my gratitude.'

Djamila was annoying, all winks and taps on René's chest. Fahima was ready to tell her off when René responded with grace.

'That won't be necessary,' he said. 'I wouldn't want for anyone to go to jail like that, so don't trouble yourself or your man.'

'Suit yourself,' Djamila said as she brushed past René and walked away. 'You two have fun.'

'What the hell was she talking about?' Fahima asked René, not even waiting for Djamila to be out of earshot.

'It's nothing. Colonel Dupont called me a few weeks ago to examine Djamila. They'd caught her with a man, and she claimed she was only dancing. I was called to verify, so I confirmed her story.'

'You lied to the colonel?' Fahima said. 'What if he found out?'

'He wouldn't know if I lied.'

'Still, what if he called another doctor? Why would you risk it?'

René fell silent for a while, then he said, 'I don't think it's fair to do that to you girls just to share your profit in the name of taxes and hygiene. Also, I imagined you in that position. In Djamila's place, and I...'

He didn't need to finish. Without saying a word, she took his hand and led him back home.

ii

Fahima kept telling herself to get the condom, but she was riding too high and didn't want to break away from him.

He was on top of her, his fingers tracing words of excruciating sweetness along her body, his hungry kisses on her neck, making her yearn for more, long for him to come closer, to hold her tighter.

'Come with me.'

'What?' she asked, already missing him.

He held her face and their noses touched. Her body itched with desire.

'Let's go out of here, together,' he said. 'We could go to Algiers or Paris and live together.'

Was Fahima dreaming? This was what she had lived for. Was it finally happening? And she was getting the sweetest man on earth, too? She couldn't possibly be that lucky.

'Of course,' she whispered.

Of course, she would go with him. She would go with him to the end of the earth and back if he wanted her to. She had nothing to worry about. Life in Bousaada had grown so dangerous lately anyway, and Salima was getting married soon. She would miss her family, certainly, but that was a small price to pay.

Exhilarated, she held René's face and kissed him, her entire body simmering under his.

He slipped inside her, and she stuttered out a moan. They rocked their bodies together, hands gripping, thighs aching, and when they both moaned that final groan, she felt him come inside her with a hot shudder.

It was too late for that condom.

Seventeen

i

At the Ferrero party, Fahima ate shrimp for the first time.

They also served small pieces of spinach pie, meat balls you could fit through a ring and tiny little cookies. The drinks, however, were served without moderation.

'Do they expect this piece of flesh to quench our hunger?' Nouara commented on her one-shrimp skewer.

'It feels weird,' Fahima said, chewing the little shrimp.

They were still panting, having just danced to the fast music of drums and *kerkabos*. Beads of sweat trickled down Fahima's back. French violinists were now playing a much quieter melody that harmonised with the swishing sound of the waterfall.

'Do you think they'll have us dance again tonight?' Fahima asked Nouara. She'd been to these fancy Ferrero parties before.

'I guess so. The old musicians are still here.'

'Great,' Fahima said bitterly. 'They'll wait until everyone gets drunk then have us dance again.'

Fahima had enjoyed the party so far, she had to admit. People went to great lengths to remain kind and courteous. These were mostly outsiders, Fahima guessed, and they had treated the Nailiyas like a mountain lion performing tricks; they gazed with admiration but stood cautiously out of the way.

The few locals and soldiers who were here tonight didn't behave like their usual selves, either. Of course, this could all change once people got drunk. She had seen it happen at camps many times.

'There you are!' someone shouted.

She turned to see Djamila rushing towards them, dragging a man by his sleeve. The charming young man, all dressed up in a tuxedo, was blushing red.

'Guess what we have here?' Djamila asked with excitement.

Nouara and Fahima stared blankly.

'Show them,' Djamila told him.

His face brightened with a childish grin as he produced a thick hashish joint from his pocket. Djamila looked over her shoulder to check if anyone was watching.

'Oh, Djamila, how I love you right now,' Nouara said.

'Let's find a place and smoke it together,' Djamila said.

'You all go,' Fahima said absentmindedly. 'I'll catch up with you.'

She left the small group, ignoring their booing and hissing.

'She's got her own joint to smoke,' Nouara said, and they all laughed.

Fahima crossed the terrace to René. She hadn't seen him all evening, and she had assumed he'd had to work at the hospital. But here he was standing with his friend Jean Larrey, who was doing all the talking as usual.

René's khakis and brown shirt looked dishevelled, his lower lip was bleeding and his eyes surveyed the place frantically. When they fell on Fahima, he left his friend and came to meet her.

'I've been looking for you,' he said, speaking fast.

'What's going on?' she strained not to let worry overcome her. 'What happened to your lip?'

'We have to go.'

'Where?'

'We have to get out of town.'

'Why? What happened?'

'That officer. Cambron? He has his eyes on you, and he wants to arrest you. He won't stop until you're behind bars.'

'What? Why?' Fahima vaguely remembered the man with the scarred tattoo from Mouloud's café. She'd suspected he was trouble.

'He... He was already,' René's eyes incessantly darted right and left. 'Well, we don't have time. Let's get out of here. I can explain everything.'

'René. René,' Fahima said, taking his face in her hands. 'Listen to me. I need you to calm down and tell me what happened.'

'Alright,' he took a deep breath. 'So this guy. Cambron. He'd already been suspicious of you, it seemed. He's been following you for over a month now. Trying to prove that you...' Fahima nodded, relieving him from having to say words like pleasure or sex. 'So when you told me about him last month, I went and talked to him. Man to man, you know. I said you're my girl and told him to stay away from you. But he didn't listen. Said he was on to something, and that he wouldn't stop until he put you in jail. Things heated up, and I warned him that if he ever got close to you, he'd have me to deal with.'

Fahima was lost for words. René had stood up for her. Tried to protect her.

'You didn't have to,' was all she could say.

'Anyway,' he continued. 'I ran into him in town this evening, and he was drunk. He kept taunting me on the street. Saying he'd... make you do all these things before he arrested you. And I... I just couldn't take it.'

The cut lip made sense now.

'Oh René, did you fight him?'

He nodded. 'But I'm afraid I only made things worse,' he said. 'People broke our fight, but he kept threatening to go after you. I came straight here in case he came for you. Have you seen him?'

Fahima shook her head. 'No.'

'Good. Well, let's get out of here before he arrives.'

'How does he know I'm here?'

'I don't know. We must leave. Now.'

'Where?'

'I don't know. There's a bus leaving for Algiers at six in the morning. If we could hide somewhere until then, we can escape in time.'

'You want to skip town because you had a fight with a soldier?' She asked, puzzled. There had to be something else.

'Did you not hear me? He's determined to put you in jail, and now I've given him more reason. He has Major Turrene on his side, he'll have no difficulty arresting you without real proof, and he has the power to make my life a living hell at the hospital. I'm sorry I'm throwing all of this on you, but we can't stay here anymore.'

This was all happening too fast. Just an instant ago, she'd been enjoying her weird shrimp, now she had to leave town? She had been wanting to leave with René for so long now, but this wasn't the romantic elopement she had been longing for. This was escape.

'I need time, René,' she said. 'I can't just up and leave tomorrow morning.'

'Why not?'

'I have family.'

'They're all back in your village.'

She considered telling him about Salima, but thought better of it. Salima would kill her. Also, it would only aggravate things now that René was panicking.

'Listen, ma chère,' he said, taking her face in his hands. 'I love you. You know that.' She did. 'But if we stay here, it could be the end of us both. Cambron and Turrene can easily frame me for some crime and throw me in jail, and I don't want to risk it. You shouldn't risk it either. Let's *please* get out of Bousaada. We'll be happy together. I promise.'

His eyes glistened with tears, and an odd memory swept through Fahima's mind in that moment. She remembered Baya warning René about Fahima about two years ago. *Be cautious,* that old hag had told him. *She's going to break your heart. I can see it. And you'll break hers, too.*

Fahima had never believed her, but now her heart was shattering and ready to fall apart. Had Baya been right? The *guezzana* had foreseen a lot worse than heartbreaks. *She'll be your demise,* she had told René. *The fire will eat you alive.*

'Fine,' Fahima said with newfound resolve.

She would need to tell Salima, but Fahima would go with René. Salima was getting married soon anyway.

'I'll go with you. We'll get out of Bousaada.'

'We'll get out of Bousaada.' He nodded.

'I'll go back to the military circle to collect my things,' he said. 'You go home, get ready and stay there. Meet me at Place du Pein at dawn?'

'At the crack of dawn.' She nodded.

'You'll be there, right?' he asked, and she made things worse by hesitating a moment. 'If I don't see you at the bus stop, I might have to go anyway. It'll destroy me, but I'm afraid I'll have to go.'

'I'll be there,' she said.

He kissed her passionately, much to the crowd's booing and cheering. He left her with the salty taste of blood on her lips.

ii

Fahima lingered a little after René left, the burden of her commitment growing heavier. But so did her resolve. She was going with her lover. She would go talk to Salima first, then collect her stuff.

Salima could still be at Mouloud's café. Fear gripped her heart like a falcon snatching its prey.

Cambron didn't know where Fahima was as René seemed to think. Cambron knew where *Salima* would be tonight. At Mouloud's café.

Fahima broke into a run. She had to warn her. Outside the Moulin, she rented a carriage, but the journey seemed to take ages. Fahima didn't even want to consider what would happen if Cambron got to her sister first.

She jumped out of the carriage outside the gate without the driver noticing. She was much faster on foot. She ran past the crowds, willing Salima to still be at the café.

When she arrived, she quickly swept the place from outside, hardly caring if people noticed there were two Ammariyas. Salima would be wearing a beige dress tonight, matching Fahima's, but to Fahima's utter distress, her sister was nowhere to be found.

She darted across the café and went through the back door to the small crawl space. Nothing. She went out to the narrow alley behind the café, hoping she'd find Salima blowing smoke into the night, but still nothing.

With a thudding heart, Fahima ran back to the gate and dashed into the marketplace. Maybe Salima was dancing out here. She circled the whole place, shoving her way through throngs of people, looking over shoulders and pushing people out of the way. No sign of Salima.

Fahima fought back tears. Salima could still be safe, she told herself. Maybe she went back home.

As she sprinted down the street, Fahima dreaded the possibility of finding her sister with Cambron, arresting her or even worse. What if he killed her to spite René?

When she made it home, she unlocked the door as fast as she could and went in. She was about to shout Salima's name when she heard them.

Voices came down from the balcony, all fast and jumbled up, but Fahima recognised her sister's scream. Salima's voice was pure agony, and with it came the sound of a thud and stomping, too.

Fahima strode silently through the short corridor and out to the open courtyard, her eyes locked on the source of commotion.

Salima was on the balcony, pinned against the wooden column. She was struggling. A big man was gripping her neck with one hand. Fahima's heart was in her throat. Salima groped for his face, but she couldn't reach it.

'What are you going to do now?' the man said.

He grasped Salima's neck with the second hand. Salima's resistance was weakening. One hand rising and falling uselessly on his outstretched arm.

He's going to kill her.

Eighteen

i

Most people were at the Ferrero party, but Salima stayed back in town so she wouldn't be seen with Fahima.

She had first gone to dance in the marketplace, but few people made it out there tonight, so she went to the café. Mouloud was pleased to see her and the café was surprisingly full. *Not everyone was invited to the party after all,* Salima thought.

Salima received more attention than usual; the customers' choice was limited to four dancers. Two people showed particular interest, though; two young Frenchmen in civilian clothes. She wasn't sure if they were soldiers or tourists.

They both seemed familiar to her, one with two moles on his upper cheeks and the other one had lazy eyes. She must have just seen them in town; they were probably military. Now all she had to do was make sure they weren't going to report her.

Both men danced close to her, now together and now taking turns, their faces red from alcohol. One of them, the one with the lazy eyes, had a nasty bruise on his face too.

The man with two moles started throwing coins at her, clearly drunk. His friend tried to stop him with weak shoves and whispers. Disappointed, he shifted his attention to another dancer, flashing her a lustful grin.

With most of the local customers not daring to approach a dancer that had a Frenchman's attention, Salima was left alone with the lazy-eyed man.

The man looked too drunk to be doing any thinking, so he probably wouldn't arrest her if she took him home. It was still pretty early when she told him to wait for her outside the café. She danced a little more to throw any suspicion, then went to meet him.

When Salima left the café, the man with two moles left with another girl under his arm, laughing and shouting. None of them seemed to care that they were attracting attention.

Salima's client was waiting right outside the café and she motioned him to follow her discreetly, though she didn't expect much from his current state.

Close to her home, she let him hold her hand in the dark empty streets. Her heart still beat faster each time she walked through these alleys at night, scared of what might be lurking around the corner. She calmed herself, taking deep intentional breaths.

As she unlocked the front door of her home, she looked right and left to make sure no one was watching, no thief or French soldier trying to catch her in the act. She jumped when she saw a tall man with a duffle bag standing further down the street. It took a moment before she realised the man wasn't standing, but walking away. His back was to them so he couldn't have seen anything. Or so she thought.

She let her client in, entered and quickly locked the door behind her.

ii

As Salima led the French officer up the dark stairs, he was barely able to walk straight. She took one step at a time, allowing him to adjust to the darkness and the view of her behind.

He held on to her hand softly as she led him through the dark archway. When they drew level with her bedroom, Salima freed her hand for a moment to open the door. By the time she'd unlocked it, a sharp creak behind her made her hairs stand on end. She swung around to find her client leaning against the wooden railing. The railing, which had been squeaky since the day they moved in, was now swinging from one loose end. The officer had almost fallen to his death. Fortunately, he must've found his footing in time. He was still swaying dumbly when Salima pulled him into the room and closed the door.

The man frowned and flared his nostrils. The room smelled of jasmine and the ambergris Salima had left smoking in here. *You can't complain about pleasant odours,* she thought.

She left him standing by the door while she lit a candle. Fahima had broken Salima's oil lamp and bought a few candles to replace it. The candles smelled of roses, and Salima kind of preferred it.

She led her customer to sit on a large sheepskin rug under the window and lit a small clay stove to make him tea. He scanned the room a little too quietly. The candlelight shone bright on his face, highlighting the nasty bruise on his cheek. He looked familiar, but she couldn't seem to place that face.

When the tea was ready, Salima picked up the pot from the clay stove, drawing a cloud of sparks from the charcoal, and filled two glasses on a small silver tray. She handed the officer a glass with a sweet smile, and when her fingers brushed his, he froze momentarily, staring.

'Danse?' she finally said, her voice rusty.

When her client didn't say anything, Salima stood up again and started dancing. The officer put down his tea and tried to stand up.

'Viens,' he said. *Come.*

He reached to the window ledge for support, but his hand landed on the candle and he withdrew it with a long string of curses. He bit his hand and lost his footing.

Salima rushed to help him, tucking her hands under his armpits for support. He leaned his head against her shoulder. The smell of beer and smoke washed over her as his nose brushed against her naked neck.

Then she saw it. Resting his head on her shoulder, he revealed the base of his neck. Salima's knees shook. A tattoo which had been covered by his shirt collar. A small black rose crossed by two thin-lined scars.

The sight brought back memories buried deep within Salima's heart. Memories of the night she and Naima had been attacked. This very man, Salima remembered, clearly, had straddled her and was about to plunge a knife into her chest when Naima had tried to drive her spiked bracelet into his neck and missed, leaving the two parallel lines across the tattoo.

The murderer started kissing Salima's neck. It took all the will and strength Salima could muster not to push him away and run. Naima's killer was in her bedroom, resting his head on her shoulder. She felt disgusted, nauseated, but also scared. Was he intending to kill her?

She needed to deal with this carefully. It wasn't easy, but it would be safer. When he slid his hand down her lower back, however, she felt so repulsed, she couldn't help yanking it away. But he pressed her harder.

'Arrête,' she coaxed as she pushed down on his shoulders. 'Arrête.'

If she could get him to sit down, it would be easier for her to leave. Surprisingly, she managed to sit him on the floor. But that wasn't the end of it.

He pulled her down, with more strength than she had thought him capable of in this state. He forced her down to the floor, and before she had a chance to react, he had turned her onto her back and gotten on top to kiss her.

Her pleas quickly turned into shouts and curses. 'Salaud,' she kept repeating as she tried to scratch his face. 'Connard.'

He twisted her hands above her head and pinned them to the floor with one hand. Her efforts to free herself were in vain, a child's hands in the grip of a monster. She kept shouting and cursing, and she kept wiggling her head to prevent him from kissing her on the lips. He covered her mouth with his free hand, but it did nothing to muffle her screams.

Her heart was beating out of control. She began to writhe her entire body to slip out from under him. He slapped her across the face. It hurt so much she stopped moving and went quiet for a moment.

The officer tried to pull her dress up. Salima looked around for anything to hit him with. The small clay stove was within reach, so she groped for it, toppled it, and gingerly picked up two burning charcoals. The heat ate through her skin, but she didn't drop them. She screamed bloody murder as she rubbed the charcoal on his face, smearing it right in his eyes.

Salima felt a rush of pleasure as the man screamed and his entire body shook in excruciating pain. But she had to focus.

She had managed to slip her entire upper body from underneath his when he grabbed her arm. She yanked it free, and now even her legs were out. She scrambled onto all fours; she was almost safely away from him, but then he gripped her ankle.

Salima tried to pull her foot free, but it didn't work. She turned onto her back and used her free foot to kick him in the face. He didn't let go. She kicked a second time, and a third until his grip loosened. She yanked it away, staggered to her feet and ran for the door, all whimpers.

Salima had opened the door and almost made it out when he got a hold of her braid and yanked her back inside. He slammed her against the wall so roughly she could hear the thud of her own skull. She let out a scream of agony. He was smiling now, a frighteningly evil smile. He was enjoying this.

He put his face against hers, their eyes locked as he reached his hands down between her thighs.

Salima remembered something. Her hands were trapped between her body and his, but she wiggled them until she had positioned the bracelet on her wrist.

He squeezed her between her legs and she squinted with pain, and, despite her effort, she couldn't hold back a cry. He laughed.

When she was ready, she snuck her hands out and up to his neck. She kept her eyes open to see his face when she did what she was about to do. She perceived the slightest look of shock in his eyes when he realised what was happening, but it was too late for him.

She held his neck in one hand, and she drove the spikes of her bracelet into the other side, just under his jaw, releasing warm blood. He didn't scream. He just touched his wound, gently.

Seizing the moment, Salima freed herself again and ran out of the room. This time she made it to the balcony before he caught up with her.

He grabbed her robe and slammed her against the wooden column. Her back felt like it was breaking.

He rushed to check her hands for a weapon. He looked surprised to see the blood on her bracelet. Salima kept up the resistance, but he pinned her to the column behind her.

'What are you going to do now?' He asked.

He clasped her neck with one hand and tightened his grip. The other hand held her bracelet.

She tried to loosen his grip on her neck, using her free hand, but it was in vain. His blood still oozed out of his wound, and her own throat was burning as she struggled to breathe. She was growing dizzy, and she wondered if he was going to get her this time. If he was going to kill her just like he had killed Naima.

Suddenly, his grip weakened, giving her an opportunity to breathe a little, but that only lasted a moment, for he soon let go of her bracelet and used his other hand to choke her tighter, blocking all air from her chest.

His eyes trained on her bracelet lest she used it again, but she was too busy scratching his forearms and hands, trying, and failing, to loosen his grip.

Then out of nowhere something crashed and dirt went flying through the air, raining down on her face. The aggressor released her and turned to see where the blow had come from.

It was Fahima. She had smashed a flowerpot on the back of his head.

The officer swayed and groped for something behind him. He stepped back until he leaned against the wooden railing. The wood creaked again, louder than earlier, then snapped with a sharp crack.

Salima gasped for air as the French officer fell to the courtyard. She stepped closer to the edge and peered down. He lay still on his back, a small pool of dark blood forming around his head.

'Is he dead?' Fahima asked, stepping forward to see for herself.

Salima nodded and coughed. 'He's dead,' she said.

1935
April

Nineteen

i

Colonel Joseph Dupont's son, Bernard, arrived with his girlfriend on a Wednesday morning.

Joseph and his wife waited outside the Hotel de l'Oasis, sipping coffee under the weak shade of a tree. The *Car Rapide* from Algiers always arrived at noon. He could usually see it from the window of his office, but today it was already half an hour late. Joseph was smoking his sixth cigarette which did nothing to quench his hunger.

A few other families were waiting for their loved ones. They were growing restless too. Place de Pein was otherwise deserted. It wasn't a market day, and the midday heat had forced what few people had ventured out to scurry back home.

'Why is it late?' Delphine asked.

Joseph wanted to tell her that he was here with her and not a clairvoyant, but he didn't.

'I'm not sure,' he said instead. 'Maybe a flat tire?'

'I hope it's nothing serious,' Delphine said. 'Lord knows what would happen to them if the bus broke down in the middle of the desert.'

Joseph's biggest fear was the bloody Ouled Brahims. They might have attacked the bus, killed everyone on board and taken all their luggage and pulled every last earring out to take with them. This had apparently never happened before, but still they loomed large and dark in the corner of Joseph's eye. They were a sneaky breed.

'Here they are,' Delphine squealed.

A long-hooded bus emerged into the square, and the small crowd rose to their feet. Delphine dashed towards the bus, one hand gripping her hat and the other one holding up her skirt. Joseph put out his cigarette in the ashtray and placed a five-franc note beneath it.

No longer had the bus stopped that it was surrounded by barbaric locals, screaming and beating on the windows. Joseph was not going near it. He watched as the driver elbowed his way past the Arabs.

The travellers emerged one by one. A middle-aged man in a grey suit looked exhausted. A younger man in shorts and a white shirt, evidently a tourist, paused at the door, looking charmed already. He looked far too happy to be here, not the brightest apparently. There was a family of Arabs, too.

Bernard came out with a small leather bag in his hand. With his glossy dark hair and black sunglasses, he reminded Joseph of his own youth. His tall and slender figure, his handsome face and delicious perfume used to turn heads.

Bernard's face lit up when he spotted Delphine. He hopped to the ground and gave her a big long hug. Behind him was a thin brunette, no older than twenty. Bernard took her hand. His son finally caught Joseph's eyes and waved energetically. Joseph waved back.

Bernard and his girlfriend picked up their pieces and walked towards Joseph. Father and son embraced briefly. Bernard introduced his girlfriend, Roselyn and Joseph shook her hand, enquiring about their journey.

'It wasn't too bad,' Roselyn responded in a perfumed Parisian accent. 'But we took off from Algiers an hour late.'

'Well, you must be exhausted,' Joseph said, 'Let's get you off the road. We have a delicious lunch waiting for you. Then you can get some rest.'

Joseph needed that lunch and nap so badly.

The heat had started sooner and stronger this year, and, when they turned to Rue Gaboriau, Joseph was grateful for the shade of the trees.

'So how is school?' Joseph asked. The two women were already chatting animatedly behind them.

'Good,' Bernard answered. 'But they're keeping us busy with lots of reading.'

Joseph snorted. 'How else would you prefer to learn? There's so much to know about law.'

This generation expected to get a degree without doing the work.

'True,' Bernard said politely. 'But many of my colleagues who are well connected managed to secure an internship with lawyers in Toulouse, and that helped them a lot. Experience at an actual lawyer's office or a firm is much more beneficial than reading.'

Joseph nodded. 'So why don't you try and get one of those internships?' he asked.

'It's not that easy. These students – their parents know someone or other, and that's the only way you can get your foot through the door.'

Joseph shook his head disapprovingly.

'I was actually hoping you could help me with that,' Bernard added.

'I don't know anyone in Toulouse,' Joseph said.

'I know,' Bernard said quickly.

Bernard already had a plan, and Joseph had the feeling he wasn't going to like it.

'An internship with a lawyer here in Bousaada would be equally beneficial,' Bernard ventured. 'And there aren't many law students to compete with.'

So that was the real reason Bernard was here. A quick trip to secure an internship that he could come back for in the summer. Joseph had to admit it was clever. He admired Bernard's willingness to spend his summer here in the desert for the sake of his career. Still, Joseph wished his son had relied on himself instead of his father's connections.

Also, last time Bernard had been here he had almost cost Joseph his career.

'I don't know,' Joseph said. They were now approaching his home.

'There's Monsieur Rainier who works here,' Bernard prompted.

Rainier was one of the few lawyers in Bousaada, and he hardly ever had cases to work on. In such a small town, people rarely sued each other. Few Europeans lived here, and most disputes amongst Arabs or between Arabs and Europeans seldom made it to court.

'I met him briefly last time I was here, and I know that he...'

Joseph had stopped listening. Major Pierre Turrene was standing outside his house. Turrene knew he wasn't supposed to disturb Joseph at his home. He must be here for something urgent, or at least something Turrene had imagined was urgent. Joseph was starving; he just wanted to eat.

'Look who's back,' Turrene said cheerfully. He shook Bernard's hand then kissed Delphine and Roselyn. No one introduced her to Turrene.

'You all go in,' Joseph told his family. 'I'll catch up in a minute.'

When they had left, Joseph faced Pierre and gave him an expectant look, letting his annoyance show.

'Forgive my intrusion, Colonel,' Turrene started. 'But it's an emergency.'

Joseph said nothing. Turrene continued, 'Officer Mercier and I have been working on a lead since our last meeting with you two weeks ago. But I regret to tell you that,' he cleared his throat, 'that Officer Mercier has gone missing, too.'

Joseph counted his breaths, hardly keeping himself from punching the wall out.

ii

It was almost three in the afternoon when Turrene left Joseph's office, allowing him to ponder the new developments. He still hadn't eaten anything, but he'd lost his appetite. His head was about to explode though, so he lit another cigarette.

He stood by the window, staring past Place de Pein at the hills rising like walls across the horizon. Joseph wasn't sure what to make of the news. Officer Mercier hadn't been seen since Friday night when he and Turrene had gone to Mouloud's café to talk to the Arab and some of his dancers.

Naturally, Joseph had been livid. Why was he hearing about this now, almost a week later? Turrene claimed Mercier had mentioned a hunch about one of the dancers, but he hadn't said much more. Turrene told him to follow that hunch and report back to him. He hadn't expected any news over the weekend and had wanted to give Mercier a few workdays. But when he didn't show his face by yesterday, Turrene had sought him out only to find that he had been the last person to see Mercier.

What did this all mean? Joseph still couldn't make it out. Was it related to the two other disappearances? It had to be. But how? Joseph kept returning to the Ouled Brahims. Who else could have the audacity to do this? And with such precision?

He couldn't think clearly. He needed a break from it all, but he couldn't afford to waste time. More of his men could be disappearing, murdered one by one, as he wasted precious seconds pacing back and forth.

He bolted out of his office and left the military circle. Joseph crossed Place de Pein towards l'Hotel de l'Oasis. He went around the hotel and knocked at Alexandre Ivy's door.

Joseph wasn't sure what he expected from the painter. If Alexandre knew anything, he probably wouldn't share it with Joseph anyway. He had to find a way to break him. He must know something, anything.

Joseph had to knock again before Alexandre opened the door. To both men's surprise, the painter was naked but for white trousers. His hairless chest was pale, a sharp contrast against his desert-tanned face and arms. Alexandre hadn't been expecting anyone at this hour. *All the better*, Joseph thought.

'Bonsoir, Alexandre,' Joseph said cheerfully, and without any invitation, went in, leaving Alexandre standing dumbfounded at the door.

'I was taking a nap,' Alexandre said.

Joseph had never seen anyone blush this much about a little nap. Alexandre stood by the open door, as if hoping Joseph would just turn around and leave again.

'This will only take a minute,' Joseph assured him. 'I have a few more questions to ask you.'

The drawing room was a familiar chaos of books, clothes and canvases, and it reeked of smoke.

'Is this about the disappearance of the two soldiers again?' He smoothed his hair as he spoke. 'I told you I don't know anything, and I still haven't heard anyone talk about it.'

Alexandre was lying, Joseph knew. His eyes constantly wandered towards his studio door. Was he hiding something? Joseph shook off the idea. He was being paranoid.

'Well, someone else has gone missing,' he announced and watched for Alexandre's reaction. 'Another French soldier.' Alexandre didn't budge.

'Sorry to hear that,' he said gravely. 'I wish I could help.'

Joseph felt frustrated. Why wasn't this man cooperating? What did the Arabs have on him? Why did he go to such lengths to protect them?

'Listen, young man,' Joseph said patiently. 'I understand you must empathise with these Arabs. But you must believe me when I say, I'm not trying to persecute them. My men, your countrymen, are disappearing, and I need to put an end to this. I need your help to save the lives of innocent men.'

'I do understand,' Alexandre said. 'I promise you I would tell you if I knew anything.'

This was going nowhere. It was a waste of time. He still needed to break him somehow, but this wasn't the right time for it.

'Very well,' Joseph said as he headed for the door Alexandre was still holding wide open. 'I'm sorry I disturbed your afternoon nap,' he said as he walked out the door.

As Joseph turned around, and before Alexandre had the chance to say anything, another man appeared next to him, saying in a rather playful voice, 'Who was that?'

Joseph only caught a quick glimpse of the young man before he ducked behind the door again, realising his mistake. The young man was an Arab. He wore nothing but large white pants, just like Alexandre.

'We're...' Alexandre explained, 'Ahm, I'm drawing a painting. He's my model. It's a nude painting.'

Alexandre tried to remain composed, but his own half naked body betrayed him nastily. A red rash washed over his face and extended to his neck, like someone was choking him. Joseph knew very well what was going on between the artist and his Arab boy, and it wasn't painting.

'Alright,' Joseph said, a satisfied smile unfolded across his face. 'I'll leave you two to it then.' And just to make sure Alexandre knew he hadn't tricked him, Joseph added, 'I'll be back to see you soon.'

The colonel walked back to his office feeling content. It appeared that Alexandre was one of those men who slept with other men.

Alexandre would certainly deny it but spreading such a rumour alone would taint the artist's reputation forever in this town. It would destroy his career. Alexandre would be much more talkative next time he came to visit, no doubt about it.

iii

Back in his office, Joseph sat at his desk and looked at his notepad.

This morning he had been half-convinced that one of the two soldiers had killed the other and skipped town. Now Mercier's disappearance had left him in utter bewilderment.

Turrene and Mercier had interviewed the driver that had worked the *Car Rapide* between Bousaada and Algiers, and he assured them that he hadn't seen any of the two men in the pictures – Brossolette and Cambron. Brossolette could have skipped town some other way, but that would be extremely difficult to plan last minute, and, if he had, Joseph had no way of finding out.

This could also mean that Brossolette never left town, in which case the theory that he, too, had been kidnapped or killed was back on the table.

Joseph wasn't surprised that no one at Mouloud's café seemed to know what happened. Admitting such involvement alone might get the dancers in trouble and the owner wouldn't want his business to be connected to any crime.

During conversations with Turrene, Joseph had added three more notes only, and none of them were useful. They did bring up more questions though.

– *Bus driver hadn't seen Brossolette or Cambron on March 10. Skip town? How?*

– *Mouloud and dancers hadn't seen a thing. Lying?*

– *Mercier disappeared after interviews at Mouloud's café*

Mercier had a hunch about one of the dancers at the café, Turrene had said. Which Dancer? Joseph couldn't believe Turrene hadn't asked. Moron.

He was at a dead end again. Joseph wanted to beat his desk with his clenched fist. He took a deep breath, lit another cigarette and forced himself to think instead.

He needed to know which of the dancers Mercier had been following, and if she had been involved in his disappearance. Had she also been involved in Brossolette and Cambron's disappearances? Was it possible that she had been the one over whom the two men had fought? She had to be, Joseph concluded. He needed to find her.

Did he though? Another thought started growing in his mind, like a palm tree he hadn't been paying attention to. The only reason he needed to find her was to punish her, right? What if he could punish her without finding out who she was?

He couldn't believe he hadn't thought of this earlier.

All he needed to do was send a message. A strong message that she couldn't miss.

And he knew exactly how to cause her that much suffering without ever laying eyes on the whore.

Twenty

i

Fahima's bowels were about to burst out of her mouth. She had to try one more time. She had to get everything out.

Bending over the small hole in the toilet, she opened her mouth so wide her jaw hurt. Her stomach twisted in an involuntary spasm of pain, her knees shuddering uncontrollably.

This time it worked. Last night's dinner came up her throat and rushed out of her mouth. Most of it spilt into the small hole, but pieces of bread and meat got everywhere.

She felt much better now. Her head already began to clear and the dizziness lightened. But she didn't stand up yet. Another gush was coming. Fahima couldn't believe all this food had been inside her.

The third wave was smaller and Fahima felt well enough to stand up cautiously after. To her relief, the vertigo didn't come back. This was the third time she'd thrown up in a week, the fourth if she counted the night of the second Frenchman. All that blood and the nightmares were making her sick, eating her away.

Fahima went to the kitchen to wash her face.

There was a knock at the front door. Fahima went to answer it, slowly and cautiously, like an old woman. *Soldiers who come to arrest or kill you don't knock politely,* she thought. She knew that from experience.

It was Akshish, Mouloud's errand boy, a skinny lad of eleven or twelve in dirty white clothes.

'Akshish,' she said excitedly. 'Come on in. How are you?'

With his hands in his pockets, Akshish gazed with mild curiosity at the floor. Like a true gentleman, Fahima thought.

He cleared his throat and announced, '*Ammi* Mouloud sent me to get you.'

It wasn't uncommon for Mouloud to summon girls for a special client or to help with something at the café, but Fahima couldn't help thinking about what happened last time Mouloud had called for Salima. Fahima shivered as the sound of clay on bone echoed in her mind.

'Is it the French officers again?' Fahima asked with an exaggerated air of annoyance. It was very likely they had come back now that another one had gone missing.

Akshish looked puzzled. 'The French? No, they're not there. He just wants you immediately. I'll wait for you.'

That was a little reassuring, but it could still be about the missing officer. Perhaps Akshish didn't know.

'Well, you don't need to wait for me, Akshish. I know the way, you know. I'll get ready quickly and go to the café on my own.'

'He's not expecting us at the café,' Akshish said as if he was addressing a slow-witted five-year-old.

'Then where?' Fahima was truly confused now.

'I said I'll take you there,' he said, frowning. 'You wouldn't know the place. I'll be outside when you're ready.' He stopped at the door and said, 'And bring your sister along, too. He wants you both.'

Fahima's heart sank. Too many questions rushed to her mind, but Akshish didn't stay to answer them. He closed the door to wait outside.

She looked up, and, to her surprise, Salima was on the balcony leaning against the wooden railing outside Fahima's bedroom. Akshish couldn't have seen her.

'Did you hear?' Fahima asked. Salima was already nodding. 'You think they know?'

Salima shrugged. 'Why else would he want us both there?'

Salima looked calm. Fahima felt nauseous again.

'What do you think they're going to do?'

'There's only one way to find out.'

Fahima didn't like that.

'If they'd wanted to arrest or kill us,' Salima added, 'they wouldn't have sent Akshish.'

That was a good point, but Fahima still wanted to barf.

ii

When Fahima and Salima were ready, Akshish came back inside and gave them instructions.

'Ammi Mouloud doesn't want us to be seen together,' he said with authority. 'I'll lead the way, and you can follow a little distance behind me.'

Fahima and Salima exchanged a confused look. This was getting worse. But they felt it would be safer for them to walk separately too. They ended up walking in a long line of three with Akshish first, Fahima in the middle and Salima bringing up the rear.

Fahima made her way through the narrow winding streets of Bousaada with trepidation. If Mouloud knew about their secret, other people might know it, too. Apparently, Fahima and her sister hadn't done such a good job hiding it.

They emerged on the main street and turned left. Further down the street, not far from Place de Pein, he turned right into a narrow alley.

Just when Fahima was about to turn, an unusual commotion drew her attention to Place de Pein. She paused to watch a large crowd of French soldiers loading bags and weapons into the back of trucks.

Fahima was startled by a shove from behind. Salima hissed, 'Move or we'll lose him, stupid fool.'

Luckily, the street wasn't crowded at this time of day. She spotted Akshish's small figure in time before he disappeared around a bend. Akshish didn't seem to notice their delay, clearly not wanting to risk looking over his shoulder. Fahima hurried to catch up.

They were still in the Ksar, the old part of town where most locals lived, well distanced from the Ouled Nails on the one hand and the French on the other. Fahima had rarely ventured out here.

Taking another right after Akshish, Fahima grew more anxious. Why would Mouloud want to meet with them here? Akshish stopped outside a small house on his left, pushed the door open, lifted a curtain, then looked over his shoulder to make sure Fahima saw him before he entered.

She stepped through the door.

Her heart beat loud in that dark windowless space. Staying close to the door, she let her eyes adjust to the dim light. She made out Akshish's face, and next to him stood Mouloud, smiling. This reassured her a little. All the same, she couldn't stop her hands from shaking.

To Fahima's right was a flight of stairs, and to her left a closed door. Did any of them lead outside? Behind Mouloud was a room with better lighting. Someone moved inside that room, but didn't come to greet them.

A moment later, Salima entered with caution and looked around, squinting.

'Good afternoon, Ammariyas,' Mouloud said, still smiling. He looked from Fahima to Salima and then back to Fahima. 'So it *is* true.'

Fahima frowned. *How did he know?*

'What do you want from us?' Salima shot back, struggling to mask the fear in her voice.

'We just want to talk,' Mouloud said, keeping calm.

'We? Who's we?'

'Come on in,' Mouloud said, and he turned to the door behind him. Akshish stood by the door and motioned the two sisters to enter. Fahima followed her sister in, slowly.

iii

The small room was grey and mostly bare save for three mattresses and a low table in the middle of the space. The light coming through the window on the left was dimmed by a sheer curtain.

Two men sat cross-legged on one of the mattresses. Fahima had never seen any of them before. One was older, in his sixties and wore a grey turban. The other man was in his late twenties. His face was clean-shaven. His dark hair was short and he wore a black suit in the French style.

Smiling at the sisters, nothing really looked dangerous about these two men. Fahima's throat was still dry.

Mouloud sat down below the window, and, at his request, the sisters took the vacant mattress across from the two strangers. Akshish dashed up the stairs.

Fahima looked at Salima, who was staring at the two strangers. She didn't seem to recognise them either.

As if reading their thoughts, Mouloud spoke in a surprisingly pleasant voice, 'Thank you for coming, Ammariyas. These two are my friends, Kamel and Brahim.' Kamel was the younger one, and Brahim the older. 'They're among Bousaada's leading farmers.'

Judging from their clean outfits and soft skin, they clearly hadn't spent a lot of time farming.

'Why did you call us here?' Salima was gaining her confidence back.

'We just want to talk,' Mouloud repeated.

'About what? We're listening.'

'We know about your secret,' Brahim spoke. His voice was deep, his speech a slow rumble. Fahima had guessed as much by now.

Brahim went on, 'We know you've murdered two French officers. Or is it three now? We also know how you've been able to evade taxes for so long.'

Fahima had forgotten about that part.

'I have to admit,' the younger one, Kamel, said in a softer voice. 'It's very clever. You never suspect twins, too obvious.'

He snickered, but no one else laughed. Despite the men's pleasant attitudes, Fahima and her sister sat stiff.

Fahima wondered how they knew all of this. The taxes were fair enough. That would have been possible considering Fahima and her sister were committing that crime in Mouloud's café in front of everyone, but the French officers? How could they have seen into the courtyard?

They had concealed their second murder quickly compared with the first one. There hadn't been much blood. The dirt from the flowerbed helped dry most of it. Fahima and Salima had made a swift job of cleaning the courtyard. Like a bad dream.

She could still remember the stench that had blown out of the well when they opened it. They'd dumped in a lot of dirt to bury the bodies, but the sweet rotten smell still wafted up. Fahima had thrown up all through that evening, and nightmares kept her up that night. The thud, splinter, blood played over and over and over. The smell, always the smell.

'I asked you why you've called us here,' Salima reminded their hosts. Mouloud cleared his voice and said, 'We have an offer for you.'

An offer? Of all the possible outcomes Fahima had imagined, an offer wasn't one of them.

'We've suffered at the hands of the French longer and worse than you have,' the older man started, like an Imam launching into his Friday *khutbah*. 'They've caused us much pain and misery. They've killed our men, women and children. Turned our brethren in Bousaada against us and thrown us out of our own lands. Our homes. We've had to live in the desert for so long and still they won't leave us in peace. Colonel Dupont has a bounty on us. We have no allies.'

The French had set up a bounty to exterminate the Ouled Brahims. This man, Brahim, had to belong to the infamous Ouled Brahim tribe. Named after his ancestral leader no doubt.

'We cannot live in peace no matter how far we run from them. Every once in a while, they organise a random raid and burn our camps to the ground.'

The French weren't above such monstrosities. She believed him, but she still didn't understand why he was telling them all this.

'We've been patient for too long, but it's time to hit back. We must get back at them. Make them miserable. We'll drive every last one of them out of this town, or we'll kill them. We don't care if we all perish. They will kill us all anyway. But at least we'll go fighting.'

Sensing the sisters' confusion, Brahim finally came to the point. 'Which is where you come in.'

Fahima leaned forward.

'We know you're also victims,' Kamel said. 'Everyone in Bousaada is. No, everyone in this whole country is a victim to France's cruelty. They brought poverty and ignorance and violence. They're trying to erase our identity. Our language. Our religion. Our history and traditions. They're trying to erase us all and keep this country for themselves, even if it's mutilated and cold without us.'

Fahima had heard a lot of these words before, but they'd always sounded empty to her. What could we do? They were already here. We were already defeated.

'We must fight back. Everyone must. And you two, you've already done something very brave, and we want to help you keep doing that. For the cause.'

Fahima frowned and asked, 'You want us to keep evading taxes?'

'You can do that all you want. Everything helps,' Brahim answered. 'But most of all we want you to keep killing French soldiers.'

Fahima was still confused. Salima leaned back too far, nearly hitting her head on the wall.

'Listen,' Brahim resumed. 'We know you've already killed two or three of them, and did a wonderful job hiding their bodies and going about your life as if nothing happened.'

'How do you know that?' Salima spoke up.

'That doesn't matter now,' Brahim said, 'We want you to keep going. And we can help. We can help you get rid of the bodies. We've done it before. We have resources. Financial resources.'

'Then why don't you do it yourselves?' Salima didn't seem to trust any of this.

'They're watching us too closely,' Kamel answered.

The two men were working well together, taking turns patiently answering their questions. Fahima guessed this wasn't their first time recruiting someone.

'We can hardly breathe without them taking notes. So our movement and actions are limited. But you? You've managed to fool soldiers and even Turrene. Just impressive. We owe you our gratitude.'

Mouloud, who had been silent all this time, spoke. 'Listen girls. You don't have to decide now. Go home and think about it. Alright?'

'What if we refuse? What happens?' Salima asked.

Fahima, too, wondered if they really had any choice in this.

'We'd only ask you to forget this ever happened,' Brahim returned. 'You can't tell anyone about this conversation, of course.'

'And if you're wondering,' Mouloud continued, 'we won't tell anyone about your secret either.'

Sure, Fahima thought, *why would you need to tell a dead girl's secret?* The French would kill them at the mere hint that they'd touched one of the soldiers.

'Look,' it was Kamel's turn now. 'You have to understand that we're taking a big risk approaching you like this. We're also putting Mouloud in great danger. But we have to. You can't deny that you're suffering at the hands of the French. Everyone is. So take your time, and think about it. You know how to get in touch with us when you decide.'

He looked at Mouloud who nodded.

Akshish walked into the room with a tray of tea. Salima stood up to leave, and Fahima did the same.

'We'll think about it,' Salima said.

iv

Fahima and Salima made their way back home in silence. The street was deserted, but a deafening rumble of a thousand trucks rose from the far distance.

Fahima couldn't focus on anything. They had sat with members from the dreaded Ouled Brahims tribe. And they wanted them to join them. To kill French soldiers for them.

'So what do you think?' Fahima finally asked her sister. Her question came out uncannily light, like she'd just asked what they should make for dinner.

Salima looked back to make sure no one was following them before responding.

'Well, there's nothing to think about,' she said decisively. 'We can't do it.'

There was no way she was going to kill more soldiers. They were already in enough danger. The constant fear was unbearable.

And the guilt. She was not a killer, and she wasn't about to become one.

They approached the main street, and the rumbling trucks she had been hearing were growing louder. More thunderous.

'There's something else that worries me.' Salima had to raise her voice to be heard over the noise. 'How did they find out anyway?'

Fahima had forgotten about that part.

'Didn't Mouloud see you leave with…'

Before Fahima could finish that sentence, Salima pulled her back so hard the neck of her dress choked her. A burst of air swept over her, pressing her dress against her body, a loud roar drummed inside her ears. The military truck drove past Fahima. The metal was so close it could have easily scraped up her face had Salima not grabbed her.

The truck was driven by a young soldier and next to him sat Colonel Dupont. This man had recently turned the lives of Ouled Nail dancers into a living hell with his daft new regulations.

The truck carried at least two dozen French soldiers under a tarpaulin cover. They wore stern faces and held long rifles between their legs. This was the first of a huge convoy. Similar trucks followed, and smaller ones. At least twenty vehicles drove by, Fahima couldn't hear her own thoughts for all the noise.

Other people had gathered on the sides of the street to watch the procession. A sinister silence cloaked the bystanders and lingered in the air. It felt like a funeral.

v

Outside their door, as Fahima fumbled with the key, Salima looked behind her at the Jew's house and a thought struck her.

Fahima also felt a movement but didn't think much of it. But as soon as the sisters went into their house, Salima announced, 'I'll put my hand on fire if it isn't the Jews who told them about the soldiers.'

Fahima knew that people often blamed the Jews for a lot of things, but Salima harboured particular hate for Fadhila. Fahima couldn't blame her, but still, she didn't believe that woman would have told the Ouled Brahims. The image of that stout grumpy lady talking to a dangerous tribe was laughable.

Fahima had more pressing concerns.

'What are we going to do now?'

'What do you mean what are we going to do?' Salima asked incredulously.

'About the Ouled Brahims. They're going to expect an answer soon.'

'Of course, the answer is no,' Salima said. 'We can't kill French officers for them.'

'I know, but do you really think they are going to take no for an answer? Do you believe what they said?'

'I'm not sure. All I know is that if they tell the French about us, they'll go down with us. We already know too much. The house where we met. Mouloud's involvement. Their names are fake, I'm assuming, but we know what they look like. I think the French would be more interested in them. They might even let us go if we help them catch the Ouled Brahims.'

Fahima thought her sister was exaggerating, but she was right about one thing. She and her sister knew too much already. But would the French believe them?

'What do you think about what they said?' Fahima ventured.

'I don't know,' Salima said. 'I don't know about fighting. The Ouled Brahims are just a small tribe and they have swords and two rifles. Have you seen the French military convoy that just left town? They could burn the Ouled Brahims to the ground before they unsheathe their swords. It's a pointless cause.'

'They've survived this long,' Fahima said.

'Only because they've been running all this time. Besides, if they want to fight, it's their business. I don't want to be involved. It's too risky, and we have nothing to gain. We're dancers. Not killers.'

Tell that to the two men in the bottom of our well, Fahima wanted to say. She couldn't help looking at the well and Salima caught it.

'It's not the same,' Salima explained. 'We didn't have a choice. It was us or them. It's not like we went around killing people for no reason.'

Salima seemed to have somehow made peace with the killings, but it still troubled Fahima. She thought about it every single day now.

'But I guess that's how the Ouled Brahims feel.' Fahima said. 'It's either them or the French.'

'Maybe,' Salima shrugged. 'It still doesn't make it our problem, though. Our problem is finding out how they know about the two dead soldiers, and who else knows about it.'

That was true, and just thinking about the other people that might know made Fahima's back cold with fear.

'How do we do that?'

'We need to watch that bitch across the street,' Salima said. 'I know she had something… oh shit.'

Salima froze in place for a moment. Then she touched herself between her thighs. 'Oh shit,' she said, annoyed.

She marched across the courtyard and up the stairs, repeating, 'This is just great.'

'What is it?' Fahima asked, trying hard not to laugh.

'It's my fucking period.'

With a large grin on her face, Fahima watched her sister stomp bow-legged into her bedroom.

Then it hit her. Like a sandstorm in the middle of the night slamming into your house, shaking the doors and battering the windows. The courtyard span. She needed to sit down.

She had been too distracted to think about it. Too nauseous.

'Oh, fuck,' she murmured.

It had been more than two months since Fahima last bled.

Twenty-one

i

When Salima woke up, close to midday, Fahima had already cleaned the house, bought vegetables from the market, and was almost done preparing her favourite pepper and tomato *checkchouka*.

It gave Fahima a chance to think. There were so many signs she had missed entirely, Fahima thought, as she beat garlic in a brass mortar with a heavy pestle. She had been around many pregnant women. She knew that the constant morning nausea, the sore breasts and the craving she felt today for *checkchouka* meant only one thing: she was pregnant.

She felt dizzy every time she thought about it, but it had to be done. There were questions she had to consider.

First, who was the father? Fahima was sure it was René. She remembered the night they had made love as if they had known it would be their last time. It had felt significant at the time, and now she knew why. After that, Fahima had only serviced four men as far as she could remember, but never without condoms. Not even with her regular clients.

Or perhaps she willed René to be the father. Not that it meant anything now. It wasn't like they could live as one happy family. He was gone now, she reminded herself.

Fahima stirred sorrow into the simmering pan. Her *checkchouka* was almost done, so she went about breaking eggs in a small bowl. Fahima always threw four or five eggs in her *checkchouka* despite Saadia's protests that it no longer tasted the same. Today, she was indulging herself even more, pouring six eggs in the pan.

Was she going to keep it? She wouldn't be able to do a lot of dancing once her belly grew bigger, and most clients would be repelled by her pregnancy. How was she going to take care of the baby? Would she still be able to work after that? It would never be the same once the baby was here. It would surely ruin her plans of dancing in Algiers or Paris.

There were options, Fahima knew. Women lost their babies on purpose all the time. There were healers and *guezzanas* who gave you herbal drinks that would send you into fevers and diarrhoeas, and when you recovered you would no longer be pregnant. But that didn't always work, and sometimes the pregnant women died after drinking those potions.

Deep down Fahima knew perfectly well she could never bring herself to put an end to her pregnancy. She was imagining how she would hold him in her arms, breastfeed him and watch him sleep. He would grow to look like René. These fantasies stirred things in Fahima's heart that she had never experienced before.

The *checkchouka* was ready, and Fahima heard movement upstairs. Salima was awake.

Fahima wondered if she should tell her sister about the pregnancy. Salima would throw a big fit and call Fahima a stupid fool, but there wasn't much else she could do. This happened often enough. It could have happened to Salima, Fahima thought before she quickly realised that no, it wouldn't. Not in a million years.

Still, Fahima couldn't hide the pregnancy forever even if she tried, so she might as well let Salima know and get it over with.

And then there was her mother. Saadia would be humiliated and disappointed and would cry like it was the end of their lives. Fahima was sure to have a few things thrown her way, too.

When Fahima sat out in the courtyard to eat, Salima shuffled her way downstairs, her eyes saggy and her hair a gigantic mess.

'It smells delicious,' Salima said, taking a stool across from Fahima, then she saw the eggs and made a gagging sound.

Fahima knew her sister would eat it anyway. Salima lit a cigarette.

'Did you talk to Mouloud?' Salima asked.

Fahima was supposed to give Mouloud their final answer last night, declining the Ouled Brahim offer for Salima and Fahima to join their fight against the French.

'I couldn't get him alone,' Fahima said.

'You're not having second thoughts, are you?' Salima asked with narrowed eyes.

'Of course not.'

It had been over a week since the sisters had met Mouloud and the two Ouled Brahim men. Since then, Mouloud had been acting as if nothing had happened, treating the sisters no differently than before.

His ability to conceal this huge secret amazed Fahima, but it also made her wonder what else he was hiding. *We're not the only ones with secrets after all.*

'Well, I guess we'll have to try again tonight,' Salima said between drags. Salima served herself some *chekchouka* and the sisters ate in silence.

Fahima had just wiped her plate clean with a piece of bread when Nouara knocked on the door and shouted something. Fahima and Nouara had made plans to go to Alexandre's house.

'Are you ready to see the most beautiful thing in this world?' Nouara said half-jokingly when Fahima opened the door.

Nouara was referring to the painting Alexandre had been drawing of her. Djamila was outside, too, looking a little bored.

'Let's do it,' Fahima said cheerfully, thankful for any distraction. She closed the door, and the three girls set out towards the main street.

'Now it's not quite finished yet,' Nouara explained, 'but Alexandre finally agreed to show it to you all. And I want you to tell me what you really think, alright?'

'I am sure it's uglier than the inside of a cow's ass,' Djamila teased.

'But I also wanted him to talk to you both, you know,' Nouara ignored Djamila's jibe. 'I want him to make one for each of you. It would be great. Maybe the three of us together? Can you imagine? And I won't lie to you, the money's great and all, but I would've done it for free.' She roared with laughter. Fahima and Djamila joined, too. 'Not a lot of Nailiya dancers have the chance to do this, you know. And Alexandre always works half-naked, and I don't mind looking at his sweaty body.' She shook her shoulders seductively. 'A lot of the times, we'd stop and make love, and that's always nice. I wish all my clients were like him, you know. You have to try it sometime.'

This talk reminded Fahima of René. How she longed for his whispers. She touched her stomach discreetly, as if to make sure the baby was still there. The last proof of a memory that was so distant in time and space that she almost suspected it had never happened. How could she have been so happy?

Nouara was still talking when the three women emerged onto the main street and turned left towards Place de Pein. Something was wrong. They went silent and stopped in their tracks. People around them were watching something near the gate. A loud guttural shriek echoed through the place.

More screaming rose from the crowd. Not just one person. Several women were crying. Sobs and howls and moans all mixed up with muffled words. A girl was on her knees, her head thrown back as she pleaded with the sky. Two women were hugging each other, and another woman rubbed a girl's back while she sobbed.

'Come on,' Nouara called impatiently. 'Let's go. We don't know these girls. They must've lost someone back in their village.'

It felt more like a collective funeral. As if many people had died at once, and all these women – mostly dancers, Fahima was now noticing – had just heard the news.

They broke her heart, the way they cried and wailed, but there wasn't anything she could do. So when Nouara tugged at her sleeve, Fahima turned away from them, and the group of women resumed walking towards Place de Pein. The cries faded behind them.

ii

Alexandre welcomed the girls with a genuine smile and bare feet. He wore a light beige shirt embroidered with brown shapes and matching linen pants.

'Come on in,' he said. 'I was expecting you all.'

All smiles and giggles, the girls crowded into a messy room with fancy furniture. The air was dense with the smell of cigarettes and feet.

'This way,' Nouara said, leading her friends through a corridor to a small parlour with large windows.

Fahima was amazed by the number of paintings in this place. *I can't believe he's only been here two years,* Fahima thought.

Her eyes fell on a group of women showering in the river, splashing gayfully in their nakedness. Chilled, Fahima wondered if the painter had been spying on naked girls. There was another painting of a man and a woman lying in bed together, all naked, too, and Fahima imagined them on the floor right there as Alexandre worked his brush and stared at them from behind his canvas.

'Are you ready for the big reveal?' Alexandre asked as he hurried into the room. He stood next to a painting covered by a white bedsheet.

The three girls formed a line facing Alexandre and nodded. With exaggerated slowness, the Frenchman lifted the bedsheet. There was a light brown patch, like sand, and feet pointing outward. An anklet appeared on each foot. Fahima and Djamila looked down at Nouara's feet and saw that she was wearing the same anklets. Alexandre then exposed her legs, long and slender with light dark skin and strong meaty thighs. Djamila stifled a giggle when she saw a patch of dark hair between the legs. Then, to their relief, Alexandre lifted the whole sheet at once with a flick of his wrist.

Nouara's belly was flat and her breasts small and perky. Her face glowed, and she stared absentmindedly at something in the distance. One hand was perched on her hip while the other one fell gracefully at her side. Her hair was wrapped in a red and yellow scarf with elaborate knots and a thick braid folded in on each side. Nouara was entirely naked. Except for the anklets and one bracelet, she wasn't even wearing any jewellery. Behind her was part of a bedsheet, but the rest was all black and brown.

'Isn't it amazing?' Alexandre asked in broken Derja, and they all roared in laughter.

'Fantastic,' Djamila called out.

'When it's finished,' Nouara explained, 'he'll take it to some exposition in Paris, and he'll try and take me with him so people can see me next to the painting, you know. Can you imagine?'

Fahima could imagine. Nouara was about to live Fahima's dream. She'd no doubt dance while she was there.

As if hearing her thoughts, Alexandre addressed the two girls, 'Do you want a painting?'

'I don't want to stand here naked for days, thank you,' Djamila chuckled.

Fahima didn't mind standing there naked if it meant she could go to Paris.

'What a pity,' Alexandre said. 'Your green eyes would drive people in Paris crazy.'

Djamila shrugged.

'I want one,' Fahima heard herself say. 'I'll do it.'

Alexandre looked at her with surprise, which Fahima didn't understand.

'Are you sure?' Nouara asked.

'Yeah, of course. Why are you surprised?

'No, I'm just... I mean he and I told you he was looking for subjects when he first started, and you said you were interested. It was out by the river if you remember. But you never showed up.'

'That's Ammariya,' Djamila teased. 'Always changing her mind. One day she can't keep a cigarette out of her mouth, the next day, she can't even stand the smoke. One day she wants a painting, and the next day she doesn't.'

Fucking Salima, Fahima thought.

'I'm not sure I remember,' she said, 'but I promise I'll show up this time.'

'Well, listen, I only need a few weeks to finish this painting and a few other projects I started, but when I'm ready, I'll send for you. If you don't show up this time, I'll look for you myself, deal?'

'Deal!' she said, struggling to hide her excitement.

'Now how about we all sit down for some tea yes?'

Alexandre was proud to announce he had finally learnt to make tea *à la* Bousaada. It was good, the girls agreed, strong and rich. They sipped at it while they shared town gossip.

Colonel Dupont's son, Bernard, was in town with his girlfriend, Nouara reported. They wondered if the girlfriend knew about his flings with the Bousaada girls. Someone needed to point her in the right direction, Djamila suggested, laughing, and Fahima secretly wondered how Bernard had explained the scar she knew he had on his neck, the one inflicted by Salima over a year ago. Would he seek revenge?

The conversation soon went to the missing soldiers, and Alexandre said Dupont had come to see him about the case. Fahima kept silent through it all. But Alexandre's face reddened, too, when he talked about Dupont, and he constantly caressed the top of his head. He quickly changed topic.

They talked about the new *Caid* who hadn't done anything since his appointment over a year ago.

'They say Malek Kacimi resisted for as long as he could, but when the colonel offered to help get his daughter into the French school, he gave in,' Djamila said.

'Like I always say,' Nouara said, 'Everyone's a prostitute. We all sell our values for money or something else. It's just a matter of price.'

Fahima had heard this talk from Naima a few times. *Poor Naima was right,* she thought.

It was the middle of the afternoon when the three girls left the painter's home.

'I told you he was nice,' Nouara said as soon as they turned right around l'Hotel de l'Oasis. 'Now Be careful, Ammariya,' she added, addressing Fahima. 'You can have all the fun you want, but he's mine to keep. Hear me?'

'You keep him,' Fahima said, feigning disinterest.

Something else was growing in Fahima's mind. Alexandre had said he would call her in a few weeks, and it would probably take months to finish that painting. Her belly would be up to her nose by then. But this was Fahima's only chance to travel. She had no idea what Alexandre would say to all this.

'What on earth?' Djamila stood with her mouth open.

A group of Nailiya women marched from the main street and crossed Place de Pein towards the military circle. There was something sinister about the soundless brisk way they walked, thrusting sticks and canes in the air. There were a few men, too. With axes. What on earth was going on?

iii

Fahima, Djamila and Nouara hurried across the square to inspect the clamour. A group of French soldiers marched to meet the Nailiya men and women before they fully reached the military circle. The French pointed their weapons at the crowd, but to no avail. They didn't stop until they were within arm's reach of the soldiers.

'Arrêtez,' one soldier shouted at them to stop. 'Que croyez-vous faire?'

The rioting crowd was small, no more than thirty people, but their anger seemed to scare the armed soldiers. Fahima had no doubt they would use their weapons if the crowd came too close.

They formed a thick line against the wavering French soldiers, and they started shouting in Derja and French, brandishing their sticks and canes and axes above their heads.

Bastards. Killers. You killed innocent people. Children. You murderers. What did they ever do to you?

More people were pouring in from the many streets that flowed into Place de Pein. Some joined the rioters, but most of them just watched from a safe distance.

A woman tried to push her way past a soldier. He hit her across the face with the butt of his weapon. The sound of metal on bone smacked loud for everyone in the audience to hear. The woman collapsed to the ground, and three other girls attacked the soldier with their sticks. More joined in, but the wood was no match for machinery. It did little to discourage the rioters, though. The shouting continued, and the crowd swelled like a fevered limb. Groans swept the crowds as a large group of soldiers ran out of the military circle towards the riot.

'What happened?' Nouara asked a bystander.

'They killed their folks,' he said.

'Who?'

'Who? The French. They've been out for over a week attacking villages out in the desert.'

'Attacking Ouled Brahims?' Fahima asked, trying hard not to let a numbness overwhelm her. 'You mean the French have been killing Ouled Brahims?'

The young man shook his head.

'They've been killing everyone,' another voice said. Fahima turned to face an older woman. It was Soltana, the owner of the Haouch where Nouara worked. 'The first survivor arrived over a week ago. He came from some Beni Adas tribe not far from here. He said his entire village had been burnt to the ground. Then two days later, there was news from another village. And then another. At least five or six villages have been burnt. Everyone killed.'

'Why?' Nouara asked.

Fahima's entire body went limp. Had the French gotten to her village? Was her family safe? She searched among the rioting crowd for a familiar face, but she couldn't see anyone. Maybe that meant her village hadn't been attacked.

The protest continued to swelter, and more and more soldiers were joining the defence line. This place is going to explode, Fahima thought. The last group of soldiers didn't stop at the line. Instead, they worked in twos. Each pair snatched a woman from the crowd and carried her off into the military circle. If anyone tried to rescue her, other soldiers would beat them into the dusty ground.

'… not like they need a reason to do that,' Soltana was saying, 'they say Colonel Dupont did this to avenge the soldiers that went missing.'

Fahima's stomach dropped. Did they figure out she and her sister had killed the missing soldiers? Why didn't they just arrest or kill them? Why go around burning their villages?

'Do you know if they've attacked my village?' Djamila asked.

'I couldn't really tell,' she said. 'We've been receiving different stories. Most are rumours. Some we know for sure…'

Fahima couldn't stay here any longer. She peeled away and headed home. Was her family safe? Saadia and Afir? And two siblings? Her aunt and cousins and friends?

She remembered Mourad. He usually had the latest news from the village. She needed to find Salima so she could go talk to him.

The alleys seemed to stretch out, and Fahima felt like her brisk steps were taking her backwards. Her throat went dry as sand, and her hands were shaking. What if the French had killed everybody?

They usually killed criminals or Ouled Brahims. The outcasts. This was different. Suddenly, what those Ouled Brahim men had said in that house started to make sense. *Everyone in this whole country is a victim to France's cruelty,* they had said. *They're trying to erase us all and keep this country for themselves.*

When she finally reached her house, she knew something was wrong. The front door was open. They never left the door open. She tip-toed across the small passage, not sure what to expect, then she heard sobs. Was it Salima? Yes, definitely. But there was someone else with her. Another woman.

She found them both in the courtyard standing by the well: Salima and Mother. They were crying, their chests heaving up and down as they sobbed. *Oh no.*

She approached them carefully. Part of her knew what this meant and she wanted to turn around and leave.

'What happened?' she asked, her voice shaking. Tears already trailing down her cheeks.

Saadia turned to face Fahima. Her eyes and nose were swollen and red, and her face tired and dusty. Her clothes were blackened with ash. There was blood, too.

'Yemma,' Fahima stifled a sob, 'Tell me what happened.'

'They killed them, all,' Saadia said in a cavernous, deep voice. 'They killed everyone in the village. They burnt it down.'

The world turned upside down. A thousand daggers stabbed her heart, again and again, relentless. Next to her, Salima tumbled down to the ground and let out a high howl, like a wolf in pain. It was the most horrible sound she'd ever heard. Fahima's head was racing to grasp what this all meant. Her mother had survived, so surely others did, too. Her father? Her little sister? Her brother?

'Where's Father?' she asked.

Saadia shook her head, her eyes shut tight as tears traced the ash on her face. 'I saw them all. I held their bodies in my own hands, hugged them for so long. They killed them all.'

Fahima turned around, no longer able to face her mother. She clutched her stomach and opened her mouth to scream, but no sound came out. Just a small, low wail. Her knees were so weak she could no longer stand. She allowed herself to collapse next to her sister. Two corpses.

Her mind went back to the village, the people she had spent most of her life with. Her father's calm that had brought her so much peace of mind. Was she never going to have that again? Was her brother Amar dead, too? And her sister, oh, her baby sister, Farida. Fahima could still see her skipping around with her missing teeth and the piece of bread in her hand. Her dreams of becoming a dancer floating about her. Did they kill her baby sister?

'I'd been visiting your aunt. Cruel luck,' Saadia was saying. She dumped down next to them, wet and dusty. 'When I came back, the French. The French, were already on their way out with their trucks and guns. They just left. I could see the smoke. I didn't believe it. It was still on fire when I got there. Bodies, blood, everywhere. I looked for them. I looked and looked and looked. I looked, Fahima. One by one. Their bodies. They were holed with bullets. Like sieves. Everywhere.'

Fahima gritted her teeth. She wanted Saadia to stop.

'Your father. My Afir. His eyes, they were still open, his mouth... drooling. It wasn't his face. And and and then I found Farida,' she whimpered, 'My baby! My baby Farida. She was so limp. So so so cold. I couldn't warm her. Her small, beautiful hand with that stupid piece of bread. She wouldn't wake up. I tried. She wouldn't wake up. She wouldn't.'

Saadia couldn't go on. All three of them sobbed. They were melting away. Fahima wailed.

Someone came in through the front door. She didn't care to see who it was.

'I heard what happened,' a male voice said.

Saadia shifted, and Salima sat up.

'We'll do it,' Salima said.

Fahima looked up to see who her sister was talking to, and her eyes fell on Mouloud standing right outside the passage.

'Tell the Ouled Brahim we'll do it,' Salima added. 'We'll kill them all.'

Twenty-two

i

We've done this before, Salima told herself. *Many times.* There was no reason to be afraid.

Not yet at least.

She and Fahima called it the switch trick, and they had been using it to fool the French since Colonel Dupont had imposed those stupid regulations. It had worked just fine. Well, except when Cambron had found out about them, but that was different. He had been stalking them. As far as Salima knew, no one else was on to them yet.

She danced at Mouloud's café, feigning normalcy as she kept a watchful eye on the trays that Mouloud carried back and forth. All the glasses he served were white or light brown. Some were green, but none red. Red was her signal.

They had gone through the plan over and over again. Fahima, Salima, Mouloud and the two Ouled Brahim men. They had explored different schemes, but none seemed as efficient as what Fahima and Salima were already doing. They only added a few tweaks so they could communicate without exposing themselves.

Salima avoided looking at the faces of the men in the café. She had avoided looking at French soldiers since the day she heard about the massacre. Each time she saw a Frenchman, she wondered if he was the one who had killed her family and found herself shaking with rage and fiddling with her bracelet.

There it was. A red glass, just slightly concealed among white ones. Mouloud carried the tray with such a casual air that Salima wondered for a moment if this was really her cue or if he'd forgotten all about their code.

With a racing heart, Salima watched the tray travel across the café. Mouloud made several detours, nodding to customers, placing glasses here and there. But the red glass remained. He finally stopped by a table of young French soldiers in civilian clothes. Mouloud placed the red glass on the table and someone immediately picked it up.

Salima followed the glass as it floated to the soldier's mouth and she finally allowed herself to look at him. He was a short man with a puffy face and short cropped hair. Engaged in conversation with his friends, he took a sip of his drink and replaced the red glass without as much as looking at it.

This man was Salima's target.

Salima continued to dance, but she couldn't help feeling both afraid and angry at the same time. She had seduced men before, but only for money, never for this. She could not forget; this man had taken part in the carnage in her village. Not only that, but other villages around Bousaada had been completely ravaged. He was nothing more than a murderer.

This had been Salima and Fahima's condition. They would only help if they targeted soldiers who had participated in the massacre. The sisters were after revenge, and the Ouled Brahims had the means to identify the soldiers. While Salima would have preferred to get her hands on the colonel himself, he was impossible to reach, so she had to make do with his underlings.

She detached herself from the girls and danced her way around the café until she was close to the target. When he was looking, she flashed him a smile and wink so subtly that she wasn't even sure he'd caught it.

When men stood to dance, she danced near him and let him touch her a little, but not too much. That was the secret of seduction: give the man just enough to entice him and let him run after you like a child.

Sure enough, when Salima told him to go meet her out by the gate, he waited a little and left from the front door. Salima went out through the back, and Fahima replaced her. Fahima looked a lot more scared than Salima; she was pale and quiet. They had done the right thing by not letting Fahima take the first target. Fahima might be able to do it eventually, but she wasn't ready yet.

Salima met the Frenchman out by the gate and she motioned him to follow her. Things felt a lot more real as she neared the house. Salima's lips quivered, and her stomach twisted.

She let the man into the house. *I haven't done anything wrong yet. I can still give him pleasure, get paid and just let him go.*

She led him upstairs, her hand holding his. The sisters had never replaced the broken railing on the balcony. The flowerpots stood there instead, like two headstones. *Am I really going to do this?*

In the bedroom, the soldier sat down on the sheepskin rug, right where his countryman had sat a few weeks ago. It was as though she'd been dreaming for weeks; now here she was, awake in her nightmare.

She prepared tea as usual, and then danced for him. He smoked hashish while he watched, eager for more. She kept pretending to herself that all she was going to do was dance. She was just going to dance for him.

But the grin on his face disgusted her. This monster had killed innocent people. He could have been the one who murdered her father or baby sister. And now he was here, enjoying life, and grinning.

Salima's brother would never grow up. He'd never be the man he so desperately wanted to be.

She wanted to cry. Instead, she decided to act while her rage burnt fierce. She felt strangely calm, focused.

Salima stepped closer to the man, and his teethy smile widened. She let him grab her behind, and she lowered herself down in front of him. She hovered her lips close to his, breathing in the smell of smoke, hashish and alcohol all at once. She rubbed her lips against his teasingly, and he breathed hard, barely able to contain himself.

He took her naked breast in his hand, and when she touched his manhood, he gasped as if she had taken him by surprise.

She put her hand on his neck, gently, and kissed him. As he kissed her back, eyes closed and absorbed in every movement, she raised her right hand in the air. Salima rotated her bracelet until the two sharp spikes were right on the heel of her hand.

With her mouth still on his, Salima, with one swift move, thrust the spiked bracelet into the side of his neck right under his jaw.

First, his tongue went limp between her lips, and his eyes shot open. He tried to move, but she held his head steady. Just a moment longer. She needed to feel the blood, warm and sticky, seep down his neck. Then she stood up, ripping the spikes out, and stepped back.

She watched him, ready to call the Ouled Brahim boys stationed in Fahima's room for support if the solider launched at her.

But the soldier didn't stand up. He tried to, but his face was pale, and his movements feeble. He pressed his hand against his injury as the blood spilt down his neck and dyed his shirt crimson. He kept checking his reddened hand, frowning, as if he expected the bleeding to stop on its own. It didn't.

Salima slipped back into her dress, her eyes always fixed on the soldier. A calm had descended. She felt inexplicably serene.

She lit a cigarette and stood by the door, gazing at him. The

Frenchman could no longer sit. He lay down on the sheepskin rug, as if to sleep. He coughed, and blood spouted between his lips. He twitched one more time, and that was it. He never moved again.

Salima inhaled some more smoke before she left the room to knock on Fahima's door. Three young men, big and strong, came out to the balcony.

'He's dead,' she said.

The men looked at her. They probably expected some scene, some tears or some statement even. She merely looked back at them, and they went past her to the room. They paused at her door, staring at the corpse. They were probably new to this too.

They picked the dead man up and took him downstairs, leaving a long trail of blood behind them. They dropped the soggy body by the well and removed the pots from the lid. In one strong movement, they pushed the cement lid aside, opening the mouth of the well. Then they dropped the corpse down into oblivion.

With speed and efficiency, two boys picked up buckets and cloths and cleaned the pool of blood in Salima's room while the third took care of the blood trail.

Salima watched with admiration as the young men completed their task in silence. It had taken her and Fahima an entire day to clean up after Cambron's death, and these men had covered everything up in no time. It was like it had never happened.

Salima was half-way through her second cigarette, still perched up on the balcony, when the men threw the last bucket of bloodied water and sodden cloths into the well. They emptied sacks of sand and dirt in to cover up the smell. Finally, they pushed the lid shut.

Salima blew a small cloud of smoke in the air and looked down at the well that now concealed three dead bodies. Three French soldiers.

'This one's for Amar,' she whispered to the night.

"Violence is a cleansing force. It frees the native from his inferiority complex and from his despair and inaction; it makes him fearless and restores his self-respect."

Franz Fanon, *The Wretched of The Earth*(1963), p. 94

1935
October

Twenty-three

i

The rain started before midday. A drizzle, no more. By midnight, the city was almost flooded by the downpour, and Salima was soaked with water. Water and blood.

Walking around the marketplace with Mourad that morning, Salima wasn't bothered by the light shower. She enjoyed the feel of moisture in the air and the smell of wet earth.

Salima was looking for a chicken. It was about time she bought a hen for her lonely rooster to finally come home and… roost. It was either that or kill that fucking bird so she wouldn't have to deal with the Jewess each time he found his way to Fadhila's chickens.

Walking by her side, Mourad played with his cane and chatted about his sheep, something about the black-headed twin ewes being ready to breed. Salima nodded as she usually did when the topic didn't interest her, but she was glad Mourad was finally back to his usual self. He had taken the news of his family's massacre quite badly, locking himself up in his stables for weeks and abandoning his sheep. Every single person in his family had been murdered in that attack.

It broke Salima to see Mourad in that state, no longer enjoying life, giving up on the project that he had spent his life working on. Fortunately, Kader, his aide, had risen to the task and taken care of the sheep. Salima felt a newfound respect for the man despite his condescendence.

For months, Salima had tried talking to Mourad, distracting him, seducing him even, but nothing worked. A stone would have budged, but Mourad never did.

A few weeks ago, he had suddenly emerged all chatty. Almost cheerful, as if something had snapped in him and he'd forgotten all about his misery. Salima wondered what had happened, but she never asked him lest it send him back to his dark place.

'What do you think of this chicken?' Salima asked. Pointing at four chickens tied together inside a makeshift cage. 'The brown one?'

The vendor spoke to Salima and Mourad. 'You'll love this hen, sister. It lays the largest eggs you've ever seen. Every day. Never misses a day.'

He held up a large egg with a bluish colour.

'That's a duck egg,' Mourad replied.

'You would think! But it's all chicken. No one lays bigger eggs!'

Salima and Mourad rolled their eyes and walked away.

'Besides, that brown chicken is old,' Mourad said. 'Did you see the comb on her head? It's floppy.'

'Well,' Salima said, 'I'm glad you're here with me.'

Having grown up around chickens, Salima could practically speak to them, but she was happy to let Mourad believe she needed him.

'Here, this one,' Mourad said, pointing to three chickens on a wooden plank.

These chickens did look young, and their hearts beat through their chests.

'The grey one?'

'Yes, exactly.'

The hen was pretty with its layered shades of grey and long naked neck. Her comb was small, and just turning from pink to red, which meant she would lay her first egg anytime now.

'I love it,' Salima said discreetly, careful not to let the vendor hear her and charge her more.

The vendor wanted four francs for the hen. Salima said she would pay one. She bought her for one and a half.

They had only walked a few steps when Mourad stopped in front of a man selling souvenirs, small decorative ornaments, jewellery boxes and tiny, little jars. The rain was growing stronger now, turning the pieces dark brown. The colour of mud.

Salima didn't know what Mourad could possibly need from the stall. He never cared for decorations or souvenirs.

He picked up a light brown sand rose and handed it to her. Salima held it in her free hand and looked at him, puzzled.

'What?' she asked.

'I'm buying it for you,' he said.

Salima eyed the sand rose. It almost looked like a real flower in full bloom, skilfully crafted by nature. The piece had a flat bottom, so it didn't need a saucer underneath for it to stand.

'Why?' she asked. She didn't need a sand rose.

'Do I need a reason to give my future wife a gift?'

Her heart crumbled into tiny sand grains. She fought back tears and inspected the sand rose more closely. This was her man's gift to her.

Mourad paid for the rose and resumed walking. Salima didn't know what to say.

'You know what they say about Nailiya dancers and sand roses?' he asked.

Salima nodded, but Mourad still wanted to explain. 'They say Nailiya dancers are like sand roses. They're beautiful. Like flowers. But they're tough. Hard at the core. Ouled Nail are strong, and my own Nailiya is the strongest of them all.'

He spoke with such pride you would think he was Nail himself. Father of all Ouled Nail.

Salima felt undeserving of Mourad's love. She had been keeping a huge secret from him for months.

She could never bring herself to tell him. She didn't know how he was going to look at her knowing she was a killer. She often wondered if maybe he would be proud and support her for taking action against the French. But she knew better than to believe this fantasy. If anything, he would blame her for the death of his family, and rightly so. It had all started when Salima and Fahima killed Cambron.

Nonetheless, Salima felt like she was betraying Mourad by hiding a part of her. She didn't deserve his kindness.

'Are you crying?' Mourad teased.

Salima shook her head. She remained silent, lest her voice betray her. He jumped in front of her and placed his hands on her shoulders. The rain was pouring, and her hair was dripping. She didn't care that people were staring. While people in Bousaada never showed affection in public, the French and Ouled Nail weren't expected to obey that rule. The locals treated them like kids who didn't know how to behave yet.

'Listen,' he said. 'Don't you think it's time we got married?'

Salima did think it was time, but that didn't matter because she was a murderer. Besides, if they did get married, where would they go? There was no village to go back to.

As if hearing her thoughts, Mourad continued, 'We don't have to leave town. We could stay here and work together, raise sheep and have kids.'

He didn't bring up their desecrated village. They never mentioned it. Salima knew he was right, though. They could stay here. It would mean she would stop working as a dancer – even Ouled Nail men, who were fine marrying dancers, wouldn't accept their wives pleasuring other men after the wedding– but that didn't bother Salima. She couldn't wait to quit.

The problem was that she couldn't marry him while she wasn't being completely honest with him. It wasn't fair.

'What do you say?' Mourad asked, hands still on her shoulders.

'I have to go,' she said, barely able to contain her tears. 'It's raining.'

She broke from him and hurried back home.

Once she was past the gate, she let her tears mix with the raindrops trickling down her face.

ii

Vincent was the chatty type.

He went on and on about how he had never imagined he would grow to like life in the desert, but a year into it, he didn't want to ever leave it again.

Salima was making him tea with nothing on but her white underdress. She had serviced many people like Vincent before, and she knew the best thing to do was to remain silent, nodding and smiling here and there. One client had once paid her to only do that.

'And the dates,' Vincent was saying as she stirred the teapot. 'Oh my God, the dates. I've never tasted anything like them. I sent some to my children, and they loved it. They've been asking for more but I said—'

'You have children?' Salima interrupted him, wishing she hadn't been listening.

'Yes, three. The oldest is twelve, but he's so big you would think he's twenty. And I have a girl named Collette. She's the sweetest—'

'Do you smoke?' Salima interrupted him again. To her relief, he didn't. 'I'll be right back,' she said as she stood up. 'I have to smoke.'

She went out to the balcony where she could finally breathe. The rain was still pouring down from the sky like Salima had never seen before. It rarely rained in Bousaada, and when it did, it was usually a light shower, never this strong or this long. Salima wondered if the river could flood the city.

She needed to know what to do about Vincent, and she wanted to consult someone. The boys hiding in Fahima's bedroom wouldn't do. They were men of force.

Fahima wasn't here either. Tonight was her turn to stay behind at

Mouloud's and dance, but she wouldn't stay long. Eight months pregnant, Fahima moved slower and tired faster. Apart from that, her pregnancy barely showed, and hiding it had never been a difficult task. Fahima was one of those women who would give birth before you even noticed she was expecting.

After dancing, Fahima would go to the stupid painter. For months now, she had been posing for one of his paintings. Salima had been obliged to pose a few times, too, and she hated it. She couldn't fathom why Fahima was so excited about the whole thing.

Downstairs, Salima found her mother in the living room. She put her head through the door and whispered, 'Yemma? Are you sleeping?'

'No,' Saadia's whispered, and Salima heard her move in the dark. 'I'm listening to the rain. What happened? Is it done?'

'I can't do it,' Salima said. She sat down by the door. 'He has kids. Three. One is a sweet little girl. Collette.'

'Why were you talking to him about his children?' Saadia hissed.

Salima couldn't see her mother in the dark. Saadia had pretended to remain strong through the whole tragedy, but something had clearly been eating her up from the inside. Her face had gained years, and her eyes grown tired. Her body had been reduced to bones and sheer skin. She had lost her brisk walk. She waddled now.

'He wouldn't stop talking,' Salima said.

Saadia made no reply.

'What am I going to do? Kill him and make his kids orphans?'

As soon as she said it, Salima realised the other soldiers she and Fahima had killed over the months might have had children, too. Did it really make a difference, or was she growing soft?

'You think he considered that when he killed your father?' Saadia hissed. 'You think he ever paused to think that your poor baby sister was as sweet as his daughter Collette? No. He and the other monsters killed everyone in cold blood.'

'Do we know for sure he was part of that massacre?' Salima asked. Even she knew it was a weak argument.

'Mouloud said they'd only target those who'd been there,' Saadia replied. 'Even if he wasn't, what do you think he and his countrymen are here for? They're here to take our lands away from us. They'll kill every last one of us, kids or not, until we're all gone.'

Salima had never heard Mother speak like this. She sounded like the Ouled Brahim men.

Saadia sniffed. Salima couldn't see anything, but she knew her mother was crying. She hadn't cried since the day she came back from the village. Salima imagined her mother cradling her dead children in her arms.

She went back upstairs.

iii

Vincent was still where Salima had left him sitting awkwardly on the sheepskin rag. The tea in front of him was boiling.

Silently, Salima placed a low table next to him, then she set the tray she had prepared earlier and brought the hot teapot over.

'Are you alright?' Vincent asked. 'You look upset.'

Salima flashed him a weak smile and said she was fine. She picked up a small glass with yellow drawings and filled it with tea. The glass had poison at the bottom.

Killing soldiers with the spiked bracelet had proven to be a messy affair and at times dangerous. Cleaning the blood took longer, and sometimes the stab didn't effectively kill the man, so he would fight back and struggle until the boys next door neutralised him. After trying the spiked bracelet three or four times, Salima and Fahima had resorted to other means, cleaner, more efficient.

They still had their bracelets and ropes for strangling in case of emergency, but their weapon of choice was now poison. It was Mouloud's task to acquire it, and he had Akshish deliver the poison discreetly every few weeks.

Before going to the café earlier this evening, Salima had prepared the tea tray and put a few drops of it in the yellow glass. Then she prepared the tea in front of Vincent, leaving him oblivious to any danger.

Vincent picked up his glass but didn't drink. Salima filled her glass and took a sip.

'Is it because I said I have kids?' Vincent asked. 'Do you feel uncomfortable lying with a married man?'

Salima never cared if her clients were married or not. Nailiyas couldn't afford to have too many principles.

'Because I assure you,' Vincent went on. 'I'm not married. My wife passed away four years ago.'

Salima felt boneless. She was killing this man for being inhumane.

For killing innocent people and children. But she was going to kill him and leave his three kids fatherless. And they had already lost their mother. How was she any different from him?

But her mother downstairs had become a soulless, fleshless body. Half her family had been killed senselessly. And here she was hesitating to avenge their deaths?

What had changed? She had killed so many soldiers over the months, almost twenty between her and her sister without a moment of hesitation.

Even though the killings never satisfied her, she constantly came back to the image of people in her village pierced with bullets and covered in blood. It had never failed to motivate.

Had running into Mourad this morning affected her?

All these thoughts raced through her mind in an instant while the yellow glass in Vincent's hand travelled to his mouth. Salima had to decide quickly. She felt like a god right then. Doling out life and death.

With a swift strike of the hand, Salima knocked the glass out of Vincent's hand and sent it flying across the room, hot tea spilling in all directions. The glass hit the wall before rolling across the floor. Vincent's eyes widened.

'Get out of here,' she shouted, pretending to be offended. 'You're lying to me. You're sleeping around with girls behind your wife's back, and you have the audacity to lie to me?'

She willed the boys in the next room to stay hidden and not take the screaming as a call for help. They had been clear on the code for help. It was her name. Salima. There was no other explanation for why she would call out her own name unless it was for their aid.

Vincent didn't budge. He gaped at her and his face turned red.

'I said get out of here, you sick bastard,' Salima kept shouting. 'You dirty old pig.'

Vincent's expression changed from surprise to anger. He frowned and his lips tightened.

'I didn't pay you to be insulted,' he said in a calm voice. 'I refuse to be treated like this.'

Salima fumbled among her clothes on the floor and found the little leather pouch. She took out two ten-franc coins and threw them at Vincent.

'Here's your money. Take it and go. Now!'

She wanted to tell him to run for his life. That he didn't know what he was doing. Vincent stood up, but instead of going out, he came around the table and stood in front her. He towered over her.

'You're going to give me what I came here for.'

His face was so rigid it was starting to scare Salima. He pushed her, holding her neck down with an elbow while he unzipped his pants.

'You whores think you're so special,' he said. Struggling to breathe, she tried to remove his forearm. She only managed to scrape off some skin.

'You think you're above the other prostitutes. That you're queens or something.'

He lifted her underdress with his free hand. Salima wanted to shout for help. She reached for his eyes, but he pulled his head higher, so she scratched his cheek instead.

'My wife used to think that, too,' he said. 'She thought she could give me pleasure only when it suited her. Not when I wanted it.'

Amid her agony, Salima could imagine him. The charming talkative man who became a monster if he didn't have what he wanted. She imagined him raping his own wife.

Salima tried to relax. She stopped resisting, and made as if she was giving in. He grinned and loosened the pressure on her neck. Salima gasped for air. She forced herself not to cringe when she felt his dick between her legs, unable to find its way. Vincent removed his elbow from Salima's neck to steady himself while his other hand worked between her legs.

With practiced speed, Salima held his head steady with so much strength her left-hand fingernails dug through his skin. And, with her right, she drove the bracelet studs into his neck. As the blood gushed out, he roared and twisted his neck. She held him tight, driving the spikes deeper into his flesh.

Vincent pushed himself up, dripping blood on Salima before he crawled away. Still in shock, Vincent pressed his hand against his injured neck. He looked around the room, suddenly a lot more sober.

'It's you,' he whispered. 'You're the killer. You've been killing French soldiers.'

He stood up slowly, watching her movement. The blood seeped through his fingers, but Vincent didn't seem affected. Salima realised she hadn't finished him off properly. Vincent was going to run away.

'Salima!' Salima screamed at the top of her lungs.

Understanding what Salima's call meant, Vincent darted for the door. As Salima struggled to her feet, she heard the boys in the next room move. Vincent opened the door. The boys were too late.

Salima chased him, but by the time she made it to the balcony he had already disappeared down the stairs. One of the boys darted past her. The other two stopped outside her room.

'Are you alright?' one of them asked.

'What happened?'

'Just get him. We can't let him go. He knows everything.'

The two boys headed for the stairs, and Salima followed. Vincent ran for the front door, and the Ouled Brahim boy followed him, splashing in the rainwater, before he threw himself on Vincent. The two men fell to the floor, and Salima held her breath.

Vincent turned around and kicked the boy in the face, hard. The boy fell over, and Vincent scrambled to his feet and fled out the door. The two other boys finally arrived. One of them followed Vincent and the other stopped to check on his friend.

Salima dashed down the stairs, vaguely aware of Saadia standing by the living room.

'Both of you get up!' she shouted as she ran past the two boys in the courtyard. 'We can't let him go.'

She went out in the rain, looking right and left and right. The street was empty. Both Vincent and his pursuer had disappeared.

The two boys joined her outside, looking at her, waiting for her to tell them what to do. This was beyond their instructions. They had never done this before. Neither had she.

'We can't do this alone,' she said, 'I'll go down this way towards the Street of Joy. You take this way and see if you can find them. Your friend will need help.'

She looked at the other boy, the one whom Vincent had kicked in the face.

'You. Go back to Mouloud. Have him send as many men as he can. We need to find Vincent before he runs into anyone in Bousaada.'

The two boys bolted, and Salima dashed towards the Street of Joy.

iv

Salima looked for any sign of the two men passing this way.

Vincent was bleeding, she knew, but if any drops had fallen here, the rain had washed them off the cobblestones by now. Still Salima pressed on, her underdress soaked by rainwater.

It was on the Street of Joy that she saw the first footprint on the muddy road. It looked like a boot, thick and heavy. Next to it was another footprint that must have belonged to the boy who was chasing Vincent. She didn't even know his name.

The footprints led her down the Street of Joy towards the oasis, and she was past Hadda's haouch when she saw him. The man lay on the ground, twisting and writhing in pain. Salima ran to him.

It wasn't Vincent. The Ouled Brahim boy had a young face despite the size of his body. Salima felt a twitch of guilt. His body twisted in a pool of blood flowing from his mouth. He had a large gash across his stomach.

Wincing, the boy pointed toward the oasis. 'That way.' His throat gurgled. 'He's injured.'

The boy must have caught up with Vincent. He might have been brave, but Vincent was bigger, stronger, and trained for combat. Killing French soldiers had been easy when they took them by surprise. Now, Vincent was prepared and dangerous.

Salima stood in the rain watching the poor boy suffer. She didn't know what to do. He wasn't going to make it.

'Go,' he managed to say. 'Go.'

Tears springing to her eyes, Salima went toward the forest, treading carefully in the mud.

What have I done? Her hesitation had turned into a disaster. A young man was dying. She'd risked the lives of everyone involved. This was all her fault.

She tried to focus on finding Vincent. She could still prevent another massacre if they found him in time.

The oasis was dark and muddy, but Salima knew her way perfectly. Vincent was at a disadvantage here. And injured. But the place was large and dark, and he could be hiding anywhere.

The river gurgled in the distance, rippling and splashing louder than usual. It sounded alive. Salima strained her ears to hear anything.

And there it was. Underneath the burbling river and throbbing rain she could make out a groaning. She followed the sound.

Vincent's silhouette was barely visible leaning against a palm tree with his hand pressed against his hip. He was clearly too weak to walk, but he held a glinting dagger out in front of him, ready to slash at her if she came close.

Salima watched from a distance as he breathed heavily. She had no idea what to do. Would Mouloud's boys arrive in time to help her? He was badly injured. Maybe if she remained here, he would eventually crumble in on himself.

' So it is you, isn't it?' Vincent said between breaths. 'You have a whole operation going. Killing French soldiers.'

'Were you with Colonel Dupont? When he was out massacring villages back in the spring?'

She didn't know why she had asked. Would she feel better if he said yes?

'Yes, I was there with him every day. Burning down tents. And raping women. And murdering children.' Salima was horrified. He said it with such calm and bitterness. 'And I'm glad I did. Because killing you barbaric monsters is the only way to prevent you from killing us. Those vermin you call children can't grow to become murderers like you. They're dead.'

She wanted to cry, but she didn't allow herself. Not in front of him.

'Shut up,' she shouted.

'Did we kill your family?'

'Shut up.'

'Your parents?'

'SHUT UP!'

'Your brothers? Sisters?'

'SHUT UUUUP!'

'You should've seen the shock in their eyes. Couldn't understand why we were killing them. What had they done?'

'Shut up, shut up, SHUT UP,' she screamed as she plunged at him, 'SHUT THE FUCK UUUUUP!'

Vincent didn't move. He kept looking at her. Grinning. He was saying something, but she was no longer listening.

As soon as she was within reach, he slashed his dagger at her. She tried to stop at the last moment, but it was too late. The blade cut her arm. She tried to back away, but her feet slid beneath her and she was on the ground.

Vincent dropped on top of her and pushed the dagger against her neck. He could have made up the whole thing about the massacre. He had enraged her so she would come to him, angry and reckless. A weak prey.

She brought her hands to her neck and tried to push away the dagger. Surprisingly, it was easier than she expected. Vincent's body was heavy, but he offered little resistance against her push. Grasping the blade, her fingers were bleeding, stinging, but she pushed harder still until the blade touched Vincent's neck.

His eyes, up against hers, widened. He was too weak. She drove the blade through his neck, slitting it open.

His blood spilt onto her chin and chest, mixing with her own.

She pressed harder, and the slit widened. His grip weakened as more blood leaked out of his cursed mouth. Then his head dropped and his body slumped on top of Salima. She closed her eyes, letting the rain wash the blood off her face.

'For my mother,' she whispered in Vincent's ear.

v

Salima couldn't tell how much time had passed before she heard feet mushing mud and splashing water. The night was still dark, and the rain hadn't ceased. Vincent's body was still on top of her, like lovers after sex.

'They're here,' someone called out. 'Hurry up. They're here.'

He pushed Vincent's corpse off Salima before others arrived to help her up.

'Are you alright?' he asked. She coughed in response.

'We have to get rid of the body,' a second man said.

'We can't take him back to town,' the first man said. 'It's too risky.'

'What do we do?'

'The river,' the third man said.

She recognised that voice.

'The tide is high. If we throw him in, his body will flow down into the middle of the desert. No one will find him.'

Salima's heart sank. Was it possible?

The voice belonged to Mourad. Was he part of this too? How? Then it all made sense, like a key in a keyhole.

Mourad had come out of his depression for a reason. The Ouled Brahims had offered him a way to avenge the death of his family, and he took it. But had he known about Salima's involvement too?

The three men agreed to Mourad's plan, so they picked up Vincent's body and threw it in the river. The water swallowed it with a splash.

Two other men arrived carrying another body. 'What do we do?' one of them asked. 'He's dead.' The corpse belonged to the boy Salima had left on the Street of Joy.

'We should throw him in the river, too,' someone said gravely. 'We can't risk taking him back through town.'

Salima was overwhelmed by guilt. She was responsible for the death of this young man.

'What's his name?' Salima asked no one in particular.

'Hakim,' a man replied.

They dropped Hakim's body, and the river swallowed him too, mercilessly.

Salima sobbed.

'Salima?' Mourad asked. 'Is that you?'

Twenty-four

i

Salima was grateful for the clear blue sky.

It hadn't rained since that cursed day she went up against Vincent. Today it was sunny, and the air no longer smelled of wet dirt. Salima hoped it would remain that way.

Salima was combing Fahima's hair on the rooftop above the animal shed. Fahima sat on a rug, legs crossed, and Salima sat behind her on a low wooden stool. A spark of pain shot through Salima's palm.

'Your hands?' Fahima asked.

'Yes,' she said. Her palms were healing nicely, but they still hurt each time she flexed her skin. 'They're going to leave scars,' Salima added.

It would be a memory of how close she had been to death, again. Two thin lines where the dagger cut through her hands.

'It's going to be difficult to hide them,' Fahima said.

Salima's comb ploughed through a knot in Fahima's hair and her sister winced.

'Maybe we should give you matching ones on your hands,' Salima said half-jokingly.

'I already have an unfinished tattoo to hide.'

'That sounds miserable.'

They fell silent while Salima weaved through Fahima's left braid, crossing one thick strand tightly over another.

'Alexandre knows about my tattoo,' Fahima said.

'The painter?'

'Yeah. When the whole fight was happening here,' Fahima went on, 'I stayed back at Mouloud's café after you left, then I went to Alexandre's house for the painting. The rain must have wiped the kohl off my face and that was the first thing Alexandre noticed when I arrived. I couldn't think of anything to say.'

Salima finished the left braid, tied it with a strip of cloth, and moved to the right.

'You're not going to say anything?' Fahima asked. 'You're not going to call me naïve or a stupid fool?'

Salima stared at the small date palm grove behind the animal shed, probably the only unoccupied piece of land in this part of town. To her own surprise, she wasn't angry.

'Is he going to show it in his painting?' Salima asked.

'He wanted to. He thought it was so intriguing, and when I told him the story behind the tattoo, he found that even more exciting. But I managed to talk him out of it.'

'Just don't tell Yemma,' Salima said.

She tied the second braid, and patted Fahima's head to indicate she was done. Salima dropped down to the rug while her sister struggled to take her place, all moans and groans.

'You sound like a woman with her belly up to her chin,' Salima said.

Fahima jerked Salima's hair in response. 'Try having a baby about to burst out of you, and then we'll see what you sound like.'

Fahima's pregnancy was still a barely visible bulge, but she could go into labour any time now.

'You think it's going to be a boy or a girl?' Salima asked.

'I hope it's a boy. I want him to look like his father.'

'Oh, you stupid fool,' Salima was obliged to say. 'He'll have bulging green eyes like Djamila, I'm sure.'

When Fahima had told Salima and Mother about her pregnancy, no one scolded her for her recklessness. The three women had been too stuck in the thick of mourning to summon any anger at her. And now Saadia was even excited about the baby. It was giving her a reason to hold on to life. Salima was happy to see her mother living again.

As if hearing Salima's thoughts, Fahima said, 'I bet Yemma wants a girl, though.'

'Or two. She'd teach them to sing and dance before they grew teeth.'

They fell into silence again. Salima traced the cut across her palm.

'It was my fault,' Salima said out of nowhere.

'How do you mean?' Fahima ploughed through the knots in Salima's hair.

For the first time, Salima told her sister about her hesitation to kill Vincent, which led to his escape. She didn't know why she was telling this story, but she felt better now that she had. A weight lifted off her chest.

After her own blunder that had brought them all close to the end, the tattoo incident seemed like a triviality.

'But you stopped him,' Fahima said. 'The secret is still safe.'

'Yeah, but that boy, Hakim. He died because of me. Because I hesitated.'

'You didn't kill him. And it could've been worse. That soldier could've escaped with the secret, and the French army would've fallen on us all.'

Salima nodded. Her sister, the stupid fool, was now offering words of wisdom. She could never have imagined this moment.

'You know what?' Salima said. 'Sometimes I'm not even sure we're any different from the French. I mean for all we know, the only reason they attacked our village was because we killed two of their men. Yes, the first one was an accident, but does that really justify anything?'

'Salima, they killed innocents. Kids and old people.'

'All to avenge Cambron. Remember what Khalti Baya told you on our first night here? Something about darkness and death?'

'I see a lot of death and fire,' Fahima repeated the guezzana's premonition. 'I see darkness, and the living sleeping with the dead in the dark. You'll be our downfall. You and your sister will bring death and misery to this town.'

Salima was surprised Fahima remembered the prophecy word for word. She, too, must have thought about it often.

'You think she knew what she was talking about?' Salima asked.

'We have seen an awful lot of death since then.'

'We haven't seen any fire,' Salima said. 'And we haven't slept with the dead.'

'Not yet. Or maybe she meant we'd sleep with people before we kill them?'

Fahima had a good point.

'Didn't she tell your stupid French lover the fire would eat him, too?'

'Maybe it did. We wouldn't know if it happened,' Fahima said.

Salima sensed sadness in Fahima's voice.

'What should we do?' Salima asked. 'Just keep killing the French?'

'Do you think the Ouled Brahims would let us quit?'

'They said we could stop anytime.'

'That was before we knew so much. What if they kill us? Or deliver us to the French?'

'The French might catch us anyway, and then we'll all die.'

Fahima sighed. 'I don't want to die,' she said. 'My baby.'

'Salima! Fahima!' Saadia hollered from downstairs. 'Time to go. Zeyara time is almost over. Which of you's coming with me?'

'Salima's coming,' Fahima called back without consulting her sister. 'She really needs that zeyara right now.'

ii

The zeyara was far from over when Salima and Saadia made their way up the small rise upon which Etienne Dinet's koubba was built. Scores of people were still picnicking outside the small white building with a cone-shaped dome. The ground had dried up, and local women came out with their kids who ran around giggling and screaming. Some Nailiya dancers were eating and laughing too.

Saadia had brought a basketful of flatbread, and she started handing it out to the crowd of beggars squatting in the shade of the stone wall surrounding the small shrine.

Salima and Saadia joined a long line of women that started at the door of the koubba and wound its way through the groups of visitors enjoying the sun outside.

'This shouldn't take long,' Saadia announced, sensing Salima's impatience.

Salima was amused by the lengths her mother went to observe the zeyara every week, something the old Saadia would never have done. Mother had never raised their family to be religious.

Having spent so much time here, Salima had come to learn that everyone in Bousaada identified with the Muslims, Christians or Jews, but her family didn't identify with any of them.

Many of Salima's clients had asked about her religion, but she never knew how to answer. One customer once tried to convince her that Ouled Nails had once been Muslims, but they had grown so out of touch with the rest of the world that they had forgotten about it and fallen into sin and vice. Another client had mockingly declared that all Ouled Nail dancers worshipped only one god: Money. Salima actually found that more plausible.

No one back in her village ever prayed to a god, and no one told her what she could or couldn't do in the name of religion. A lot of people believed in the word of *guezzanas* and gave money to healers though. They thought certain waters were holy and wiped their hands on a piece of cloth stuck on a tree for its miraculous blessings. But Saadia had never done any of that, and she hadn't raised her daughters to do it either.

Not the old Saadia anyways. The new Saadia was different. The new Saadia would never miss a zeyara.

257

When it was their turn to go into the koubba, Saadia and Salima kneeled on either side of Etienne Dinet's tomb. Dozens of candles had been lit on a raised ledge and practically on every flat surface inside. The deceased artist had been highly respected in his life, and because he converted to Islam prior to his death about seven or eight years ago, he was now a popular saint. Many people came here seeking his blessings and praying for their wishes to come true.

The outside noise was instantly muffled inside. Saadia lowered her head and started murmuring rapidly. Salima wondered what her mother was whispering, but when she saw the tears flow down her face, she knew, with a stab to her heart, that Saadia was praying for the souls of her husband and two children.

Salima lowered her head, too, looking at the rather small grave covered in white tiles and some Arabic inscriptions. She wondered if this dead man really had the power to answer her mother's prayers. She hoped so.

Salima didn't have any specific wishes of her own, but she enjoyed the quiet. The world went still while they sat in that dim light.

On second thought, Salima did have a wish. She wished for this serenity to last longer. For all this suffering to end. For all the death and killing to stop. She wished she and her sister could just wake up one day and not have to fear for their lives. That she could simply start a family with Mourad. She wished to go back in time and undo everything. To go back to the night they had killed Cambron.

But as she voiced all these wishes in her mind, Salima knew perfectly well that it wasn't up to this dead artist interred in front of her to answer her wishes. It was up to her to put an end to all of this.

All she had to do was stop the killings.

An overwhelming sense of peace settled over her. Mountains she hadn't known she'd been carrying crumbled off her shoulders.

iii

Salima was still relishing that peace later that evening, and she didn't go to work at Mouloud's. Mouloud could serve all the red glasses he wanted. She wasn't going to kill anyone tonight.

Fahima didn't go tonight either. She went to her painter. Alexandre was almost done with the painting apparently, although Salima had been hearing this for weeks now.

Salima strolled around town with Mourad like tourists, something she had never done at night. They stood outside cafés listening to music and watched tricksters and dancers perform outside the gate. They bought makroudh from a street vendor and ate it, dripping honey down their chins.

'You're no longer mad at me,' Mourad said as they made their way up the main street for the fourth time that night. He smoked his cigarette and tapped his cane on the cobblestones.

'I should've never been mad at you in the first place,' she said.

Salima had been mildly cross with Mourad since she had discovered he had joined the Ouled Brahims. Of course she had known all along that she had no right to be angry with him for hiding it from her, especially because she herself had kept bigger secrets for months. She had mostly been worried about his safety.

'I think I'm ready to get married,' she said, surprising both Mourad and herself.

Mourad stopped and turned to face her.

'Are you sure?' he asked.

Right then, Nouara walked between the two of them with a young man in a black suit, clearly a tourist she was taking to the haouch.

'Looking brighter than ever, Ammariya,' Nouara teased without stopping to look at Salima. 'It was that good, huh?' She was referring to sex with Mourad.

'Looks like you're about to get brighter, yourself,' Salima called back.

'I always look bright, sweetheart.'

By then Nouara was too far for Salima to call something back. The client followed close on her heels. Salima turned back to Mourad, intending to pursue the conversation she had been avoiding for over a year now. Two more men, French soldiers, one young and one older, walked between Salima and Mourad before she could say anything. Annoyed, she pulled Mourad to the wall so no one could interrupt them.

'Yes, I'm sure,' she said. 'I want us to get married. To get out of this once and for all.'

Something started to bother Salima in the back of her mind, but she couldn't tell what.

'What changed?' Mourad said. 'Why now?'

'Are you having cold feet?'

The thing in the back of her mind was growing, faster, taking up more space, threatening to spill over.

'No, I'm honestly thrilled,' Mourad said. 'But I want to make sure this is what you really want.'

'Oh fuck,' Salima said. 'Nouara!'

'I should've known this was a joke,' Mourad said, dispirited.

'No, no, no,' Salima said while she stretched to look down the main street for any sign of Nouara. Nothing. 'It's Nouara. I think she's in danger. We have to warn her.'

Salima darted down the main street. Mourad, dumbfounded, followed.

Salima turned left towards the Street of Joy. She was almost sure Nouara had been headed to her *haouch*, but she could have taken any turn.

Mourad tried to keep up with her, asking what was wrong. She had no time to explain. She pushed past throngs of people. She had to find Nouara before it was too late.

It had been right there in front of her. But somehow Salima had missed it. Two French soldiers were following her, and Salima had seen that look of desire and anticipation on their faces. They were following Nouara to catch her in the act. Many girls had been arrested that way over the past year. Salima had to warn her.

She continued to shove her way past people, looking every which way. Nouara was nowhere to be seen. She had to have taken another route. That wasn't too bad, Salima told herself as she neared the Street of Joy. She might get there first and wait outside Nouara's haouch. Salima couldn't hear Mourad behind her anymore.

The Street of Joy was unusually quiet when Salima emerged from a narrow alley. It wasn't empty. It was as crowded as usual, but everyone was still. They were all watching something. Salima followed the bystanders' gazes until her eyes fell on Nouara and her heart sank.

iv

Nouara was standing in the middle of the street with her client facing the two soldiers that had been following them. Nouara looked tense.

'I said I'm not working,' Nouara told the soldiers. 'Leave me alone.'

'I see you're working for this man just fine,' the younger soldier said, pointing to the client. Salima knew he was drunk; his speech slurred.

'He's just a friend,' Nouara lied, but the soldiers weren't buying it.

'We want to be friends, too,' the older soldier said and chuckled. He tried to grab her wrist, but she jerked her arm away.

Completely unaware of her own movements, Salima found herself approaching the commotion. She forced herself to stop, racking her brain for how to help Nouara. She came up empty.

Nouara's client stepped between her and the two soldiers.

'Listen, boys,' he commanded, trying to calm the situation. 'I'm sure we can work this out like civilised people.'

Salima rolled her eyes. What is it with French people and civilisation?

'We're not talking to you, boy,' said the older soldier, stepping closer. 'Why don't you get out of the way like civilised people, and let us deal with this?'

'She's with me,' said the suited man, starting to lose patience. 'Why don't you go find other girls? There's plenty of them on this street.'

'We want this one,' said the younger soldier. 'Go get yourself another girl.'

The younger soldier looked around and his eyes fell on Salima. Before Salima had a chance to act, the man was upon her. He grabbed the back of her neck and, effortlessly, pushed her at Nouara's client. The stench of alcohol was heavy on the soldier's breath.

'How about this girl?' he asked. 'Take her and get out of here.'

The client stepped aside, letting Salima go past him until she was next to Nouara. The two girls exchanged a fearful glance.

'I'm going to report you to your supervisors,' the client told the soldiers.

'Oh, ho ho. We're so scared. Why don't you...'

Salima pulled Nouara's hand and backed away. 'Let's get out of here,' she whispered.

Nouara stepped back. When the two girls were some distance from the men, they broke into a run.

'They're running!' someone called behind them, but Salima didn't stop. She ran faster.

Nouara was close behind, and not too far, were too many footfalls. Salima lifted her dress and threw all her might into her strides.

A scream pierced the night air and Salima stopped and turned around. The young soldier was pulling Nouara's braid.

The tourist came to her rescue, pressing his body between her and the young soldier, but it did nothing. He pushed the soldier back, but the soldier kept Nouara's braid in his hand, drawing her back with him.

Out of nowhere, a fist hit the client right in the face and he dropped to the ground, nose bloody. The older soldier had punched him.

'Ready to go?' the older soldier told Nouara.

A confusion of memories swept Salima's mind. Naima bleeding and bleeding and bleeding, Bernard shouting, Cambron's weight on her chest as he fumbled with his pants, Vincent's blade in her hands.

She lunged at the soldier, hitting his chest and screaming. 'You let her go you son of a bitch. Leave her be. Salaud! Let her go! Connard!'

With one foul swipe of his left arm, the man pushed Salima away with such force she felt her chest collapse. Stepping back, she stumbled on a stone and fell. Salima scrambled back onto her feet, picked up the stone she had stumbled on, and lifted it in the air, ready to spring at the attackers again. But she stopped when she realised everything had changed.

Drops of blood fell on Salima's face. The cut in her hand had opened and was bleeding, but she couldn't have cared less.

Nouara had been freed, and the two soldiers were engaged in a violent brawl against two other men. One of them was the client, his black suit already torn and dirtied, and the other man, to Salima's horror, was Mourad.

Mourad slammed the young soldier with his head, right on the nose, but the soldier fought back, throwing punches and kicks at Mourad. Mourad gave his opponent a low blow in his side then one to the temple. The soldier staggered a little, but when Mourad came at him again, the soldier tucked his knee and hit him between the legs. Mourad folded over in pain. The soldier kneed him again, this time in the nose, sending Mourad to the ground.

Salima, with the stone high above her head, lunged at Mourad's opponent from behind. The soldier was kicking Mourad in the ribs when she drove the rock down as fast and as hard as she could. The stone hit the back of the man's skull, exploding into small fragments. Salima's weapon was weaker than she had assumed, but the blow had left enough damage.

He turned to face her, his hand on the back of his head. He was furious, and stepped forward, ready to hit her.

One instant the soldier was coming at Salima, and the next one he was on the ground with another man. It was one of Mouloud's boys. He straddled the soldier and started punching him in the face.

Not far from Salima, another of Mouloud's boys was fighting the older soldier. The tourist was on all fours, writhing in pain. Salima went to help Mourad stand up.

But she was swept back by another man dashing past her. A French soldier, rushing to his countrymen's aid. Yet another Frenchman arrived and started kicking Mourad in the ribs, right where the first soldier had left off.

'Stop!' Salima yelled. 'Stop, stop, stop, STOOOOOOOOOOOOOP!'

Her voice was drowned out by the commotion. No one was listening.

Nouara, finally regaining her wits, came to Mourad's rescue. She pushed against his attacker, but her body couldn't budge the monster. Salima looked for another stone or anything, but there was nothing but pebbles.

The fight had grown so big it looked like a battlefield. At least thirty men, French and locals, were throwing kicks and punches at each other. Nouara and Salima weren't the only girls involved in this brawl, either. At least four or five other dancers were hitting French soldiers, trying to help their men.

Mourad was still wriggling and twisting as the soldier repeatedly drove his boot into his ribs. Salima shook her right bracelet until the spikes faced inward, and she jumped on Mourad's attacker. She planted the two spikes in his neck.

They didn't go deep enough.

He stopped kicking and turned to face her. He saw his own blood on Salima's bracelet and he slammed her in the face, sending her reeling. Salima's hands shook as she fixed her bracelet again, ready to lunge right back at him when two sets of strong arms grasped her shoulders from behind.

The two men twisted her arms easily, and she felt cold metal against her wrists. These were no bracelets, she realised, as she tried, in vain, to wriggle herself free. The men had put her in handcuffs. Panting, Salima had no more fight left in her.

Around her, tens of French soldiers had joined the scene, overwhelming the locals. Three men lifted Mourad off the ground, throwing in some more punches and kicks until they put him in handcuffs and threw him back down on the ground. Nouara, too, was trying to free herself from the grasp of two men, her legs kicking the air like a cockroach turned upside down.

The other Ouled Nail girls who had joined the fight had all been handcuffed, and so were Mouloud's boys. The two last ones still kicking were outnumbered by a dozen French soldiers who were enjoying taking turns against the boys before arresting them.

The suited tourist walked away, and the French soldiers hauled everyone else to the military circle.

Twenty-five

i

The autopsy report arrived on Saturday morning, but Colonel Joseph Dupont had left clear instructions to inform him at home no matter what day or time the report came in.

I've been trying for years to get them to stop bothering me at home, Joseph thought, and now I'm excited to be brought in on a Saturday morning.

Four days ago, they had found two bodies stranded on the riverbank a few kilometres outside of town. One belonged to an Arab, and the other a French soldier. These were the first bodies they had found since the first Frenchman had gone missing, and Joseph hoped they would help him find the culprits.

The discovery confirmed one thing everyone had assumed: someone was targeting the French. Now the autopsy report had better reveal a lot more.

On the third floor, Joseph found Major Turrene in the meeting room with two men from the morgue. They rushed through the military salute before Turrene introduced the two officers as Dr. Sorraine and Dr. Roguette.

'Brief me,' Joseph said, 'What did the bodies tell you?'

The three men seemed to have already started going through the report. The table was covered with unorganised folders, papers and pictures.

'Our assumptions were mostly right,' Dr. Sorraine started with a rusty and annoyingly slow voice. 'The bodies belonged to a French officer, identified as Officer Vincent Galou, thirty-nine years of age, and another Arab man, about twenty-one years old. We still haven't confirmed the identity of the young Arab.'

It had been easy to identify the body of the French soldier – Joseph kept pictures of every officer who had gone missing – but he didn't allow anyone to contact the Arabs to identify the other body. Whoever dumped the corpses in the river had clearly intended for them to stay hidden, and Joseph had no intention of alarming the perpetrators yet. Not until they knew more.

'Both bodies suffered severe injuries,' Dr. Sorraine went on, 'from a sharp object, a long knife or dagger we're assuming, which led to their death. The bodies travelled several kilometres through water judging from the post-mortem bruises they suffered from rocks and other solid objects. We're assuming they were dead before they were thrown into the water upriver, presumably very close to town. The high tide caused by heavy rains last weekend made it easier for the corpses to travel that far.'

None of this information was new to Joseph, and he could hardly contain his impatience. He didn't care about the hows, he needed to know who.

'Judging from the decomposition of the bodies, we're assuming the killings occurred on the night of October nineteenth to twentieth.' That was when the officer went missing. 'And both bodies had other types of injuries due to physical struggle.'

'So the two men fought each other before dying?' Turrene asked.

'We know they've fought, probably with each other, but also with other people,' Dr. Roguette answered softly.

Dr. Roguette flipped through the files until he found a picture. He held it up in front of Joseph. It showed bluish dark skin with bruises. Another picture was a closeup of knuckles with pale white skin and pink scratches. Joseph didn't know what to make of that.

'We believe this bruise on the Arab boy's temple here was caused by a punch from Officer Galou,' Dr. Roguette explained.

'There were other similar matches,' continued Dr. Sorraine, 'but there were also other injuries on Officer Galou that weren't caused by his fight with the Arab.'

Dr. Roguette pointed to three other pictures. They all focused on the scratches on his pale skin; thin pink stripes across his forearm, down his cheeks and on the side of his neck. Joseph found that interesting, but he didn't want to get too excited. He wanted to hear it from the experts.

'These are scratches,' Dr. Sorraine explained, 'that we believe resulted from another aggressor. Definitely not the Arab for his fingernails were too short.'

'Are they...' Joseph couldn't help it.

Dr. Sorraine nodded. 'We're assuming they're women's fingernails. They align with the type of cut that killed the man. The neck slit. It was done in a messy and slow manner, indicating the person committing the crime had neither the physical strength nor experience. We're assuming a woman did it. Or at least a much smaller man than the Arab we found.'

So many thoughts, scrambled and squished, ran through Joseph's mind.

'Probably the most bizarre finding,' Dr. Roguette said, picking up yet another photograph, 'is this injury on Officer Galou's neck. It looks like a snake bite, except it's not.'

Joseph studied the picture. Right above the cut that had slit the French soldier's throat were two tiny holes, barely two centimetres apart – precisely one point seventy-five centimetres according to the wooden ruler placed in the picture.

Joseph had seen a similar injury before.

'Then what is it?' Turrene asked.

'We're not sure yet. It could be just an attempt to distract us. Or maybe a random accident. What we know is that this was caused by a metal weapon with small sharp spikes. Just a little deeper and he would have bled to death. Maybe some sort of ritual that we're not familiar with?'

'Oh, this is no ritual,' Joseph murmured as he took the picture and opened a desk drawer. He found a wooden ruler, put it in his pocket and walked to the door.

'Good work, doctors,' he said on his way out. 'Turrene, keep going through the report. Brief me later.'

Turrene followed Joseph out the meeting room. 'Colonel,' he called. 'Sir.'

Joseph stopped and turned to face him. What is it now?

'Sir, I just wanted to let you know about something that happened last night.'

'Out with it.'

'There was a small fight on the Street of Joy. Maybe a small riot, but we've arrested a number of people, Arab men and Ouled Nail dancers. They're still in the cell downstairs if you...'

'Any French soldiers killed?' This was the last thing Joseph needed right now.

'No, sir,' said Turrene. 'A few were injured, but nothing fatal.'

'Then it doesn't need my attention,' Joseph said, letting his impatience show. 'I have a French officer's body and potentially eighteen other corpses stuffed somewhere. I think that takes precedence. You take care of the small riot, will you?'

'Oui, Colonel.'

Joseph left the building and hurried across Place de Pein. He was finally close to finding the people behind the disappearing soldiers, and, if his guess was right, he had the next piece of the puzzle.

He turned onto Rue Gaboriau and headed back home.

ii

Bernard was still fast asleep when Joseph arrived. He started shouting his son's name the moment he opened the front door.

Delphine rushed to meet him in the foyer, her face creased with worry. 'What's going on?'

'Where's Bernard?' Joseph ignored his wife's question. 'Bernard!'

He rushed up the stairs, his voice roaring through the house, and barged into his son's bedroom.

'Bernard! Wake up!' He drew the curtains, flooding the room with light.

'What?' he asked drowsily. 'For the love of God, it's Saturday.'

Joseph dashed to the bed and pulled his son up by his undershirt. Delphine came into the room.

'What did he do?' she asked, her voice high and squeaky.

This wasn't about Bernard doing something wrong for once. Not lately anyway. In fact, since he'd come back in the spring, Bernard had been nothing but serious, even turning his internship into a part-time job.

'Show me your neck,' Joseph ordered his son, already trying to bend Bernard's head to the side.

'What?' Bernard wiggled to free himself. 'Why?'

'Just show it to me, damn it!' Joseph roared.

Bernard tilted his head with a huff, revealing a scar. Just like he thought: two tiny holes resembling a snake bite.

From his pocket, Joseph produced the picture and wooden ruler. He looked at the picture again comparing the injury on Galou's neck and the one on his son. Exactly the same.

He placed the ruler under Bernard's scar to measure the distance between the two dots. One point seventy-five centimetres. Joseph could hardly contain himself.

'I need you to listen to me carefully, Bernard.' Joseph said, struggling to keep calm. 'What I'm about to ask you is very important. It could help me solve the biggest case in the history of this town. I could stop the killings of French officers. Do you hear me?'

Delphine was still asking what on earth was going on, but Joseph ignored her.

'I need you to tell me how you got that injury'.

Bernard had refused to talk about the incident. Word on the street was that he had attempted to rape a girl, and she or someone else attacked him. Bernard had neither confirmed nor denied any of this, and, refusing to take risks, Joseph had sent him away as soon as Bernard was able to travel.

'It's literally a matter of life or death,' Joseph said gravely. 'My career, too.'

'I don't remember,' Bernard said, embarrassed. 'It was dark, and I was drunk.'

'You have to try,' said Joseph patiently. 'Anything can help.'

'All I remember is that it was a woman. A Nailiya dancer maybe?'

'A Nailiya dancer?' Joseph repeated.

Could Galou's killer be a Nailiya dancer? The same one who had attacked Bernard last year? Everything seemed to be falling into place. But he still couldn't touch anything concrete. It was like trying to reach for a cloud of dust, and it just would not settle.

'Son, were you trying to… get with a Nailiya dancer?' Joseph had to ask. 'I need you to be honest with me.'

Bernard shook his head and lowered his gaze. 'She was just there on the street.'

'What did she use to attack you? Did she have some kind of weapon?'

Bernard shrugged. 'She came at me from behind.'

'Who were you with? Maybe she could remember who attacked you.'

'I don't think she'll tell you.'

'You let me handle that.'

'It was the Jew's daughter,' Delphine said. Bernard and Joseph both looked up at her, wide-eyed. 'Ayash,' Delphine went on. 'Bernard was with his daughter that night. Her name's Yamina.'

iii

Joseph went back to the military circle searching for Turrene. He found him in a waiting room downstairs with the two doctors from the morgue. All three fussing over a French officer sitting on a high stool.

The older doctor – was it Dr. Sorraine? – was examining the soldier's neck. On any other day, Joseph would have pointed out that they should stick to their job of tending to the dead.

'Major Turrene,' he said, standing at the door. Everyone began to salute Joseph, but he dismissed them, 'Let's go. I need you, Turrene.'

Turrene joined Joseph outside the room, 'Sir, there's something you might want to look at.'

'Not now, Major Turrene. There's something more important. Do you know the Jew? Ayash, the jeweller?' Turrene nodded. 'I need you to send for his daughter. Yamina, her name is. I believe she can help us find out more about this two-hole injury.' He tapped the picture in his hand.

'Yes, sir, I will,' Turrene said, and Joseph was about to walk away when Turrene added, 'Sir, about that two-hole injury.' Joseph stopped. 'I think you'll want to see this.' Turrene pointed at the two doctors and the soldier inside the room.

Joseph joined the two doctors studying the man's neck. The soldier had an injury like the one on the picture and the one on his son's neck.

'Sir,' said the younger doctor. 'We're assuming—'

'For scientists,' Joseph interrupted while he fished the wooden ruler out of his pocket, 'you do a lot of assuming, and not enough proving.'

Joseph placed the ruler against the soldier's neck, and his heart leaped. One point seventy-five centimetres.

'How did you get this injury, officer?' Joseph asked.

Turrene answered for him, 'He got it last night during the fight on the Street of Joy, sir.'

'Do you know who gave it to you?'

'Sir, I only remember it was a girl who attacked me from behind. A Nailiya dancer.'

'We arrested five dancers last night, sir,' Turrene said, reading Joseph's thoughts.

'What did she use to attack you?' Joseph asked.

The young man's head was lowered this entire time, undoubtedly embarrassed by the fact that he had been attacked by a woman. He answered with an incomprehensible murmur.

Joseph grabbed the officer's jaw and lifted his head to face him. 'Speak up, Officer.'

'A bracelet, sir. I think she attacked me with a bracelet.'

'A bracelet?' Joseph and Turrene asked at the same time.

'Oui, Colonel,' the officer answered. 'It had these tiny spikes.'

'Can you identify the one who attacked you?' Joseph asked.

The officer shook his hand. 'It was dark, sir. And I was drunk. Besides, they all look …'

'Tell me those sluts are still in the cell,' Joseph asked Turrene, releasing the officer's jaw.

'All five of them,' Turrene said, his smile positively radiant.

iv

Of the five dancers, three had bracelets with spikes. Joseph tasked three officers to interview them all individually, and they also interviewed four or five men as a decoy. The real task was to strip the dancers of their jewellery and bring Joseph the bracelets. That way, he could identify the killer without alerting her or others that this investigation was no longer about the street fight.

'And don't forget to label them,' he instructed.

Joseph's impatience was eating him up. He went upstairs to his office and started going through his notes and files.

From day one, Joseph had suspected that the Ouled Nail dancers had been related to the disappearances. He hadn't known how or which one– there were hundreds of them in town – but he knew they were involved somehow. He had assumed if he killed enough of their folks in their villages it would intimidate them and get them to stop. Little did he know that the disappearances would only increase in numbers. The Ouled Nail were taking revenge.

But never had Joseph imagined that these tiny girls were doing the killing themselves.

Joseph found the folders containing information about the three dancers downstairs. He had assigned soldiers to each and every one of the dancers this past month, and their task was to follow the girls and take notes of their movements, what they did and who they met. Everything. He also had them follow other people including the Caid, Mouloud, the café owner, and Madani, though the latter never hesitated to volunteer information about anyone, including himself, in hopes of gaining favours with Joseph.

Joseph picked up the three folders and his notepad, and made his way back downstairs where Turrene was waiting with news.

'We found her,' Turrene said. 'Of the three spiked bracelets, only one matches the measurements on the injuries.'

'Which one?'

'They call her Ammariya.'

v

Joseph knew of Ammariya. She was one of the more prominent dancers in town, a young beauty with exceptional dancing skills and, judging from her popularity, extensive knowledge of how to please a man.

Was this the murderer Joseph had been chasing all these months? It felt unlikely, but all evidence pointed to her.

Ammariya's file didn't include a picture, but it contained quite a lot of information.

'Let's go meet the killer,' Joseph said, too impatient to read the notes first.

Inside the interview room, the dancer sat behind the table as if she was the one in control. She looked like a mess, her green dress stained with mud and blood and her hair dishevelled. Her makeup was smudged all over her olive skin. All the same, her almond-shaped eyes stared at him menacingly, like Queen Mary of Teck.

Joseph suddenly felt a strong desire to strangle her. But he needed to remain calm. He already had her, but if anyone else was involved in the killings, he needed to find out.

As he dropped the folders and notepad on the table with a dramatic thud, he managed a weak smile, hoping it looked confident, and sat down across from the girl.

'Alors,' he said, 'Mademoiselle Ammariya. Do you have anything to tell me?'

She nodded and said, 'I need to piss.' Her voice was deep and rusty. Her French was broken, and her attitude was savage, just like her appearance. Joseph was tempted to deny her access to the bathroom until she talked, but then he remembered that time another girl just lifted her skirts and pissed right there in the room. So, he chose another tactic.

'Of course. Major Turrene here will escort you.'

Turrene looked at Joseph with incredulity, but he didn't say anything. The girl looked surprised too. She stood up with caution, and Turrene opened the door for her.

Joseph said, 'And do us all a favour and wash your face, mademoiselle, will you?'

While Turrene and the dancer were out, Joseph opened her folder again and skimmed through the notes on the front page. They detailed her working nights in town and when she went away for camps and the people she was in regular contact with.

At first, nothing stood out to Joseph, but then his eyes caught on a particular date: October nineteenth. That was the day Officer Galou had been murdered.

Based on these notes, this Ammariya girl was busy that day. She was seen with her village lover, Mourad the shepherd, then at night she worked at Mouloud's café until close to midnight when she went directly to Alexandre's house and spent the night there.

That didn't make any sense. The two-holed injury on Officer Galou's neck linked her directly to his death. Yet, someone seemed to have had eyes on her that entire day. Were his men getting sloppy?

Maybe this girl didn't work alone. She couldn't. She had to have help. How else would she be able to get rid of the bodies, drag them through town and throw them in the river or wherever else she disposed of them?

There were many possibilities, but Joseph definitely needed to have a word with the painter.

Turrene and Ammariya came back into the room, and the girl stomped to her chair. She had taken Joseph's advice and washed her face. It was still dripping but a lot cleaner, the ugly tattoo prominent on her forehead.

Determined to keep up his approach, Joseph took out a white handkerchief from his pocket, and handed it to her. 'To dry your face,' he said.

The girl's eyes narrowed, but she took the handkerchief and wiped her face all the same.

'How about now, Mademoiselle?' Joseph asked. 'Anything you'd like to share with me about last night?'

Out of the corner of his eye, Joseph saw Turrene shift in his place, unable to fathom why on earth Joseph was talking about last night instead of the killings.

'Like you're going to believe what I say. Your men already told you what happened, and that's the only story that matters to you, no?'

'This is not how you speak to a colonel, young lady,' Turrene roared.

'I still want to hear your side of the story,' Joseph said, his voice calm. He was in control.

'I was walking with my fiancé when we found two drunk soldiers trying to force my friend with them. When I tried to help her out, they attacked me too. Then my fiancé came to my defence, and before I knew it the whole town was involved.'

She said everything at once in a flat tone as if talking about something she had cooked the night before. Then she shrugged as if to minimise the whole fight. A quarrel between children.

'Some of our men were badly hurt, you know,' Joseph said.

'Have you seen my man?' she retorted. She was quick-witted, Joseph noted. 'Have you seen me?'

She opened her hands, and Joseph recoiled in disgust. Two long gashes ran across her palms like they had been slit by a knife. The two cuts were just drying up, their lips coated in some foul mixture of mud and blood.

Turrene, no longer able to contain himself, jumped in, ignoring the wounds in front of him: 'Where were you the night of—'

Joseph placed a hand on Turrene's shoulder and interrupted him just in time, 'That's enough, Major Turrene.'

Turning his attention back to the dancer, Joseph said, 'I need to make something clear, Mademoiselle Ammariya. You cannot attack my men on the street like that. Do you understand?'

Ammariya looked at him defiantly, 'What am I supposed to do when they attack me? Open my legs?'

'You come to me. If anyone tries to hurt you, you come to me. I'll protect you.'

Ammariya snorted. 'Like you protected all those innocent children in my village? The women and helpless old men? That's how you protect people?'

'I did it to protect this town. Someone started kidnapping my men.'

'This town was a lot safer before your countrymen arrived, and it'll only be safe again when you leave.'

This was leading nowhere. The dancer would push back on anything he said. And this conversation had already achieved its purpose anyway. The girl clearly had motive, and she was definitely involved in the killings. He only needed to discover who helped her and he had a feeling she wouldn't tell him of her own volition.

'Very well, mademoiselle,' Joseph said, standing up. He picked up his white handkerchief, now dampened and stained, and folded it gently. 'I have to warn you, though. Next time you attack one of my men, I won't be this forgiving.' He pocketed the handkerchief and looked her in the eyes. 'I'll make sure you regret it.' He turned to Turrene. 'We're done here.'

Joseph picked up his folders and notepad and left the room.

As soon as they closed the door behind them Turrene began to protest but Joseph raised a hand to stop him. 'Listen, Listen. We know she's behind the killings. I'm certain of that. But I also know she has help.'

Joseph explained everything about October nineteenth.

'You let everyone go with a warning,' Joseph repeated. 'But I need you to watch her closely. I need to know where she goes. What she does. Who she meets. Everything.'

'Yes, sir.'

'Now take these to my office.' Joseph handed him his folders.

'Are you going to see the *Caid*, sir?'

'I'm going to see the artist,' Joseph replied.

vi

The painting of Ammariya looked majestic, even though it wasn't finished yet. Despite his current chagrin with both artist and model, Joseph couldn't deny it was a flattering portrait of a beautiful woman.

Sitting down, the girl gazed at something behind Joseph, her almond-shaped eyes wide open as if staring at someone she hated, reminding Joseph of the way she had looked at him just a few minutes ago.

A headwrap rose high on her head, richly decorated with silver trimmings and an ostrich feather. She wore large earrings and two thick looped braids. The dress looked like an upside-down balloon, its long red skirts covering her crossed legs and the white and yellow striped sleeves flaring to the sides.

Ammariya sat straight in the painting, showing off the thick golden belt under her breasts. She held a leaf-shaped wicker fan that only accentuated the grandeur of the scene.

'Why do I have a feeling you're not telling the whole truth?' Joseph asked, turning to face Alexandre.

'But I am,' Alexandre responded. He stood with his arms folded, the side of his mouth pulled up in a half-nervous, half-mocking smile. 'I told you I don't know anything about her involvement with the Ouled Brahims or anything related to killings for that matter.'

Joseph strolled around the studio, casually examining other paintings until his eyes fell on a painting of a dark-skinned boy. Joseph had seen this painting before, and he had seen the model, too.

'Tell me, Monsieur Ivy,' Joseph asked. 'Do you sleep with all of your subjects?'

'Excuse me?' Alexandre asked, sounding genuinely shocked.

'I mean that's the only explanation why you'd hide something from me,' Joseph said, still pretending to study the painting of the local boy. 'You must be having an affair with her and feel the need to protect her. Yes?'

Alexandre said nothing.

'Well, I don't think anyone will chastise you for sleeping with a prostitute, of course. These girls were practically raised for this job.' Then Joseph turned and looked Alexandre in the eyes. 'But I can't guarantee how people would react if they heard about your sexual explorations with the local boys.'

Alexandre bit his tongue. Joseph could swear he saw his shoulders tremble ever so slightly. It was all Joseph could do not to smile.

'What are you talking about?' Alexandre asked, his face growing red.

'You know it's my job to know things, young man,' Joseph said, intending to give the artist the impression he knew more than he was letting on. 'And I'm willing to forget about this secret of yours if you give me what I want.'

'I don't know what you want.'

'I want you to tell me everything you know.'

'What do you think? That these girls go out killing French soldiers then come stand in my studio and confess their sins while I paint them?'

Alexandre was getting worked up.

'Was she here the evening of October nineteenth?' Joseph asked.

Alexandre thought for a moment than he nodded. 'Yes, she was.'

'Are you sure?' Joseph suspected Alexandre was only telling Joseph what he wanted to hear.

'Certain. It was the night it rained, right?' he said. Joseph nodded. 'I remember her coming here so wet that her makeup was all over her face and the fake part of her tattoo had rained away.'

'Did she spend the night here?'

'Yes.'

'All night? She didn't leave?'

'She left at the crack of dawn.'

That didn't make any sense. If she had stayed here all night, how could she have killed Officer Galou?

'How often does she come here?' Joseph asked, taking out a small notepad and a pen. He was going to compare all these dates with the dates of the disappearances.

Alexandre threw his head back and blew air in exasperation. Joseph was ready to threaten him again.

'I don't know if I can remember everything,' Alexandre said.

'Give me what you remember. Start from the most recent date. When did you last see her?'

'This morning.'

'This morning?'

'Yes, she spent the night here.'

'Monsieur Ivy, I need you to stop lying to me,' he said.

'I'm not. She spent the whole night here.'

'I know she spent the night in a cell at the military circle.'

Alexandre looked genuinely stupefied. Then, like a sudden gust of wind, Alexandre's words came back to Joseph.

'Wait a minute,' he said, frowning as he tried to put the pieces of the puzzle together. 'What did you say about the tattoo?'

Alexandre frowned, too. 'What do you mean?'

'When it rained. October nineteenth. You said something about a fake tattoo.'

Alexandre bit his lip, as if realising he had mentioned something he shouldn't have.

'What do you mean the fake part of her tattoo?' Joseph pressed.

Alexandre stared at Joseph blankly for a moment then hung his head and answered, 'She has an Amazigh tattoo between her eyebrows. But...

the lower stroke was never complete. Something happened when she was getting the tattoo. So now she draws that lower stroke with kohl.'

Joseph stepped closer to the painting of Ammariya in the middle of the studio and looked at the tattoo between her eyebrows.

'So when it rained, and it got wet, this little line right here disappeared?' he asked touching the fork-like shape on the canvas.

Alexandre said nothing.

Joseph fished out his white handkerchief from his pocket and unfolded it. Ammariya had used this very handkerchief to wipe her face after she had washed it. Joseph envisioned her coming back into the room with Turrene, her face clean and dripping. The Amazigh tattoo remained untouched between her eyebrows. Could this be possible?

He cast his mind back to the Ammariya who'd sat across the table from him less than half an hour ago. Then he looked at the one in the painting.

'Did she have any cuts on her hand?' Joseph asked. 'This morning or last night. Did she have any cuts across the palm of her hand?'

He drew his finger across his palm to show Alexandre what he meant.

Alexandre shook his head slowly at first, then more quickly as he grew more certain.

'Are you sure?'

'I kissed the inside of her hands just this morning. They were soft as silk.'

He had been right about one thing. Ammariya didn't work on her own. She had collaborators. What he had been missing all this time – what he hadn't even considered – was the fact that there might be two of her.

Two Ammariyas. That was the only explanation. That was how she had managed to be in two places at once. Here in the studio and back in the cell. Dancing at Mouloud's café and killing Officer Galou.

'Oh, we've been fooled,' Joseph said aloud. Alexandre looked at him, puzzled. 'You and I have both been fooled.'

Ammariya has a twin sister.

Twenty-six

i

Fahima noticed the approaching sandstorm when her teeth started gritting on the grains. Only then did her ears pick up the wind howling and the palm trees whispering.

She went up the stairs to the rooftop above the animal shed, looking for a distraction. Fahima was itching to know what was going on out there. Upon her return from Alexandre's home that morning, Mother had told her that Salima had been arrested after some kind of street brawl.

Leaving Fahima at home, Saadia had gone out to see what she could do and had made Fahima promise to stay in case someone came with news.

'And I don't want you out there with your belly up to your chin risking your pregnancy,' Saadia had said before heading off.

Fahima's belly wasn't really up to her chin, but she did feel heavy and slow as a cow, and she wouldn't be much help anyway. So, she had stayed behind, biting her nails and straining to hear a knock at the door.

A shock of pain shot up Fahima's back as she made her way up the stairs. So strong it brought her down on all fours. Fahima was paralysed, her eyes welled up with tears. She had been having some of these shocks lately, but none as bad as this.

Fahima took deep breaths as she scrambled to her feet and continued her ascent to the rooftop. Her back still hurt as though a knife was lodged there, but the pain was dulling bit by bit.

Looking west beyond the little palm grove, she saw it. It was still far behind the distant hills, but the sandstorm raged on, a gigantic brown cloud heading towards the city, low, heavy and angry.

Fahima hoped her sister and mother would get back home before the storm hit.

There was a knock at the door. A light tap. Fahima rushed downstairs and hit the courtyard floor running, dashing through the passageway and almost slamming into the door before she could bring herself to stop.

'I'm here,' she said as she fumbled with the door handle. 'Don't go. I'm here. I'm here. Wait up.'

She swung the door wide open and was about to throw herself out on the street when she suddenly halted. Her heart raced. She felt sick.

'Wha… what,' she stammered, 'what are you doing here?'

'I've missed you, ma chère,' René said.

Fahima was too scared to let herself fall for this illusion. Was she dreaming? Her throat swelled up, blocking the air off from her chest.

'Are you alright?' he reached for her arm.

No sooner had she felt his touch than she threw herself in his arms, sobbing uncontrollably. René took her in and let her cry, soaking his shirt.

'You're alright,' he whispered. 'You're alright.'

Fahima poured her entire misery out. Her tears dissolved the heavy weight she'd been harbouring, one sob at a time, yet the very air seemed to stifle her.

'You left without me,' Fahima said when she finally regained some control of herself.

'It's a long story,' he said.

She led him into the courtyard where they sat down together at the bottom of the stairs.

'You're pregnant,' he announced.

'Almost nine months already.' She touched her belly. 'I think it's yours.'

René's face lit up, then he frowned, as if remembering something sad.

'Were you going to tell me?' he asked.

'I wouldn't know how if I wanted to.'

He nodded gravely, and they both fell silent.

'I saw you,' he said, avoiding her eyes. 'That night after the Ferrero party. We agreed to meet back at Place du Pein.' Fahima remembered. It was the last time she had seen him. 'I collected my stuff and I went to find you. I'd found us another safer way out of town. One of Djamila's clients. He owed me. He offered to drive us to Biskra, and from there, we would go to Algiers or Tunis. Then Paris.

'But when I came here, I saw you with Cambron.' Fahima's heart took a stab. 'I'd warned you about him, and it was very clear to me that he wasn't forcing you or anything.'

René finally turned to face Fahima, his eyes glistening. 'It broke my heart.'

He held her gaze, expecting an explanation.

'It wasn't me,' she said, fully aware that her mother and sister would kill her for saying this, but she didn't care anymore. She had already lost her love once, and she wasn't going to go through it again. She wasn't going to lose the father of her son.

René coughed a half laugh and turned away. 'I saw you,' he said.

'It wasn't me,' Fahima repeated. 'It was my sister, Salima.'

'Your sister?' he frowned. 'You never—'

'We're twins. We've kept it a secret. To cheat the system.'

His eyes widened. "But—".

'After what you told me about Cambron, I went looking for my sister to warn her, but I was too late. He'd already gotten to her. It was her you saw coming home with Cambron. He almost killed her that night.'

'My friend, Jean Larrey,' he said, trying to make sense of everything. 'He told me Cambron was last seen at the café. So if he came here after that, does that mean you—'

'It was either him or my sister,' she said.

'And then there was Mercier,'

'He found out.' She avoided his eyes.

'And all those other officers?'

'They killed my family. My little sister, and brother and my father. They killed hundreds of people in my village and other villages.'

'Oh God, ma chère. What did you do?'

She didn't reply. He stood up and walked around the courtyard. Then stopped.

'Why? Why all the killings?' he said. 'How could you? They could kill you!'

'It may be too late for that.'

'What do you mean?'

She told him about Salima's arrest. She was scared Colonel Dupont was on to them.

'This is too much,' he said. 'I... I have to go.'

He turned to leave, and Fahima stood up. She didn't want him to disappear on her again. Not him too.

There was another knock at the door, then someone started beating it hard. Fahima made to go open it, but the hinges screeched and the door slammed against the wall. Loud footfalls and shuffling echoed through the passageway. Salima and Nouara burst into the courtyard, shouldering Mourad between them.

'Here, here,' Nouara shouted. 'Just put him down here for now.'

Mourad was a mess. His face swollen and bloody, his entire body drooping from his shoulders.

Behind them came Saadia, out of breath. Her eyes immediately fixed on René. She looked at Fahima, demanding an explanation.

'Fahima, bring me a rug and pillow. Now!' Salima shouted.

She and Nouara lowered Mourad down to the floor by the well.

'Let me look at his wounds,' René said.

Fahima felt her mother's strict eyes on her as she went to Saadia's bedroom and brought out a pillow and a rug.

'What happened?' René asked, kneeling at Mourad's side. Mourad groaned.

'We have to get out of here,' Salima said. She took the pillow from Fahima and got down on her knees to place it under his head. 'I think Dupont suspects something.'

'What did he say?' Saadia asked.

'He didn't say anything, but I know it. We must get out of here before it's too late. We'll have to stay out of sight until Mourad recovers, then we'll hit the road.'

'I hope we have that kind of time,' Saadia said.

'We should be fine. If he'd known something for sure, he wouldn't have let me go today.'

'Oh fuck!' Nouara suddenly shouted, her eyes jumping back and forth between Fahima and Salima.

'Who's this?' Nouara demanded Salima, pointing a trembling finger at Fahima.

Before anyone could reply, someone barged through the front door, which Mother must have left open behind her. Everyone in the courtyard looked up in nervous silence as the newcomer stepped out of the passageway.

It was Djamila. A strong gush of wind followed her, heavy with grains of sand.

'The colonel knows,' Djamila announced, looking dazedly from Fahima to Salima. 'Alexandre sent me here.'

'What?' Fahima was lost. 'What does Alexandre have to do with this?'

'It's true,' Djamila said absentmindedly. 'He was right.'

Salima strode to Djamila and shook her by the shoulders.

'Spill it out already!' Salima shouted. 'What was he right about?'

'Colonel Dupont went to see Alexandre, asking about you, and Alexandre might've mentioned something he shouldn't have. He says he's so sorry. He didn't know.'

'Djamila! What did Alexandre tell the colonel?'

'He said something about a tattoo and the injured hands. He didn't know what it meant, but it meant something to the colonel. Only when he left did Alexandre put it all together.'

Alexandre had noticed the missing stroke on her tattoo, Fahima realised. Then there were the two cuts across Salima's hands, which Fahima didn't have.

'Colonel Dupont knows you're twin sisters,' Djamila said, confirming Fahima's fears.

What are we going to do? Fahima asked herself. Things were going too fast.

As if hearing her thoughts, Salima announced, 'We need to move now. We can't stay here and wait for the Colonel to bring this house down on our heads.'

'Let's quickly collect what we need and get out of here,' Saadia said.

'You may not even have time for that,' someone announced from the passage behind Djamila.

Djamila stepped aside allowing Mouloud to emerge. Everyone looked at him expectantly, not knowing if he was threatening or advising caution.

'I came here as soon as I heard,' Mouloud said, addressing Saadia, then he added to everyone in general, 'Colonel Dupont is already putting together a small force outside the military circle. They could be here anytime now.'

The whole place went quiet but for the wails of the winds, scratching sand against walls and windows. Fahima stood close to the well. At her feet lay Mourad, almost unconscious. René had forgotten all about him and was looking at Mouloud, waiting to hear an escape plan Mouloud didn't have. On Mouloud's left Djamila and Salima watched their dresses ripple to the blows of the wind, and on his right Saadia stood silently, her face tired, resigned.

The silence lasted for a brief moment, but to Fahima, it felt like a whole day. It was finally broken by a head-splitting cry that came out of her own guts. A sharp cramp had stabbed her lower abdomen, and it was all she could do to stay on her feet.

'Fahima,' Saadia called, pointing at Fahima's feet. 'Your water just broke.'

Only then did Fahima feel the wetness trickling down her legs. She looked down to see a small pool on the cemented floor of the courtyard.

'The baby's coming,' René announced.

The sandy winds howled in response.

Twenty-seven

i

The wind howled like a pack of wolves, and sand scarred the walls and windows.

Joseph would have preferred a bigger army to overwhelm the dancers and their collaborators, but that would raise unnecessary concerns in town. He didn't want anyone, including the dancers in question, to think he was bringing a huge army to arrest two scrawny girls.

Joseph had finally decided thirty was a good number, but he spared no weapons or ammunition. He even brought two dynamite plungers, several bundles of explosive sticks and rolls of wire. As a precaution, he had placed guards at all city exits and warned his men to be extremely alert. These girls and their collaborators had already killed close to twenty men, and they wouldn't think twice before killing more.

Joseph and his men stole their way among the palm trees. Directly in front of him was a one-storey animal shed with a wooden door and a window looking out on the grove. A man emerged from behind a palm tree, startling everyone and almost getting himself shot. Joseph hushed his men.

'Tell me,' Joseph skipped the pleasantries. 'Can you confirm this is their house?'

'Yes,' Madani said. 'I'm certain of it.'

Since losing the *Caid* position to Malek Kacimi, Fatah Madani had been dying to prove his worth, and Joseph had actually grown to appreciate Madani's skill, especially since *Caid* Kacimi had turned out to be quite useless. Today more than ever, Joseph needed a reliable source who knew his way around this part of town, and he couldn't think of a better person than Madani.

'What can you tell me about the property?' Joseph asked.

'This is the only open area. The main entrance opens onto the street right across from the Jew's house.'

Joseph nodded. The mention of the Jew reminded him of his idiot son and the Jew's daughter. He pushed that infuriating thought out of his head.

It might be difficult to surround the house, but it might be equally hard for its residents to escape unless…

'Are the roofs connected to their neighbouring houses?'

'Most likely, but both neighbouring houses are one floor lower than the Ammariya's.'

Beside Ammariya's house, four one-storey buildings formed a square around an inner courtyard. No one could jump off of Ammariya's roof to that house without inflicting some serious injury.

'How about windows?' he asked.

'The windows are too small for anyone to go through. They're built this way so you don't look into your neighbour's courtyard. They're only there for light.'

Well, that was out of the question. His men could potentially climb up the wall and over the roof, though that would make them very vulnerable to attack. Joseph still needed access to the two neighbouring buildings.

He turned to Turrene and ordered him to take ten men and surround the area.

'Put two men on the main street, but out of sight, then get the residents of both houses to leave immediately and quietly. I don't want to give them any reason to suspect we're here. Clear?'

'Oui, Colonel.' Turrene beckoned ten men to gather around him.

He sent two of them to find discreet locations with a commanding view of the house's street entrance. He ordered four people to circle the Jew's house through narrow alleys and then to evacuate Ammariya's neighbours.

Joseph stayed back, already feeling hot with anticipation. Today he would capture the woman who had been killing his men. The one he had been chasing for months, assuming it was the Ouled Brahims.

Today he would put an end to it all. He refused to be remembered as the colonel under whose watch Bousaada fell into the filthy hands of prostitutes.

'Monsieur le Colonel,' Madani said. 'There's something you need to know.'

Joseph looked at Madani expectantly, squinting against the sandy winds.

'It's about *Caid* Kacimi. He's inside the house right now.'

'Which house?'

'Ammariya's house. I saw him walk in on my way here. I think he's involved. My men saw him talk to two Ouled Brahim leaders more than once.'

Joseph wasn't sure he should take Madani's word for it. Madani had made it his life's mission to take down the current *Caid*. But could this be true? Joseph hadn't liked the way *Caid* Kacimi withheld information, but he had assumed it was out of loyalty to his own people. Joseph cursed himself for also underestimating Kacimi.

'Are you sure he's inside the house right now?' he asked Madani.

Madani nodded.

If this was how Kacimi was going to repay him for promoting him, Joseph wasn't going to show any mercy. He would hit him where it hurt most: his family.

Major Turrene appeared from behind Ammariya's house and gave Joseph a thumbs-up indicating both houses had been secured. Joseph acknowledged Turrene with the same gesture before beckoning an officer to hand him the megaphone.

Raising the device to his mouth, he called out, 'Mademoiselle Ammariya.' His voice amplified and crackled through the large opening of the tube. 'Mademoiselle Ammariya. This is Colonel Dupont. Your house is surrounded by my men. Don't try anything foolish. Do you hear me?'

He listened, waiting for a reaction, a movement, a window opening. Nothing. It was just him and the winds, growing ever stronger. The palm trees around him creaked back and forth, their leaves slashing violently through the air. The street to the north was deserted, and Joseph didn't know if the residents were hiding from the sandstorm or his raid. He guessed it was the latter.

He waited a few more seconds then spoke through the amplifier again. 'Mademoiselle Ammariya. I know you can hear me. Reveal yourself or else I'll enter the house by force. I repeat. Your house is surrounded.'

This time, someone emerged on the roof of the building directly in front of him – the animal shed. Her head raised high, her silhouette floated to the edge of the roof.

It was undoubtedly her. She wore the same green dress from earlier this morning, stained with mud and blood. It rippled fervently in the wind. She stood her ground, confident.

To Joseph's surprise, Ammariya's eyes fell directly on him as if she had known he was there this entire time.

'I didn't think we'd meet again today, mademoiselle,' Joseph said through his amplifier. 'I know you've been killing our soldiers. You and your twin sister.'

He intended this announcement to shock her, but she didn't budge. She stared down at him as if she was the one in control. It bothered him that she had the advantage of the higher ground.

Another silhouette materialised behind her, coming up the stairs. This one moved less gracefully, as if struggling to walk. When she stood next to Ammariya, her red dress rippling in the wind, Joseph realised this must be her twin. They looked identical. The other soldiers also seemed to have noticed for he heard a wave of murmurs around him.

A third person appeared behind the sisters, and everyone around Joseph fell silent. Could it be...? No, this one looked much older, their mother perhaps. She wore a white dress and a matching headwrap.

Looking closer, Joseph thought he recognised her, but he couldn't see her face clearly. Was she involved in the killings, too? The mother took her position between her daughters, and stared back at him.

'Mes dame et moiselles. I advise you to cooperate if you want this to go peacefully. Come out the front door with your hands behind your heads, and we'll take you into custody. I promise you'll be treated with the respect you deserve, but you need to—'

All of a sudden, the three women ducked and headed back to the stairs. At the same time, the small window on the wall facing him opened ever so slightly. Joseph peered through it straight into the mouth of a rifle. Two rifles. Someone moved between the columns in the southern balcony. Something was wrong.

'Take cover,' he shouted through the megaphone right before the firing started.

With the thunder of rifles came bullets swishing. Singing in ones and twos above Joseph and all around him. He plunged to the ground and crawled to the nearest palm tree. His men screamed, and something snapped at the tree trunk to his left.

When he finally found cover behind the palm tree, he tried to survey the area. His men were all crawling to safety. Memories from the Great War stormed Joseph's mind as he watched an impatient soldier get to his feet and break into a run. Joseph was about to order him to drop down when the man took a bullet to the thigh and fell to the ground with a cry.

And just like it started, the shooting suddenly stopped. Joseph stayed still for a moment, breathing heavily and bracing himself for another wave. He couldn't make sense of all this. The women were up on the roof when it started, so who was shooting at them? *Caïd* Kacimi probably, but there were at least two other shooters.

'Madani,' Joseph called out.

Madani was crouched behind another palm tree, his chest heaving and his face glittering with sweat. He turned his head ever so slightly and looked at Joseph from the corner of his eye.

'Was Kacimi alone when he went into the house earlier?'

Madani nodded, lips trembling.

That didn't mean he was alone in there, Joseph knew. He might have brought help with him. Or maybe there were other people helping the killer twins. The Ouled Brahims maybe.

Joseph took another look around him. At least four of his men were down, wounded or dead, but the others had taken cover in time.

Joseph's eyes met those of another soldier near him. 'Go back to the military circle and bring backup. We don't know how many men we're up against.' Joseph was done underestimating the enemy.

The man looked over his shoulder to check if it was safe, then he crawled away, slowly at first, then a little faster. When he was far enough, he got up and ran. Joseph half expected him to be shot in the back, but, to his relief, the young officer made it out of the grove intact.

Maybe two more minutes had passed without hearing another shot. Joseph stood up carefully behind the palm tree and peered at the house.

He couldn't see any movement, but he knew better than to assume the danger had passed. His men rose to their feet as well, cautiously. He ordered them to be ready to fire back, but that was hardly necessary. They already had their fingers on the trigger.

Joseph could start firing at the house to draw out the enemy, but he wasn't sure it would work. The house provided good shelter, and Ammariya's men could easily wait Joseph out until he ran out of ammunition.

He had to destroy the house.

ii

Joseph beckoned three men and had each of them pick up a tank of gasoline. He assigned one of them to the animal shed and tasked the two others with taking their tanks to Turrene for the south and east buildings. He didn't want to risk the north building because his men would be without cover.

'And have him prepare holes for dynamite,' he said. 'Now go to the edge of the grove and wait for my signal.'

One man ran north and the others ran south until they reached the edge of the grove. They stopped and waited.

Joseph ordered the rest of his men to get ready to shoot. He divided them into three groups to allow time to reload while the other group took over. The aim was to overwhelm the enemy and provide cover for the runners.

On his cue the shooting started, and the three men with tanks ran towards Ammariya's house. Bullets tore dozens of holes in the wall, yet no one shot back. By the third round of firing, the soldiers to the south had already disappeared into the small gap behind Ammariya's house, and the one to the north had opened the tank and was splashing gasoline on the bullet-ridden wall.

Someone could shoot the man down at any moment now. He ordered a fourth round of firing and surveyed the buildings. No shots were returned.

The soldier produced a box of matches and tried igniting a stick. The first strike didn't catch. Neither did the second, or third. Joseph cursed under his breath. He ordered a fifth round of fire.

The soldier drew another match. This time it caught fire on the first strike, and no sooner had the soldier thrown the match on the wall than everyone around Joseph erupted into cheers.

'Fire!' he shouted at his men. 'Give your comrade cover, you idiots!'

The outside wall of the animal shed was already ablaze as the brave soldier dashed towards the thick of the grove. To Joseph's surprise, no one attempted to shoot him from the house. It was as if they had disappeared. Joseph's men stopped firing and welcomed their brave comrade with hugs and pats.

Joseph watched as the flames, provoked by the storm, snaked high and angry up the wall. Thick dark smoke rose to the sky.

Joseph waited for any sign of smoke from the other surrounding buildings. A loud guttural wail came from the courtyard. It was a woman, and she sounded like she was in excruciating pain.

Had one of the girls been shot? Was she hurt by the fire? Maybe

Turrene managed to shoot someone from the neighbouring building.

Another scream joined the wailing wind in a bone chilling harmony.

iii

The flames started reaching out of one of the doors on the eastern building across from the animal shed. Between two columns, Joseph could see the upper floor was on fire too. The flames were weak at first, but then it ate through the wooden columns and railings. Soon, the whole building was consumed by an insatiable fire.

A few more minutes passed, and the northern building caught fire, too. The flames hissed as they bit away at the wood. The crackling and crashing mixed with the howling wind.

The southern building hadn't caught on fire yet, and Joseph wondered what had gone wrong. Loud bangs sounded from the gap behind the house. Turrene was hopefully preparing the dynamite.

Joseph watched his enemies' fortress burn. He hoped they were suffering. He couldn't have imagined a better way to defeat them. He was actually glad they had put up a fight. This was so much better than taking them to court. What a spectacle this was. What an example.

Turrene popped his head through the small gap and gave Joseph another thumbs-up. The dynamite was ready. Joseph had two men carry a few bundles of dynamite sticks, and the ends of two rolls of wire. When the rest of the squad fired, the two soldiers made a run for the gap where Turrene was waiting for them.

By the end of the first round, the men were halfway to the gap. One of them stumbled and fell, dropping the dynamite sticks. *Moron!*

The second runner didn't stop until he was safely out of shooting range, the wires trailing behind him. Then, to Joseph's dismay, Turrene appeared from the gap and ran for the scattered dynamites.

You idiot, Joseph hissed, and ordered another round of fire. Joseph's eyes kept jumping from Turrene, picking up the sticks with painful slowness, to Ammariya's house, scouting for potential hostiles.

Turrene finally finished collecting the dynamites and turned to run back to his hiding place. Joseph couldn't see how the enemy could shoot from between the walls of flames, but he didn't take risks. He ordered the third group to fire.

In that very brief moment it took him to issue the order, a man appeared on the southern balcony. He leaned over the railing and aimed his rifle at Turrene. Joseph's men hailed the building with bullets, but it was too late.

Turrene's head exploded while his feet were still moving. He collapsed backward, dropping everything.

Silence fell all around him, except for the deafening shots he had already ordered a fraction of a second too late.

The runner who had fallen stumbled to his feet and, abandoning Turrene and his dynamites, ran for the gap between the two buildings, powered by naked fear. Joseph ordered another round of fire, not sure if to cover the running soldier or to get back at Turrene's killer.

Something had been familiar about the shooter on the balcony. He had ducked so quickly after his single shot he'd barely caught a glimpse. He wasn't an Arab. Joseph had seen that face before. In a photograph. A photograph he had looked at over and over.

Brossolette, Joseph realised. He had thought Brossolette had either deserted or been victim to these killers, like Cambron and the other soldiers.

But no. Here he was. Right here in Bousaada, shooting at Joseph's own men. What the hell had happened to him? A traitor to his countrymen, killing for whores.

Well, Joseph thought, *He's going down with the rest of them.*

Joseph turned at some commotion behind him, and his spirits were lifted by the sight of another squad of over fifty men joining him in the grove. The fight was almost over, but it never hurt to have support. He noticed that Madani was no longer there. The coward must have snuck away when he had the chance.

'Colonel, look,' someone shouted.

Joseph caught a glimpse of a shadow running across the balcony.

Brossolette, Joseph knew. He was trying to flee the blast. Joseph sensed the men around him tense, longing to shoot at the man who had just murdered their comrade, but he didn't allow it. *I want to see that man in pieces*, Joseph thought.

The window of the animal shed, entirely covered in flames, fell with a sizzle. Joseph strained to see through the window, but he couldn't make anything out through the fire and smoke.

Then something fell through the gap. It flew through it, and landed safe and sound. Joseph couldn't believe his eyes at first, but he wasn't hallucinating. It was a rooster. A full-grown rooster.

The rooster stood there a moment, as if he too couldn't believe he had just flown through the wall of fire either. Then he shook his feathers about him and started walking slowly to the north edge of the grove. Joseph followed the bird, amused, as he limped about, nodding his head this way and that until he disappeared down the street.

Joseph turned his attention back to the house. A soldier's face popped through the gap behind it. The dynamite was in place. One minute.

'Sixty seconds!' Joseph announced through his megaphone so his soldiers could take cover. The soldier disappeared back into the gap.

Joseph counted to sixty, then, taking a deep breath, he placed his hands on the handle of the dynamite plunger. Its wires slinked all the way across the grove to the sticks that had been placed in the southern wall of Ammariya's house. He took one last look at the enemy's house, and, with all his might and anger, he plunged the handle down into the box, sending an electric current through the wires.

It took barely a second, but Joseph's entire world slowed down before the deafening blast shook the earth beneath him.

The entire house collapsed in its place, walls fell apart in bricks and columns of wood tumbled down whole onto the courtyard. Shards and stones flew through spirals of smoke. And just like that, the southern two-storey building was reduced to a cloud of heavy dust.

Joseph watched with relish as the air turned murky with the brown of the sandstorm, dark grey smoke and bright red flames.

He waited to see the other three buildings turn into skeletons, darkened by the ceaseless raging flames.

It was almost sundown when the storm finally calmed and the three buildings had all collapsed into the mouth of the hellish fire, turning into coal and rubble. A few neighbouring houses had also caught on fire, but Joseph couldn't care less. He had brought down his enemies, and the Arabs' houses were but a small price to pay.

iv

He stepped gingerly on the rubble and burning debris. Small columns of smoke persisted, swaying in the weak winds of the dying storm.

Joseph's nostrils filled with an aggressive stench. A confusion of grilled meat, something metallic and burnt plastic all in one foul whiff. This was the smell of burning flesh. Human flesh.

Joseph trod carefully, feeling the warm ruins under his boots. Fragile mud bricks crumbled under his weight, and wood snapped and cracked all around him as his men scoured the remains of the building, their weapons levelled in case someone had miraculously survived the blast and fires.

'You're sure no one escaped?' Joseph asked.

'Yes, sir,' someone said. 'We had the entire place surrounded.'

Then Joseph saw them. They were barely recognisable at first, but when he looked closer, they were unmistakable. The skin had entirely burnt and so had most of the flesh, revealing bones here and there and cavities where the mouth and eyes had been. The feet and hands had melted into truncated stubs. Only the teeth had survived, protruding in an eternally mocking smile.

'I count eight bodies,' someone called, then he amended, 'Nine. Ten.'

'Have you counted these?' someone asked, pointing to two bodies under rubble.

'Those are animals,' the first man replied. 'Sheep or goats, judging from their size.'

'Can you tell their gender?'

'Not here. Most of the bodies seem to be too damaged, but maybe if we take them back to the morgue, we could—'

'Never mind that,' Joseph interrupted.

Who cared if these terrorists were men or women? He knew the two murderers were in here, and that was all that mattered. Maybe they had others helping them out, and they had all hopefully met their demise with them.

His attention was transfixed to one female body in the middle of it all. It lay on the floor right by the well, her hands resting on her chest, and her head facing upward. The girl looked as though she was resting, her body radiating so much serenity that she seemed entirely separate from the rampage around her.

She had lain in the centre of the courtyard with enough distance from each of the surrounding buildings that she hadn't been touched by fire. Her skin and clothes had been blackened, though, having absorbed all the fumes and dust and ash, but underneath that thick layer, Joseph recognised the shape of her face. The almond-shaped eyes that, only hours ago, had stared at him so defiantly, had now been forever shut.

Joseph approached carefully, as though afraid to wake her up. He knew she was dead. She had to be. But he had to check one little thing. He stood over her, eyeing her up and down again. Her pose and the thick layer of ash gave her the look of a saint statue made of black granite. It was impossible to believe this tiny creature had managed to murder so many of his trained soldiers.

Joseph squatted over her head and gently rubbed between her eyebrows, her skin unnervingly warm under his touch. The first rub removed some ash but revealed nothing, so he rubbed again and again until he cleaned the better part of her forehead and nose ridge, all reddened by the heat.

To his surprise, someone had beaten him to it. The skin where her Amazigh tattoo should have been had been burnt, leaving only blisters, wrinkles and faint remnants of a dark vertical line. He turned her right hand to see her palm. Also burnt. The left hand, the same.

Joseph couldn't fathom how this had happened. Her entire body seemed to have escaped the fire save these three burns. It was as if someone had done this on purpose. Like a ritual of some sort.

Maybe the Nailiya had intentionally burnt the only proof that she had a twin sister. He wondered if the other sister had inflicted the same burnings on herself before she burnt to death. They might have decided to render themselves one and the same before dying, Joseph thought as he stood up. Erase their physical differences. Freaks.

But Joseph had no way of finding out for sure. The other sister seemed to have been entirely cremated.

Twenty-eight

i

'The baby's coming,' René announced.

Salima followed René's gaze to Fahima's wet feet where a pool of fluid was forming on the cemented floor of the courtyard.

Salima couldn't think clearly. They had to get out of here right now. Fahima's labour couldn't have come at a worse time.

'Can you walk?' Nouara asked. 'We can get away from here and hide somewhere close until you've had the baby.'

'Let me check,' René said, and before anyone knew what he meant, he went to Fahima.

Fahima's face was pale and contorted, but still puzzled as René helped her sit on the staircase and lifted her dress up. Everyone looked away as he parted her knees and reached between her thighs as if it were the most common thing in the world. This was no time for delicacies.

'She can't walk much,' he answered Nouara's question. 'We barely have a few minutes before the baby has to come out.'

'I can do it,' Saadia said to everyone's confusion. 'I can stay here with Fahima and deliver the baby. No one else needs to stay. Run for your lives before the colonel arrives.'

No one moved or said anything.

'Go!' Saadia yelled. 'Now!'

'I'm not leaving,' Salima said. How could she? Her mother and sister. And her future husband, who lay injured on the floor. She couldn't live with herself if she left. 'I've put us all in this situation. I'll stay.'

'I'm not leaving Fahima, either,' René said. 'Not again. I'm a doctor. I can help.'

Mouloud cleared his throat, 'I wouldn't be true to my word if I left you to fend for yourselves.'

Nouara and Djamila exchanged a look of determination and fear. They crossed their arms. It didn't need saying.

Salima's eyes welled up. Not very long ago, she wouldn't have trusted any of these people with anything. Now they were willing to sacrifice their lives for her and her family.

'It's your lives you're giving away,' Saadia said. 'You'll only make the colonel's job easier. He'll find everyone in one place, so he'll kill us all. Take your chance and go!'

Fahima stood up to walk, moaning, her hands pressed against her back.

'We won't make it that easy for him,' Mouloud said. 'We'll fight.'

'With what?' Saadia said. 'Bracelets?'

The outer door slammed against the wall and someone stomped in. Salima's heart sank. Colonel Dupont must be coming to finish them off.

It wasn't Dupont, but Salima was horrified to see two long rifles in the newcomer's hands, pointed downward. It was *Caid* Kacimi, sent by the colonel to do his dirty work for him. To kill them all.

'So, are we going to fight that *roumi* bastard?' the *Caid* addressed everyone.

'Where are all your boys?' Mouloud asked.

'I didn't want to risk their lives. This isn't their fight.'

'Well, we're going to need a lot more rifles than that.'

'Good thing we have them stashed just across the street.'

Without saying a thing, Mouloud left the house. Salima followed him to the door and watched with incredulity as he knocked on the Jew's door. For the very first time, the door was answered by Ayash himself. He opened the door wide and let him in. A short while later, they both came out with five more rifles and a heavy bag which Salima assumed was full of ammunition.

She was at a loss. The *Caid* was here to help them *against* the colonel? And the Jew was involved?

'Do we know how far they are?' Ayash asked as he passed Salima, followed by Mouloud.

'They'll be here any minute now,' Mouloud said.

Salima locked the door behind them and followed them to the courtyard. 'Ayash?' she asked. 'And the *Caid*? How—'

She couldn't even think of a question to ask.

'Who do you think provided all the money and information, Salima?' the *Caid* asked, and Salima almost collapsed. He knew her name?

'And who do you think found out about your secret in the first place?' Ayash added to Salima's bewilderment.

Salima remembered the night they had accidentally killed that first officer. Cambron. She had felt someone was watching from the Jew's house.

'Well, if you're going to stand there and pretend to be brave,' Saadia said, 'will someone please boil some water?'

Djamila and Nouara both darted for the kitchen. Mouloud, Ayash and Kacimi emptied the bag of ammunition on the floor, and they each took their rifle and started working them.

Salima went upstairs and stood on the balcony outside her room where Cambron had fallen to his death all those months ago. She strained her eyes against the sanded winds, looking for any movement in the small palm grove. There was no sign of any colonel or French army.

Downstairs, Fahima paced around the courtyard, her forehead sweaty. Saadia and René followed her, as if ready to catch the baby if it slipped out.

Salima went into her room, spread out a large veil and dumped a few of her most expensive clothes in the centre. On top of the heap, she placed her jewellery and a few pouches of money.

She then went into Fahima's room and picked up her jewellery, too. She found a sand rose and a postcard of the Eiffel Tower that René had given her sister a while ago. She took everything back to her room and threw them on top of the pile.

Salima remembered the sand rose that Mourad had given her, too, so she fetched it from a wooden chest and placed it by Fahima's sand rose. She brought the four corners of the veil together and tied it in a large bundle. She didn't know why she even bothered. It was almost certain they wouldn't make it out alive, but somehow this made her feel better.

Salima picked up the bundle and went out to the balcony. There was still no movement in the grove. Djamila and Nouara had set up a little wood stove in the courtyard to boil water. Mouloud, Kacimi and Ayash were stuffing ammunition into their pockets, and Fahima was leaning against the tiled wall of the well, moaning. René was telling her to breathe, and Saadia held her hand.

Someone was missing. Mourad. He had been lying by the well. His rug was empty. Her eyes swept the courtyard; he wasn't there.

Salima rushed down the stairs and dropped her bundle on the ground. 'Mourad? Mourad? Have you seen Mourad?' No one heard her. 'Where's Mourad?' she yelled louder.

Everyone stopped what they were doing and looked around. Mourad emerged from the animal shed, relying on the doorframe to keep from falling.

'They're here,' he said, his voice hoarse. 'Colonel Dupont and his men just arrived.'

ii

It was happening.

René, who didn't understand a lot of Derdja, seemed to grasp the news perfectly. Still, he walked into the animal shed to confirm.

'How many men?' asked the *Caid*, apparently unafraid.

'I counted about thirty,' Mourad replied. Salima was surprised he could think clearly after the injuries he had suffered last night.

'That means he's not expecting much resistance,' Mouloud said. 'He probably thinks the girls are home alone.'

The *Caid* nodded. 'But he's not taking risks, either. He's prepared to raid the house if we don't surrender.'

'Well, we need to keep them out as long as possible,' said Ayash. 'We need them to think a raid is dangerous.'

'Maybe a few shots will do?' Nouara spoke for the first time.

René came back out to the courtyard and said, 'They've brought dynamite and petrol.'

'Dynamite?' Salima asked. She had never heard that word before, but it didn't sound good.

'It's a bomb. He's going to destroy the house with us inside if we don't surrender.'

'But we can't surrender,' Djamila said. 'They'll kill us if we do.'

'And they'll kill us if they destroy the house,' Saadia concluded.

So, we're dead either way, Salima thought, not wanting to speak it into existence. Everyone fell silent as if they'd heard her thoughts.

The winds were growing louder. Strong gushes smashed against doors and windows, shaking them.

'The well,' said Fahima.

She leaned against it, biting her lip and shifting with pain.

'We can hide in the well until it all blows away,' she added in French.

No one said anything at first. Salima didn't think it was a great idea, but it was the only real one they had so far.

'We could survive there,' René said, 'but only for a few hours. Six or seven.'

'That's better than nothing,' the *Caid* said. 'From the looks of it, we have a few minutes before Dupont starts an attack.'

'That's actually a great idea,' Mouloud said. 'We could fish the bodies out of the well and lay them around the house so the colonel will think we all perished.'

'There are dead bodies in the well?' Djamila asked, horrified. Nouara was shocked, too, and so was René.

Before anyone had a chance to explain, they heard booted footfalls all around them, and they all fell silent.

'They're in the house next door,' Ayash said.

'They're surrounding the house,' René explained. 'They'll probably evacuate neighbouring houses before they attack.'

'Your family?' Moloud asked Ayash.

'I sent them away for the day.'

'Can they come in through the windows?' René asked Salima.

Salima sensed a little discomfort in the way he looked at her. Seeing his lover yet knowing it wasn't her. She shook her head, and said, 'The windows are too small.'

'Well, let's get working,' the *Caid* said. 'Let's start taking out the bodies.'

He walked to the well and started removing the flowerpots decorating the concrete lid. Mouloud, Ayash and Mourad followed suit. Fahima stepped out of their way, and René came to check between her legs again.

'You're almost there,' he said. 'Just take deep breaths.'

'We should deliver the baby out here before going down,' Saadia said, and René nodded in agreement.

The other men placed their hands on the lid of the well and pushed it open without much effort. Salima remembered how difficult it had been for her and Fahima to move that heavy thing. Everyone covered their noses and the strong stench hit Salima by surprise. It turned out all the dirt they had thrown down the well did little good to hide the smell of rotting corpses.

Salima went into the kitchen and brought back a long roll of thick rope with a bucket tied to one end.

'I'm fine,' Mourad said, placing his foot carefully on the iron ladder attached to the inside of the well. His head was all blue and swollen, his left eye closed shut and his lip badly cut.

'Well, wait,' Ayash said. He took the roll of rope from Salima, removed the bucket and tied a knot around Mourad's waist. He pulled to check if it was secure enough. 'Just in case.'

Mourad swung his second leg over the wall and started descending with Ayash feeding him the rope. The rest watched quietly until Mourad disappeared into the darkness.

A loud voice came from everywhere, filled with crackling and popping sounds. Salima thought she heard someone say 'Ammariya,' but she wasn't sure. She strained to hear, and it happened again.

'Mademoiselle Ammariya,' the voice repeated slowly. It was as though the voice was coming from the heavens. 'This is Colonel Dupont. Your house is surrounded by my men. Don't try anything foolish. Do you hear me?'

Salima stiffened.

'We have to get ready,' Mouloud said, as he picked up a rifle.

The *Caid* did the same, and so did René. To everyone's surprise, Nouara picked up another rifle and started inserting bullets, handling it with practiced expertise.

'What are you doing?' Mouloud asked.

'I learnt to use these when I was six,' she said without looking up and when she was met with silence, she added, 'What? Ammariya has a twin sister and has killed dozens of Frenchmen, and you're surprised I can use a rifle?'

No one answered.

'We need to spread out,' René said, changing the topic. 'Take different positions.'

René took the stairs two at a time. When he emerged on the balcony, he walked slowly to the end, staying out of sight, and leaned his back against the far wall.

'Mademoiselle Ammariya,' the crackling sound of Colonel Dupont descended upon them once more.

'We need more time,' Ayash said.

He was struggling with the rope, trying to pull the first body out of the well. Djamila rushed to help him.

'I know you can hear me,' Colonel Dupont said. 'Reveal yourself or else I'll enter the house by force. I repeat. Your house is surrounded.'

'I'll buy us some time,' Salima said, surprising herself and hoping she could deliver on her promise.

She ran up to the roof above the animal shed, the winds scraping her skin with tiny, sharp grains of sand. As her head ascended above roof level, she saw the small palm grove to the west, and in the thick of it, Frenchmen in uniforms stood armed.

Their leader, the colonel, carried a cone-shaped tool in his hand.

iii

Salima stared at the colonel for a while before he put the cone up to his mouth and spoke again.

'I didn't think we'd meet again today, mademoiselle,' he said. 'I know you've been killing our soldiers. You and your twin sister.'

This revelation didn't surprise Salima. She squinted, trying to make out his face, but he was standing too far away. She heard movement behind her. When she turned, she was surprised to see Fahima coming up the stairs, all groans and moans. She wanted to tell her to go back, but it was too late. Fahima was at Salima's side.

Saadia joined, too. She stood between her two daughters and gave the French colonel the stare of death, though Salima wasn't sure he could see it.

Salima didn't know how this was buying them time, but at least the army wasn't attacking yet. That was good.

'Mes dame et moiselles. I advise you to cooperate if you want this to go peacefully.'

'Ammariya,' Djamila's voice came up from the courtyard.

'Come out the front door with your hands behind your heads,' the colonel was saying.

'Come back downstairs now,' Djamila yelled. 'They're ready to open fire here.'

'... and we'll take you into custody,' Colonel Dupont said. 'I promise you'll be treated with the respect you deserve, but you need to—'

Salima, Fahima and Saadia had already lowered their heads and headed back for the stairs. Fahima went down first, slowly and painfully, then Saadia. Salima was just taking the first step when the colonel called through his tool, 'Take cover.'

The shooting started, all of it coming from Salima's house. They had taken the French by surprise. That was good. The plan was working.

Salima felt sick when she spotted the body Ayash had fished out of the well. The flesh looked slick and rotten. Ayash was already hauling the second body.

Someone had also had time to get the two goats and their kid, the chicken and the rooster out of the animal shed. They all huddled in the far corner, sensing the danger.

Once downstairs, Fahima lay on the rug by the well and opened her legs for Saadia to check. Yemma announced the baby was ready to come out.

Saadia waddled into her room and brought back a large bedsheet. She tore it into small pieces using old scissors while Salima used two towels to bring the hot basin off the stove Nouara and Djamila had set up outside the kitchen.

The shooting stopped, and all went quiet but for the storm.

Saadia sat between Fahima's legs and instructed Salima to sit behind her sister. Salima had seen this done before. She sat behind Fahima and rested her head on her sister's shoulder. Fahima's cheek was damp and burning. Salima stuck out a hand on each side of her sister and Fahima clutched her hands.

'Are you ready to meet your son?' Salima whispered.

A wave of tiny explosions echoed outside, followed by muffled bangs. Mouloud and the *Caid* ran out of the animal shed announcing that the French had started shooting back. Nouara, too, came out of the toilet where she had been shooting at the enemy. Behind Salima, Ayash and Djamila were still pulling up bodies, but Salima wouldn't look at them.

From the balcony above, René called out, 'They're lighting the animal shed on fire.'

'Can you shoot them?' Nouara asked, her voice barely audible through the hundreds of shots firing outside.

'I can't,' René called back. 'They're shooting everywhere to provide cover for a man.'

'Breathe, Fahima,' Mother said. 'Take deep breaths.'

Fahima's chest quivered up and down as her breathing grew deeper. Her lips trembled, too. *She's scared*, Salima realised, and she wished she could take her sister's pain away. Somehow inflict it on herself instead. Salima could handle it better.

The shooting outside stopped for a moment, long enough for Salima to hear a cheerful uproar before the firing resumed.

'The wall is on fire,' René announced.

'Push, Fahima,' Yemma was saying. 'Let's do this. Push.'

Fahima's hands tightened around Salima's as her back arched upwards. She let out a sharp whine which grew thicker and louder until it became an ear splitting wail, carrying all the suffering and agony that exhumed from her feverish body. The wail ended in short, shattered sobs as Fahima's hands weakened in Salima's grasp.

'That was good,' Salima said, her voice broken. 'That was very good.'

'Let's do another push.' Saadia's eyes fixated between Fahima's legs.

Fahima pushed one more time, but her strength already seemed to be waning. Salima held her tighter and whispered, 'Come on, Fahima. Push harder. Almost there.'

The shooting had stopped now, another voice sounded from outside. Wood crackling and sizzling. A small column of grey smoke rose from the outer wall of the animal shed. The column was growing wider and darker. *The hay is catching fire.*

'The eastern building is on fire,' René announced from the balcony.

'We need to go into the well,' Mouloud said.

'We're not done yet,' Ayash said from behind Salima. 'We need help.'

Mouloud joined Ayash and Djamila to help them haul out more bodies. Nouara sat by Saadia. She looked between Fahima's legs and her face lit up.

'I see the head,' Nouara cried. 'Come on, Fahima. Keep pushing.'

Salima stole a glance behind her, trying to count the number of bodies they had pulled out without fixating on the rotten skin. There were only four, but as the three of them worked on the rope, the task seemed to go smoother and faster.

Something hit Salima. There was something they hadn't thought about.

'How are we going to open the lid from the inside?' she asked no one specifically.

No one heard her. The lid needed a group of men to push from the outside. Someone standing at the top of the ladder, with only one free hand, wouldn't stand a chance. Salima's heart throbbed in her mouth. The air was growing warmer from the burning buildings on either side.

She asked Nouara to take her place behind Fahima, and she stood up, determined to find some solution. Looking around her, she asked one more time, louder. 'How are we going to open the lid from the inside?'

'What?' the *Caid* asked.

'The lid is too heavy. We can't open it from the inside.'

'That's right,' Ayash said, stopping what he was doing. 'We'll need someone to open it from the outside.'

'But who?' asked the *Caid*.

'My wife,' said Ayash. 'My wife can do that.'

Salima wasn't thrilled about the prospect of having her life in the hands of her cruel neighbour, but Fadhila would be more inclined to help if her husband was down in the well with the rest of them.

'But how will she know where to find us?' Salima asked.

'We have to leave her some sort of a sign.' He stepped away from the well and gazed at it.

'The northern building is catching on fire, too,' René called out from upstairs. 'We have to move!'

Salima didn't need to know which direction north was. Behind her, the building facing the street had caught fire. The entire world was shrinking in on them.

'A pyramid,' Ayash yelled. 'I know how to get Fadhila to look in the well. I'll draw a pyramid on the wall of the well.'

'A pyramid?'

'Yes, when tiles started falling off the wall of our fountain, we removed a few tiles to make a pyramid shape out of the empty tile slots.'

'Do you have a hammer?' Ayash asked.

'No, but let me see what I can find.'

Salima went into the kitchen, covering her nose and mouth. The kitchen's far side was ablaze, and clouds of smoke flew to the ceiling and out to the courtyard. Salima had to crouch to see. She found a brass mortar and pestle and brought them out, coughing. Ayash took the pestle and the *Caid* the mortar, and they both started hammering the tiles off the wall of the well to create a pyramid.

Salima still wasn't satisfied with this plan. She didn't trust this pyramid to save everyone's lives down there in the well.

'It's a girl,' Saadia yelled. 'It's a girl.'

Salima sat next to her mother just in time to see the baby's feet slide out of Fahima. All wrinkled and slick, the baby let out one high-pitched shriek as Saadia covered her in one of the makeshift towels and wiped the liquids off her skin. Fahima's hair stuck to her pale face. She was breathing heavily.

'Get ready to cut her umbilical cord,' Saadia told Salima, coughing a little.

Following Saadia's guidance, Salima used two strips of the white bedsheet to tie two knots on the umbilical cord, close to the baby's bellybutton. She then fished the scissors from the water basin and cut the cord between the two knots.

Salima panicked when blood spurted out of the cord, thinking she had done something wrong, but Saadia assured her it was fine, and she made her dab the cord until the bleeding stopped.

Saadia coughed harder now, and so did Nouara. The smoke was getting to them.

When the baby's crying died down, Saadia handed her to Fahima who held her up to her chest, tears trickling down her face. She touched the baby's lower lip.

'You're so beautiful, baby girl,' Fahima said. 'You have your father's blue eyes,' she added with hushed excitement.

'What do you want to name her?' Nouara asked behind Fahima.

'Farida.'

Salima and Saadia exchanged a look, and Salima glimpsed the pain in her mother's eyes. Salima felt that too, remembering her baby sister.

Salima looked between Fahima's legs and was surprised to see a pool of blood mixed with other murky liquids.

'Is that...?' she whispered to her mother, not wanting to scare Fahima.

'Yes,' Saadia said, 'but *that* isn't.'

She was referring to the weak trickling of blood still oozing out of Fahima. Mother and daughter watched, willing the blood to stop, but it didn't. Saadia dipped a towel in clean water and dabbed the blood.

At that moment, loud bangs came from the back of the house, like hammering on the walls. Everyone stopped what they were doing and looked up at René, who was supposed to be watching the French.

'I think they're preparing holes for the dynamite,' he said between coughs. 'They're going to blow up the building anytime now. Are we ready to go into the well?'

'We only have eight bodies out,' Djamila said.

'That's fine,' René replied. 'They don't know how many people are in here anyways.'

Mouloud called out to Mourad to come out of the well now. 'We need to spread the bodies around the courtyard,' Mouloud said, and he went to work.

The *Caid* and the Jew were almost done making their pyramid, but something still bothered Salima. *How could the Jewess know to look for her husband here in this house? We need to draw her in somehow.*

Salima stood up and looked around. The fire was eating more and more of the space, leaving little to use. The animals crowded in one corner, shifting nervously under the raging fire.

The rooster, Salima thought with elation. *We can use the rooster to send Fadhila a message*. After all the times Salima and her neighbour had argued over the stupid rooster, there was no doubt Fadhila would recognise it. All Salima needed to do was get the little bird out of the house safely somehow with a message for the Jewess.

Salima picked up the grey chicken as the burning building sent gushes of warm air against her face. She needed to get rid of the chicken to ensure the rooster didn't come back to the house.

The chicken offered no resistance, trusting Salima with her life. Salima took a deep breath, and, with a swift move, she twisted the hen's long neck. The chicken only kicked one foot in the air before she fell limp in Salima's arms.

Salima placed the fowl on the floor, allowing the rooster time to realise his hen was dead. The rooster's head twitched right and left, then he pretended to have found something to eat and pecked at the floor. He repeated thick croaking sounds, inviting her to join. He even gave her a brief mating dance, but the chicken didn't budge.

The cruelty of this whole act wasn't lost on Salima, but it might be the key to saving ten people. And a baby. She walked back to Ayash, who was just finishing his pyramid on the wall of the well. She looked him up and down searching for something to use.

The shooting from the palm grove outside persisted. Salima looked up just in time to see René lean over the wooden railing, fire a single shot and pull himself back before the wall behind him was hailed with bullets.

'I think I just killed Major Turrene,' he shouted.

'Aim for the colonel,' Salima replied.

'We have to start going in now. They're placing dynamites in the building.'

The *Caid* finally listened to the French doctor. 'Let's go in,' he said. 'Girls, you go first.'

'I have to stop the bleeding here first,' Saadia said, trembling. 'You take the baby down, and we'll be right behind you.'

'I'll take some goatmilk,' Nouara said softly, as if afraid to offend someone.

Djamila gently plucked the baby off Fahima's breast and walked to the well, ready to go in.

Salima's heart skipped a beat at the sight of her sister's face. It was growing alarmingly pale. Her lips turning blue.

'René,' Salima called. 'Come down here now. You need to help Fahima. The bleeding won't stop.'

René's dashed across the balcony and down the stairs. As he joined Saadia between Fahima's legs, Salima saw the horror in his eyes as they fell on the bleeding down there.

'Oh, mon Dieu,' he said.

iv

Salima didn't want to know what René meant. She watched as he slipped his hand in, then, unable to see the rest, she went back to her task, desperate for a distraction.

The *Caid* and Mouloud were helping Djamila over the low wall of the well and onto the ladder. The baby, Farida, was attached to her back, wrapped firmly with a long strip of sheet. Nouara was ready to go next, with a bucket hanging from her elbow, containing goatmilk.

'Ayash,' Salima called out, and coughed. 'Will Fadhila recognise your ring if she sees it?'

Ayash looked at the thick ring on his thumb, as if seeing it for the first time, then he nodded.

'Hand it to me. Quick.'

Looking uncertain, Ayash removed the ring and placed it in her hand.

Salima walked back to the rooster. The bird seemed to have already come to peace with the death of his hen and stood safely away from the blazing fire.

Salima picked him up and held him to her chest. She put his lower toes together so she could slip them through Ayash's ring. The foot was thick, and as she had feared, the ring got stuck. She held the rooster firmly and pushed the ring further until she felt his back-toe break. The rooster squawked and writhed, but Salima held him tight. She slid the ring further up the shank and over his spur where it wouldn't slide down.

With the rooster under her arm, Salima went into the animal shed where she was met with violent heat. The far wall was on fire, and so was the hay.

Dark smoke filled the place and sent Salima into a coughing fit, but she made it to the far window, barely visible through the flames. She picked up a wooden rod and slammed it into the window, pushing it off its hinges and down with a sizzle. She held out the rooster. The rooster shifted and twitched nervously.

'Go get us a Jewess,' she whispered, hoping beyond hope that Fadhila would notice the ring.

With all the strength she could muster, Salima sent the rooster flying through the window and the sheet of flames out into the open. He flapped his wings uselessly until he landed outside.

The fire was spreading across the shed, snaking its way through the hay. Salima's eyes stung with smoke, so she ran back out to the courtyard.

Outside, the air was only slightly clearer. The buildings to her left and directly in front of her were drowning in crackling fire, and smoke twirled and danced with the winds, swaying in and out of the courtyard. Wooden planks fell off the buildings, their flames flailing like wings.

Salima saw the *Caid*'s head right before he disappeared down the well ladder, and Ayash was ready to go next.

Salima rubbed her eyes and fell to her knees next to Fahima. Saadia was sobbing helplessly. René's eyes were red and teary.

The blood was still trickling between Fahima's legs, weakly now that most of it was already in a pool around her. To Salima's horror, Fahima's face was whiter than milk. Her lips were dark, and she struggled to keep her eyes open.

Salima felt grief deep in her stomach. She fell on her sister's chest and sobbed. She couldn't believe this was happening. Half of her being, her entire existence, was crumbling in front of her eyes.

Fahima touched Salima's face gently, so she would raise her head to meet her sister's gaze. Their faces were so close together that Salima felt as if she were looking at herself in the mirror. She was. A relaxed and gentle reflection of hers looked at her trustingly, not feeling any of the pain and terror that was eating up Salima's insides.

'Listen to me, Salima,' Fahima said with much effort. 'Listen.'

Trying to keep herself together, Salima sniffed and nodded, stroking the hair off Fahima's sweaty cheek. Their foreheads touched. The tips of their noses, too. Salima's breathing sent her chest and lips into trembling fits.

'My baby,' Fahima said.

'I'll—,' Salima started, but she was overwhelmed by sobs. When she finally managed to, she continued, 'I'll take care of her.'

'Don't you—,' Fahima started. 'Listen. Listen to me, Salima. Don't you dare call her a stupid fool.'

They both laughed. Sad, miserable laughs.

'You're the only stupid fool, Fahima,' Salima said. 'You're my own stupid fool.'

They laughed again. And cried some more.

'I'm sure my girl will be smart like her aunt,' Fahima said, and tears fell from her eyes.

Salima hugged her tightly, weeping into her neck. She felt her sister's hands on her own back, a light effort to return the embrace.

'We have to get going,' Mouloud urged softly.

When Salima felt her sister's last breath, she held her all the tighter until someone pulled her by her shoulders. She let them pull her at first, but then dropped back as if to give Fahima one last hug. This time, she wailed and sobbed uncontrollably until Mourad pulled her away and hugged her.

Salima was faintly aware of Mouloud pulling Saadia, whose weeping had been quiet all this time. Like her voice had been consumed by all this loss.

René's crying was more reserved, but his face was a tragedy. He closed Fahima's eyes, then kissed her forehead, right between her eyebrows.

Seeing that gave Salima an inexplicable surge of strength. She broke off Mourad's arms and stood to her feet. She looked around her but didn't find what she was looking for. All the wooden pieces were either too big or burnt out.

'Take Yemma down the well,' she said. 'I'll be right behind you.'

She went into the animal shed. The fire was making its way to the door, and it had grown louder. Bellowing like winds. Salima found a small rod with one burning end. Mouloud lowered himself into the well, then René helped Saadia next. The four buildings threatened to come down on them at any moment.

Salima stood over her sister's body and pressed the stick's burning end to Fahima's face, right between her eyebrows.

'What are you doing?' Mourad asked, but Salima didn't say anything.

She held the rod there, taking in the sizzling sound of fire and the stench of burning skin and something metallic. Was that blood? When she removed the rod, the tattoo between Fahima's eyebrows had disappeared all but for a hazy line. The spot was now a horrible sight of burnt skin. That would have to work, Salima thought.

She squatted and placed Fahima's hand on the floor. Then she pressed the rod across the palm. When she removed the stick, she was satisfied with the long line of sweltering skin on Fahima's hand.

Salima was preparing to do the same for the second hand when the thick voice of Colonel Dupont came from his machine. He only said a few words and Salima couldn't make them out.

'They're blowing up the house in one minute,' René announced. 'We won't survive the blast if we're still out here.'

Salima ignored that too. She had to finish her task. Mourad tried to grab her shoulders, but she shrugged him off. Only when she was satisfied with the result did she drop the rod. She placed Fahima's hands on her chest, right hand over the left, gave her dead sister one last kiss on the cheek, then she ran to the well.

Mourad and René broke into motion, helping her go over the wall and onto the ladder. She risked one last glance at her sister, laying there on the floor, peaceful, before she stepped down into the cold, stinky darkness of the well.

Salima was vaguely aware of René's boots above her head as she took one step after the other, guiding her feet with touch to find each lower rung, her hands gripping the side rails. She felt like the ladder was going nowhere, the darkness growing thicker and the stench stronger as she went down.

A scraping voice came from above, slow and heavy, followed by a light shower of dust and the whole place went pitch dark. Someone had closed the lid of the well, leaving her sister's body out there to burn.

With a heavy heart, Salima went further down. She heard faint shuffling, coughing and splashing below her now, boots scuffing the metal rungs of the ladder above her.

Then the world blasted around them with a loud bang. The rails trembled so fervently as though to shake her off. Another dust shower fell on top of her, heavier this time, filled with tiny pebbles. Salima stayed still until it washed away and the ladder became stable again before she resumed her descent.

When she finally touched the ground, the water almost to her knees, she stepped aside to allow René and Mourad to land. The ground under her was uneven, lumpy at times, and muddy too.

René was right behind her, but slow to move away from the ladder. Salima strained to hear how far up the ladder Mourad was, but she heard nothing. She saw nothing.

She waited some more, but Mourad never made it down.

v

'You have to calm down,' René kept repeating.

But Salima wouldn't hear of it.

She felt hollow and dark, like the well they were stuck in. Half of her, half of her own being, no longer was. It died and left a void within her. All she could think of was how she couldn't go on living without her sister. Life without Fahima felt like setting out on a long voyage across the desert alone and without a guide, condemned to be lost.

'Listen to me, Salima,' René was saying in the dark. 'Listen to me.'

Salima wept her sorrow. She wept her loss. Her sister and her lover. The man who had sacrificed his life to lock everyone inside the well.

She hadn't thought about it. She and Ayash had spent so much time finding ways to get Fadhila to come and open the well for them from the outside, but they hadn't thought about closing the lid from the inside. It was an equally impossible task, and Mourad had known it. He hadn't said anything. He just lingered back and pushed the lid closed.

There was no way he could have survived the blast. Salima imagined him trapped under the rubble of the house, probably on fire, and she wept some more.

'You need to calm down.'

Salima was angry. Angry at Mourad for having sacrificed his life. For not having said anything about it. For leaving her alone when she needed him most. For adding to her loss. Was it not enough that she had just lost her twin sister? Couldn't René have stayed behind and closed the lid? Why did Mourad have to be the hero?

Two hands grabbed Salima's shoulders firmly, and René's voice, too close to her, echoed off the walls of the well.

'Think about everyone else in here,' René said. Salima didn't understand what he meant, and she didn't care, either. She tried to shrug his hands off. 'There isn't enough air in here to last us a long time. And you're consuming a lot of it when you're crying.'

That caught her attention. She didn't understand what he had just said, but it sounded dangerous.

'If you're too sad to think about yourself,' René continued, 'think about your mother. The baby.'

The baby? She had forgotten all about her. Her sister's baby. A piece of her. The baby who would grow up motherless. Supposing she made it out of here alive.

'If you don't calm down,' René said, 'you'll consume all the air, and we'll die before someone comes for us.'

Salima tried to calm herself, but sobs kept escaping her.

'Breathe,' René said. 'Take deep breaths.'

He took deep breaths himself to show her. She did the same, her lips trembling as she drew in air. She let out one more sob, which bounced off the walls above her, then she grew quiet.

The whole well seemed to grow quiet, too, as if she had been behind all the noise in her head. Then she heard her mother on her right, breathing in and out while sniffing quietly. She must be weeping, too, Salima thought, and she relapsed into another, stronger, weeping fit.

Saadia took her in her arms, and the two women wailed into each other's embrace.

'Mes dames,' René started, but Mouloud interrupted him.

'Leave them be,' Mouloud said.

'But we—'

'Just let them cry.'

When Salima finally cried and dried, her head was about to explode. Her throat was dry, too, and it burnt, probably from all the smoke she had inhaled.

The wait was long, made all the longer by the still darkness and uncertainty. Salima didn't know if the Jewess would come for their rescue. Their survival depended on too many hopes. It depended on the dumb rooster going to the Jew's house looking for hens. It depended on Fadhila seeing the rooster and noticing her husband's ring on the bird's shank. It also depended on her coming to Salima's house, or whatever was left of it, and seeing the pyramid on the wall of the well. If any of those parts didn't happen, Salima and everyone else would die in here and their souls would be trapped with the foul smell of their rotting bodies.

Salima was growing tired. Her feet were sore, and her head weighed heavy on her neck. She struggled to keep her eyes open, and she felt like sleeping while standing. She could swear someone was snoring across from her. Was it the *Caid*?

Salima shifted her foot, and it helped ease the pain, but only for a brief while. The second time she did it, her toes touched something soft and sticky. It wasn't mud. It was a corpse. A French soldier's body wasting away at the bottom of the pit. She whipped her foot away, panicking, and strained to remain motionless.

She remembered the prophecy that *Khalti* Baya, the seer, had recited.

I see a lot of death. And fire. I see darkness, and the living sleeping with the dead in the dark.

The baby cried several times. Djamila and Nouara took turns hushing her to sleep. At one time she wouldn't stop crying, so Saadia dipped a piece of cloth into the bucket of goatmilk and let the baby suckle on it until she fell asleep.

The exhaustion crept into Salima's head, her entire body ached, and she was growing weaker. She was also growing weary of the dark confinement.

No one opened the lid.

'We have to give it a try,' Mouloud said, and, not waiting for a response, he splashed around the well until he found the ladder.

'Be careful,' René said. 'And don't try too hard. You'll consume more air.'

Mouloud made no reply. The echo of his steps ascended above Salima, and a shower of dust rained down as he tried to move the heavy concrete lid. When he climbed down, she knew he had given up.

Salima was certain it was at least evening when the place started to cool down. She hugged herself and shuddered. René gave his jacket to Saadia to wrap the baby in.

'Warm her hands and feet,' he instructed. 'They're the first to suffer from the cold.'

The air grew heavy in Salima's chest, and her head was swimming now. She wanted to sleep so badly, but René kept repeating that no one was to sleep. He kept calling people by their names to check if they were awake. Or maybe he was checking if they were still alive.

When Nouara didn't reply, Djamila splashed around the water and slapped her. She woke up, and René made her climb the ladder to the top of the well. There was more air up there, he said. He climbed with her to keep her from falling, and they only climbed back down when she was feeling better.

Breathing became harder, laborious, and Salima contemplated giving in to sleep. She relished the prospect of fading away like that. From darkness to darkness. She might not even notice when she fell asleep or when she departed this world. She had no desire for this world, anyway.

Someone touched Salima's face, then kissed her lips. It was Mourad, and they were back in the village, lying on a rock watching the starry night sky. It was quiet and they were the only people in the world.

'Yemma,' someone called for her, so she broke away from Mourad and went back to the tent.

The boys were fighting, throwing pebbles at each other, but they stopped as soon as she stepped into the tent. The girl was sitting in the far corner, playing with the doll Salima had sown for her. She raised her head, her thick braids brushing against her shoulders, and gazed at Salima with large eyes.

'Don't you dare call her a stupid fool,' the girl said in Fahima's voice.

'Salima,' someone slapped her. It was Saadia. 'Wake up.'

Salima had been dreaming, and tears ran down her face.

'The baby?' Salima asked. 'Where's the baby?'

'She's alright,' Djamila said. 'I have her.'

'You have to stay awake,' René urged, but even he sounded weak and hoarse.

Salima was annoyed that they had snatched her out of her dreams into the sour darkness and the wet cold of this pit, but something had brought her back here. It wasn't Saadia's slap; it was Fahima's voice. Her last words. Salima gasped for air, and it burnt its way down her throat and into her chest.

'Ayash, wake up,' the *Caid* was whispering. 'Wake up.'

Djamila was also urging Nouara to stay alert. The baby cried.

Was this it? Was this how they were going to die? A slow and painful death? Deprived of air? Salima didn't mind dying, but she didn't want everyone here to die with her.

Poor Nouara and Djamila had nothing to do with this fight. Yemma didn't deserve this, either. And the innocent baby. It was unfair that she came into this world in the midst of it all. Born to a dying mother, only to expire at the bottom of a pit with a band of killers and a pile of French corpses. *She is a daughter of war*, Salima thought.

When the shower of dust fell around her, Salima didn't know what to make of it. Then a trickle of light seeped into the well like a thin crescent in a dark night. Was she dreaming again?

The shaft of light widened, and she gasped for air, but there was nothing. She wanted to scream but couldn't. It was the third or fourth time when her chest finally filled. Everyone around her gasped, too, and a squeaky voice came tumbling down the walls of the well.

'Ayash?' Fadhila called. 'Are you in there?'

Everyone responded with gut-wrenching coughs.

vi

When Salima emerged from the well, the sun had all but disappeared, and the sky raged with colour against the last of the storm. She was surprised to see the carnage around her. The air was warm, blurred with smoke, and it smelled of burning meat. The entire house, all four buildings, had crumbled into piles of rubble.

As Ayash and his daughter, Yamina, helped her out, Salima searched frantically for any sign of Mourad. Apart from Fahima's body, still lying on the floor, all else was beyond recognition. There were burnt bodies everywhere, and all but one of them, Salima knew, had been French soldiers.

Salima fell to her sister's side again, hugging her warm body and weeping uncontrollably. She willed her sister to move, to open her eyes and say something. She willed this all to be a nightmare that she would soon wake up from.

'Come on,' a squeaky voice came from behind, and Fadhila's warm hand grabbed Salima's elbow. 'We have to get you out of Bousaada. You have to go now.'

Salima said nothing. Saadia knelt beside her, the baby in her arms, and said, 'You promised to take care of her baby.'

That was true, but Salima couldn't stand up. Saadia handed her the baby, and Salima held her for the first time. Baby Farida clenched her hands and rubbed her face slowly, eyes squinting at the new world.

Watching the baby filled Salima with a strong urge to protect this fragile creature. This living reminder of her twin sister. This girl was new, no dark secrets, no bloody bracelets, no loss clouding her bright eyes. She was free from the well, born again.

Saadia stood up and picked up a heavy bundle dripping with water. Yemma must have kept her daughters' clothes and jewellery with her at the bottom of the well.

Saadia reached out a hand to her daughter, and Salima took it, holding Farida tight.

Epilogue

The evening was cold, shrouded in the damp air which rolled in from the Bay of Algiers. It was the kind of cold that penetrated your nostrils and seeped through your skin. The atmosphere in Dar Zehour, the heart of the Casbah, was warmed by the crowds gathered in the small courtyard and on the balcony upstairs.

Under the balcony, a group of old stocky *madahat* sat cross-legged, playing drums, *bendirs* and *kerkabous*, while a few young people, French, British and Americans, danced and laughed, their faces reddened by the strong alcohol. The night was an extension of this morning's ceremonies, only less formal.

Joseph stood under the archway smoking with two British generals. They, too, preferred to watch from the sidelines.

'It was a beautiful ceremony,' said one of the British generals, Briden. His French was accurate but sounded incorrect to Joseph's ear. 'I hadn't expected so many people to come out and greet us.'

'It's because it's more than just an anniversary,' Joseph explained. 'The people want to express their gratitude to the Allied forces for having liberated them.'

Having recently succeeded in throwing the Axis out of Algiers, the British and American armies were still in town when Algiers commemorated the Battle of Austerlitz.

The residents flooded the sidewalks to cheer for the soldiers who paraded through the streets. People cared more for the recent battle that had taken place near them than the Napoleonic wars.

'I'm certain the entire world will celebrate like this when we defeat the Nazis and their friends once and for all,' said the second British general. Baldwyn or Aldwyn. Joseph couldn't remember. 'And that's just around the corner. Our armies just attacked the Italians in Tunis, the siege on Stalingrad has practically been lifted, and the Nazis are retreating.'

'Experts are saying it won't take more than six months before the war is won,' Joseph said, remembering something he had read in l'Echo d'Alger.

'I'd say a year,' Briden said. 'Let's not forget the Japanese at the far end of the world.'

'Maybe,' said Baldwyn or Aldwyn.

The three men fell silent, dragging at their cigarettes.

'Have you seen the view from the rooftop?' said Joseph, and when they both shook their heads, he added, 'It's breathtaking. You must see it. Let's go up.'

Joseph led his British guests up the dark stairs to the balcony and all the way up to the rooftop. A young couple holding hands dashed past them, giggling.

The air on the rooftop was even cooler than downstairs and Joseph was able to breathe better here. The sky was clear, and the half-moon shone generously over the connected rooftops extending all around Dar Zehour.

The bay was dotted with Ally battleships, their lights glistening in the calm waters. The merry noise echoing across the water from their decks cast a sense of reassurance over the entire city.

'What an astounding view!' said Briden in English.

The sounds of the party downstairs, the music, singing and laughter, arose in waves, like distant memories. The three men stayed up there for well over an hour, poisoning the clear air with their cigarettes.

'Have you heard General Eisenhower's speech?' Baldwyn or Aldwyn asked.

Briden shook his head.

The party downstairs was dying down. The music had stopped and was replaced with chatter. Boots pounding and doors banging.

'I heard of it,' said Joseph. 'I'm sure it'll be all over the newspapers tomorrow morning.'

'It was very positive and all,' said Baldwyn or Aldwyn. 'But he gave most of the credit to himself and his army. A little bit to the French army and the people of North Africa, but none to the British army.'

'Why am I not surprised?' said Briden.

'Here you are,' someone said in English. Joseph turned but couldn't make out who was standing at the door. 'We're leaving. You two coming?'

'Yeah, yeah,' said Briden. 'In a minute.'

The two British generals thanked Joseph for his hospitality and went downstairs, leaving him alone with the night.

Joseph lit another cigarette and stared out at the Bay of Algiers. The battleships were growing dark and quiet, too, as if the whole armada was somehow connected to the party downstairs.

Algiers felt safe now, but Joseph refused to be lulled. It had felt safe the night the British army raided the city just a few weeks ago. A whole Nazi fleet could be lurking on the horizon right now for all he knew.

Hearing footsteps and the clanking of jewellery behind him, Joseph turned to find an Arab woman waddling her way towards him, two small tea glasses in her hands and a large smile on her face.

'You look worried,' the woman said in broken French. The kind of French that felt purposefully broken, mutilated, as though the speaker refused to pronounce the vowels and the Rs the way they were supposed to.

Joseph nodded gravely. He didn't know what to make of this. He wasn't accustomed to having Arabs address him so casually.

As the woman came closer, her face looked familiar. Her dark skin was creased on her forehead and wrinkled around the mouth. She had a tiny cross-shaped tattoo on either cheek and a three-dotted line on her chin. Her hips were wide, and her bosoms drooped unapologetically low.

She was a member of the *meddahat* from downstairs. She had played the drum, he remembered, and a little girl, about seven or eight, had slept on her lap. But something else about her struck him as familiar. He couldn't bring himself to remember where he had seen her before. Maybe she came here often too. He came to these parties quite frequently.

The woman offered him a glass of tea and an encouraging nod, her jewellery clinking and rattling as she moved. He took it gratefully and sipped. It was scalding, but, after all those years in Bousaada, Joseph had grown to like his tea hot and strong.

'Is this your *haouch*?' Joseph asked the woman.

'No, I just play the drum.' She leaned over the low wall and looked out at the bay beyond. 'And this isn't a *haouch*. It's a guesthouse.'

Different terminology, he thought, *same thing*. He took another sip of his tea and stared out at the distance.

'Don't you feel safer now that the British and Americans have helped us kick out the Axis?'

The woman looked at him blankly. She took a sip of her own tea, and he did the same. 'What difference does it make for us?' she said flatly. 'We've barely noticed the change over the years.'

Joseph didn't know what to say. She turned away from him. He gazed at the side of her face for a moment, then took another sip.

She couldn't possibly mean that, he thought. Of course, there was a difference. France meant living under a free sky, liberated from enemies who were trying to build an empire at the expense of other nations.

He suddenly found it hard to look at the bay. His head was swimming, as if he was out at sea, and his vision blurred. He stepped back and leaned his head against the wall. Closing his eyes to calm down.

Without opening his eyes, Joseph upended the tea glass in one large gulp. It didn't help. When he opened his eyes, the whole world was swaying. The floor rose and fell like the waves of a foul sea. He felt sick, unable to breathe. Something burnt in his throat.

Joseph looked at the empty glass in his hand. He turned to the woman. There was a hint of a smile in her eyes as she sipped at her tea.

'Why?' he asked, struggling to produce the word. 'Who are you?' His glass dropped with a clank. It didn't break.

'You don't remember me? I remember you,' she said calmly. 'You took my virginity years ago.'

That didn't remind Joseph of anything. He swallowed hard, fumbling for the handgun at his waist.

'Then you killed my family in Bousaada,' she said, bitterness seeping through her every word. 'I won't rest until I know you can't lay a finger on what's left of it.'

Bousaada, he thought. *That's it.* She and her daughters had died many years ago. Perished in that big fire. He had seen their burnt bodies himself. How could they have—?

He managed to grab the gun, and, in what he hoped was a fast-enough movement, he knocked the safety off and raised the pistol to shoot.

The woman was faster. She swept his hand away, sending his gun hurling through the air. Joseph had pulled the trigger at the last moment, and the pistol fired once, and missed. The gun clunked to the floor and slid away from him.

He turned back to the woman, ready to punch her in the face, but he never stood a chance. She grabbed the side of his neck and plunged something sharp into the other side. A flash of pain overwhelmed his body, paralysing him as hot blood trickled down to his chest.

Joseph felt like he'd been stabbed by a knife, but he knew perfectly well what weapon the woman was using. It was a spiked bracelet. Just like her two daughters did.

'You killed my baby girl, Farida,' the woman said, then she made to give Joseph another stab saying, 'And only son, Amar.'

Joseph pushed her away, consuming all his strength. He was about to fall. He leaned against the low wall, closing his eyes and failing to breathe. He pressed a hand to the side of his neck where the warm blood was still oozing. Loud footsteps came up the stairs, and Joseph knew they were here to save him.

He fell to his knees first, as if to pray. His upper body collapsed, and he lay on his side. The woman kicked him in the gut. Saying something about her daughter, Fahima. He didn't feel anything.

There was shouting on the rooftop. A lot of running and shouting. A loud bang.

The woman was next to him, her head resting on her arm and her face close to his, like lovers in bed. Blood trickled out her mouth and dripped down her cheek to the floor.

Saadia looked at Joseph. She smiled.

That was the last thing Joseph saw before he died.

Historical Note: The Quest for a Fading Memory

I first learned about Ouled Nail culture in 2016 when I stumbled on Ottoman History Podcast's episode with the French historian, Aurélie Perrier, discussing prostitution in Algeria during the Ottoman and French epochs (La prostitution en Algérie à l'époque Ottomane et française). When the speaker, in passing, likened Ouled Nail customs to those of Japanese Geishas, I was immediately fascinated but at the same time outraged that I had never heard of this unique side of my country's history. People often praised the beauty of the Ouled Nail women and the magic of Bou Saada, gateway to the Sahara, yet the generations-old tradition that had once enchanted tourists worldwide has been conveniently buried under heaps of denial and national shame.

Fuelled by curiosity, and admittedly thrilled by the prospect of finding an untold story of a past long forgotten, I set out to comb the Internet searching for any trace of the Ouled Nail dancers. I was fascinated by their tales of resilience in the face of violence and discrimination. I learned that the Ouled Nail dancers had roamed the world, carrying their tunes through cafes in Algiers, captivating circusgoers in Europe, and even performing across the Atlantic at the Chicago Fair of 1893.

I also uncovered why this culture had all but disappeared from modern memory. Following Algeria's independence in 1962, the dancers were left with little space to exercise their profession now that France had departed with their core clientele of French soldiers and European tourists. Most of them were integrated into the government's agrarian reforms, and the few ones that survived on a trickle of tourists had no choice but to quit in the 1980s as the country fell to religious fanatism and a devastating civil war.

Today, every mention of the dancers online attracts a tsunami of angry comments. People deny the existence of this Ouled Nail culture, relegating it to the orientalists' fetishist tendencies and accusing the French of fabricating content with the sole objective of tarnishing the reputation of the pure Algerian people. Some university students have explored this exotic past through Masters and PhD theses, but the narratives unfailingly rush to excuse their practices, blaming the French-imposed poverty and hunger that left these women with no other means of income. But the memory still lives true in the minds and hearts of Bousaadis who remember these beautiful creatures walking and dancing amongst them, emanating joy and freedom.

I quickly discovered that the history of Ouled Nail had been documented in visual form rather than written narratives or academic studies. Rudolf Franz Lehnert's photographs allow us a glimpse of these women's stunning beauty and strength, and the National Geographic magazine depicts life in Bou Saada (albeit with the occasional supremacist side comment) through Frank Edward Johnson's chronicles "Here and There in Northern Africa" (January 1914). Artists like Etienne Dinet and Juanita Guccione spent years in this town, fully assimilated into the local culture, and their paintings immortalise stories that would otherwise have been lost. Videos dating back to the early to mid-1900s have carried the fading memory of the Ouled Nail's dance and their melodies of a thousand flutes, and Émile Gaudissard's gigantic sculptures in the Hamma botanical garden of Algiers capture their glory in eternal poses of stone, likes victims of Medusa.

I am grateful for the Algerian historian and anthropologist, Barkahoum Ferhati, whose writings capture life in Bou Saada from Ouled Nail rites and customs down to their clothing and jewellery, defying all taboos around prostitution. Barkahoum's works convey universal lessons from these women's struggle to maintain control over their bodies, secure financial independence and navigate a role for themselves in the midst of what Christelle Taraud calls "la double violence sexuelle" from colonialism and patriarchy.

Archives from l'Echo d'Alger newspaper found on the website of la Bibliothèque nationale de France helped me keep track of the daily news coming out of Bou Saada in the 1930s: the movies shot in town, the things that excited inhabitants and the dangers that kept them awake at night.

My conversations with the Bousaadi poet Sahraoui Mekhannene were suffused with oral history from the region, the good and the horrendous, revealing some ugly atrocities on both sides of the colonial struggle. He spoke at length about the role of the *Caids* and how they often abused their proximity to the French, advancing their own interests on the expense of their compatriots. The story about the Ouled Brahim's banishment and fellow Algerians killing them in exchange for money, including the rings of ears, was inspired by my conversations with Ammi Sahraoui. It was heart-breaking to hear about the torments and suffering to which the Algerians were subjected, and the tales of resilience, solidarity and altruism warmed my heart. Thank you, Ammi Sahraoui, and thank you Othman Mekhannene for connecting me with your uncle.

The characters in Sand Roses are fictional with the occasional reference to real people such as Etienne Dinet, Colonel du Pein, General Eisenhower and the half-myth half-real character, Hizya, who haunts the fantasies of many writers and poets just like she dances in the dreams of Fahima and Farida. The Ferreros did live in Bou Saada though I did take liberties with the Ferrero characters. Emilie and Mathilde are actually names of the same person who was born in Bou Saada in 1885. I found records of a Marcel Gabriel Darbéda, but his age and relation to the Ferreros are the product of my own imagination. Joseph is not exaggerating when he says there are too many Ferreros in the world to keep up with.

I did my best to restrict the events in Sand Roses to incidents that did take place in Bou Saada or at least other parts of the country. The virginity bids, the laws and hygiene checks regulating the Ouled Nail's profession, the camps and parties, and the violence and thefts they suffered on a regular basis were all inspired by years of research. Joseph's campaign to eradicate the Ouled Nail tribes was a commonplace occurrence throughout the 132 years of French occupation in Algeria. I found online records of a huge fire in town and a fight on the Street of Joy involving tourists, soldiers and Ouled Nail dancers. Though I couldn't verify sources for these events, they were too convenient for my plot to give them up.

The lack of documentation around the Ouled Nail culture made me realise the importance of a project like this to preserve unique immaterial heritage from little-known corners of the world. It also gave me the chance to do what writers like to do best: invent.

Acknowledgments

I embarked on the Sand Roses project seven years ago, but I am forever indebted to those who contributed to my writing journey in countless ways. My mother's bedtime stories ignited my fascination with storytelling and left me daydreaming about the characters in those tales and recreating events using animal figurines, toys and, when away from home, even matchsticks. My high school Arabic Literature teacher, Mr. Boulekreb, taught me the difference between history and a story and drew my attention to the importance of character arcs, which made me reconsider the hundreds of pages I had written over the years and motivated me to write hundreds more, none of which will ever see the light of day— thank you very much.

I am grateful to Elizabeth Kadetsky for letting me audit her creative writing class at Penn State University. Workshopping stories with other aspiring writers, meeting award-winning authors and receiving feedback and encouragement from Elizabeth herself rekindled my passion for storytelling when I had let it slip through the years of workaholism. I started plotting Sand Roses during that gap year, and I genuinely believe that thanks to this positive experience my mind was wired to find a potential story behind every mundane detail. Otherwise, I would have dismissed the podcast and carried on writing my paper for Instructional Psychology class.

Many friends have read, partially or fully, this gigantic piece, suffering through earlier, and much lengthier versions. Their generous feedback and long conversations (and sometimes heated arguments) contributed in small and major ways to the improvement of the story. They saved me from fatal mistakes and oversights and spared you, dear reader, from hundreds of unnecessary pages. Omayma Kerthiou mailed me annotated pages that rival those of a professional editor, and Aziza El Kolei challenged me to reconsider what would go on inside a woman's head in the 1930s. Zobida Tadj continuously urged me to stop holding back and her tips helped me build more realistic characters. Anes Houari taught me to let the text breathe but choke the characters on the filthy smell of rotting corpses. The following friends read and provided comments: Amina Kateb, Amira Boutaiba and her mom, Jenny Holland Kebir, and Leah Bitat. Others have supported my journey with their relentless enthusiasm and unconditional support throughout the years including Achraf Meguelllati, Amine Benakila, Andrew Farrand, Fares Bouloudani,

El Mehdi Bentoumi, Hadjer Neggaz and Yacine Hakmi just to name a few. I consider myself extremely lucky to count among my friends these generous individuals with insightful minds and a passion for stories. I apologise if I neglected to mention any names.

I spent hours on the phone with Mohamed Abdelaziz trying to salvage the ending and save our beloved characters from certain death. Lots of calculations and medical tips went into determining, and stretching, how long eight adults and a baby can survive at the bottom of a well. If anyone has a problem with the accuracy of that scene, take it up with Dr. Mohamed Abdelaziz. Just kidding— it was probably just me hellbent on fulfilling the seer's prophecy.

I am also indebted to quite a few perfect strangers who spared no time or effort to read my work and provide valuable suggestions. Today, you couldn't say writing is a lonely job when there is countless communities of writers and beta-readers organising to support you and cheer you on. Goodreads, Scribophile and even Facebook Groups helped me find a few wonderful souls like Geralyn Dunbar-Giles, Jonathan Simpson and Lydia Wilkins. If it hadn't been for them, I probably wouldn't have felt confident enough to share my writing with anyone else.

The single biggest boost to my writing journey to-date has been the Island Prize. When I submitted Sand Roses, it was just another line at the bottom of an ever-growing list of queries and competition entries that were quickly turning red due to rejections or CNRs (Closed No Reply). Getting shortlisted for the prize introduced me to world class writers whose generous attention and guidance have been the most valuable prize I could ever dream of. Thank you, Robert Peet, Karen Jennings and everyone at Holland House and Karavan Press for offering unpublished African authors the chance to tell their stories, and thank you Obinna Udenwe and Hilda J. Twongyeirwe for reading Sand Roses and for your kind messages.

And finally, I am grateful to everyone at Holland House for believing in Sand Roses and allowing me to bring to life this unique story from a little-known part of the world. Robert Peet's guidance has been instrumental in shaping the final structure that you, dear reader, have just read. Juni Kvarving's thorough edits and attention to detail have been invaluable. She took a merciless scythe to the fluff that had plagued the narration and pushed me to lean more into key moments that heightened the impact and elevated the emotional experience of our characters' journeys. Ken Dawson has shown stoic patience as he created not one, not two, but over twenty cover designs before we settled on the perfect one that captures the story and strength of a Ouled Nail dancer.

And above all, thank you, dear reader, for choosing Sand Roses. I hope it has been an enjoyable experience and an opportunity to discover the world of Bou Saada in the 1930s.

About the Author

Hamza Koudri has an MA in English Literature and Civilization and has been working in education and international development since 2008. Currently serving as the Country Director with the British Council in Algeria, he oversees a portfolio of English, STEM, higher education and cultural programmes, working closely with public sector teachers and institutions. Over the years, he has created and led courses and projects for youth and educators across the MENA (Middle East and North Africa) region and beyond.

During a year-long fellowship in the United States, he also helped establish a mentorship programme for a social equity course at Penn State University and a teacher training certificate program for Indiana University. He also took a creative writing course with award-winning author, Elizabeth Kadetsky, during which time he started working on Sand Roses. Research for his novel took the better part of a decade, seeking traces of a muted past between the folds of visual documentation and oral histories. In 2022, Sand Roses was shortlisted for the Island Prize for unpublished African authors.

Hamza co-authored an article on "Social Responsibility Discretion in Algeria" highlighting unique management practices in the country. The article was published in "Responsible Management in Africa" with Emerald Publishing.